DEEP
STORM

DEEP STORM

• A NOVEL •

LINCOLN CHILD

All rights reserved.
Published in the United States of America
by Random House Large Print in association with
Doubleday, New York.
Distributed by Random House, Inc., New York.

Library of Congress Cataloging-in-Publication Data
Child, Lincoln.
Deep Storm : a novel / by Lincoln Child.—1st large
print ed.
p. cm.
ISBN 978-0-7393-2639-8
1. Atlantis—Fiction. 2. Geographical myths—Fiction.
3. Lost continents—Fiction. 4. Large type books.
I. Title.
PS3553.H4839D44 2007b
813'.54—dc22
2006038122

www.randomlargeprint.com

FIRST LARGE PRINT EDITION

10 9 8 7 6 5 4 3 2 1

This Large Print edition published in accord with the
standards of the N.A.V.H.

To Luchie

Acknowledgments

At Doubleday, I'd like to thank my editor, Jason Kaufman, for his friendship as well as his tireless assistance in countless matters. For their consistent enthusiasm since the beginning, thanks to Bill Thomas and Adrienne Sparks. And thanks to Jenny Choi and the rest of the gang for their dedication, hard work, and support. Eric Simonoff at Janklow & Nesbit and Matthew Snyder of the Creative Artists Agency were, as always, indispensable and irreplaceable.

Thanks also to my wife, Luchie, and my daughter, Veronica, without whom this book could not have been written.

Doug Preston—writing partner, "brother from another mother"—was right there with me in the trenches during the creation of the novel. He made literally dozens of contributions, both large and small, to my conception. His importance to the story can't be overstated.

And to the many others who helped **Deep Storm** become the book it is—especially Claudia Rülke; Voelker Knapperz, M.D.; Lee Suckno, M.D.; and Ed Buchwald—my deep appreciation.

It goes without saying that **Deep Storm** is a work of fiction. All persons, places, locales, incidents, corporations, government institutions, or facilities are either fictitious or used fictitiously.

· **PROLOGUE** ·

STORM KING OIL PLATFORM
Off the Coast of Greenland

It took a certain kind of man, Kevin Lindengood decided, to work an oil rig. A certain screwed-up kind of man.

He sat morosely before his console in the Drilling Control Center. Outside, beyond the reinforced windows, the North Atlantic was a blizzard of black and white. Spindrift frothed above its surface, churning, angry.

But then again, the North Atlantic **always** seemed angry. It didn't matter that the Storm King oil platform towered more than a thousand feet over the surface: the ocean's vastness made the platform seem tiny, a child's toy that might be swept away at any moment.

"Pig status?" asked John Wherry, the offshore installation manager.

Lindengood glanced down at his console. "Seventy-one negative and rising."

"Pipe status?"

"All readings nominal. Everything looks good."

His gaze rose once again to the dark, dripping windows. The Storm King platform was the northernmost rig in the Maury oil field. Somewhere out there, forty-odd miles to the north, was land, or what passed for it around here: Angmagssalik, Greenland. Although on a day like this, it was hard to believe there was anything on the surface of the planet but ocean.

Yes: it took a screwed-up kind of man to work an oil rig (and they were **always** men, unfortunately—the only women ever "on platform" were company relations flaks and morale officers who came by helicopter, made sure everybody was well adjusted, then left as quickly as possible). Every man seemed to bring his own portion of unfinished business, personality tic, or lovingly tended neurosis. Because what drove a person to work inside a metal box suspended over a freezing sea by steel toothpicks? Never knowing when a monster storm might come along, pick him up, and fling him into oblivion? Everybody liked to claim it was the high pay, but there were plenty of jobs on dry land that paid almost as much. No: the truth was that everybody came here to escape something or—more frightening—escape **to** something.

His terminal gave a low beep. "The pig's cleared number two."

"Understood," said Wherry.

At the terminal next to Lindengood, Fred Hicks cracked his knuckles, then grasped a joystick built into his console. "Positioning pig over well slot three."

Lindengood glanced at him. Hicks, the on-duty process engineer, was a perfect example. Hicks had a first-generation iPod on which he had stored nothing but Beethoven's thirty-two piano sonatas. He played them constantly, day and night, on shift and off, over and over and over. **And** he hummed them while he listened. Lindengood had heard them all, and had in fact memorized them all—as had just about everybody on Storm King—through Hicks's breathy humming.

It was not a tutelage likely to foster music appreciation.

"Pig in position over number three," Hicks said. He adjusted his earbuds and resumed humming the **Waldstein** sonata.

"Lower away," said Wherry.

"Roger." And Lindengood turned back to his terminal.

There were just the three of them in the Drilling Control Center. In fact, the entire massive rig was like a ghost city this morning. The pumps were silent; the riggers, drillers, and derrick men were lounging in their quarters, watching satellite TV in the crew's mess, or playing Ping-Pong or pinball. It was the last day of the month, and that meant everything had to come to a complete stop while electromagnetic pigs were sent down to clean the drilling pipes.

All ten drilling pipes.

Ten minutes passed, then twenty. Hicks's humming changed in tempo, acquired a kind of nasal urgency: clearly, the **Waldstein** sonata had ended and the **Hammerklavier** had begun.

As he watched his screen, Lindengood did a mental calculation. It was over ten thousand feet to the ocean floor. Another thousand or more to the oil field itself. One hundred and ten thousand feet of pipe to clean. And as production engineer, it was his job to run the pig up and down again and again, under the watchful eye of the rig boss.

Life was wonderful.

As if on cue, Wherry spoke up. "Pig status?"

"Eight thousand seven hundred feet and descending." Once the pig got to the bottom of pipe three—the deepest of the bores into the ocean bed—it would pause, then begin crawling upward again, as the slow, tedious process of cleaning and inspecting began.

Lindengood shot a glance at Wherry. The offshore installation manager was validation of his certain-kind-of-man theory. The guy must have been beat up one too many times on the school playground, because he had a serious authority problem. Usually, chiefs were low-key, laid-back. They realized life on the platform was no fun, and they did what they could to make it easier on the men. But Wherry was a regular Captain Bligh: never satisfied with anybody's work, barking orders at the line workers and junior engineers, writing people up at the least opportunity. The only thing missing was a swagger stick and a—

Suddenly, Hicks's console began beeping. As Lindengood looked on uninterestedly, Hicks leaned forward, scanning the readings.

"We've got a problem with the pig," he said, plucking out his earbuds and frowning. "It's tripped out."

"What?" Wherry walked over to examine the monitoring screen. "High pressure discharge?"

"No. The feedback's all garbled, never seen anything like it."

"Reset," said Wherry.

"You got it." Hicks made a few adjustments on his console. "There it goes. Tripped out again."

"Again? Already? **Shit**." Wherry turned abruptly to Lindengood. "Cut power to the electromagnet and do a system inventory."

Lindengood complied with a heavy sigh. There were still seven pipes to go, and if the pig was acting screwy already, Wherry was going to have a fit . . .

Lindengood froze. **That can't be. It's impossible.**

Without taking his eyes from the screen, he reached over and plucked Wherry's sleeve. "John."

"What is it?"

"Look at the sensors."

The manager stepped over, glanced at the sensor readout. "What the hell? Didn't I just tell you to turn off the electromagnet?"

"I did. It's off."

"What?"

"Look for yourself," Lindengood said. His mouth had gone dry, and a funny feeling was growing in the pit of his stomach.

The manager peered more closely at the controls. "Then what's making those—"

Suddenly, he stopped. Then, very slowly, he straightened, face going pale in the blue wash of the cold-cathode display. "Oh, my God . . ."

· TWENTY MONTHS LATER ·

1

It looked, Peter Crane thought, like a stork: a huge white stork, rising out of the ocean on ridiculously delicate legs. But as the helicopter drew closer and the outline sharpened against the sea horizon, this resemblance gradually fell away. The legs grew sturdier, became tubular pylons of steel and pre-stressed concrete. The central body became a multilevel superstructure, studded with flare stacks and turbines, festooned with spars and girders. And the thin, necklike object above resolved into a complex crane-and-derrick assembly, rising several hundred feet above the super-structure.

The pilot pointed at the approaching platform, held up two fingers. Crane nodded.

It was a brilliant, cloudless day, and Crane squinted against the bright ocean stretching away on all sides. He felt tired and disoriented by travel: commercial flight from Miami to New York, private Gulfstream G150 charter to Reykjavik, and now helicopter. But the weariness hadn't blunted his deep—and growing—curiosity.

It wasn't so much that Amalgamated Shale was interested in his particular expertise: that he understood. It was the hurry with which they'd wanted him to drop everything and rush out to the Storm King platform that surprised him. Then there was the fact that AmShale's forward headquarters in Iceland had, rather oddly, been bustling with technicians and engineers rather than the usual drillers and roughnecks.

And then there was the other thing. The helicopter pilot wasn't an AmShale employee. He wore a Navy uniform—and a sidearm.

As the chopper banked sharply around the side of the platform, heading for the landing zone, Crane realized for the first time just how large the oil rig was. The jacket structure alone had to be eight stories high. Its upper deck was covered with a bewildering maze of modular units. Here and there, men in yellow safety uniforms checked couplings and worked pump equipment, dwarfed by the machinery that surrounded them. Far below, the ocean frothed around the pillars of the substructure, where it vanished beneath the surface to run the thousands of feet to the sea floor itself.

The chopper slowed, turned, and settled down within the green hexagon of the landing zone. As Crane reached back for his bags, he noticed someone was standing at the edge, waiting: a tall, thin woman in an oilskin jacket. He thanked the pilot, opened the passenger door, and stepped out into bracing air, instinctively ducking under the whirring blades.

The woman held out her hand at his approach. "Dr. Crane?"

Crane shook the hand. "Yes."

"This way, please." The woman led the way off the landing platform, down a short set of stairs, and along a metal catwalk to a closed, submarine-style hatch. She did not give her name.

A uniformed seaman stood guard outside the hatch, rifle at his side. He nodded as they approached, opened the hatch, then closed and secured it behind them.

Beyond lay a brightly lit corridor, studded along both sides with open doors. There was no frantic hum of turbines, no deep throbbing of drilling equipment. The smell of oil, though detectable, was faint, almost as if efforts had been made to remove it.

Crane followed the woman, bags slung over his shoulder, glancing curiously into the rooms as he passed. There were laboratories full of whiteboards and workstations; computer centers; communications suites. Topside had been quiet, but there was plenty of activity here.

Crane decided he'd venture some questions. "Are the divers in a hyperbaric chamber? Can I see them now?"

"This way, please," the woman repeated.

They turned a corner, descended a staircase, and entered another hallway, wider and longer than the first. The rooms they passed were larger: machine shops, storage bays for high-tech equipment Crane didn't recognize. He frowned. Although Storm King resembled an oil rig in all outward appearances, it was clearly no longer in the business of pumping crude.

What the hell is going on here?

"Have any vascular specialists or pulmonologists been flown in from Iceland?" he asked.

The woman didn't answer, and Crane shrugged. He'd come this far—he could stand to wait another couple of minutes.

The woman stopped before a closed gray metal door. "Mr. Lassiter is waiting for you."

Lassiter? That wasn't a name he recognized. The person who'd spoken to him over the phone, briefed him about the problem at the rig had been named Simon. He glanced at the door. There was the nameplate, white letters on black plastic, spelling out E. LASSITER, EXTERNAL LIAISON.

Crane turned back to the woman in the oilskin jacket, but she was already moving back down the corridor. He shifted his bags, knocked on the door.

"Enter," came the crisp voice from within.

Lassiter was a tall, thin man with closely cropped blond hair. He stood up as Crane entered, came around his desk, shook hands. He wasn't wearing a military uniform, but with his haircut and his brisk, economical movements he might as well have been. The office was small and just as efficient looking as its tenant. The desk was almost studiously bare: there was a single manila envelope on it, sealed, and a digital recorder.

"You can stow your gear there," Lassiter said, indicating a far corner. "Please sit down."

"Thanks." Crane took the proffered seat. "I'm eager to learn just what the emergency is. My escort here didn't have much to say on the subject."

"Actually, neither will I." Lassiter gave a smile, which disappeared as quickly as it came. "My job is to ask you a few questions."

Crane digested this. "Go ahead," he said after a moment.

Lassiter pressed a button on the recorder. "This recording is taking place on June second. Present are myself—Edward Lassiter—and Dr. Peter Crane. Location is the ERF Support and Supply Station." Lassiter glanced over the desk at Crane. "Dr. Crane, you are aware that your tour of service here cannot be fixed to a specific length?"

"Yes."

"And you understand that you must never divulge anything you witness here, or recount your actions while at the Facility?"

"Yes."

"And are you willing to sign an affidavit to that effect?"

"Yes."

"Have you ever been arrested?"

"No."

"Were you born a citizen of the United States, or are you naturalized?"

"I was born in New York City."

"Are you taking medication for any ongoing physical condition?"

"No."

"Do you abuse alcohol or drugs with any regularity?"

Crane had fielded the questions with growing surprise. "Unless you call the occasional weekend six-pack 'abuse,' then no."

Lassiter didn't smile. "Are you claustrophobic, Dr. Crane?"

"No."

Lassiter put the recorder on pause. Then he picked up the manila envelope, tore it open with a finger, pulled out half a dozen sheets of paper, and passed them across the table. "If you could please read and sign each of these," he said, plucking a pen from a pocket and placing it beside the sheets.

Crane picked them up and began to read. As he did so, his surprise turned to disbelief. There were three separate nondisclosure agreements, an Official Secrets Act affidavit, and something called a Binding Cooperation Initiative. All were branded documents of the U.S. government, all required signature, and all threatened dire consequences if any of their articles were breached.

Crane put the documents down, aware of Lassiter's gaze upon him. This was too much. Maybe he should thank Lassiter politely, then excuse himself and head back to Florida.

But how, exactly, was he going to do that?

AmShale had paid a great deal of money to get him here. The helicopter had already left. He was having trouble deciding between two research projects at the moment. And besides, he had never been one to turn down a challenge, especially one as mysterious as this.

He picked up the pen and, without giving himself time to reconsider, signed all the documents.

"Thank you," Lassiter said. He started the recorder again. "Let the transcript show that Dr. Crane has signed the requisite forms." Then, snapping off the recorder, he stood. "If you'll follow me, Doctor, I think you'll get your answers."

He led the way out of the office through a labyrinthine administrative area, up an elevator, and into a well-furnished library stocked with books, magazines, and computer workstations. Lassiter gestured toward a table on the far side of the room, which held only a computer monitor. "I'll come back for you," he said, then turned and left the room.

Crane sat where directed. There was nobody else in the library, and he was beginning to wonder what would happen next when the computer screen winked on in front of him. It showed the face of a gray-haired, deeply tanned man in his late sixties. **Some kind of introductory video,** Crane thought. But when the face smiled directly at him, he realized he wasn't looking at a computer monitor, but rather a closed-circuit television screen with a tiny camera embedded in its upper frame.

"Hello, Dr. Crane," the man said. He smiled, his kindly face breaking into a host of creases. "My name is Howard Asher."

"Pleased to meet you," Crane told the screen.

"I'm the chief scientist of the National Oceanic Agency. Have you heard of it?"

"Isn't that the ocean-management arm of the National Oceanographic Division?"

"That's correct."

"I'm a little confused, Dr. Asher—it's 'Doctor,' right?"

"Right. But call me Howard."

"Howard. What does the NOA have to do with an oil rig? And where's Mr. Simon, the person who I spoke with on the phone? The one who arranged all this? He said he'd be here to meet me."

"Actually, Dr. Crane, there is no Mr. Simon. But I'm here, and I'll be happy to explain what I can."

Crane frowned. "I was told there were medical issues with the divers maintaining the rig's underwater equipment. Was that a deception, too?"

"Only in part. There **has** been a lot of deception, and for that I'm sorry. But it was necessary. We had to be sure. You see, secrecy is absolutely critical to this project. Because what we have here, Peter—may I call you Peter?—is the scientific and historical discovery of the century."

"The century?" Crane repeated, unable to keep the disbelief from his voice.

"You're right to be skeptical. But this is no deception. It's the last thing from it. Still, 'discovery of the century' may not be quite accurate."

"I didn't think so," Crane replied.

"I should have called it the greatest discovery **of all time**."

2

Crane stared at the image on the screen. Dr. Asher was smiling back at him in a friendly, almost paternal way. But there was nothing in the smile that suggested a joke.

"I couldn't tell you the truth until you were physically here. And until you'd been fully vetted. We used your travel time to complete that process. Fact is, there's much I can't tell you, even now."

Crane looked over his shoulder. The library was empty. "Why? Isn't this line secure?"

"Oh, it's secure. But we need to know you're fully committed to the project first."

Crane waited, saying nothing.

"What little I can tell you is nevertheless highly secret. Even if you decline our offer, you will still be bound by all the confidentiality agreements you signed."

"I understand," Crane said.

"Very well." Asher hesitated. "Peter, the platform you're on right now is suspended over something more than an oil field. Something much more."

"What's that?" Crane asked automatically.

Asher smiled mysteriously. "Suffice to say the well drillers discovered something nearly two years ago. Something so fantastic that, overnight, the platform stopped pumping oil and took on a new and highly secret role."

"Let me guess. You can't tell me what it is."

Asher laughed. "No, not yet. But it's such an important discovery the government is, quite literally, sparing no expense to reclaim it."

"Reclaim?"

"It's buried in the sea bed directly below this platform. Remember I called this the discovery of all time? What's going on here is, in essence, a dig: an archaeological dig like none other. And we are, quite literally, making history."

"But why all the secrecy?"

"Because if people caught wind of what we've

found, it would instantly become front-page news on every paper in the world. In hours, the place would be a disaster area. Half a dozen governments, all claiming sovereignty, journalists, rubberneckers. The discovery is simply too critical to be jeopardized that way."

Crane leaned back in his chair, considering. The entire trip was becoming almost surreal. The rushed flight plans, the oil platform that wasn't a platform, the secrecy . . . and now this face in a box, speaking of an unimaginably important discovery.

"Call me old-fashioned," he said, "but I'd feel a lot better if you'd take the time to see me in person, talk face-to-face."

"Unfortunately, Peter, it's not that easy. Commit to the project, though, and you'll see me soon enough."

"I don't understand. Why, exactly, is it so difficult?"

Asher chuckled again. "Because at the moment, I'm several thousand feet beneath you."

Crane stared at the screen. "You mean—"

"Precisely. The Storm King oil platform is just the support structure, the resupply station. The **real** action is far below. That's why I'm speaking to you over this video feed."

Crane digested this a moment. "What's down there?" he asked quietly.

"Imagine a huge research station, twelve levels high, full of equipment and technology **beyond** cutting edge, placed on the ocean floor. That's the ERF—the heart and soul of the most extraordinary archaeological effort of all time."

"The ERF?"

"Exploratory and Recovery Facility. But we refer to it simply as the Facility. The military—you know how fond they are of buzzwords—have labeled it Deep Storm."

"I noticed the military presence. Why are the soldiers necessary?"

"I could tell you it's because the Facility is government property; because the NOA is a branch of the government. And that's true. But the real reason is because a lot of the technology we're using in the recovery project is classified."

"What about those men I saw topside, working on the rig?"

"Window dressing, for the most part. We do have to look like a functioning oil platform, after all."

"And AmShale?"

"They've been paid exceptionally well to lease us the rig, act as front office, and ask no questions."

Crane shifted in his chair. "This Facility you mention. That's where I'd be quartered?"

"Yes. It's where all the marine scientists and engineers live and work. I know how much time you've spent in submerged environments, Peter, and I think you'll be pleasantly surprised. Actually, 'amazed' is more like it. You've got to see the place to believe it—the Facility is a miracle of undersea technology."

"But why is it necessary? Working from the bottom of the sea, I mean. Why can't you run the operation from the surface?"

"The, ah, **remains** are buried too deep for most submersibles. Besides, submersible yield per dive is abysmally low. Trust me—once you're fully briefed, it will all make sense."

Crane nodded slowly. "I guess that leaves just one question. Why me?"

"Please, Dr. Crane. You're too modest. You're ex-military, you've served aboard stealth submarines and carriers. You know what it's like to live in confined spaces, under pressure. And I mean that both literally and figuratively."

He's done his research, Crane thought.

"You graduated second in your class from the Mayo Medical School. And due to your stint in the Navy, you're a medical doctor who has—among other things—familiarity with the disorders of divers and other seagoing workers."

"So there **is** a medical problem."

"Of course. The installation was completed two months ago, and the reclamation project is fully under way. However, in the last couple of weeks, several of the inhabitants of Deep Storm have been manifesting unusual symptoms."

"Caisson disease? Nitrogen narcosis?"

"More the former than the latter. But let's just say you are uniquely qualified—both as a doctor and as a former officer—to treat the affliction."

"And my tour of duty?"

"Your tour of duty will be, in effect, as long as it takes to diagnose and treat the problem. My best guess is you'll be with us for two to three weeks. But even if you were to effect a miracle cure, you'd still be at the Facility a minimum of six days. Not to go into details, but because of the tremendous atmospheric pressure at this depth we've developed a unique acclimatization process. The upside is that it allows people to operate at depth with significantly greater ease than in the past. The downside is that the process for entering or leaving the station is quite lengthy. And, as you can imagine, it can't be rushed."

"I can imagine." Crane had seen more than his share of fatal cases of decompression sickness.

"That's all there is, actually. Except of course to remind you again that, even if you decide against the assignment, you are under a strict code of secrecy never to mention your visit here or to reveal what has passed between us."

Crane nodded. He knew Asher had to be evasive. Still, the lack of information was irritating. Here he was, being asked to give up several weeks of his life for an assignment he knew next to nothing about.

And yet he had no ties preventing him from spending a few weeks on Deep Storm. He was recently divorced, without kids, and at present trying to decide between two research positions. No doubt Asher knew this, too.

An unimaginably important discovery. Despite the secrecy—or perhaps because of it—Crane felt his heart accelerating at the mere thought of being part of such an adventure. And he realized that, without even being aware of it, he'd already reached a decision.

Asher smiled again. "Well, then," he said, "if there are no more questions, I'll terminate the video feed and give you some time to think it over."

"That won't be necessary," Crane replied. "I don't need to think over history being made. Just point me in the right direction."

At this, Asher's smile grew broader. "That direction would be down, Peter. Straight down."

3

Peter Crane had spent almost four years of his life inside submarines, but this was the first time he'd ever had a window seat.

He'd killed several hours on the Storm King platform, first submitting to lengthy physical and psychological examinations, then hanging about the library, waiting for concealing darkness to fall. At last he was escorted to a special staging platform beneath the rig, where a Navy bathyscaphe awaited, tethered to a concrete footing. The sea heaved treacherously against the footing, and the gangplank leading to the bathyscaphe's access hatch had redundant guide ropes. Crane crossed over to the tiny conning tower. From there, he climbed down a metal ladder, slick with condensation, past the pressure hatch, through the float chamber, and into a cramped pressure sphere, where a very young officer was already at the controls.

"Take any seat, Dr. Crane," the man said.

Far above, a hatch clanged shut, then another, the sound reverberating dully through the submersible.

Crane glanced around at the cabin. Aside from the empty seats—arranged in three rows of two—every square inch of the walls and decking was covered by gauges, ducts, tubes, and instrumentation. The only exception was what looked like a narrow but extremely massive hatch set into the far wall. A smell hung in the close space—lubricating oil, dampness, perspiration—that instantly brought back his own years wearing the dolphins.

He sat down, put his bags on the adjoining seat, and turned toward the window: a small metal ring, studded around its circumference by steel bolts. He frowned. Crane had a submariner's innate respect for a thick steel hull, and this porthole seemed an alarming, needless luxury.

The sailor must have noticed his look, because he chuckled. "Don't worry. It's a special composite, built directly into the hull. We've come a long way since the old quartz windows of the **Trieste**."

Crane laughed in return. "Didn't know I was being so obvious."

"That's how I separate the military from the civilians," the youth said. "You used to be a sub jockey, right? Name's Richardson."

Crane nodded. Richardson was wearing the chevrons of a petty officer first class, and the insignia above the chevrons showed his rating was that of operations specialist.

"I did a two-year stint on boomers," Crane replied. "Then two more on fast attacks."

"Gotcha."

A distant scraping sounded from above: Crane guessed it was the gangplank being withdrawn. Then, from somewhere amid the tangle of instrumentation, came the faint squawk of a radio. "Echo Tango Foxtrot, cleared for descent."

Richardson grabbed a mike. "Constant One, this is Echo Tango Foxtrot. Aye, aye."

There was a low hiss of air, the muffled whisper of propellers. The bathyscaphe bobbed gently on the waves for a moment. The hiss grew briefly louder, then gave way to the sound of water flooding the ballast tanks. Immediately, the submersible began to settle. Richardson leaned over the controls and switched on a bank of exterior lights. Abruptly, the blackness outside the window was replaced by a storm of white bubbles.

"Constant One, Echo Tango Foxtrot on descent," he said into the mike.

"What's the depth of the Facility?" Crane asked.

"Just a shade over thirty-two hundred meters."

Crane did a quick mental conversion. Thirty-two hundred meters was over ten thousand feet. The Facility lay two miles beneath the surface.

Outside the porthole, the storm of bubbles slowly gave way to greenish ocean. Crane peered out, looking for fish, but all he could see was a few indistinct silvery shapes just beyond the circle of light.

Now that he was actually committed, he felt his curiosity swelling. As a distraction, he turned to Richardson. "How often do you make this trip?" he asked.

"Early on, when the Facility was coming online, we were making five, sometimes six trips a day. Full house each time. But now that the operation is nominal, weeks can pass without a single descent."

"But you still need to bring people up, right?"

"Nobody's come up. Not yet."

Crane was surprised by this. "Nobody?"

"No, sir."

Crane glanced back out the window. The bathyscaphe was descending rapidly, and the greenish cast of the water was quickly growing darker.

"What's it like inside?" he asked.

"Inside?" Richardson repeated.

"Inside the Facility."

"Never been inside."

Crane turned to look at him again in surprise.

"I'm just the taxi driver. The acclimation process is much too long for me to do any sight-seeing. One day in and three days out, they say."

Crane nodded. Outside the window, the water had grown still darker, and the surrounding ocean was now streaked with some kind of particulate matter. They were descending at an accelerating rate, and he yawned to clear his ears. He'd done his share of crash dives in the service, and they'd always been rather tense: officers and crew standing around, grim faced, while the sub's hull creaked and groaned under the increasing pressure. But there was no groaning from the bathyscaphe—just the faint hiss of air and the whirring of instrument fans.

Now the blackness beyond the porthole was absolute. He peered down into the inky depths below. Somewhere down there lay a beyond-state-of-the-art facility—along with something else, something unknown, waiting for him beneath the silt and sand of the ocean floor.

As if on cue, Richardson reached for something

beside his seat and passed it over. "Dr. Asher asked me to give you this. Said it might give you a bit to think about on the ride down."

It was a large blue envelope, sealed in two places and stamped with numerous warnings: CLASSIFIED. EYES ONLY. PROPRIETARY AND HIGHLY SECRET. At one corner was a government seal and a lot of small print full of dire warnings to whoever dared violate its confidentiality pact.

Crane turned the envelope over in his hands. Now that the moment had finally come, he felt a perverse reluctance to open it. He hesitated another moment, then carefully broke the seals and upended the envelope.

A laminated sheet and a small pamphlet dropped onto his lap. He picked up the sheet and glanced at it curiously. It was a schematic diagram of what appeared to be a large military installation, or perhaps a vessel, with the legend DECK 10—PERSONNEL QUARTERS (LOWER). He looked it over a moment, then put it aside and reached for the pamphlet.

The title **Code of Classified Naval Conduct** was stamped onto its cover. He flipped the pages, scanning the numerous articles and lists, then closed it with a snap. What was this, Asher's idea of a joke? He picked up the envelope and peered inside, preparing to put it aside.

Then he noticed a single folded paper stuck

within. He pulled it out, unfolded it, and began to read. As he did so, he felt a strange tingle start at his fingertips and travel quickly until it had consumed his entire frame:

EXTRACT FOLLOWS

Ref No. ERF-10230a

Abstract: Atlantis
        i. First recorded description
       ii. Precipitating events for submer-
          gence (conjecture)
      iii. Date of submergence: 9500 B.C.

Source: Plato, **Timaeus** dialogue

History tells of a mighty power which made an expedition against the whole of Europe. This power came out of an island in the Atlantic Ocean; it was larger than Libya and Asia put together, and was the route to other islands, and from these you might pass to the opposite continent which surrounded the true ocean.

Now in this island of Atlantis there was a great empire which ruled over the whole island and several others, and over parts of the continent. But then there occurred violent earthquakes and floods, and in a single day and night of misfortune the island of Atlantis disappeared far into the depths of the sea . . .

END OF EXTRACT

This brief quotation from Plato was all the sheet contained. But it was enough.

Crane let the document fall to his lap, staring out the porthole without seeing. This was Asher's coy welcome aboard—his way of telegraphing precisely what was being excavated two miles below the ocean's surface.

Atlantis.

It seemed beyond belief. And yet all the pieces fit: the secrecy, the technology, even the expense. It was the world's greatest mystery: the flourishing civilization of Atlantis, cut short in its prime by a cataclysmic eruption. A city beneath the sea. Who were its inhabitants? What secrets did they possess?

He waited, motionless in his seat, for the tingle of excitement to recede. And yet it did not. Perhaps, he decided, this was all a dream. Perhaps the alarm would go off in a few minutes, he'd wake up, and it would be just another sweltering day in North Miami. All this would evaporate and he'd be back to the old grind, trying to decide on a new research position. That had to be the answer. Because it wasn't possible he was descending to an ancient, long-hidden city or that he was about to become a participant in the most complex and important archaeological excavation of all time.

"Dr. Crane?"

At the sound of Richardson's voice, Crane roused himself abruptly.

"We're nearing the Facility," Richardson said.

"Already?"

"Yes, sir."

Crane glanced quickly out the porthole. At two miles down, the ocean was an intense silty black the exterior lights could barely penetrate. And yet there was a strange, ethereal glow that came—against all logic—from below, rather than above. He leaned closer, glanced downward, and caught his breath.

There, perhaps a hundred feet below them, lay a huge metallic dome, its perimeter buried in the sea floor. About halfway down its side, an open, circular tunnel about six feet across led inward, like the mouth of a funnel; otherwise, the surface was smooth and without blemish. There were no markings or insignia of any kind. It looked exactly like the crown of a gigantic silver marble, peeping up from a bed of sand. A bathyscaphe identical to the one he was in sat tethered to an escape hatch on the far side. At the dome's summit, a small forest of sensors and communications gear sprouted around a bulky object shaped like

an inverted teacup. From all over the dome's surface, a thousand tiny lights winked up at him like
jewels, flickering in and out in the deep ocean
currents.

Hidden beneath this protective dome was Deep
Storm: a cutting-edge city of technological mar-
vels. And somewhere **beneath** Deep Storm—as
ancient as the recovery Facility was new—lay the
unknown mystery and promise of Atlantis.

Staring, entranced, Crane realized he was grin-
ning like an idiot. He glanced over at Richardson.
The petty officer was watching him and grin-
ning, too.

"Welcome to Deep Storm, sir," he said.

4

Kevin Lindengood had worked everything out with fanatical attention. He knew the game was potentially dangerous—maybe even very dangerous. But it was a game about preparation and control. He was well prepared, and he was in complete control. And that was why there was nothing to worry about.

He leaned over the hood of his beat-up Taurus, watching the Biscayne Boulevard traffic pass by. This gas station was on one of Miami's busiest thoroughfares. You couldn't ask for a more public place. And a public place meant safety.

He loitered by the air pump, hose in hand, pretending to check the tires. It was a hot day, well over ninety, but Lindengood welcomed the heat. On the Storm King oil platform, he'd had enough ice and snow to last several lifetimes. Hicks and his damn iPod, Wherry and his swaggering . . . there was no way in hell he wanted to go back to that life. And if he played his cards right today, he wouldn't have to.

As he straightened up from the front passenger tire, a black sedan pulled into the station and parked in the service area, a dozen feet away. With a thrill that was half excitement and half fear, Lindengood saw his contact get out of the driver's seat. The man was wearing the clothes he had insisted on for the meeting: tank top and swimming trunks. No chance to conceal a weapon of any kind.

He glanced at his watch. Seven o'clock: the man had arrived precisely on time.

Preparation and control.

Now the man was walking toward him. In prior meetings, he'd said his name was Wallace, but had never volunteered a last name. Lindengood was fairly certain even Wallace was an alias. He was thin, with a swimmer's physique. He wore thick tortoiseshell glasses and limped slightly as he walked, as if one leg was a bit shorter than the other. Lindengood had never seen the man in a tank top before, and he couldn't help but be amused at how pale his skin was. Clearly, this was a fellow who spent most of his time in front of a computer.

"You got my message," Lindengood said as the man approached.

"What's this about?"

"I think we'd be more comfortable in my car," Lindengood replied.

The man stood still a moment, then shrugged and slipped into the passenger seat.

Lindengood walked around the front of the car and got in behind the wheel, careful to leave the door wide open. He kept the air hose in his hand, playing with it idly. The man wasn't going to try anything, not here—besides, he hardly looked the physical type—but on the off chance he did, Lindengood could use the air hose as a blackjack. Yet once again he reminded himself that wouldn't be necessary: he'd transact his bit of business and then vanish. Wallace didn't know where he lived, and Lindengood sure as hell wasn't about to tell him.

"You've been paid, and paid well," Wallace said in his quiet voice. "Your part of the job is finished."

"I know that," Lindengood replied, careful to keep his own voice firm and confident. "It's just that, now that I know a little more about your, um, **operation,** I'm beginning to think I was underpaid."

"You don't know anything about any operation."

"I know that it's far from kosher. Look, I'm the one who found **you,** remember?"

Wallace didn't answer. He simply stared back, his expression neutral, almost placid. Outside, the air compressor chuffed, then chimed, as it maintained pressure.

"See, I was one of the last of the crew to leave Storm King," Lindengood went on. "It happened a week after we'd finished our little business, and I'd fed you the last of the data. All these government types, all these scientists, began swarming over the place. And I got to thinking. Something huge, **really** huge, was taking place. It was a lot bigger than I'd ever thought. So just the fact you were interested in what I had to sell meant your people must have resources—**and** deep pockets."

"What's your point?" Wallace said.

Lindengood licked his lips. "My point is certain officials would be very, **very** eager to learn of your interest in Storm King."

"Are you threatening us?" Wallace asked. His quiet voice had gone silky.

"I don't want to use that word. Let's say I'm trying to redress an imbalance. Clearly my original fee wasn't nearly enough. Hey, I'm the guy who first discovered the readings, reported the anomaly. Doesn't that count for anything? And I passed the information on to you: all the readouts, the triangulation data, the telemetry from the deep-sea probe. **Everything.** And I'm the only one who could have done it—I made the connection, saw the data. No one else knows."

"No one else," Wallace repeated.

"Without me, your people wouldn't even have known about the project. You wouldn't have your own—I presume?—assets in place."

Wallace took off his glasses, began polishing them on the tank top. "How much were you thinking?"

"I was thinking fifty thousand."

"And then you'll go away for good. Is that it?"

Lindengood nodded. "You'll never hear from me again."

Wallace considered this for a moment, still polishing. "It'll take me a day or two to get the money together. We'll have to meet again."

"Two days is fine," Lindengood replied. "We can meet here, the same—"

Quick as a striking snake, Wallace's right fist shot out, index and middle knuckles extended, hammering Lindengood in the solar plexus. A crippling pain blossomed deep in his gut. Lindengood opened his mouth but no sound emerged. Involuntarily he bent forward, fighting to get his wind back, hands clutching his midriff. Now Wallace's right hand grabbed Lindengood by the hair and pulled him down onto the seat while brutally twisting his head around. Staring eyes wide with agony, Lindengood saw Wallace look first left, then right—glasses forgotten—checking that his actions were unobserved. Still holding Lindengood by the hair, he reached over to close the driver's door. As the man sat back again, Lindengood saw he had the air hose in his other hand.

"You, my friend, have just become a liability," Wallace said.

At last, Lindengood found he could speak. But as he drew in breath to yell, Wallace thrust the air hose into the back of his throat.

Lindengood retched and bucked violently. He pulled up from the seat despite the restraint, hair tearing out at the roots. Wallace grabbed a second, larger handful of hair, pulled him back, and with a brutal movement shoved the air hose directly down his windpipe.

Blood filled Lindengood's mouth and throat and he let out a gargling scream. But then Wallace clamped down on the compressor handle; air shot from the nozzle with terrible, overwhelming force; and a pain unlike anything Lindengood had ever remotely imagined exploded in his chest.

5

The voice that echoed over the talkback mike was pitched slightly high, as if the person on the other end was sucking helium. "Another five minutes, Dr. Crane, and you can pass through airlock C."

"Thank God." Peter Crane swung his legs off the metal bench where he'd been dozing, stretched, and checked his watch. It was 4 A.M.— but he suspected that, if the Facility was anything like a submarine, day and night held little meaning.

Six hours had passed since he'd left the bathyscaphe and entered the maze of airlocks known as the Compression Complex. He'd been cooling his heels since, waiting through the Facility's unusual acclimatization period. As a doctor, he was curious about this: he had no idea what it might consist of or what technology was involved. All that Asher had told him was that it made working at great depths easier. Perhaps they'd modified the atmospheric composition: reduced the amount of nitrogen and added some exotic gas. Whatever the case, it was clearly an important breakthrough—no doubt one of the classified elements that made this mission so hush-hush.

Every two hours, he had been instructed by the same disembodied chipmunk voice to pass into a new chamber. Each was identical: a large saunalike cube with tiers of metal bunks. The only difference had been the color. The first compression chamber had been military gray; the second, pale blue; and the third—rather surprisingly—red.

After finishing a short dossier on Atlantis he'd found in the initial chamber, Crane spent the time dozing or paging through a thick anthology of poetry he'd brought along. Or thinking. He spent a lot of time staring up at the metal ceiling—and the miles of water pressing down on him—and thinking.

He wondered about the cataclysm that could

have sunk the city of Atlantis to such a depth; about the lost civilization that had once flourished. It could not be the Greeks, or the Phoenicians, or the Minoans, or any of the other usual suspects favored by historians. As the dossier made clear, nobody knew anything about Atlantean civilization—not really. Although Crane was surprised the city was situated this far north, the dossier also explained that, even in the original sources, its actual location was obscure. Plato himself knew next to nothing about its citizenry or civilization. Perhaps, Crane mused, that was one reason it had remained hidden so long.

As the hours slowly passed, his feeling of disbelief refused to ebb. It all seemed miraculous. Not just that it had all happened so quickly, not just that the project was so breathtakingly important—but that they'd wanted **him**. He hadn't stressed the point to Asher, but the fact was he remained unsure why they'd so particularly required his services. After all, his specialty wasn't hematology or toxicology. **You are uniquely qualified— both as a doctor and as a former officer—to treat the affliction,** Asher had said. True, he was well versed in the disorders of those who lived in undersea environments, but there were other doctors who could make the same claim.

He stretched again, then shrugged. He'd learn the reason soon enough. And besides, it didn't really matter; being here was simply his good fortune. He wondered what strange and wonderful artifacts had been unearthed, what ancient secrets might already have been rediscovered.

There was a loud clank, and the hatchway in the far wall opened. "Please step through the airlock and into the passageway beyond," the voice said.

Crane did as instructed and found himself in a dimly lit cylindrical passage about twenty feet long with another closed hatch at the end. He stopped, waiting. The airlock behind him closed again with another sharp clank. There was a rush of escaping air, so violent that Crane's ears popped painfully. Then at last the forward hatch opened and yellow light flooded in. A figure stood in the hatchway, haloed in light, one arm outstretched in welcome. As Crane stepped out of the passageway and into the chamber beyond, he recognized the smiling face of Howard Asher.

"Dr. Crane!" Asher said, taking his hand and shaking it warmly. "Welcome to the Facility."

"Thanks," Crane replied. "Though I feel I've been here awhile already."

Asher chuckled. "We kept meaning to install DVD players in the compression chambers to help pass the acclimation time. But now that the station is fully staffed there didn't seem any point.

And we weren't anticipating any visitors. How did you find the reading material?"

"Incredible. Have you really discovered—"

But Asher stayed the question by raising his finger to his nose, winking, and giving Crane a conspiratorial smile. "The reality is more incredible than you can imagine. But first things first. Let me show you to your quarters. It's been a long trip, and I'm sure you'd like to freshen up."

Crane let Asher take one of his bags. "I'd like to know more about the acclimatization process."

"Of course, of course. This way, Peter. Did I already ask if I could call you Peter?" And he led the way with another smile.

Crane looked around curiously. They were in a square, low-ceilinged vestibule with gray-tinted windows lining the opposing walls. Behind one of the windows sat two technicians at a bank of controls, staring back at him. One of them saluted.

At the end of the vestibule, a white hallway led off into the top level of the Facility. Asher was already heading down it, bag slung over one shoulder, and Crane hastened behind him. The hall was narrow—of course—but not nearly as cramped as he'd expected. The lighting was unexpected, too: warm and incandescent, quite unlike the harsh fluorescence of submarines. The atmosphere was yet another surprise: warm and pleas-

ingly humid. There was a faint, almost undetectable smell in the air Crane didn't recognize:
coppery, metallic. He wondered if it was related
to the atmosphere technology the Facility employed.

As they walked, they passed several closed
doors, white like the hallway. Some bore individual's names, others abbreviated titles like ELEC
PROC or SUBSTAT II. A worker—a young man
wearing a jumpsuit—opened one of the doors as
they passed by. He nodded to Asher, looked curiously at Crane, then headed back toward the
vestibule. Peering inside, Crane got a look at a
room full of rack-mounted blade servers and a
small jungle of networking hardware.

Crane realized the walls and doors were not
painted white, after all. Instead, they were constructed of some unusual composite that seemed
to take on the color of their environment: in this
case, the light of the hallway. He could see his
own ghostly reflection in the door, along with a
strange, platinum-colored underhue.

"What is this material?" he asked.

"Newly developed alloy. Light, nonreactive, exceptionally strong."

They reached an intersection and Asher turned
left. From the image, Crane had assumed the
chief scientist of the National Ocean Service to be
in his late sixties, but he was obviously a decade

younger. What Crane had taken for age lines was really the weathering of a life spent at sea. Asher walked quickly, and he toted Crane's heavy bag as if it were nothing. For all his apparent healthiness, however, the man kept his left arm cradled against his side. "These upper levels of the Facility are a warren of offices and dormitories, and they can be disorienting at first," he said. "If you ever get lost, refer to the schematic diagrams at major intersections."

Crane was impatient to learn more about the medical issues and the dig itself, but he decided to let Asher set the agenda. "Tell me about the Facility," he said.

"Twelve decks high, and exactly one hundred eighty meters per side. Its base is embedded into the matrix of the ocean floor, and a protective titanium dome has been placed over it."

"I saw the dome on the way down. That's some piece of engineering."

"It is indeed. This Facility we're in sits beneath it like a pea under a shell, and the open space between is fully pressurized. With the dome and our own hull, there are two layers of metal between us and the ocean. And it's some metal, too: the skin of the Facility is HY250, a new kind of aerospace steel, with a fracture toughness above twenty thousand foot-pounds and a yield strength in the range of three hundred KSI."

"I noticed the surface of the dome was punctured by a horizontal tube, running inward," Crane said. "What's the purpose of that?"

"You must mean the pressure spoke. There are two of them, actually, one on either side of the Facility. Given the water pressure at these depths, the ideal shape would be a perfect sphere. The dome being only one half of an ideal sphere, those two tubes—open to the ocean—help counterbalance the pressure. They also anchor the Facility to the dome. No doubt the propeller-heads on deck seven could give you more details."

This second hallway they were walking through resembled the first: a ceiling busy with cabling and pipes, lots of closed doors with cryptic labels. "I also noticed a strange object attached to the top of the dome, maybe thirty feet across," Crane said.

"That's the emergency escape pod. Just in case someone accidentally pulls the plug." Asher laughed as he said this—an easy, infectious laugh.

"Sorry, but I have to ask. That dome around us isn't exactly small. Surely certain foreign governments have taken interest?"

"Naturally. We've carefully disseminated a disinformation campaign about a secret research sub that went down at this site. They think we're involved in reclamation operations. That doesn't stop the occasional Russian or Chinese sub from doing a drive-by, of course, causing our military contingent all sorts of angst."

They passed by a door with a retinal scanner beside it and a complement of two marines, rifles at their sides, standing guard. Asher didn't offer an explanation, and Crane didn't ask.

"We're on deck twelve right now," Asher went on. "It's mostly support services for the rest of the Facility. Decks eleven and ten are crew quarters, including the sports complex. You're bunking on deck ten, incidentally. We've got you sharing a bath with Roger Corbett, the mental health officer. Most rooms share baths—as you can imagine, space is at a premium. We've already got a full complement, and you're an unexpected addition."

He paused before an elevator, pressed the button. "Deck nine is crew support. The medical suite—where you'll be working—is there as well. And deck eight holds the administrative offices and research facilities."

There was a quiet chime and the elevator doors whispered open. Asher waved Crane in, then followed.

The elevator was of the same strange material as the corridor. There were six unmarked buttons on the panel: Asher pushed the third from the top and the elevator began to descend.

"Where was I? Oh, yes. And deck seven is the

science level. Computer center, scientific laboratories of every description."

Crane shook his head. "It's unbelievable."

Asher beamed, looking as proud as if the Facility were his own, rather than on loan from the government. "I've left out a hundred things you'll discover for yourself. There are mess halls served by kitchens specializing in haute cuisine. Half a dozen lounges, comfortable accommodations for over four hundred persons. Basically, Peter, we're a small city, two miles below the surface of the ocean, far from prying eyes."

"'In th' ocean's bosom unespied,'" Crane quoted.

Asher looked at him curiously, a half smile on his face. "That's Andrew Marvell, isn't it?"

Crane nodded. "'Bermudas.'"

"Don't tell me you're a reader of poetry."

"Now and then. I got the habit during all that downtime on sub duty. It's my secret vice."

The smile widened on Asher's wind-tanned face. "Peter, I like you already."

The elevator chimed again, and the doors rolled back onto another corridor, much wider and busier than the others. Glancing out, Crane was shocked at how well-appointed the staff quarters appeared to be. There was elegant carpeting on the floor, and—miraculously—framed oil paintings on wallpapered walls. It reminded him of the lobby of a luxury hotel. People in uniforms and lab coats were walking past, chatting. Everyone had an ID badge clipped to a collar or shirt pocket.

"The Facility is a marvel of engineering," Asher went on. "We were extremely lucky to get the use of it. In any case, this is deck ten. Any questions before I show you to your quarters?"

"Just one. Earlier, you said there were twelve decks. But you've only described six. And this elevator has only six buttons." Crane pointed at the control panel. "What about the rest of the station?"

"Ah." Asher hesitated. "The lower six decks are classified."

"Classified?"

Asher nodded.

"But why? What goes on there?"

"Sorry, Peter. I'd like to tell you, but I can't."

"I don't understand. Why not?"

But Asher didn't answer. He simply gave him another sly smile: half chagrined, half conspiratorial.

If the Facility's living quarters reminded Crane of a luxury hotel, then deck 9 seemed closer in spirit to a cruise ship.

Asher had given him an hour to shower and stow his gear, then he'd shown up to escort him to the medical suite. "Time to meet your fellow inmates," he'd joked. On the way, he gave Crane a brief tour of the deck below his own quarters, known officially as Crew Support.

But "Crew Support" didn't begin to do deck 9 justice. Asher steered him briefly past a hundred-

seat theater and a fully stocked digital library before leading him to a large plaza bustling with activity. Music echoed faintly from what looked like
a miniature sidewalk café. On the far side of the
plaza, Crane made out a pizzeria, and beside it a
small oasis of greenery surrounded by benches.
Everything was miniaturized to fit into the small
footprint of the Facility, but it was so artfully con-
trived there was no sense of crowding or claustro-
phobia.

"Deck nine has a unique layout," Asher said.
"Basically, it's constructed around two large per-
pendicular corridors. Someone dubbed their intersection Times Square."

"Remarkable."

"The multimedia nexus and laundry are down
that way. And over there is the PX." Asher
pointed at a storefront that looked more like an
upscale department store than a commissary.

Crane stared at the small knots of workers all
around him: chatting, sipping coffee at small tables, reading books, typing on laptops. A few
were in military uniform, but the majority wore
casual clothes or lab wear. He shook his head; it
seemed almost unthinkable that miles of ocean
lay above their heads.

"I can't believe the military built something like
this," he said.

Asher grinned. "I doubt the original designers

had this in mind. But you have to remember this project will last many months. And leaving isn't an option, except under the most extreme circumstances. Unlike you, most of the workers here have no experience in submarines. Our scientists aren't used to living inside a steel box without doors or windows. So we do what we can to make life as bearable as possible."

Crane, inhaling the scent of freshly ground coffee wafting from the café, decided life here would be very bearable indeed.

On the far side of the tiny park, he could make out an oversize flat-panel display, perhaps ten feet by ten, with a group of benches set before it. On closer inspection, he noticed it was actually an array of smaller displays placed in a grid to project a single image. That image was dim, green-black ocean depths. Strange, almost otherworldly fish floated by: bizarrely articulated eels, colossal jellies, balloon-shaped fish with a single lighted tentacle on their heads. Crane recognized some of the species: fangtooth, deep sea angler, viperfish.

"Is that the view outside?" he asked.

"Yes, via a remote camera outside the dome." Asher waved his arm around the little square. "A lot of the workers spend their off hours here, relaxing in the library or watching interactive movies in the multimedia nexus. The sports center on deck ten is also very popular: remind me to show you around it later. Also, we'll need to get you chipped."

"Chipped?"

"Tag you with a RFID chip."

"Radio frequency identification? Is that necessary?"

"This is a very secure installation. I'm afraid so."

"Will it hurt?" Crane asked, only half joking.

Asher chuckled. "The tag's the size of a grain of rice, implanted subcutaneously. Now, let's get to the medical suite. Michele and Roger are waiting. It's this way, at the end of the corridor."And Asher pointed with his right hand down one of the wide hallways. At the end, past the PX and café and a half dozen other entranceways, Crane could just make out a double set of frosted glass doors, marked with red crosses.

Once again, he noticed Asher kept his left arm tucked in stiffly against his side. "Something wrong with your arm?" he asked as they made their way down the hallway.

"Vascular insufficiency of the upper extremity," Asher replied.

Crane frowned. "Is the pain significant?"

"No, no. I just need to be a little careful."

"I'll say you do. How long have you had the condition?"

"A little over a year. Dr. Bishop has me on a Coumadin regimen, and I exercise regularly. We have a fine set of squash courts in the sports complex." Asher bustled ahead, apparently eager to change the subject. Crane reflected that if Asher had not been the chief scientist, such a condition would probably have kept him on dry land.

The medical suite was engineered like the other spaces Crane had already seen: meticulously designed to fit as many things as possible into the smallest area, yet without appearing cramped. Unlike usual hospital practice, the lighting was kept indirect and even mellow, and piped classical music came from everywhere and nowhere at the same time. Asher led the way through the waiting area, nodding to a receptionist behind the front desk.

"Like everything else in the Facility, the medical suite is state-of-the-art," he said as he ushered Crane past a records office and down the carpeted corridor. "Besides our doctor, we have four nurses, three interns, a diagnostician, a nutritionist, and two lab specialists. A fully stocked emergency unit. Equipment for just about every test you can name, from simple X-rays to whole body scans. All backed up with a comprehensive pathology lab on deck seven."

"Beds?"

"Forty-eight, with contingencies for double that if necessary. But let's hope it never is: we'd never get anything done." Asher stopped outside a door marked CONFERENCE ROOM B. "Here we are."

The room was small and even more dimly lit than the waiting area. A large videoconferencing screen hung on one wall, while the others sported innocuous watercolors of landscapes and sea-scapes. Most of the space was taken up by a large, round table. At its far end sat two people, a woman and a man. Both wore officer's uniforms beneath white lab coats.

As Crane entered, the man sprang up from his seat. "Roger Corbett," he said, reaching across the table to shake Crane's hand. He was short, with thinning mouse-colored hair and watery blue eyes. He had a small, neatly trimmed beard of the kind favored by psychiatric interns.

"You're the mental health officer," Crane said, shaking the proffered hand. "I'm your new neighbor."

"So I understand." Corbett's voice was low for a man of his size, and he spoke slowly and deliberately, as if weighing each phrase. He wore round glasses with thin silver rims.

"Sorry to barge in on your domestic arrangements."

"Just so you don't snore."

"No promises. Better keep your door closed."

Corbett laughed.

"And this is Michele Bishop." Asher indicated the woman seated across the table. "Dr. Bishop, Dr. Peter Crane."

The woman nodded. "Nice to see you."

"Likewise," Crane replied. The young woman was slender, as tall as Corbett was short, with dark blond hair and an intense gaze. She was attractive but not stunningly so. Crane assumed she was the station's chief medical officer. It was interesting that she had neither stood nor offered to shake his hand.

"Please, Dr. Crane, have a seat," Corbett said.

"Call me Peter."

Asher beamed at each of them in turn like a proud parent. "Peter, I'll leave you to the kindly ministrations of these two. They'll bring you up to speed. Michele, Roger, I'll check in later." Then, with a wink and a nod, he stepped out into the corridor and closed the door.

"Can I get you something to drink, Peter?" Corbett asked.

"No thanks."

"A snack of some kind?"

"I'm fine, really. The sooner we get to the medical problem, the better."

Corbett and Bishop exchanged glances.

"Actually, Dr. Crane, it's not 'problem,'" Bishop said. "It's 'problems.'"

"Really? Well, I guess I'm not surprised. After

all, if we're dealing with some variant of caisson disease here, it often presents in a variety of ways."

Caisson disease was so named because it was first diagnosed in the mid-nineteenth century in men working in environments of compressed air. One environment was in the first caisson dug beneath New York's East River to support the Brooklyn Bridge. If the diggers in the caisson reemerged into open air too quickly after working under pressure, nitrogen bubbles formed in their bloodstreams. This caused, among other symptoms, intense pain in the arms and legs. Sufferers frequently doubled over in agony, and the ailment became known—mordantly—as the Grecian bend. This led to the nickname "the bends." Given the depth at which they were currently working, Crane felt certain caisson disease was involved one way or another.

"I assume you have a hyperbaric oxygen therapy chamber or some other kind of recompression equipment on site you've been treating the patients with?" he asked. "When we're done here, I'd like to question them directly, if you don't mind."

"Actually, Doctor," Bishop said in a clipped voice, "I think we could proceed more quickly if you let me outline the symptomology, rather than make assumptions."

This took Crane by surprise. He looked at her,

unsure why she had responded so tartly. "Sorry if I'm overeager or presumptuous. It's been a long trip, and I'm very curious. Go right ahead."

"We initially became aware something was wrong about two weeks ago. At first it seemed more a psychological issue than a physiological one. Roger noticed a spike in the number of walk-in visits."

Crane glanced at Corbett. "What were the symptoms?"

"Some people complained of sleep disturbances," Corbett said. "Others, malaise. A few cases of eating disorders. The most common complaint seemed difficulty in focusing on what they were doing."

"Then the physical symptoms began," Bishop said. "Constipation. Nausea. Neurasthenia."

"Are people working double shifts down here?" Crane asked. "If so, I'm not surprised they're feeling fatigued."

"Others complained of muscle tics and spasms."

"Just tics?" Crane asked. "No associated pain?"

Bishop looked at him with mild reproach, as if to say, **If there had been pain, I would have mentioned it, wouldn't I?**

"These people aren't presenting with caisson disease," Crane said. "At least, no variant I'm aware of. I guess I don't see the concern. Problems with concentration or focus, constipation, nausea . . . that's all non-specific. It could simply be work-induced stress. It's an unusual environment and an unusual assignment, after all."

"I'm not through," Bishop said. "Over the last week, the problems have grown worse. Three cases of cardiac arrhythmia in people with no history of heart disorders. A woman with bilateral weakness of the hands and face. And two others suffered what appeared to be transient ischemic attacks."

"TIAs?" Crane said. "How extensive?"

"Partial paralysis, slurred speech, lasting in each case less than two hours."

"What were their ages?"

"Late twenties and early thirties."

"Really?" Crane frowned. "That seems awfully young for a stroke. **Two** strokes, at that. You did neurological workups?"

"Dr. Crane, please. Of **course** we did neurological workups. Noncontrast cranial CT scans; EKGs to check for cardioembolic event triggers; the rest. There's no EEG on the station—you know they're mainly used for seizure disorders or coma—but in any case it wasn't necessary here. Except for evidence of stroke, **everything** was completely normal."

Once again the tartness had crept into her tone. **She's territorial,** Crane thought. **This is her turf and she doesn't like me stepping on it.**

"Even so," he said, "it's the first evidence of dysbarism I've heard today."

"Dysbarism?" Corbett asked, blinking through his round glasses.

"Decompression sickness. Caisson disease."

Bishop sighed. "Actually, I believe that caisson disease is the one thing we can safely rule out."

"Why? I assumed—" Crane fell silent. He realized that Asher had never told him outright what the problem was. Given the nature of the Deep Storm station, he'd assumed caisson disease.

"I'm sorry," he went on more slowly. "I guess I don't understand why, exactly, you people asked for me."

"Howard Asher asked for you," Bishop said. And for the first time, she smiled. A brief silence fell over the conference room.

"Have you been able to isolate any commonalities?" Crane asked. "Do the patients all work on the same level or in the same general area of the Facility?"

Bishop shook her head. "We've received patients from most of the decks and from all general work areas."

"So there's no common vector. And no common complaint. It all seems like coincidence to me. Just how many patients, total, have you received?"

"Roger and I figured that out while we were

waiting for you." Bishop took a sheet of paper from her lab coat pocket and glanced at it. "The Facility has been operational almost five months. On average, between mental health services and medical, we see perhaps fifteen patients a week. In the past, nothing worse than a case of strep. But since this thing started, we've seen one hundred and three."

Crane was stunned. "One hundred and three? My God, that's—"

"A quarter of the population, Dr. Crane. And far, **far** too large a number to be coincidence."

And she stuffed the paper back into her pocket with something almost like triumph.

7

Crane stood in the silence of his quarters on deck 10, rubbing his chin thoughtfully. The room was small, and—like the rest of the Facility—softly lit. There was a narrow bed, two chairs, a walk-in dressing alcove, and a desk with a terminal that was linked to the Facility's central network. Beside the desk, a comm unit set into the wall allowed Crane to dial the Medical suite, reseve a lane at the bowling alley, even order a pizza delivery from Times Square. Save for a large flat-panel television, the light-blue walls were devoid of prints or decoration.

There were two doors of the same strange platinum-hued metal he'd seen elsewhere, but here they were tastefully edged in blond wood. One led to the outside corridor, the other to the bath he shared with Roger Corbett. The mental health officer had offered to take him to lunch at Top, the prosaically named mess on deck 11. Crane said he'd meet him there. He wanted a few minutes alone first.

A sealed folder lay on the desk, his name and a bar code imprinted along one edge. Crane picked up the folder, broke the seal with a fingernail, and dumped the contents onto the desk. Out fell a bulky name tag with a magnetic stripe and pocket clip; another copy of **Code of Classified Naval Conduct**; a two-page bibliography of books on Atlantis, all available in the library or for download to his terminal; and an envelope that contained a list of temporary passwords for the general and medical computer networks.

He clipped the ID to his pocket. Then he sat down at the desk and stared a moment at the blank screen. At last, with a sigh, he booted up the terminal and logged on with his temporary password, pausing to massage the spot on his upper arm where the radio tag had been inserted a few minutes earlier. Opening the text editor, he began to type.

Non-specific symptomology:
   physiological—& neurological??—deficits
   & psychological—detachment / dissociation
Check clinical presentations
Look for index case?
Atmospheric / environmental?
Poisoning: systemic or general?
Preexisting condition(s)?

He pushed back from the desk and glanced at the screen. **Caisson disease? Nitrogen narcosis?** he'd asked Asher from the Storm King oil platform. **More the former than the latter,** had been the reply. Crane was only now beginning to understand just how evasive that answer had been. In fact, Dr. Asher—as affable and open as he appeared to be—had so far told him next to nothing.

This was annoying, maybe even a little alarming. But in one respect it didn't really matter. Because, at last, Crane was beginning to understand why Asher had so specifically requested him—

"Is it all becoming clear, then?" asked a voice at his shoulder.

Crane almost leapt out of his seat in surprise. He wheeled around, heart racing, to see a rather

astonishing sight. An old man in faded bib overalls was standing there. He had piercing blue eyes,
and a shock of silvery hair stuck up, Einstein-like,
from his forehead. He was very short—no taller
than five feet—and gaunt. For a moment, Crane
wondered if he'd come to repair something. The
door to the room was closed. There had been no
knock, no sound of entry. It was as if the man had
materialized out of thin air.

"Excuse me?"

The man looked over Crane's shoulder at the
screen. "My, my. So few words, so many question
marks."

Crane cleared the screen with the touch of a key.
"I don't believe we've had the pleasure of meeting," he said drily.

The man laughed: a high, piping sound like the
twitter of a bird. "I know. I came to make your acquaintance. I heard there was a Dr. Crane on
board and that intrigued me." He held out his
hand. "The name's Flyte. Dr. Flyte."

"Pleased to meet you."

An awkward silence followed and Crane sought
a neutral, polite question. "What's your role here,
Dr. Flyte?"

"Autonomous mechanical systems."

"What's that?"

"Spoken like a true newcomer. The Facility is
like a frontier town—and, if you're a fan of West-

ern movies, as I am, you would know that in a
frontier town there are two questions you don't
ask: Where do you come from? And: Why are you
here?" Flyte paused. "Suffice to say, I'm indispensable—more's the pity. My work is **highly** classified."

"That's nice," said Crane lamely, at a loss for a
reply.

"You think so? Not I. This is no happy assignment, Dr. Crane, here so far beneath νύμε εος
όαίρω."

Crane blinked. "Beg pardon?"

"Bless me, not **another**!" Flyte raised his eyes
skyward. "Does no one speak the mother tongue
anymore? There was a time when ancient Greek
was sung upon every civilized lip." He wagged a
finger at Crane. "'Ocean, who is the source of all.'
Homer, you see, was a countryman of mine. You
would do well to read him."

Crane resisted an impulse to glance at his
watch. Roger Corbett was waiting for him in Top.
"It was nice meeting you—"

"And you," Flyte interrupted. "I am a great ad-
mirer of any practitioners of the noble art."

Crane began to feel a swell of annoyance. He
wondered how a man like Flyte had managed to
slip through the vetting process everyone must
have undergone before being admitted to the Fa-

cility. The best way to handle things, he decided, was to cut short any attempts at friendship on his part.

"Dr. Flyte, I'm sure you've got as busy a day ahead as I do—"

"Not at all! I've all the time in the world . . . at the moment. It's only when the drilling resumes that they might need me and my artistry." He held up his small hands and wiggled his fingers as if he were a concert pianist.

The man's bright eyes began to wander and fell once again on the open duffel. "What have we here?" he asked, reaching down and picking up a couple of books peeking out of the open duffel. He held up one of them, **An Anthology of Twentieth Century Poetry.**

"What is the meaning of this?" the man demanded crossly.

"What does it look like?" said Crane, exasperated. "It's a book of poetry."

"I have no time for modern poetry, and neither should you. Like I said: read Homer." The man dropped the book back onto the duffel and glanced at the other volume, **Pi: Its History and Mystery.** "Aha! And this?"

"It's a book about irrational numbers."

The man laughed and nodded. "Indeed! And how appropriate, no?"

"Appropriate for what?"

The man looked up at him in surprise. "Irrational numbers! Don't you see?"

"No. I don't see."

"It's so obvious. A number of us here are irrational, aren't we? If we're not, I fear we soon will be." He extended a wiry index finger and tapped Crane on the chest. "That's why you're here. Because it's **broken**."

"What's broken?"

"**Everything** is broken," Flyte repeated in an urgent whisper. "Or at least, will be very soon."

Crane frowned. "Dr. Flyte, if you don't mind—"

Flyte held up one hand. The mood of sudden urgency seemed to pass. "It hasn't occurred to you yet, but we have something in common." He paused significantly.

Crane swallowed. He was not about to ask what it was. But it seemed that Flyte needed no encouragement.

The man leaned forward, as if to share a confidence. "Our names. Crane. Flyte. You understand?"

Crane sighed. "No offense, but I'm going to have to ask you to leave. I have a lunch appointment I'm already late for."

The tiny old man cocked his head to one side and grasped Crane's hand. "Delighted to make your acquaintance, Dr. Crane. As I said, we've got something in common, you and I. And we need to stick together."

With a parting wink he ducked outside, leaving the door open. A moment later Crane went to close it, and he glanced curiously down the long corridor. It was empty, and there was no sign of the strange old man. It was as if he'd never been there at all.

8

Howard Asher sat at the desk in his cramped office on deck 8, staring intently at a computer screen. The wash of color from the flat-panel monitor turned his silver-gray hair a strange, ethereal blue.

Behind him was a metal bookcase stuffed with technical manuals, textbooks on oceanography and marine biology, and a few well-worn collections of poetry. Above the bookcase were several framed etchings: reproductions of Piranesi studies taken from **Vedute di Roma**. Another, smaller bookcase, this one with a glass door, held a variety of maritime curiosities: a fossilized coelacanth, a battered handspike from a clipper ship, a tooth from the impossibly reclusive Blue Grotto shark. Neither the diminutive size of the office nor its eclectic collections gave any evidence its occupant was the chief scientist of the National Ocean Service.

Faintly, through the closed door, came the sound of approaching footsteps. Then a face appeared in the glass window of the door. Glancing over, Asher recognized the red hair and freckled face of Paul Easton, one of several marine geologists at work on the reclamation project.

Asher swiveled in his chair, leaned over, opened the door. "Paul! Good to see you."

Easton stepped in, closed the door behind him. "I hope I'm not catching you at a bad time, sir."

"How often do I have to tell you, Paul? My name's Howard. Here at the Facility, we're on a first-name basis. Just don't tell Admiral Spartan I said so." And Asher chuckled at his little joke.

Easton, however, did not laugh.

Asher regarded him carefully. Normally, Easton was a puckish fellow, fond of practical jokes and very dirty limericks. Today, however, he was frowning, and his youthful features looked somber. More than that: Easton looked worried.

Asher waved a hand at the lone empty chair. "Sit down, Paul, and tell me what's on your mind."

Although Easton sat down immediately, he did not speak. Instead, he raised a hand to his forearm and began rubbing it gently.

"Is something wrong, son?" Asher asked.

"I don't know," Easton said. "Maybe."

He was still rubbing his arm. Some people, Asher knew, had minor skin reactions from the RFID chip implantation process.

"It's the vulcanism," Easton said abruptly.

"The vulcanism."

"At the burial site. I've been working with several samples of basalt from the sea floor, trying to get a firm date for when the burial event occurred."

Asher nodded in encouragement.

"You know how it is." Easton seemed to grow flustered, or maybe defensive. "Because the undersea currents in this region are so strong, the sedimentation of the ocean floor is all messed up."

"Is that the technical term for it?" Asher said, trying to lighten the tone.

Easton didn't notice. "There's no layering, no stratification. Core sampling is virtually useless. And you can't get any kind of clear dating from visual examination, either. There isn't the kind of weathering or erosion you'd find on land. So I've been trying to date the basalt formation by cross-comparison with known samples in our geological database. But I couldn't get any definitive match. So then I decided to date the sample from the decay of radioactive isotopes within the basalt."

"Go on," Asher said.

"Well." Easton seemed to grow even more nervous. "You know how we've always put a rough estimate on when the burial event took place. It's just that . . ." He faltered, started again. "I made the same assumption in my tests. I never checked for magnetic field reversal."

Now Asher realized why Easton seemed so flustered. The man had made the one mistake a scientist should never make: he'd made an assumption, and as a result skipped a basic test. Something inside Asher relaxed.

Time to play the frowning paterfamilias. "I'm glad you told me, Paul. It's always embarrassing when we realize we haven't followed the scientific method. And the dumber the mistake, the dumber we feel. The good news here is that no vital work was compromised as a result. So my advice to you? Feel bad, but don't feel broken."

The worried look had not left Easton's face. "No, Dr. Asher, you don't understand. You see, just today, I performed that test, measured the magnetism. And **there was no magnetic reversal in the sample**."

Abruptly, Asher sat up in his chair. Then he settled back slowly, trying to keep surprise from blossoming over his face. "What did you say?"

"The samples. There's no evidence of magnetic reversal."

"Are you sure the orientation of the samples was correct?"

"Absolutely."

"And you made sure there was no anomaly? That you weren't using a bad sample?"

"I checked all my samples. The results were the same in each case."

"But that can't be. Magnetic reversal is a fail-safe method of dating rock samples." Asher exhaled slowly. "This must mean the entombment happened even longer ago than we thought. Dating back **two** reversals, rather than just one. North to south, then south to north again. I'm sure your examination of the isotopes will confirm that."

"No, sir," Easton said.

Asher looked at him sharply. "What do you mean, no?"

"I've already checked the radioactive isotopes. There's hardly any decay. Hardly any at all."

Asher said simply, "Impossible."

"I've spent the last four hours in Radiography. I ran the tests three times. Here are the results."

And Easton removed a DVD from his lab coat pocket and laid it on Asher's worktable.

Asher stared at it but did not touch it. "So all our conclusions were wrong. The burial event is much more **recent** than we expected. Have you got a new date, based on the tests?"

"Just a rough one, sir, for now."

"And that is?"

"Approximately six hundred years ago."

Very slowly, Asher leaned back in his chair. **"Six hundred years."**

Once again, the tiny office fell into silence.

"You need to requisition one of the rovers," Asher said at last. "Have it fitted with an electron-phasing magnetometer, do several passes over the burial site. You'll take care of that?"

"Yes, Dr. Asher."

"Very good."

Asher watched as the young geologist stood up, nodded, made for the door.

"And, Paul?" he said quietly.

The man turned back.

"Do it right away, please. And don't tell anyone. Not a soul."

9

Crane looked up from the digital clipboard that he'd been scribbling notes on with a plastic stylus. "And that's it? Just some pain in the legs?"

The man in the hospital bed nodded. Even beneath the sheet it was clear he was tall and well built. He had good color, and his eyes were clear.

"On a scale of one to ten, how severe is the pain?"

The man thought a moment. "Depends. I'd say around six. Sometimes a little more."

Nonfebrile myalgia, Crane jotted on the clipboard. It seemed impossible—no, it **was** impossible—this man had suffered a ministroke two days ago. He was too young, and, besides, none of the tests indicated one had occurred. There were only the initial complaints: partial paralysis, slurred speech.

"Thank you," Crane said, shutting the metal clipboard. "I'll let you know if I have any more questions." And he stepped back from the bed.

Although termed a "suite," the medical facility of the Deep Storm station boasted equipment that a moderate-sized hospital might envy. In addition to the ER, surgical bays, and two dozen patient rooms, there were numerous breakout areas for specialties from radiography to cardiology. There was a separate complex in which the staff had working areas and conference rooms. It was here that Crane had been given a small but well-equipped office with an attached lab.

Of all the recent complaints Dr. Bishop had described, only three had been severe enough to warrant hospitalization. Crane had already interviewed two of the patients—a forty-two-year-old man suffering from nausea and diarrhea, and this supposed stroke victim—and the fact was, neither really needed to be hospitalized. No doubt Dr. Bishop was just keeping them under observation.

Crane turned and nodded to Bishop, who was standing well back.

"There's no indication of TIA," he said as they stepped into the corridor.

"Except for the initial presentation."

"You witnessed it yourself, you said?"

"I did. And the man was clearly having a transient ischemic attack."

Crane hesitated. Bishop had said little during his examination of the two patients, but the hostility had been just below the surface. She wouldn't like having her diagnosis called into question.

"There are numerous syndromes that can present in similar fashion—" he began as diplomatically as possible.

"I did my internship in a vascular care unit. I've seen more than my share of patients stroke out. I know a TIA when I see one."

Crane sighed. Her defensiveness was starting to wear on him. True, nobody liked an interloper, and perhaps that's what he seemed. But the fact was the medical team here had only done superficial tests, treating each case as a separate event. He was convinced that if they dug deeper, ran more extensive tests, some commonality would surface. And despite what Bishop had told him, he was still betting on caisson disease as the main differential.

"You never answered my question before," he said. "There is a hyperbaric chamber here, right?"

She nodded.

"I'd like this man placed in the chamber. Let's see if repressurization and pure oxygen ease the pains in his extremities."

"But—"

"Dr. Bishop, Asher told me this Facility uses some kind of classified pressurization technology. Basically untested in the field. That makes the bends the most likely culprit by far."

Bishop did not reply; instead, she frowned and looked away.

Crane felt himself growing impatient. "Feel free to talk to Asher if you don't like it," he said crisply, "but he brought me down here to make suggestions. Now please get this patient to the chamber." He paused to let this sink in. "Shall we visit patient number three?"

He had saved the most interesting case for last: a woman who presented with numbness and weakness in both hands and face. She was awake when they entered her room. Latest-generation monitoring equipment surrounded her, bleating quietly. Immediately, Crane sensed a difference. He noted the distress in her yellowish eyes, the wasting body rigid with worry. Even without per-forming a diagnostic procedure, he knew this case might be serious.

He opened the clipboard, and the LCD screen sprang to life. The patient history came up automatically. **Must be tagged to her RFID chip,** Crane thought.

He glanced over the summary data:

Name:	Philips, Mary E.
Sex:	F
Age:	36
Brief Presentation:	Bilateral weakness / numbness of hands and face

When he looked up from the clipboard he noticed a naval officer had slipped into the room. The man was tall and lean, and his pale eyes were set unusually—even oddly—close together. The right eye appeared to be exotrophic. Commander's bars were on his sleeves, and his left collar sported the gold insignia of the Intelligence Service. He leaned against the door frame, hands at his sides, acknowledging neither Crane nor Bishop.

Crane looked back toward the patient, tuning out this new arrival. "Mary Philips?" he asked, falling automatically into the neutral tone he'd long ago learned to use with patients.

The woman nodded.

"I won't take up much of your time," he said with a smile. "We're here to see you back on your feet as quickly as possible."

She returned the smile: a small jerk of the lips that vanished quickly.

"You're still feeling significant numbness in your hands and your face?"

She nodded, blinked, dabbed at her eyes with a tissue. Crane noticed that when she blinked her eyes did not seem to close completely.

"When did you first notice this?" he asked.

"About ten days ago. No, maybe two weeks. At first it was so subtle I barely noticed."

"And were you on or off shift when you first became aware of the sensation?"

"On shift."

Crane glanced again at the digital clipboard. "It doesn't say here what your station is."

It was the man in the doorway who spoke up. "That's because it isn't relevant, Doctor."

Crane turned toward him. "Who are you?"

"Commander Korolis." The man had a low, soft, almost unctuous voice.

"Well, Commander, I think her station is very relevant."

"Why is that?" Korolis asked.

Crane looked back at the patient. She returned his gaze anxiously. The last thing he wanted to do, he decided, was increase that anxiety. He motioned Commander Korolis in the direction of the hall.

"We're performing a diagnostic procedure," he said, in the corridor and out of the patient's earshot. "In a differential diagnosis, every fact is relevant. It's quite possible her work environment is in some way responsible."

Korolis shook his head. "It's not."

"And how do you know that?"

"You'll just have to take my word for it."

"I'm sorry, but that's not good enough." And Crane turned away.

"Dr. Crane," Korolis said softly. "Mary Philips works in a classified area of the Facility on a classified aspect of the project. You will not be permitted to ask work-specific questions."

Crane wheeled back. "You can't—" he began. Then he stopped, forcing down anger with effort. Whoever this Korolis was, he clearly wielded authority. Or thought he did. Why all this need for secrecy, Crane wondered, at a scientific establishment?

Then he paused, reminding himself he was the newcomer here. He didn't yet know the rules—overt or covert. It seemed likely this was a battle he couldn't win. But he'd sure as hell bring it up with Asher later. For the moment, he'd just have to diagnose this patient as best he could.

He stepped back into the hospital room. Dr. Bishop was still beside the bed, her expression studiously neutral.

"I'm sorry for the interruption, Ms. Philips," Crane said. "Let's proceed."

Over the next fifteen minutes, he performed a detailed physical and neurological examination. Gradually, he forgot the watchful presence of Commander Korolis as he grew absorbed in the woman's condition.

It was an intriguing case. The bilateral weakness to both the upper and lower facial muscles was marked. When tested for pinprick sensation, the woman demonstrated significant impairment in the trigeminal distribution. Neck flexion was intact, as was neck extension. But he noticed that the sensation of temperature was greatly reduced across both the neck and upper trunk. There was also—surprisingly—noticeable, and apparently quite recent, wasting of the hand muscles. As he checked the deep tendon reflexes, then the plantar responses, a suspicion began to take root in his mind.

Every physician dreams of stumbling across a particularly rare or interesting case, the kind one reads about in the medical literature. It rarely happened. And yet, in all observations so far, Mary Philips was presenting with precisely such a condition. And Crane, who often stayed up late catching up on medical journals, thought perhaps—just perhaps—he had just identified such a case. **Maybe there is a special reason I'm here, after all.**

On a hunch, he examined her tonsils: markedly large, yellowish, and lobulated. **Very interesting**.

Thanking the woman for her patience, he stepped away, picked up the clipboard, and glanced at the blood work:

White-cell count (per mm)	3,100
Hematocrit (%)	34.6
Platelet count (per mm)	104,000
Glucose (mg/dl)	79
Triglycerides (mg/dl)	119
Erythrocyte sedimentation rate (mm/hr)	48.21

He withdrew to speak with Dr. Bishop. "What do you think?" he asked.

"I was hoping you could tell me," she replied. "You're the expert."

"I'm no expert. Just a fellow doctor looking for a little cooperation."

Bishop simply looked back at him. Crane felt the anger returning, stronger now: anger at all the inexplicable secrecy, anger at the meddling Commander Korolis, and particularly anger at the unhelpful, resentful Dr. Bishop. He'd take her down a peg, show her how much he **did** know.

He closed the clipboard sharply. "Did you think to do any antibody tests, Doctor?"

She nodded. "Viral hepatitis A and C, sulfatide IgM. All negative."

"Motor-conduction studies?"

"Normal bilaterally."

"Rheumatoid factor?"

"Positive. Eighty-eight units per milliliter."

Crane paused. These were, in fact, the tests he would have performed next.

"There was no history of arthralgia, anorexia, or Raynaud's phenomenon, for that matter," she offered.

Crane looked at her in surprise. It wasn't possible the same exotic conclusion had occurred to her as well. Was it?

He decided to call her bluff. "The incipient wasting of the hand muscles would seem to suggest syringomyelia. So would the loss of sensation in the upper trunk."

"But there's an absence of leg stiffiness," she replied immediately, "and little to no medullary dysfunction. It isn't syringomyelia."

Crane was now even more surprised by the depth of her diagnostic technique. But it couldn't hold.

Time to lay my cards on the table, he thought. "What about the sensory defects? The neuropathy? And did you notice the tonsils?"

Bishop was still staring at him, her face expressionless. "Yes, I did notice the tonsils. Enlarged and yellowish."

There was a silence.

Gradually, a smile crept over her features. "Why, Doctor," she said. "Surely you're not suggesting Tangier disease?"

Crane froze. Then slowly—very slowly—he relaxed. He found that he couldn't help smiling back. "As a matter of fact, I was," he said a little ruefully.

"Tangier disease. So, what: now we've got a hundred rare genetic diseases floating about this station?" But her voice was mild, and there was no hint of reproof that Crane could detect. Even the smile, he decided, might be genuine.

At that moment a series of alarms sounded, loud and fast, cutting through the wash of classical music. An amber light snapped on in the hallway outside.

The smile left Bishop's face. "Code orange," she said.

"What?"

"Med-psych emergency. Let's go." She was already running toward the door.

10

Bishop stopped at the front desk just long enough to grab a radio. "Get Corbett!" she called to a nurse behind the desk. Then she ran out of the medical suite and down the corridor, Crane at her heels, heading toward Times Square.

As she ran, she punched a code into the radio, dialed through the bands. "This is Dr. Bishop, requesting location of code orange."

There was a brief pause before the return squawk. "Code orange location: deck five, rover repair hangar."

"Deck five, roger," Bishop replied.

An elevator stood waiting beside the sidewalk café; they ducked inside and Bishop pressed the lowest button on the panel, 7.

She turned once again to the radio. "Request nature of emergency."

Another squawk. "Incident code five-twenty-two."

"What's that stand for?" Crane asked.

She glanced at him. "Floridly psychotic."

The doors opened again, and Crane followed her out into a brightly lit intersection. Corridors led away in three directions, and Bishop ran down the one directly before them.

"What about medical supplies?" Crane asked.

"There's a temporary infirmary on deck four. We'll get an MICU kit from it if necessary."

Crane noticed this deck felt a lot more confining than the ones he'd previously seen. The corridors were narrower, the compartments more cramped. The people they passed wore either lab coats or jumpsuits. He recalled this was the science level and computer center. Despite the audible rush of ventilation, the air was heavy with the smell of lab bleach, ozone, and hot electronics.

They reached another intersection and Bishop jogged right. Glancing ahead, Crane saw something unexpected: the corridor widened dramatically and ended in a black wall. This wall was smooth and broken only by a single airlock set in its center. The airlock hatch was guarded by four MPs with rifles, and a fifth sat in a high-tech pillbox to one side. A large LED above the airlock glowed red.

"What's that?" he asked, slowing instinctively.

"The Barrier," Bishop replied.

"I'm sorry?"

"Portal to the classified levels."

As they approached, two of the MPs took up positions directly before the airlock, rifles across their chests. "Clearance, ma'am?" one of them asked.

Bishop trotted over to the pillbox. The fifth MP stepped out and passed a bulky scanner over her forearm. There was a loud beep.

The MP glanced at a small LED screen set into the top of the scanner. "You're not cleared."

"I'm Michele Bishop, chief medical officer of the Facility. I have qualified emergency access to decks four, five, and six. Check again."

The MP stepped into the pillbox and consulted a computer monitor. After a moment, he came out. "Very well. Go on through. A security escort will be waiting on the other side."

Bishop stepped toward the airlock. Crane swung into place behind her, but the guards closed rank in front of him. The MP with the scanner came forward and ran it over Crane's arm.

"This man isn't cleared, either," he said.

Bishop glanced back. "He's a doctor, here on temporary assignment."

The MP turned to face Crane. "You cannot proceed, sir."

"I'm with Dr. Bishop," Crane said.

"I'm sorry, sir," the man said, his voice hardening. "You cannot proceed."

"Look," Crane said. "There's a medical emergency, and—"

"Sir, please step back from the Barrier." The pillbox MP exchanged quick glances with the others.

"I can't do that. I'm a doctor, and I'm going to assist with the emergency, whether you like it or not." And he stepped forward again.

Immediately, the men guarding the Barrier raised their rifles, while the MP with the scanner dropped a hand to his belt and drew out his sidearm.

"Stand down, Ferrara!" came a deep voice from within the darkness of the pillbox. "Wegman, Price, you others, at ease."

As quickly as they had raised their weapons, the MPs lowered them again and stepped back. Glancing toward the pillbox, Crane saw that it was in fact a portal to a far larger chamber, apparently a control room for the Barrier. A dozen screens were set into its walls, and countless small lights blinked and glowed in the dimness. A shape within drew closer then emerged into the light: a heavyset, broad-shouldered man in a white admiral's uniform. He had iron-gray hair and brown eyes. He glanced from Crane, to Bishop, then back to Crane.

"I am Admiral Spartan," the man said.

"Admiral Spartan," Crane said. "I'm—"

"I know who you are. You're Howard Asher's asset."

Crane did not know quite how to respond to this, so he merely nodded.

Spartan looked at Bishop again. "The emergency's on five, correct?"

"Yes, sir. The rover repair hangar."

"Very well." Spartan turned to the MP named Ferrara. "Clear him for this incident only. Make sure they're accompanied by an armed escort at all times, and take a nonsensitive route to the site. See to it personally, Ferrara."

The MP stiffened, gave a smart salute. "Aye, aye, sir."

Spartan let his gaze rest another moment on Crane. Then he nodded to Ferrara, turned, and disappeared back into the control room.

Ferrara stepped into the pillbox and typed a series of commands on a console. There was a low buzz, then a series of tiny lights winked on around the perimeter of the airlock. The LED above the Barrier turned green. There was a clank of heavy locks disengaging, a hiss of pressurized air, and the airlock opened. Ferrara spoke into a mike built into his console, then motioned Bishop and Crane to step through, following behind.

Beyond the airlock was a chamber about twelve feet square. Two more MPs waited here, standing stiffly at attention. The beige walls were bare, and there was no instrumentation save for a small panel beside one of the guards. Crane noted that it consisted of simply a palm-geometry reader and a rubberized handle.

The airlock door closed. The MP placed one hand on the reader and the other on the handle. There was a red glow as his palm was scanned. Then he twisted the handle clockwise. Crane's stomach gave a brief lurch as they started to descend. The chamber was, in fact, an elevator.

His thoughts went to Admiral Spartan. He had known several flag officers during his tours of duty, and they were all comfortable with command, used to being obeyed immediately and without question. But even on such short acquaintance Crane sensed something a little different in Spartan. He had a depth of self-possession unusual even in an admiral. Crane thought about that last look the man had given him. There was something unreadable in his dark eyes, as if you could never be sure just what his next move might be.

They glided smoothly to a stop. There was another low hum, another clank of locks springing free. The airlock was opened from outside by another group of armed MPs. "Dr. Bishop?" one asked. "Dr. Crane?"

"That's us."

"We're here to escort you to the repair hangar. Follow me, please."

They moved out quickly, two guards leading and two bringing up the rear. Ferrara, Admiral Spartan's man, followed. Normally, Crane would be irritated by such an entourage, but now he almost welcomed it. **Floridly psychotic,** Bishop had said. That meant the person was grossly disorganized, delusional, perhaps even violent. In such instances you tried to be calm and reassuring, establish a rapport. But when a patient was truly out of control, the first priority—the very first—was to outnumber him.

Labs and research facilities passed in a blur: the so-called classified section of the Facility seemed, outwardly at least, little different from the upper decks. Several people ran past them in the opposite direction. And now, up ahead, Crane could hear something that made his blood run cold: the sound of a man screaming.

They ducked through a hatchway and Crane found himself in a large, almost cavernous room. He blinked a moment, unaccustomed already to so much space. It appeared to be a machine shop and repair facility for robot submersibles—the rovers Bishop had mentioned.

The screaming was louder here: ragged, ululating. Small groups of workers stood nearby, held back by military police. Farther ahead, a cordon of naval personnel and more MPs blocked the way. Several were talking on mobile radios; others were staring ahead at an equipment bay set into the far wall. It was from there the screaming came.

Bishop stepped forward, followed closely by Crane and the MPs. Seeing them approach, one of the officers broke away from the cordon to intercept them.

"Dr. Bishop," the man said over the screams. "I'm Lieutenant Travers. Ranking officer on the scene."

"Give us the details," Crane said.

Travers glanced at him, then looked back at Bishop. She gave a slight nod.

"The man is Randall Waite," he said. "Machinist first grade."

"What happened?" Crane asked.

"Nobody's quite certain. Apparently, Waite had been acting moody the last day or two—quiet, not like himself. Then, just as he was about to go off shift, he started acting out."

"Acting out," Bishop repeated.

"Starting to shout. Crazy stuff."

Crane glanced in the direction of the screams. "Is he angry? Delusional?"

"Delusional, yes. Angry, no. Seemed more like he's—in despair, sort of. Said he wanted to die."

"Go on," Crane said.

"A few people approached him. Tried to calm him down, see what was wrong. That's when he grabbed one."

Crane's eyebrows shot up. **Oh, shit. That's not good.**

Ninety-nine percent of all suicidal attempts were attention-getters, pleas for help. Cutters, making slash marks mostly for effect. But when a hostage was involved, it became a different situation entirely.

"That's not all," Travers muttered. "He's got a brick of C4 and a detonator."

"What?"

Travers nodded grimly.

There was a squawk from Travers's radio, and he raised it to his lips. "Travers." He listened a moment. "Very well. Hold until you get my signal."

"What was that about?" Bishop asked.

Travers nodded in the direction of a side wall, where the smoked window of a control room overlooked the hangar. "We've got a sharpshooter up there, trying to get a hard target."

"No!" Crane said. He took a breath. "No. I want to talk to him first."

Travers frowned.

"Why did you bring us down if not to defuse things?" Crane asked.

"He's grown more agitated since that call. And we didn't know about the C4 when we put out the code."

"Does your man have a hard target?" Crane pressed.

"Intermittent."

"Then there's no reason not to let me try."

Travers hesitated for a second. "Very well. But if he threatens that hostage—or if he tries to arm that detonator—I'm going to have to smoke him."

Crane nodded to Bishop, then walked slowly forward until he reached the cordon. Gently, he pushed his way through. Then he stopped.

About twenty feet ahead, a man in an orange jumpsuit stood in the shadow of the equipment bay. His eyes were red-rimmed and tearing. His chin was flecked with mucus, phlegm, and frothy blood. Sprays of vomit slashed across the orange field of his jumpsuit. **Poison?** Crane wondered in a detached way. But the man showed no obvious signs of abdominal pain, paralysis, or other systemic symptoms.

The man held a woman before him—about thirty, petite, with dirty-blond hair. She was dressed in an identical jumpsuit. His arm encircled her neck, and her chin was pointed upward at a painful angle, rising from the crook of Waite's elbow. A long, narrow screwdriver was pressed against her jugular vein. The woman's lips were tight, and her eyes were wide with fear.

Jutting out of the man's other hand was a whitish brick of C4 and an unarmed detonator.

The screams were shockingly loud here, and stopped only long enough for Waite to draw in fresh breaths. Crane found it hard to think over the noise.

Talk him down, the rule book went. **Calm him, get him secured.** Easier said than done. Crane had talked down a would-be jumper standing on a support cable of the George Washington Bridge. He'd talked down men sticking Lugers into their ears or chewing on shotgun barrels. But he'd never talked down somebody holding ten grenades' worth of plastique.

He took a breath, then another. And then he stepped forward.

"This isn't really what you want," he said.

The man's red eyes landed on him briefly, then jittered away. The screams continued.

"This isn't **really** what you want," Crane repeated, louder.

He couldn't hear himself over the screaming. He took another step forward.

The man's eyes shot back to him. He gripped the woman tighter, pressed the point of the screwdriver deeper into her neck.

Crane froze. He could see the woman staring at him pleadingly, her face a mask of fear. He was uncomfortably aware of how exposed he was: standing between the cordon of military officers and the man with a hostage and a brick of C4. He fought back an urge to retreat.

He remained motionless, thinking. Then— slowly—he eased himself down on the metal floor. He undid one shoe, then the other, and placed them carefully aside. He removed his socks and put them to one side, arranging them with finicky precision. Then he leaned backward, resting himself on the palms of his hands.

As he did so, he became aware of something new in the hanger: silence. The screaming had stopped. Waite was staring at him now, the screwdriver still pressed dangerously against the woman's throat.

"You don't want to do this," Crane said in a patient, reasonable tone. "There's no problem that can't be taken care of. There's nothing worth hurting yourself or somebody else over. That's just going to make it worse."

Waite did not reply. He simply stared back, wide-eyed, drawing in ragged breaths.

"What is it you want?" Crane asked. "What can we do to help you?"

At this, Waite whimpered, swallowed painfully. "Make it stop," he said.

"Make what stop?" Crane asked.

"The sounds."

"What sounds?"

"**Those** sounds," Waite replied in a voice that was half whisper, half sob. "The sounds that never . . . that never stop."

"I'll talk to you about the sounds. We can—"

But Waite had begun to whimper again, and the whimper was rising in pitch and volume. More screams were not far away.

Quickly, Crane grasped his own shirt collar, jerked downward violently. There was a loud rending of fabric and a clatter of buttons. He took off the ruined shirt, placed it beside the shoes.

Waite was staring at him again.

"We can work this out," Crane resumed. "Make the sounds stop."

Listening, Waite began to cry.

"But you're making me very nervous with that detonator."

The crying grew louder.

"Let the woman go. It's the sounds we have to fight, not her."

Waite was bawling now, tears almost squirting from his eyes.

Crane had waited, waited carefully, to use the man's Christian name. He decided to use it now. "Let the woman go, Randall. Let her go and drop the explosive. And we'll work this out. We'll make the sounds go away. I promise."

Suddenly, Waite seemed to slump. Slowly, he lowered the screwdriver. The other hand dropped to his side, the C4 falling heavily to the ground. With a cry, the woman sprinted for the military cordon. Quick as lightning, an MP who had been crouching to one side darted in, secured the C4, retreated.

Crane took a deep breath. Then, slowly, he rose. "Thank you, Randall," he said. "Now we can help you. Now we can make the sounds go away." And he took a step forward.

At this, Waite reared back. His eyes rolled dangerously in his head. **"No!"** he said. "You can't make the sounds go away. Don't you understand? **No one can make the sounds go away!"** And with sudden, unexpected speed, he raised the screwdriver to his own throat.

"Stop!" Crane cried, dashing forward. But even as he did he saw, with horror, the point of the screwdriver disappear into the soft flesh of the man's neck.

11

When Howard Asher reached the executive conference room on deck 8, Admiral Spartan was already there, seated at the table, hands resting on the polished rosewood. He waited silently while Asher closed the door and took a seat across the table.

"I've just come from Medical," Asher said.

Spartan nodded.

"Waite sustained a deep puncture wound to the neck, and he's lost a lot of blood, but he's stable. He'll pull through."

"You didn't summon me to an emergency meeting just to tell me that," Spartan replied.

"No. But Waite is one of the reasons I asked you here."

Spartan did not reply; he merely gazed at Asher with his dark unfathomable eyes. In the brief silence that followed, Asher felt the old apprehension—which he'd managed to contain so long—creeping back again.

Science and the military made for strange bedfellows. Deep Storm, Asher knew, was at best a marriage of convenience. He and his team of scientists needed this station, and the bottomless resources of the government, in order to undertake such a mind-boggling excavation in the first place. Spartan needed the scientists and engineers to plan the dig and analyze the finds. But the recent, unexpected developments were putting a strain on an already fragile relationship.

The door opened quietly, then closed again. Asher looked back to see Commander Korolis. The man nodded, then wordlessly took a seat at the table.

Asher's apprehension increased. To him, Korolis symbolized everything was wrong about this project: secrecy, disinformation, propaganda. Asher knew that Waite was asleep in Medical, heavily sedated; otherwise, Korolis would be at the patient's side, ensuring that no word of what went on below deck 7 reached non-classified ears.

"Proceed, Dr. Asher," Spartan said.

Asher cleared his throat. "Waite is just the latest and most acute in a series of medical and psychological traumas. Over the last two weeks, this Facility has seen an alarming spike in illness, across the board."

"Which is why you've brought in Crane."

"I asked for several specialists," Asher said. "A diagnostician, a—"

"One is sufficient enough risk," Spartan replied, his voice low and even.

Asher took a deep breath. "Look. Once Waite is stable, we have to get him to the surface."

"Out of the question."

Now annoyance began mixing with Asher's apprehension. "Why is that, exactly?"

"You know the reasons as well as I do. This is a secret installation, undertaking a classified mission—"

"Classified!" Asher cried. "Confidential! Don't you understand? We have a serious medical issue here. You can't just ignore it, sweep it under the rug!"

"Dr. Asher, **please**." For the first time, Admiral Spartan allowed his tone to stiffen slightly. "You're overreacting. We have a fully equipped medical facility here, staffed by skilled personnel. Against my better judgment, I've bowed to your request to bring in an additional resource—over the objection, I might add, of Commander Korolis here."

This was bait, and Asher did not rise to it.

"Besides," Spartan went on, "I don't see the need for panic. Have you, or the good Dr. Crane, identified a cluster?"

"You know we haven't."

"Then let's be reasonable here. Many of your scientists aren't used to working in conditions like these. Confined to the Facility, cramped quarters, stressful working environment—" Spartan waved a meaty hand. "Irritability, sleeplessness, loss of appetite—these things are to be expected."

"It's not just scientists who are being affected," Asher replied. "So are members of the military. And what about the ministrokes? The arrhythmias? What about Waite?"

"You're talking about a very small section of the population," Korolis said. It was the first time he'd spoken. "You get enough people together, something's bound to pop up."

"The facts are these," Spartan went on. "There is no commonality. People are complaining about all sorts of things—that's what people do. Aside from Waite, there's no severity. I'm sorry, Dr. Asher, but that's the truth. Bottom line: there's no outbreak. Period."

"But—" Asher began. He fell silent when he saw the expression on Spartan's face. **Scientists have no place in a military operation,** that expression seemed to say. **And all this whining proves it.**

He decided to change the subject. "There's something else."

Spartan's eyebrows rose.

"Earlier today, Paul Easton, the marine geologist, came to see me. Turns out we're wrong about the dating."

"What dating is that?" Spartan asked.

"Of the burial event."

There was a brief silence.

Spartan shifted in his chair. "How wrong?"

"Very."

Korolis exhaled slowly between his teeth. To Asher, it sounded like the hiss of a snake.

"Specify," the admiral said at last.

"We've always assumed—based on rough visual inspection and other factors—that the entombment happened ten thousand years ago or even longer. Easton took that assumption a little too far. He never bothered to date the site using magnetic field reversal."

"Using what?" Korolis said.

"A method for dating the vulcanism around the burial site. Not to get into the scientific details"— and here Asher glanced at Korolis—"but once in a great many years, the earth's magnetic field reverses. Flips. The north pole becomes the south, and vice versa. Our original dating of the burial event would have placed it in the **last** magnetic reversal. But it seems we were wrong."

"How do you know that?" Spartan asked.

"Because when the earth's crust becomes molten, its iron particles swivel around, align themselves with the planet's magnetic field. Then, as the rock cools, they stay aligned. It's like tree rings in a way: you can date geologic events by examining that alignment."

"Well, maybe it's far older, then," Korolis said. "**Two** magnetic reversals ago. The north pole would have still been north then, correct?"

"Correct. But the event was **not** far older."

"So it wasn't as old as you thought," Spartan said.

Asher nodded.

"I presume that, since we're here, you were able to get a more accurate date."

"I had Easton send out a rover, equipped with a highly sophisticated magnetometer. It can measure, very accurately, the drift of a magnetic field. We used samples from the burial site as a starting point."

Spartan frowned, shifted again. "And?"

"The site isn't ten thousand years old, or fifty thousand. It's **six hundred years old**."

There was a moment of frigid silence.

Spartan was the first to speak. "Does this—**oversight** have any bearing on our chances of success?"

"No."

Asher thought he detected a fleeting look of relief cross the admiral's face before the expressionless mask descended again.

"Then what, exactly, is the bottom line?"

"Isn't it obvious? This has gone from an event in the unthinkable past to an event within recorded history."

"And your point, Doctor?" Korolis said.

"My **point**? My point is that there may have been **eyewitnesses** to the burial event. There may be **written accounts**."

"Then we should dispatch a researcher to look into it," Spartan said.

"I've already done that."

Spartan frowned. "With the proper credentials? And discretion?"

"His credentials are excellent—medieval historian from Yale. And, yes, he has no clue as to the real reason I'm interested."

"Good." Spartan rose. "Then if there's nothing else, I'd suggest you return to Medical and see if Dr. Crane has made a miracle diagnosis."

Asher stood, as well. "He'll need to be brought inside," he said in a low voice.

Spartan's eyebrows shot up. "Excuse me?"

"He should be fully briefed. He'll need access to the classified levels. Unrestricted access. And not with a phalanx of MPs, either."

"That's impossible, Dr. Asher," said Korolis. "We could never allow such a security risk."

Asher kept his gaze on the admiral. "Crane needs to talk to the patients, learn their movements, search for vectors, identify possible exposures. How can he do that if we keep him both gagged **and** blindfolded?"

"I have the greatest faith in your choice of specialists, Dr. Asher," Spartan said mildly. "You should, too."

For a moment Asher just stood there, breathing heavily, mastering himself. "We were given a mandate, Admiral," he finally said, voice husky. "A joint mandate to run this Facility. **Together.** So far, I haven't pushed the point. But if it comes down to a question of secrecy or the safety of this installation, I'll put aside secrecy in a heartbeat. And you'd be wise to remember that."

Then he spun on his heel, pulled open the door, and was gone.

12

There were two squash courts on Deep Storm, and a three-day waiting list to get court time. It was an example of Asher's clout, Crane thought, that the man had been able to get them a half-hour slot with a few minutes' notice.

"I never figured you for a reader of poetry," Asher said when they met on the court. "But your being a squash player is a no-brainer."

"Maybe it's my gazelle-like physique," Crane replied. "Or maybe you've just been re-reading my jacket."

Asher, juggling the little gray ball idly in his serve hand, laughed.

Crane wasn't surprised Asher wanted a meeting. After all, he'd been on station now over thirty-six hours: the chief scientist would want a report. The only surprise was the suggested location. But then, he was already getting used to Asher's modus operandi: maintain an affable exterior, imply a low-key atmosphere; but make it clear that results were expected, and expected right away.

That was fine with Crane; in fact, part of him welcomed the meeting. Because he happened to have an agenda of his own.

"Let's warm up for a minute or two," Asher said. He held out the ball. "Serve?"

Crane shook his head. "Go right ahead."

He watched Asher stroke the ball toward the front wall with a hard, clean swing. He fell back, balancing on the balls of his feet, waiting for the return. The ball bounded back, and he hit a volley, aiming for the far corner.

For several minutes they played without speaking, gauging each other's skill, experience, preferred strategies. Crane figured Asher had at least twenty-five years on him, but the older man seemed in better practice. At least, Crane was playing miserably; half his volleys were going out.

"Is there something unusual about this court?"

he asked at length, as he retrieved the ball and tossed it back to Asher.

The scientist caught it deftly in his racquet hand. "Actually, there is. We had to accommodate the floor plan of the Facility. The ceiling's about twelve inches shorter than regulation. To compensate, we've made the court a little deeper than usual. I should have mentioned it before. Once you're used to it, you'll actually find the dimensions a little forgiving. Some more practice?"

"No, let's try a game."

Crane won the spin of the racquet, chose his side, and fired off a serve. Asher countered with a quick volley to the far corner, and the game began in earnest.

As they traded volleys, Crane had to admire the scientist's game. Squash was part sport and part chess match—a mixture of wits, strategy, and stamina. Asher was excellent at controlling the T and—particularly impressive—at firing the ball straight along the sidewall, keeping Crane constantly on the defensive. He'd assumed the scientist's stiff and painful left hand would make playing difficult, but Asher seemed to have mastered using his right hand for balance as well as swing. Almost before he knew it, Crane had fallen hopelessly behind.

"That's the game," Asher said at last.

"Nine–four. Not a very good showing, I'm afraid."

Asher gave an easy laugh. "You'll do better next game. Like I said, the unusual dimensions tend to grow on you. Go ahead, your service."

During their second game, Crane found Asher was right: as he grew more used to the shorter, deeper court, he found it progressively easier to control the ball. He made fewer outs and was able to rebound the ball behind the service box, forcing Asher to play the backcourt. Now he was no longer forced to concentrate simply on returning the ball, but could move back to the T after playing shots, thus setting himself up in better position. The game ran long, and this time he beat Asher, nine–eight.

"See what I mean?" Asher said, puffing. "You're a quick study. A few more games and you'll need to find a more challenging partner."

Crane chuckled. "Your serve," he said, tossing Asher the ball.

Asher caught the ball, but made no move to serve it. "So. How's Waite?"

"Still sedated. A cocktail of Haldol and Ativan. Antipsychotic and anti-anxiety."

"I understand you used a unique method of talking him down. Bishop said something about a striptease."

Crane smiled faintly. "Somebody that florid needs to be shocked out of his psychotic loop. I did something he didn't expect. Bought us a little time."

"Any idea what happened?"

"Corbett is running a complete psych profile—at least, as complete as the meds will currently allow. As of yet, we can't settle on a diagnosis. It's strange. For the most part, the man's now completely lucid, if sedated. But earlier, he was grossly disorganized, responding to internal stimuli."

"Excuse me?"

"Out of control. Hallucinating. Now he can't remember the incident. He can't even remember the terrible sounds that apparently brought it on. Eyewitnesses and friends said they saw little preindication other than general moodiness. And Waite has no history of psychological problems. But then, you no doubt know that." Crane hesitated. "I think you should get him off the Facility."

Asher shook his head. "Sorry."

"If not for Waite's sake, then for mine. I'm getting really tired of having Commander Korolis or one of his minions in the Medical Suite day and night, babysitting Waite, making sure he doesn't say anything he's not supposed to."

"I'm afraid it's out of my hands. As soon as you clear Waite for discharge, I'll have him confined to quarters. That should make Korolis go away."

Crane thought he detected an undercurrent of bitterness in Asher's tone. It hadn't occurred to him that the chief scientist might be chafing equally under Deep Storm's culture of secrecy.

Asher, he realized, had just given him an opening; he wasn't likely to get a better chance to say what had to be said. **It's time,** he thought. He took a deep breath.

"I think I'm finally beginning to understand," he began.

Asher, who was staring at the squash ball in his hand, glanced up. "Understand what?"

"Why I'm here."

"That was never in doubt. You're here to treat our medical problem."

"No. I meant why **I** was chosen for the job."

Asher stared at him, his face blank.

"See, at first I was confused. After all, I'm not a pulmonary specialist or a hematologist. If the workers were suffering some form of caisson disease, why ask me to make the house call? But it turns out that's not what they're suffering from."

"You're sure?"

"It's the one thing I **am** sure of." He paused. "Because it just so happens there's nothing exotic or unusual about Deep Storm's atmosphere, after all."

Asher continued to hold his gaze but said nothing. Crane, taking in the man's expression, began

to wonder if speaking up had been a wise idea after all. But now that he'd begun, he had to say
everything.

"I had one of the TIA patients put in a hyperbaric chamber," he went on. "And guess what we
found."

Still Asher did not reply.

"We found it didn't help in the least. But that
wasn't all. The chamber's readout showed us that
the atmosphere was normal, inside **and** out."
Crane hesitated a moment before speaking again.
"So this talk about pressurization, special air mix-
tures—it's all bull, isn't it?"

Asher began to study the ball again. "Yes," he
replied after a moment. "And it's very important
you keep that information to yourself."

"Of course. But why?"

Asher bounced the ball off the floor, caught it,
squeezed it thoughtfully. "We wanted a reason
why nobody could leave the Facility in a hurry. A
security precaution against information leaks, es-
pionage, that sort of thing."

"And all this talk of proprietary atmospherics, of
a long acclimation process, and an even longer
cool down, provides a nice cover story."

Asher gave the ball another bounce, then tossed
it into the corner. Any pretense of game playing
had now fallen aside.

"So those rooms I had to wait in when I first got to the Facility. They're completely phony?"

"They're not phony. They are functional decompression chambers. Just with their atmospheric functions turned off." He glanced over. "You were saying you know why you were chosen for the job."

"Yes. After seeing the readout from the hyperbaric chamber, I finally put two and two together. It's what I did on the USS **Spectre,** right?"

Asher nodded.

"I'm surprised you heard about that."

"I didn't. The mission is still classified. But Admiral Spartan knew about it. He knew all about it. Your skill as a diagnostician, your past experience dealing with—shall we say?—**bizarre** medical situations under extremely stressful circumstances are unique assets. And since for security reasons Spartan would only allow one person access to Deep Storm, you seemed the best choice."

"There's that word again: security. And that's the one thing I haven't figured out."

Asher threw him a questioning glance.

"Why all the secrecy? What, exactly, is so vital about Atlantis that you need such drastic measures? And for that matter, why is the government willing to front so much money, and such expensive equipment, for an archaeological dig?" Crane waved an arm. "I mean, look at this place. Just to run something like the Facility must burn a million dollars of taxpayer money each day."

"Actually," Asher said quietly, "the amount is rather higher."

"Last time I checked, the bureaucrats at the Pentagon weren't big on ancient civilizations. And agencies like NOD usually have their caps out, thankful for whatever crumbs the government will toss them. But here you've got the most sophisticated, most secret working environment in the world." He paused. "And that's another thing: the Facility is nuclear powered, isn't it? I've been on enough boomers to know. And my ID badge seems to have a radioactive marker embedded in it."

Asher smiled, but did not reply. It was funny, Crane thought, how closemouthed the man had become in recent days.

For a minute, the squash court was filled with a tense, uncomfortable silence. Crane had one more bomb to drop, the biggest of all, and he realized there was no point delaying it any longer.

"Anyway, I've been thinking a lot about all this. And the only answer I can come up with is that it's not Atlantis down there. It's something else." He glanced at Asher. "Am I right?"

Asher looked at him speculatively for a moment. Then he nodded almost imperceptibly.

"Well? What **is** down there?" Crane pressed.

"I'm sorry, Peter. I can't tell you that."

"No? Why not?"

"Because if I did, I'm afraid Spartan would have to kill you."

Hearing this cliché, Crane began to laugh. But then he looked at Asher and his laughter died. Because the chief scientist—who always laughed so easily—wasn't even smiling.

13

At the uttermost frontiers of Scotland—beyond Skye, beyond the Hebrides, beyond even the tiny battered chain of islands known as the Seven Sisters—lies the archipelago of St. Kilda. It is the remotest part of the British Isles, rough hummocks of brown stone struggling to rise above the foam: a bleak, sea-torn, savage place.

On the westernmost point of Hirta, the main island, a thousand-foot granite promontory rises above the bitter Atlantic. Seated on its crown is the long, gray line of Grimwold Castle, an ancient and rambling abbey, hardened against weather and catapult alike, surrounded by a star curtain of local stone. It was built in the thirteenth century by a cloistered order of monks, seeking freedom from both persecution and the growing secularization of Europe. Over many decades, the order was joined by other monks—Carthusians, Benedictines—looking for a remote place for worship and spiritual contemplation, fleeing the dissolution of the English monasteries. Enriched by the personal contributions of these new members, the library of Grimwold Castle swelled into one of the greatest monastic collections in Europe.

A small fishing population grew up around the skirts of the monastery, serving the few earthly needs the monks could not fulfill themselves. As its fame spread, the monastery hosted—in addition to new initiates—the occasional wanderer. At the castle's zenith, a Pilgrim's Way led from its medieval chapter house, across a grassy close, through a portcullis in the curtain wall, and then down a winding path to the tiny village, where passage to the Hebrides could be found.

Today the Pilgrim's Way is gone, visible only as an occasional cairn rising above the bleak stonescape. The tiny supporting village was depopulated centuries ago. Only the abbey remains, its grim and storm-lashed facade staring westward across the cold North Atlantic.

In the main library of Grimwold Castle, a visitor sat at a long wooden table. He wore a pair of white cotton gloves and slowly turned the vellum pages of an ancient folio volume, set on a protective linen cloth. Dust motes hung in the air, and the light was dim: he squinted slightly to make out the words. A pile of other texts stood at his elbow: illuminated manuscripts, incunabula, ancient treatises bound in ribbed leather. Every hour or so, a monk arrived, removed the books the man had finished with, brought another set he had asked to view, exchanged a word or two, and then retired. Now and then, the visitor paused to make a cursory jotting in a notebook, but as the day went on these pauses grew less and less frequent.

At last, in late afternoon, a different monk stepped into the library, carrying yet another set of books. Like the others of his order, he was dressed in a plain cassock bound with a white cord. But he was older than the rest and seemed to walk with a more measured tread.

He proceeded down the center aisle of the library. Approaching the visitor's table—the only occupied table in the room—he laid the ancient texts carefully upon the white linen.

"Dominus vobiscum," he said with a smile.

The man rose from the table. **"Et cum spiritu tuo."**

"Please remain seated. Here are the additional manuscripts you requested."

"You are very kind."

"It is our pleasure. Visiting scholars are few and far between these days, alas. It seems creature comforts have become more important than scholarly enlightenment."

The man smiled. "Or the pursuit of truth."

"Which is frequently the same thing." The man pulled a soft cloth from his sleeve and lovingly dusted the ancient books. "Your name is Logan, correct? Dr. Jeremy Logan, Regina Professor of Medieval History at Yale?"

The man looked at him. "I am Dr. Logan. Currently, though, I'm on academic leave."

"Please do not think I am prying, my son. I am Father Bronwyn, abbot of Grimwold Castle." He took a seat on the far side of the table with a sigh. "In many ways it is a trying job. You would think an abbey as ancient as this would be free from internal bureaucracy and petty grievance. But the truth is just the opposite. And we are so remote, our life so simple and humble, that new initiates come only rarely to our gates. Our number is less than half what it was fifty years ago." He sighed again. "But my position has its consolations. For one, I preside over all bibliographic and library matters, and, as you know, the library remains our only, and our most prized, possession—God forgive my covetousness."

Logan smiled faintly.

"So naturally I am made aware of our comings and goings—especially of persons as well recommended as you. Your letters of introduction made impressive reading."

Dr. Logan inclined his head.

"I couldn't help but notice that, along with your application to visit our library, an itinerary was included."

"Yes, that was an oversight on my part. I've been doing research at Oxford, and my departure was a hasty one. I fear my papers got a bit scrambled. I wasn't trying to boast."

"Of course not. That wasn't my meaning. But I couldn't help but be surprised at the places you've already visited on holiday. St. Urwick's Tower, as I recall. Newfoundland, correct?"

"Just south of Battle Harbour, on the coast."

"And then your second stop. The Abbey of Wrath."

Dr. Logan nodded again.

"I've heard of it, as well. Kap Farvel, Greenland. Almost as remote a location as ours."

"They are possessed of an ancient and exceedingly broad library, particularly in local history."

"I'm sure they are." The abbot leaned closer over the table. "I hope you'll forgive my familiarity, Dr. Logan: as I said, we get so **few** visitors these days, and my capacity for social nuance is sadly atrophied. But you see, what surprises me most about these visits of yours is the timing. Those spots boast libraries that would reward weeks of study. And each is difficult, time-consuming, and expensive to get to. Yet according to the itinerary, this is only the third day of your trip. What are you looking for that requires you to move with such speed, and that requires such trouble and expense on your part?"

Dr. Logan glanced at the abbot for a moment. Then he cleared his throat. "As I said, Father Bronwyn, my including the itinerary among the papers I sent here was an oversight."

Father Bronwyn sat back. "Yes, of course. I am an old and curious man, and I didn't mean to pry." He removed his glasses, raised a corner of his cassock sleeve, cleaned them with it, replaced them on his nose. Then he placed his hand on the ancient calfskin volumes he had brought with him. "Here are the books you requested. The **Lay Anecdotes** of Maighstir Beaton, circa 1448; Colquhoun's **Chronicles Diuerse and Sonderie,** of a hundred years later; and of course

Trithemius's **Poligraphia**." At this last title, the abbot shuddered slightly.

"Thank you, Father," Dr. Logan said, nodding as the man rose and took his leave.

An hour later, the monk who had originally helped him returned, removed the manuscripts and incunabula, and took Logan's written request for additional volumes. Within a few minutes he returned with still more moldering titles, which he laid on the crisp linen.

Dr. Logan placed the volumes before him and, one after the other, paged through them with white-gloved hands. The first volume was in Middle English; the second in the vulgate; and the third a poor translation of the Attic Greek dialect known as Koine. None of the tongues gave Logan much difficulty, and he read with ease. Yet as he continued, an air of depression settled over him. At last, he pushed the final book away, blinked his eyes, and rubbed the small of his back. Three days of grueling travel to godforsaken spots, three nights of sleeping in cold rooms of drafty stone, were catching up with him. He glanced up at the massively built library, with its Romanesque vaulted ceiling and narrow windows of crude but charming stained glass. Late-afternoon light was slanting through them now, daubing the library in a mosaic of color. The monks, as was their custom, would put him up for the night—after all, there was no other accommodation for many miles and no roads to bear him away. In the morning, a hired trawler would take him back to the mainland . . . and then where? He realized, with a sinking feeling, he did not know where to turn next.

In the silence behind him came the clearing of a throat. Dr. Logan turned to see the abbot, arms behind his back, regarding him. Father Bronwyn gave a kindly smile.

"No luck?" he asked in a quiet voice.

Logan shook his head.

The abbot came forward. "I wish you would let me assist you. I don't know what you seek, but it is clearly something of great importance—at least to you. I may be an inquisitive old fool, but I know how to keep secrets entrusted to me. Let me help you. Tell me what you seek."

Logan hesitated. More than once, his client had emphasized the need for complete discretion. But what good was discretion if one had nothing to be discreet about? He had visited three repositories of critical knowledge, and several others of lesser relevance, while furnished with only the vaguest of assignments. Unsurprisingly, he had found nothing.

He looked carefully at the abbot. "I'm looking for local accounts—eyewitness accounts, preferably—of a certain event."

"I see. And what event is that?"

"I don't know."

The abbot raised his eyebrows. "Indeed? That does make things difficult."

"All I know is that the event would be significant enough, or perhaps unusual enough, to prompt recording in a historical text. Most likely, an **ecclesiastical** historical text."

Slowly, the abbot moved around the table and sat down once again. As he did so, his eyes never left Dr. Logan's.

"An unusual event. Such as a—miracle?"

"That is quite possible." Logan hesitated. "But it's my understanding the miracle—how can I say it?—might not have its roots in a divine source."

"In other words, the source could be demonic." Dr. Logan nodded.

"Is that all the information you have?"

"Not quite. I also have a time frame and an approximate location."

"Pray continue."

"The event would have taken place roughly six hundred years ago. And it would have happened **there**." And he raised his hand and pointed toward the northwest wall of the library.

At this, the abbot started visibly. "Over water?"

"Yes. Something seen by a local fisherman, say, straying far from shore. Or perhaps, if the day was exceptionally clear, something observed on the horizon by a person walking the coastal cliffs."

The abbot began to speak, then paused as if reconsidering. "The other two monastic libraries you visited," he began again quietly. "They, too, were situated on the coast—were they not? Both of them overlooking the North Atlantic. Just as we do."

Logan considered this a moment. Then he nodded almost imperceptibly.

For a moment, the abbot did not reply. He looked past Logan and his eyes went distant, as if viewing something far away or, perhaps, long past. At the front of the library, a monk gathered several books under his arm, then slipped out on noiseless feet. The dusty old room fell into an intense silence.

At last, Father Bronwyn stood up. "Please wait," he said. "I'll be back shortly."

Logan did as requested. And within ten minutes the abbot returned, carrying something gingerly between his hands: a bulky rectangular object wrapped in a rough black cloth. The abbot laid the object on the table, then drew the cloth carefully back. Beneath lay a lead box figured in gold and silver leaf. Drawing out a key from around his neck, the abbot unlocked the box.

"You have been candid with me, my son," he

said. "So I will be the same with you." He patted the lead box gently. "What is inside this box has remained one of the greatest secrets of Grimwold Castle. Originally it was felt very dangerous to possess a written record of the events herein. Later, as myth and legend grew, the record itself became too valuable and controversial to show to anyone. But I think I can trust you with it, Dr. Logan—if only for a few minutes." And, slowly, the abbot pushed the box across the table. "I hope you don't mind if I remain here while you read it? I can't allow it to leave my sight. That was an oath I swore on being named abbot of Grimwold Castle."

Logan did not open the box immediately. Instead, he simply stared at the gold and silver scrollwork adorning its top. Despite his eagerness, he hesitated.

"Is there something I should know before I begin?" he asked. "Something you would care to tell me?"

"I think it will speak well enough for itself." Then a smile—not grim, exactly, but not entirely pleasant—spread across the abbot's features. "Dr. Logan, surely you are aware of the saying, 'Here there be monsters'?"

"I am."

"It is found in the blank spaces of the oceans on old maps." The abbot paused again. Then, very gently and deliberately, he tapped the box. "Read this carefully, Dr. Logan. I am not a gambling man—except perhaps on the quality of Brother Frederick's wine when each new vintage is laid down—but I would bet **this** is where that expression first came from."

14

When Crane entered Conference Room A, the smaller of the two in the Medical Suite, he found Michele Bishop there already, entering a notation into her palmtop computer with a metal stylus. The glossy surface of the conference table was conspicuously bare. In his prior experience, medical fact-finding meetings were always accompanied by a blizzard of paperwork: charts, reports, histories. But save for the thin folder beneath Crane's arm, there was no paperwork here today.

Hard copy took up valuable space, and so wherever possible, data inside the Deep Storm station was kept scrupulously within the digital realm.

As he took a seat, Bishop looked up, gave him the ghost of a smile, then glanced back at her palmtop and made another entry.

"What's Waite's status?" he asked.

"I'm recommending he be released tomorrow."

"Really?"

"Roger's given him psych clearance, and Asher's agreed to confine him to quarters. No reason to keep him here any longer."

As she spoke, Roger Corbett entered the room, a large latte from the nearby coffee bar in one hand. He smiled broadly at them in turn, then took a seat at the far side of the table, placing the latte and his own palmtop before him.

"Michele was just telling me you've cleared Waite for discharge," Crane said.

Corbett nodded. "I've done a full psych workup. He's got some anxiety issues that didn't show up during the initial approval tests, perhaps some non-specific depression as well. But he's responding well to the meds. We've backed off on the antipsychotics without adverse effects. I think we're looking at a simple mood disorder that should respond well to therapy."

Crane frowned. "It's your call to make, of

course. But seventy-two hours ago, this 'simple mood disorder' took a hostage, then jammed a screwdriver into his own throat."

Corbett took a sip of his latte. "Waite clearly has some issues to grapple with, and we have no idea how long he's been internalizing. Sometimes this stuff manifests as a cri de coeur. People here are under a great deal of stress—no matter how well we vet them, we can never predict all possible behavior trees. I plan to follow up with daily sessions in his quarters, keep him under close observation."

"Fine," Crane said. **At least it will get Korolis and his goons out of the Medical Suite.**

He glanced back at Bishop. "Any new cases?"

She consulted her palmtop. "A technician came in complaining of spastic colon. Another reported palpitations. And there's a maintenance worker with non-specific symptomology: sleeplessness, inability to focus."

"I see. Thank you." Crane looked from one to the other. "Shall we get on with it, then?"

"Get on with what?" Bishop asked. "I'm not exactly sure why you called this meeting."

Crane looked across the table at her, wondering if every step would be a struggle. "I called this meeting, Dr. Bishop, to determine just what we're dealing with here."

Bishop leaned back in her chair. "Have we narrowed it down to any single agent?"

"It's a single agent, all right. We just don't know what it is."

Bishop crossed her arms, looked at him intently.

"A quarter of the people on this station have symptoms of illness," Crane went on. "That's no coincidence. Health problems don't occur in isolation. It's true that I assumed, early on, it was caisson disease. I was wrong to make that assumption before knowing the facts. But nevertheless **something** is going on here."

"But there's no common symptom," Corbett said. "At least, none specific."

"But there **must** be some commonality—we just haven't found it yet. We've been too busy running around putting out fires to look at the big picture. We have to step back, make a differential diagnosis."

"How do you suggest we do that?" Bishop asked.

"Just like they taught us in med school. Observe the symptoms, propose possible explanations, eliminate each hypothesis as it's proven wrong. Let's start by making a list." He took a sheet of paper from his folder, pulled out a pen. Then he glanced at the two palmtops, gleaming on the polished wood. "Sorry," he said with a small laugh. "I prefer doing this the old-fashioned way."

Corbett smiled and nodded, took another sip. The rich smell of espresso perfumed the conference room.

"We know now that the air of the station has no unusual gases or other atmospherics—we're to keep that to ourselves, by the way—so we can eliminate that as a possibility. What does that leave us? Dr. Bishop, you've mentioned several complaints of nausea. That suggests poison: either systemic, something eaten or drunk, or general: interaction with some toxin here on the station."

"Or it could just mean bad cases of nerves," Bishop replied.

"True." Crane made a notation. "There's a good argument for this being psychological—Waite has shown us that. We're in a strange and stressful environment."

"What about infection?" Corbett asked. "An outbreak of some unknown nature?"

"Another possibility. Deep Storm, or one of its inhabitants, might be a reservoir of some disease. Viral, fungal, bacterial. Some or all the patients coming to us might be vectors."

"I'm not sure I agree," Bishop said. "The only thing I can think of that would manifest in so many different ways would be the side effects of drug use."

"An excellent suggestion. Drugs could also be the causal agent." Crane made another notation. "Was everybody given a series of shots, say, before being admitted to the station? Or a certain prescription vitamin? Are workers being administered any kind of medication to keep them alert?"

"Not that I know of," Bishop said.

"We should look into it. There's also the possibility of illegal drugs."

"Like methamphetamine," Corbett added.

"Or Ecstasy. It inhibits glutamate transmission; it can cause behavior similar to that displayed by Waite."

"Diet might be a possibility," Bishop said. "The nutritionist staff here has developed a special high-protein, low-carbohydrate diet. The Navy is using our Facility as a test bed."

"Interesting. We should examine the bloods again, see if nutrition might play a role." Crane looked from Bishop to Corbett, pleased to find the two participating. "We're developing a good set of possibilities—let's see if there's anything we can rule out. We know the symptoms aren't confined to a certain area of the station or a specific job type. Could they be age or gender related?"

Bishop tapped at her palmtop. "No. The patients skew across all ages, and the gender ratio of the patients is the same as for the entire population."

"Very well. At least we have something to go on." Crane examined his notes. "At first glance it seems that poison, or perhaps drugs, is most promising. Heavy metal poisoning, for example, could explain the wide variety of symptoms. Infectious disease is a distant third, but still worth checking out." He glanced at Corbett. "Who's the strongest tech in the Medical Suite?"

Corbett thought a minute. "Jane Rand."

"See if you can get her to pull together all the records we have on every patient who's come in, program a data agent to mine everything for any hidden correspondences. Have her check everything, from employment records to medical results." He paused. "Can she check the patients' cafeteria selections as well?"

Corbett tapped a few keys on his palmtop, then glanced up and nodded.

"Add that to the list. See if anything comes up. Then compare the records of the patients to the Deep Storm population that is not ill: maybe there is an area of difference." He glanced at Bishop. "Dr. Bishop, if you could reexamine the blood work for anything that might hint at poison or drug use?"

"Okay," Bishop said.

"Please have your people take hair samples from every patient who's come by the medical suite in the last two weeks. And going forward, we should probably take blood and urine samples from all new patients—even if all they've got is a splinter. In fact, let's run a complete battery of tests, EKG, echo, EEG, the works."

"I told you before, we don't have an electroencephalograph here," said Bishop.

"Any chance we can get one?"

She shrugged. "In time."

"Well, put in the request, please. I'd hate to leave any stone unturned. Oh, and speaking of that, you might ask your medical researchers to examine the earliest patient reports. If this is an outbreak of some sort, maybe we can isolate the index case." Crane stood up. "I think I'll have a talk with the nutritionists, learn what I can about that special diet. Let's meet in the morning to discuss our findings."

At the door, he paused. "By the way, there's something else I've been meaning to ask you. Just who is Dr. Flyte?"

Bishop and Corbett exchanged glances.

"Dr. Flyte?" Bishop asked.

"The old Greek fellow in the bib overalls. He dropped in on my cabin, uninvited, shortly after I arrived. Strange chap, seemed to enjoy talking in riddles. What's his job here?"

There was a pause.

"Sorry, Dr. Crane," Corbett said. "I'm not familiar with him."

"No?" Crane turned to Bishop. "Short, wiry, with a wild mop of white hair? Told me he did highly classified work."

"There's nobody here who fits that description," Bishop replied. "The oldest worker here is fifty-two."

"What?" Crane said. "But that's impossible. I saw the old man myself."

Bishop glanced down at her palmtop, typed in a short command, peered briefly at the tiny screen. Then she looked up again. "Like I said, Dr. Crane. There's nobody named Flyte on Deep Storm."

15

Robert Loiseau stepped back from the industrial range, removed the toque from his head, and wiped his sweaty face with the chef's towel hanging from his belt. Even though it was cool in the kitchen he was sweating like a pig. And he was only half an hour into his shift. It was shaping up to be a long, long day.

He glanced at the wall clock: half past three. The lunchtime frenzy had passed, the cleaning staff had washed the pots and pans, and the kitchen was quiet. But quiet was a relative term:

he'd learned long ago that working cuisine in the Navy was nothing like on dry land. There were no set eating schedules; people came and went as they pleased. And with the Facility running on three shifts, it wasn't unusual to serve somebody breakfast at 8 P.M. or lunch at 2 in the morning.

He wiped his face again, then let the towel fall back into place. It seemed he was sweating all the time these days, and not just in the kitchen. And that was only one of the things he'd noticed, along with hands that shook a little and a heart that beat faster than he liked. He felt tired all the time, too; and yet he was unable to sleep. He wasn't sure when it had started, but one thing was certain: slowly but surely, it was getting worse.

Al Tanner, the pastry chef, walked past, whistling "Some Enchanted Evening." He had a pastry cone draped casually over one shoulder as if it were a freshly killed goose. He ceased his whistling long enough to call out, "Hey, Wazoo."

"It's Wah-**zoh**," Loiseau muttered under his breath. You'd think that in a gourmet kitchen, people would know how to pronounce a French name. Maybe they were all just teasing him. But the fact was only Renault, the executive chef, pronounced his name properly—and he rarely condescended to call people by name, preferring to beckon with a curt movement of his index finger.

With a sigh, he turned back to the range. No time for daydreaming. Right now he had to prepare some béchamel sauce: a whole lot of béchamel, in fact. Chef Renault was serving tournedos sauce Mornay and côtelettes d'agneau Écossais on the dinner menu, and both sauces used a béchamel base. Of course, Loiseau could practically prepare béchamel in his sleep. But he'd learned the hard way that cooking was like running a marathon: when you paused, everyone else kept going, and if you paused too long it became impossible to catch up.

Sweat the onion, incorporate the roux . . . As he went over his mise en place, Loiseau felt his heartbeat accelerate again and his breathing grow shallow. It was possible he was getting sick, of course. But he thought he had a better explanation for the sweaty palms and sleepless nights: anxiety. It was one thing to work on an aircraft carrier, with its cavernous hangars and endless echoing corridors. But this was different. During the protracted vetting process, with its endless interviews, he hadn't stopped to think much about actually **living** in Deep Storm. The pay was fantastic, and the thought of participating in a classified, cutting-edge project was a little intoxicating. He'd spent five years in the Navy, working in admirals' kitchens: how different could it be, cooking beneath the sea instead of floating on it?

As it turned out, nothing could have prepared him.

Christ, it's hot. He slowly added a pale roux to the mixture of milk, thyme, bay leaf, butter, and onion. As he bent over the pot, whisking vigorously, a brief sensation of dizziness washed over him and he had to step back, gulping for air. He was hyperventilating, that was the problem. **Get your nerves under control, Bobby-boy. Shift's just starting and there's a ton of shit to do.**

Now Tanner was coming back from the pantry, a large sack of cake flour in his hands. When he saw Loiseau, he stopped. "Everything okay, fellah?"

"Yeah, fine," Loiseau said. Once Tanner had moved on, he wiped his face again with the towel and went immediately back to whisking: if he stopped now, the sauce would scorch and he'd have to begin all over again.

Thing was, he hadn't counted on missing sunlight and fresh air quite so much. And at least aircraft carriers **moved**. Loiseau had never thought of himself as being claustrophobic, but living in a metal box, with no way to get out and all that ocean pressing down on your head . . . well, it got to you after a while. Whoever had designed Deep Storm had done an ingenious job of miniaturization—and at first, when he was working in Top, the galley on deck 11, he hadn't noticed it so much. But then he'd been transferred to Central, the deck 7 kitchen. And things down here were a little more cramped. When it got busy, when the flour really started to fly, so many bodies were packed in you could barely move. And that was when, these last few days, Loiseau had felt the worst. Waking up today, the first thing he'd thought about was the dinnertime crush to come. And the sweats had kicked in, right there in his own damn bunk . . .

He gripped the stainless-steel range handle tightly as a spasm of indigestion lanced through his stomach. The dizziness returned and—with a faint sense of alarm now—he shook his head to clear it. Maybe he **was** getting sick, after all. Maybe he was coming down with the flu. When he went off shift, he'd stop by Medical. Either way, nerves or illness, they could help.

With an effort he went back to whisking the sauce, backing it carefully off from the boil, trying to concentrate as he checked it for color and aroma. As he did so, he noticed a "runner"—one of the workers assigned to Bottom, the mess located in the Facility's deepest depths—heading out with a tall stack of prepared dishes. Bottom had only a small galley of its own and frequently used runners—who worked and lived in the clas-

sified section of Deep Storm and had the necessary clearance—to bring dishes prepared in Central down to the lower levels.

That was something else that bothered Loiseau:
all the security. It was a lot more noticeable down
here than it had been in Top. He could always tell
the ones who worked in the classified areas: they
huddled together at a table away from the others,
heads together, talking in low tones. Why did a
scientific expedition have to be so hush-hush,
anyway? With all the secrecy, he had no idea how
the expedition itself was going or what kind of
progress they were making. And that meant he
also had no idea when he would be able to get out
of here and go home again.

Home . . .

Suddenly, a stronger wave of dizziness washed
over him. Loiseau staggered, grabbing for the
range handle again. This was no fit of nerves: this
was something else. Something serious. Fear
stabbed through him as he fought to keep upright.

Abruptly, his vision began to dim. Around the
kitchen, people were pausing their work, putting
down their knives, spatulas, and wooden spoons
to stare at him. Somebody was speaking to him,
but sound had attenuated to a murmur and he
couldn't make it out. Reaching out to maintain
his balance, Loiseau grabbed for the heavy pot full

of béchamel but just missed, slipping off its side. He felt nothing. Yet another wave of dizziness, even more overpowering. And now an unpleasant scent rose to his nostrils: the smell of singed hair and overcooked meat. He wondered if it was a hallucination. People were running toward him. He glanced down and noticed, with a distant curiosity, that his hand had pushed the béchamel pot aside and fallen over the open range. Blue flames licked up between his fingers. Still he felt nothing. A curious blackness enfolded him like a blanket—and then to Loiseau it seemed the most natural thing in the world to sink to the floor and slip into dark dreams.

16

"Are you almost done, Doctor?"

Crane turned to see Renault, the executive chef, hovering nearby, arms crossed, a look of strong disapproval on his face.

"Almost." And, turning back to a rack holding at least a hundred small tubs of butter, he selected one at random, peeled the plastic wrapping from its top, and scraped about a teaspoon into a small test tube.

The walk-in cooler of Central had been a revelation. It was stocked not only with typical restaurant fare—poultry, beef, eggs, garden vegetables, milk, and the like—but also ingredients that would be more at home in three-star establishments on the Continent. Black and white truffles; near-priceless aged balsamic vinegar in tiny glass bulbs; pheasant, grouse, goose, plover; large tins of Russian and Iranian caviar. And everything was packed into a space no larger than ten feet by twenty. Given such an embarrassment of riches, Crane had been forced to limit his samples to the most common items that most people were likely to ingest every day. Even so, almost all the two hundred test tubes of his sampling kit were now full—and the hour-long process had strained the patience of the executive chef to the breaking point.

Replacing the tub of butter, Crane moved to the next rack, which contained the basic liquids for the house vinaigrette: fine old French white wine vinegars and cold-pressed olive oil.

"It's from Spain," Crane said, picking up a bottle of the oil and glancing at the label.

"The best," Renault said simply.

"I would have thought that Italian—"

Renault made a half-scornful, half-impatient sound with his lips. **C'est fou!** There is no comparison. These olives are all hand picked, from first-growth trees planted no more than thirty to an acre, sparsely watered, enriched with horse manure—"

"Horse manure," Crane repeated, nodding slowly.

Renault's face darkened. "**Engrais.** The fertilizer. All natural, no chemicals." He had taken Crane's approach as a personal affront to the quality of his kitchen, as if Crane were an inspector from the board of health and sanitation instead of a doctor tracking down a medical mystery.

Crane pulled the top from the bottle, drew out a fresh test tube from his kit, poured in a dram, then stoppered the tube. He replaced the oil, drew out another bottle from another row. "So much of the foodstuff here is fresh. How do you keep it from spoiling?"

Renault shrugged. "Food is food. It spoils."

Crane filled another tube. "What happens to it?"

"Some gets incinerated. The rest is packed up with the other waste and gets sent up in the Tub."

Crane nodded. The Tub, he had learned, was a large, unmanned supply module that made daily shuttles between the Facility and the support station on the surface. Officially known as the LF2-M Deeply Submersible Resupply Unit, it was a prototype of a Navy design to provide crippled subs with emergency supplies. It had gotten its nickname from its ungainly oblong shape, highly reminiscent of a monster bathtub.

"And your fresh provisions come down on the Tub, also?" he asked.

"Of course."

Crane filled another tube with vinegar. "Who orders your new supplies?"

"Food Service Purchasing, based on inventory control and advance menu planning."

"And who physically moves the supplies from the Tub to the kitchens?"

"The inventory officer, under my direct supervision. Today's shipment is due shortly. In fact, we should already be on our way to Receiving." Renault frowned. "If you are suggesting, **Docteur,** that—"

"I'm not suggesting anything," Crane replied with a smile. And, in fact, he wasn't. He had already spoken with the nutritionists and dieticians, and their voluntary meal plans seemed healthful and sensible. And although Crane had taken the time to carefully sample dozens of items from the pantries of Top and, now, Central, he didn't hold out much hope of finding anything harmful. It seemed unlikely anything was being introduced into the food, either accidentally or deliberately. More and more, his suspicions were settling on heavy metal poisoning.

The symptoms of heavy metal toxicity were

vague and non-specific, just like those cropping up all over the Facility: chronic fatigue, gastrointestinal upset, short-term memory loss, joint pain, disorganized thought processes, and a host of others. Already, he had two members of the medical staff investigating the work and leisure environments of Deep Storm for the presence of lead, arsenic, mercury, cadmium, and a host of other heavy metals. Meanwhile, all those patients who had complained of symptoms were being asked to return to Medical to provide hair, blood, and urine samples for testing. The exposure would naturally have to be acute, not chronic: people hadn't been on the Facility long enough for anything else . . .

Crane stoppered the final test tube, then placed it in the portable rack and zipped up his analysis bag with a faint sense of satisfaction. If heavy metal poisoning or mercurialism was found to be the culprit, strong chelators like DMPS and DMSA could be used not only for challenge testing but also for treatment. No doubt he'd have to request the necessary quantities be sent down in the Tub: there wouldn't be enough in the pharmacy to treat all patients on the Facility.

He turned around to find that Renault had already left. Picking up his analysis bag, he stepped out of the cooler and closed the door behind him.

He found Renault on the far side of the kitchen, talking to somebody wearing chef's whites. As Crane approached, Renault turned toward him.

"You are done," he said. It wasn't phrased as a question.

"Yes, except for a few questions I have about the cook who was taken ill. Robert Loiseau."

Renault seemed incredulous. "More questions? That other doctor, the woman, she asked so many before."

"Just a few more."

"You will have to walk with us, then. We are overdue at Receiving."

"Very well." Crane didn't mind—it would give him a chance to observe the transfer of foodstuffs from the Tub to the kitchens, set his mind at ease, remove this as a potential source of contamination. He was quickly introduced to the man in chef's whites—Conrad, the inventory officer—and to two other members of the kitchen staff carrying large food lockers. Then Crane fell in behind the small group, and together they left the kitchen and made their way down the echoing corridors to the elevator.

Renault was busy discussing a shortage of root vegetables with the inventory officer, and Crane had only managed to get in a single question about Loiseau by the time they arrived at deck 12.

"No," Renault said as the doors swept open and he stepped out. "There was no warning. No warning at all."

Crane had not been here since his arrival, but he remembered the way to the Compression Complex. Renault, however, struck out in the opposite direction, threading an intricate path through a maze of narrow corridors.

"The man is still comatose; we haven't been able to ask any questions," Crane said as they walked. "But you're sure nobody saw anything strange or out of the ordinary?"

Renault thought a moment. "I recall Tanner saying that Loiseau looked a little tired."

"Tanner?"

"Our pastry chef."

"Did he elaborate?"

Renault shook his head. "You will have to ask Monsieur Tanner."

"Do you know if Loiseau abused drugs of any kind?"

"Certainly not!" Renault said. "Nobody in my kitchens uses drugs."

Ahead, the corridor ended at a large, oval hatch, guarded by a single marine. Above was a sign that read ACCESS TO OUTER HULL. The marine looked at them in turn, examined a form that Renault passed over, then nodded the group through.

Beyond the hatchway was a small steel passage,

illuminated by red bulbs recessed into thick housings. Another hatch lay ahead, closed and barred from the far side. The hatch clanged shut behind them. There was the sound of retractors being swung into place. Slowly, the echoes died away. As they waited in the dim crimson light, Crane became aware of a damp chill, and a faint, briny odor that reminded him of a submarine's bilge.

After a few moments there was another loud scraping noise, this time from in front of them, and then the forward hatchway drew back. They stepped into a smaller chamber. Once again, the hatch behind swung shut, locking automatically. The chill and the smell were more noticeable here. At the end of the chamber, a third steel hatch—larger and heavier than the others—was set. Huge, swinging bolts anchored the hatch shut, and it was guarded by a brace of armed marines. Several signs warning of danger and listing numerous restrictions were fixed to the chamber walls.

For a moment, they waited in silence while the marines again examined Renault's paperwork. Then one of them turned and pressed a red button on a console. A shrill buzzer sounded. With obvious effort, the marines swiveled each of the heavy bolts half a revolution, then together turned the hatch's massive wheel in a counterclockwise direction. There was a clank, then a hiss of escaping air, as the hatchway unsealed itself. Crane felt his ears pop. The marines pushed the hatch outward, then gestured for the group to proceed. The kitchen workers carrying the food lockers stepped through first, followed by Conrad and Renault. Crane fell into place behind them, ready with another question. But then he froze in the hatchway, staring straight ahead, question abruptly forgotten.

17

He was standing at the threshold of a vast, dim chasm. At least, that was his first impression. As his eyes adjusted to the low light, he realized he was on a narrow accessway, bolted to the exterior skin of the Facility. The sheer wall fell away behind and below him—freckled by a lattice-work of rungs—plummeting twelve stories into darkness, and for a moment he felt a wave of vertigo. Quickly, he grasped the steel railing. He realized dimly that one the marines was speaking to him.

"Sir," the marine was saying, "please step out. This hatchway cannot remain open."

"Sorry." And Crane hastily withdrew his other foot from the threshold. The two marines pulled the heavy hatch shut. From within came the rasp of bolts being fixed into place.

Still clinging to the railing, Crane looked around. Some distance ahead of him, and just barely visible in the faint light, rose a curved metal wall: the outer dome. Sodium lights were set into it at regular but distant intervals, providing the weak illumination. Looking upward, he followed the dome's rising curve to its apex, directly above the Facility. Metal tubes rose from the Facility roof to the underside of the dome: these, he assumed, were the airlocks that provided access to the bathyscaphes and the escape pod.

His gaze fell from the dome to the accessway on which he stood. It widened ahead of him, becoming a gentle ramp that spanned the deep gulf between the Facility and the dome. The rest of the group was already heading up it, toward a large platform fixed to the wall of the dome. He took a deep breath, then let go of the railing and began to follow.

The air was far chillier here, and the bilge smell more pronounced. As he walked, his feet clattered against the metal grid of the catwalk, echoing dully in the vast space. For a moment, he had a mental picture of where he was—at the bottom of the sea, walking on a narrow bridge between a twelve-story metal box and the dome that surrounded it, empty space between him and the sea bed below—but found it unsettling and tried to push it away. Instead, he focused on catching up to the group, which had by now almost reached the platform.

Conrad was behind Renault and the two kitchen staffers, and Crane trotted up beside him. "And here I thought Receiving would be some nice little room," he said, "with a television, maybe, and magazines on the tables."

Conrad laughed. "Takes some getting used to, doesn't it?"

"You could say that. I had no idea the space between the Facility and the dome was pressurized. I figured it was filled with water."

"The Facility wasn't constructed to operate at such a depth. At this pressure, it wouldn't last a minute on its own. The dome protects us. Somebody told me they work together, like the double hull of a submarine or something. I don't really understand it, to tell you the truth."

Crane nodded. The concept did make perfect sense. In some ways, it **was** like a submarine, with its inner pressure hull, outer hull, and ballast tanks between.

"I noticed a series of rungs on the outside of the Facility. What on earth are those for?"

"Like I said, it was built for much shallower water, where a protective dome wouldn't be necessary. I think those rungs were meant for divers to use when moving up or down the sides of the Facility, making repairs and such."

Glancing back, Crane noticed two large, tube-like struts that led, horizontally, from opposite ends of the dome to the Facility, at a point just slightly above its center. These, he realized, were what Asher had called pressure spokes—tubes open to the sea that were yet another device to compensate somehow for the massive pressure. From this distance, they **did** sort of resemble two spokes of a wheel. But to Crane, they looked more like a rotisserie spit onto which the Facility had been impaled. Compensation or not, he didn't like having the sea that close to the box inside which he was living.

They had now reached the platform at the end of the ramp. It was about twenty feet square and fastened securely to the dome's inner wall. An airlock hatch stood at one side, immensely thick, guarded by still more marines. This hatch, Crane felt sure, led to the deep ocean outside the dome. No doubt the Tub would dock itself here, and the supplies brought in through this airlock.

There were a dozen or so people waiting on the

platform already: technicians in lab coats, maintenance workers in jumpsuits. Most had brought
containers of various sizes. The maintenance crew
had the largest ones: black plastic wheeled containers so bulky it must be difficult to fit them
through hatchways. Crane guessed these contained waste material being sent back up to the
surface.

Beside the hatch stood a control panel manned
by a tall and very attractive woman in military
garb. As Crane watched, she tapped a few keys,
peered at a tiny display. "Incoming at T minus
two minutes," she said over her shoulder.

There were a few impatient sighs from the
group. "Late again," somebody murmured.

Crane's vertigo had now receded. His eye
moved from the woman at the station to the skin
of the dome itself. Its curve was gentle and perfect, designed for maximum strength, oddly
pleasing to the eye. Amazing to think of the
terrific pressure it was under, the almost inconceivable burden of water that pressed down
upon it. It was something that, as a submariner,
he'd learned not to dwell on. Unconsciously, he
stretched forward a hand and briefly caressed the
dome's surface. It was dry, smooth, and cold.

Renault, the executive chef, looked at his watch
impatiently. Then he turned to Crane. "So, Doctor," he said, with something like satisfaction,

"the Tub arrives. My men here retrieve the food-stuffs. Conrad does a checklist to make sure nothing was forgotten. All under my supervision. Satisfactory?"

"Yes," Crane replied.

"Incoming at T minus one minute," the woman called out.

Renault drew a bit closer. "You had other questions?" he asked. And he glanced again at his watch as if to say, **Ask now, while I'm wasting valuable time anyway.**

"Has anybody else on your staff complained of health problems recently?"

"My saucier has a sinus infection. But that hasn't prevented him from reporting to work."

Crane had expected this reply. Now that he'd satisfied himself on food handling, he was eager to get to work on the heavy metal possibility. His eyes began to rove: over the assembled crowd, to the attractive woman at the monitoring station, to an electrical bulkhead beside her. Drops of condensation dripped slowly from the underside of the bulkhead. He was half tempted to say good-bye and head back down the walkway to the Facility hatch—only he felt pretty sure he'd need Renault, and his paperwork, to get back inside.

There was a thud on the far side of the dome, and the platform trembled slightly: the Tub had docked. People began to move around, preparing for the airlock to be opened.

"Docking successful," said the woman. "Initiating hatchway decompression."

"What about behavior patterns?" Crane asked the chef. "Has anybody behaved in an uncharacteristic or unusual manner?"

Renault frowned. "Unusual? In what way unusual?"

Crane didn't reply. His wandering eye had returned to the bulkhead, where the condensation was dripping more quickly now. **Odd,** he thought. **Now, why would condensation be—**

There was a strange, high-pitched sound almost like the spitting of a cat, so brief Crane wasn't sure he'd heard it. And then, quite suddenly, a jet of water—no wider than the point of a pin—appeared at the spot where the drip had been. For a moment, Crane simply stared in disbelief. The jet was perfectly horizontal, like the beam of a laser, hissing and boiling, and it arrowed straight inward for at least a hundred feet, almost reaching the Facility itself before gravity began pulling it downward in a gradual arc.

There was a moment of stasis. And then came the whoop of a klaxon, the shriek of alarms. "Perimeter breach!" an electronic voice boomed through the echoing space. "Perimeter breach! This is an emergency!"

There was a cry of surprise from the people on the platform. The uniformed woman grabbed her radio, spoke into it quickly. "This is Waybright at Tub Control. We've got a pinhole perforation in the control conduit. Repeat, it's here, **the breach is here!** Send in a containment crew on the double!"

Someone screamed, and the crowd drew back to the edges of the platform. A couple of people began edging back down the walkway toward the Facility.

"It's gonna widen!" somebody cried.

"We can't wait for the team!" said Conrad. And instinctively he put out his hand to seal the breach.

Instantly, Crane darted forward. "No!" he cried, stretching out an arm to pull Conrad back. But before he could do so, Conrad's left hand passed through the jet of water.

And, neatly as a surgeon's scalpel, the pressurized water severed each finger at the second knuckle.

Then the platform became a pandemonium: screams, cries of surprise and horror, the shrill bark of commands. Conrad slumped to the floor, grasping his injured hand, mouth wide in surprise. The catwalk rang with the sound of booted feet as the Facility hatchway boomed open and men in heavy suits came running up toward them, bulky equipment in hand. Meanwhile, Crane had crouched low and—careful to avoid the murderous jet of water—picked up the severed fingers and placed them carefully, one after the other, in his shirt pocket.

18

Admiral Richard Ulysses Spartan stood in one corner of the metal platform, severely erect, gazing wordlessly at the scene around him. Ten minutes earlier, when he first arrived, the waiting area fixed to the dome wall had been a little bedlam: rescue workers and medics; engineers; uniformed seamen and officers; and one hysterical, panicked scientist who refused to move. Now it was much quieter. Two armed seamen stood at the edge of the catwalk, barring entry to the platform. Some engineers and maintenance workers huddled around the metal and titanium seal that had been fixed over the pinhole leak. A single housekeeping employee knelt over the gridwork floor with a bucket, swabbing bloodstains from the metal.

Watching it all, Spartan frowned. He detested flaws and errors and was highly intolerant of them. Flaws, even small ones, had no place in any military operation. That was especially true in an installation such as this, where the stakes were so high and the environment so dangerous. The Facility was a highly complex system, a fantastic network of interdependencies. It was like the human body. The fact that it worked at all was a marvel of engineering. But remove just one key system and the resulting chain reaction would shut down everything else. The body would die. The Facility would fail.

Spartan's eyes narrowed further. Truth was, that had come disturbingly close to happening just now. Worse, it was apparently due to another element even more objectionable than error—a **human** element.

Movement appeared in his peripheral vision. Turning, Spartan saw the trim figure of Commander Korolis walking up the catwalk from the Facility. He arrived at the platform and the two guards immediately stepped aside.

Korolis approached the admiral and threw him a smart salute. Spartan nodded in return. Korolis had the condition known as exotrophia: one eye looked ahead normally, while the other pointed outward. But his condition was mild, making it difficult to know, when he was facing you, which eye was fixed: whether he was looking directly at you or not. It was an unsettling sensation that had proven rather useful in interrogation and other situations. Privately, Spartan disapproved of Korolis's single-minded obsession with military secrecy—he disapproved of any kind of obsessive-ness in his staff—but he had to admit the man was fiercely loyal to the service.

Korolis was carrying a thin white folder tucked beneath his arm. Now he handed it to Spartan. The admiral opened it. Inside was a single printed sheet.

Spartan closed the folder without reading the contents and glanced back at Korolis. "It's confirmed?" he said.

Korolis nodded.

"Intent, as well?"

"Yes," Korolis answered. "It was pure dumb luck that it ruptured where it did."

"Very well. And your new men?"

"They should arrive within minutes."

"Understood." And Spartan gave him a dismissive nod.

He watched for a minute, thoughtfully, as the officer made his way back down the catwalk. It was not until Korolis had dwindled to a small shadow outside the Facility entrance that he at last dropped his eyes again to the folder, opened it, and scanned the sheet inside. If the contents made an impression on him, it was visible only in a clenching of his jaw muscles.

Raised voices roused him. The admiral looked up to see Asher arguing with the guards, who were denying him permission to climb onto the platform. Asher turned toward Spartan, and the admiral nodded his permission. The guards stepped back and Asher came over, puffing slightly.

"What are you doing here, Doctor?" Spartan asked mildly.

"I've come to see you."

"I gathered as much."

"You haven't returned my calls or e-mails."

"I've been rather busy," Spartan said. "Some items of importance came up."

"What I sent you was important, too. Our researcher's report on what he found in the library of Grimwold Castle. Have you read it?"

Spartan's eyes slid away for a moment, toward the engineers working on the seal, before returning to the chief scientist. "I've skimmed it."

"Then you know what I'm talking about."

"Frankly, Doctor, I'm a little surprised. For a man of science, you seem far too credulous. The entire thing could be a work of imagination. You know how superstitious people were back then: old accounts of demons, witches, sea monsters, and other rubbish are innumerable. Even if it purports to be real, there is no reason to think this account has anything to do with what we're concerned about here."

"If you'd read the document you'd have seen the parallels." Asher, normally so calm and collected, was agitated. "Of course it's possible the two are unrelated. But if nothing else, it emphasizes the need to slow down. Learn a little more about what's down there."

"The only way to do that with any certainty is to expose it. We've already learned quite a bit, found quite a bit—you of all people know that."

"Yes, and look at the results. Healthy people falling sick in alarming numbers. People with no history of emotional problems having psychotic episodes."

"You brought somebody on board to look into that. What's he been doing?"

Asher drew closer. "Working with his hands tied. Because you haven't given him access to the lower levels. Where the **real** story lies."

Spartan gave a wintry smile. "We've been over that. Security is paramount. Peter Crane is a security risk."

"He's a lot less of a risk than—"

But Spartan made a suppressing gesture. Asher drew back, following Spartan's eyes. A new person had stepped onto the platform: a muscular, sunburnt man in dark military fatigues, carrying a black canvas duffel. His iron-gray hair was cut very short. Catching sight of Spartan, he walked over and executed a crisp salute.

"Chief Woburn, reporting as ordered, sir," he said.

"Where are your men, Chief?" Spartan asked.

"Waiting outside the Compression Complex."

"Then join them. I'll have Commander Korolis show you to your quarters."

"Aye, aye, sir." Another salute and the officer wheeled around.

Spartan turned back to Asher. "I'll take your request under advisement."

Asher had remained silent through the brief exchange, his gaze moving from the stranger's face to the insignia on his fatigues. Now he confronted Spartan. "Who was that?"

"Surely you heard the name. Chief Petty Officer Woburn."

"**More** military? There must be some mistake."

Spartan shook his head. "No mistake. They're here at the request of Commander Korolis and will be taking orders directly from him. He believes more manpower is necessary to enforce security."

Asher's expression grew dark. "Additional personnel allotments are joint decisions, Admiral. Made by us as a team. And that insignia, the man's a—"

"This isn't a democracy, Doctor. Not when the safety of this Facility is concerned. And at the moment, that safety appears to be in jeopardy." And Spartan gave a subtle nod toward the group of engineers at the far corner of the platform.

Asher turned in their direction. "What's the status of the breach?"

"Successful containment, as you can see. A submersible is being dispatched from the surface, with additional plating for the exterior of the dome. A temporary seal has been applied until a more permanent one can be fabricated. That will take some time. The affected area is about four feet in length."

Asher frowned. "Four feet? For a pinhole?"

"Yes. It was only a pinhole. But that's not what it was **intended** to be."

For a moment Asher remained still, digesting this. "I'm not sure I understand."

Spartan nodded again toward the engineers. "You see that bulkhead where the breach occurred? It runs directly to the airlock housing, where the electrical and magnetic controls that open the hatch are located. When our emergency crews sealed the breach, they found a three-foot cut, all the way from the pinhole to the housing."

"A cut," Asher repeated slowly.

"Here, along the inside of the dome. Made by a portable laser cutter, we believe—a detailed analysis is ongoing. This cut compromised the integrity of the entire bulkhead. It could have failed at any time—although failure was more likely during a moment of stress, such as the docking impact of the Tub. Luckily, the laser cut was imperfect—it was deeper in some spots than in others. Hence, the pinhole breach. If the cut had worked as designed, the pinhole would have spread down the bulkhead to the airlock housing itself . . ."

"Rupturing the hatch," Asher murmured. "Causing a massive hull breach."

"A **terminal** hull breach."

"And this cut you mention. You're implying it wasn't an accident? That it was a deliberate act of—of sabotage?"

For a moment, Admiral Spartan did not reply. Then, slowly, he lifted an index finger and—keeping his gaze locked on Asher—laid it perpendicularly across his lips.

19

Crane pulled back from the black rubber eyepiece, blinked, then rubbed his face with both hands. He glanced around the laboratory, waiting for his vision to adapt. The images slowly sharpened: a medical technician across the room, working with a titration setup. Another technician entering data into a workstation. And just across the lab table, Michele Bishop, who—like himself—was using a portable viewer. As he watched, she, too, leaned away, and their eyes met.

"You look about as tired as I feel," she said.

Crane nodded. He **was** tired—bone tired. He'd been going twenty hours straight: first with a harrowing and exhausting microsurgical procedure to reattach Conrad's severed fingers, then with the seemingly endless follow-up on his hypothesis of heavy metal poisoning.

And along with the weariness was also disappointment. Because so far, no significant traces of heavy metals had been detected in the Deep Storm personnel. Hair, urine, and other samples had been examined, without result. He and Bishop were now examining slides from energy-dispersive X-ray fluorescence spectrometer tests, but once again, nothing so far. The public areas of the Facility had also come up clean.

He sighed deeply. He'd been so convinced this was the answer. It still could be, of course. But with every new test that came back negative, the chances grew increasingly remote. Just as disappointing, Jane Rand's data mining efforts had turned up nothing.

"You need to get some rest," Bishop said. "Before you become a patient here yourself."

Crane sighed again, stretched. "I guess you're right." And she was: he'd soon be too bleary-eyed to interpret the slides properly. So he stood, said his good-byes to Bishop and the staff, and exited the Medical Suite.

Although most of the Facility remained terra

incognita to him, he knew his way from the Medical Suite to his quarters well enough to make the trip without conscious thought. Down to Times Square, then left past the library and theater, one flight up in the elevator, another left, then two quick rights. He yawned as he opened his stateroom door with his passcard. He just wasn't thinking clearly anymore. A good six hours of sleep would put the problem in perspective, maybe point out the answer that was eluding him.

He stepped inside, yawning again, and placed his palmtop device on the desk. He turned—and then froze.

Howard Asher was sitting in the visitor's chair, an unknown man in a lab coat standing beside him.

Crane frowned in surprise. "What are—" he began.

Asher made a brusque suppressing gesture with his right hand, then nodded to the man in the lab coat. As Crane watched, the stranger closed and locked the room and bathroom doors.

Asher cleared his throat softly. Crane had seen little of him since their squash game. His face looked worn, pained, and there was a haunted gleam in his eyes, as of someone who had been struggling with demons.

"How's the arm?" Crane asked.

"It's been rather painful the last day or two," Asher admitted.

"You need to be careful. Vascular insufficiency can lead to ulceration, even gangrene, if the nerve function is impaired. You should let me—"

But Asher cut him off with another gesture. "There's no time for that now. Look, we'll need to speak quietly. Roger's not in the adjoining quarters at present, but he could return at any time."

This was the last thing Crane had expected to hear. He nodded, mystified.

"Why don't you sit down?" And Asher motioned toward the desk chair. He waited until Crane was seated before speaking again.

"You're about to cross a threshold, Peter," he said in the same low voice. "I'm going to tell you something. And once I've told you, there will be no going back. Things will never be the same for you again, **ever**. The world will be a fundamentally different place. Do you understand?"

"Why do I get the sense," Crane said, "you're about to tell me I was right, back there in the squash court? That this isn't about Atlantis, at all?"

A bleak smile passed over Asher's features. "The truth is infinitely stranger."

Crane felt a chill in the pit of his stomach.

Asher placed his elbows on his knees. "Have you heard of the Mohorovicic discontinuity?"

"It sounds familiar. But I can't place it."

"It's also known as the M discontinuity, or simply the Moho."

"The Moho. I remember my marine geology professor at Annapolis talking about it."

"Then you'll remember it's the boundary between the earth's crust and the mantle beneath."

Crane nodded.

"The Moho lies at different depths, depending on location. The crust is much thicker beneath the continents, for example, than beneath the oceans. The Moho is as deep as seventy miles beneath the surface of the continents, but at certain mid-oceanic ridges, it's as shallow as a few miles."

Asher leaned toward Crane, lowered his voice still further. "The Storm King oil platform is built above just such an oceanic ridge."

"So you're saying the Moho is close to the crust directly below us."

Asher nodded.

Crane swallowed. He had no idea where this was headed.

"You were told the same story that all workers in the unclassified levels of Deep Storm were—that during a routine mining operation, drillers on the Storm King platform found evidence of an ancient civilization beneath the ocean floor. And that story is true—as far as it goes."

Asher plucked a handkerchief from his pocket,

mopped his brow. "But there's more to it than that. You see, they didn't find artifacts or ancient buildings, anything like that. What they detected was a **signal**."

"A signal? You mean like radio waves?"

"The exact nature of the signal is problematic. More of a seismic ping, almost a kind of sonar. But of an unknown nature. All we can say for sure is that it's **not naturally occurring**. And before I leave this room, I'll prove it to you."

Crane opened his mouth to speak. Then he stopped. Disbelief, shock, perplexity, all rose within him.

Seeing the look on Crane's face, Asher smiled again: an almost wistful smile this time. "Yes, Peter. Now comes the difficult part. Because, you see, that signal came from beneath the Moho. Beneath the earth's crust."

"Beneath?" Crane murmured in disbelief.

Asher nodded.

"But that would mean—"

"Exactly. Whatever it is that's transmitting the signal—we didn't put it there. Someone else did."

20

For a moment, the stateroom was quiet. Crane sat motionless, struggling to absorb what he had just heard, as the meaning of Asher's words worked its way through him.

"Take a minute, Peter," Asher said kindly. "I know it's a hard thing to get your mind around."

"I'm not sure I believe it," Crane replied at last. "You sure there's no mistake?"

"No mistake. Mankind has no technology capable of inserting a mechanical device beneath the earth's crust—let alone a device that can emit such a signal. Because of the natural phase change that occurs at the Moho, listening devices on the earth's surface are neither sensitive nor technologically advanced enough to pick up certain kinds of waves from below the crust. But because of the mid-Atlantic ridge, the Moho is unusually shallow here. That—along with the depth of the Storm King well holes—led to the accidental discovery of the signal."

Crane shifted in his seat. "Go on."

"Of course, the government's immediate goal became to excavate to the source of the signal, determine what it was. It took quite some time to get the project ramped up, the necessary equipment in place. The depth we're operating at makes things extremely difficult—this Facility was built for other purposes and was not meant to operate anywhere near this deep. Hence the surrounding dome."

"How long did the preparations take, exactly?"

"Twenty months."

"That's it?" Crane felt stunned. "General Motors can't even design a car prototype in twenty months."

"That shows you just how seriously the government is taking this project. In any case, the excavation has been online for almost two months now, and the pace is frantic. Significant progress has been made. A vertical shaft has been dug beneath the Facility. We're excavating toward the source of the signal."

"How is that possible? Isn't the rock molten at that depth?"

"The crust is relatively thin, the geothermic values are low, and radiogenic heat production is far less than it would be in the continental crust. P-wave and S-wave readings indicate the lithosphere is only about three kilometers beneath us—'only' being a relative term, of course."

Crane shook his head. "There must be some logical, some **terrestrial,** explanation. Some Russian device, or maybe Chinese. Or some naturally occurring phenomenon. If I learned anything from that marine geology course, it's that we know precious little about the composition of our own planet, save for the thinnest outer layer."

"It's not Russian or Chinese. And I'm afraid there are too many things that don't add up for it to be naturally occurring. The geology of the impact, for example. Normally, for something to be embedded so deep in the earth, you'd expect to find a serious geologic disturbance—the undersea equivalent of Meteor Crater. But in this case, the layers of sedimentation above the anomaly are in almost perfect synch with the surrounding matrix. Think of a child digging a hole on the beach, dropping a shell into it, and putting the sand back in place. There's no earthly phenomenon to explain that."

"But there **has** to be," said Crane.

"No. I'm afraid the true explanation lies **beyond**. You see, certain . . . **artifacts** have been retrieved." And at this, Asher nodded to the silent man in the lab coat. The man walked toward a far wall, knelt, and opened a plastic locker that sat there. He withdrew something, rose, and handed it to Asher.

Crane looked on curiously. It was a cube-shaped object, encased in some kind of metal shielding. Asher glanced toward him, met his eyes.

"Remember what I told you, Peter," he said. "About the threshold." And then, gently, he pulled away the shielding and offered the cube to Crane.

It was hollow, made of transparent Plexiglas. Every edge was carefully sealed. Something was inside. Crane took it from Asher's hands, drew it close—then gasped aloud in surprise.

Floating in the dead center of the cube was a small object, no larger than a domino. It emitted a laserlike beam of light, pencil thin and intensely white, toward the ceiling. Impossibly, the object itself was of no single, definable color, but rather a coruscation, shimmering and rainbow hued: gold and violet and indigo and cinnamon and other colors Crane had never imagined, all in a constant state of change. The colors seemed to come from deep within the object, rising outward from some central core, as if the little object burned with some strange inner fire.

He turned the Plexiglas cube over and over, staring at the thing within it. No matter how he turned it, the object inside stayed dead center. He peered at the makeup of the cube itself, searching for hidden wires or magnets. But it was a simple cube of clear plastic—there were no tricks.

He shook the cube, first gently, then with severity. The glowing, pulsing thing at its center bobbled ever so slightly up and down at this treatment, always coming to rest in the exact center, where it continued to float serenely, its thin beam of white light pointing straight upward.

He brought the cube up close, staring at the object with openmouthed curiosity. He noticed the edges of the domino-sized thing were not, in fact, exactly defined. Rather, the object seemed to pulsate faintly: edges grew sharp, then softened again. It was almost as if the object's mass and form were in continuous flux.

He looked up from the cube. Asher was standing there, smiling, hand outstretched. After the briefest hesitation, Crane reluctantly handed him the cube. The chief scientist replaced it inside the shielding and gave it to his assistant, who returned it to the storage locker.

Crane sat back, blinking. "What the hell is it?" he asked after a moment.

"We don't know its purpose is, exactly."

"What's it made of?"

"Unknown."

"Is it dangerous? Could it be the source of the problems here?"

"I wondered the same thing, of course. We all did. But, no: it's harmless."

"You're sure about that?"

"The very first tests we did were to see if it was throwing off any radiation other than light. But it's not. It's completely inert—all subsequent tests have confirmed that. The reason I placed it inside that Plexiglas cube is because it's a little hard to deal with otherwise—it always finds the precise center of a room in which to hover."

"Where'd you get it?"

"It was uncovered during the excavation of the shaft. Along with well over a dozen others to date." Asher paused. "Our job when we started was clear-cut: dig as quickly as possible, within safety parameters, down toward the source of the signal. He gestured toward the locker. But then, when we began to discover those . . . well, things grew more complicated."

He sat down again, leaned in, and continued in a conspiratorial whisper. "They're remarkable, Peter—even more remarkable than they look. For one thing, they seem to be essentially indestructible. They're impervious to anything we've subjected them to in controlled environments. Some kinds of damage, like radiation, they absorb; others they reflect. And another thing: they seem to act as capacitors."

"Capacitors?" Crane repeated. "Like batteries?" Asher nodded.

"What kind of power output?"

"We haven't been able to measure the top end. When we put conductors on them, they red-lined even our most powerful measuring devices."

"And what was the measurement?"

"One trillion watts."

"**What?** That little thing? Storing a thousand gigawatts' worth of energy?"

"You could put that in a car and it would provide enough electricity to power the vehicle for its lifetime—one hundred thousand miles. And there's something else." Asher reached into a pocket of his lab coat, pulled out a small manila envelope, and handed it to Crane.

Crane opened it and pulled out the sheet within. It was a computer printout, a repeating burst of short numbers:

00000111110010101101010110011101110001 01
01100011000101000110100110000100000000 00

00000111110010101101010110011101110001010110001100010100011010011000010000000000

00000111110010101101010110011101110001010110001100010100011010011000010000000000

"What's this?" he asked.

"That beam of light the marker's emitting? It's not continuous; it's actually pulsing, millions of times a second. The pulses are very regular: on and off."

"Ones and zeros. Digital."

"I believe so. It's what drives every computer on every desktop in the world. It's how neurons fire in our brains. It's a fundamental law of nature. This little device might be incredibly sophisticated, but why wouldn't **it** communicate digitally?" Asher tapped the sheet. "A sequence eighty bits long, repeating over and over. It's substantially shorter than the other message, by the way—the one transmitted from beneath the Moho, the one that was initially discovered."

"The **other** message, you say. So you think this pulse of light is trying to tell us something?"

"Yes I do—if we can decrypt it."

Crane raised the sheet. "May I keep this?"

Asher hesitated. "Very well. But don't show it to anybody."

Crane returned the sheet to the envelope, placed it in his desk. "These artifacts—"

"We call them markers. Or sentinels."

"Why sentinels?"

"Because it's almost as if they've been waiting, watching, all these years, to offer us something."

Crane thought for a moment. "So you're digging toward the source of the signal. What then?"

"There, too, things have gotten a little more complicated." Asher paused again. "Ultrasonic sensors we've lowered into the shaft . . . they've picked up evidence of something **below** the artifact field. A large object, buried even more deeply than the source of the signal."

"What kind of object?"

"We know it is torus shaped. We know it's extremely large—**miles** across. Beyond that, nothing."

Crane shook his head. "But you must have some theories."

"About what it's doing here? Certainly." Asher seemed a little more at ease now, like someone who'd unburdened himself of a painful truth. "After extensive discussion, the consensus among the scientists and the military here was that something has been left behind for humanity to discover, **when sufficiently advanced**."

"You mean, like a gift?"

"You could call it that. Who's to say which discoveries mankind is responsible for, and which were **given** us, one way or another? Who's to say, for example, that fire wasn't a gift from beyond the stars? Or iron? Or the know-how for building pyramids?"

"A gift from beyond the stars," Crane repeated dubiously.

"The Greeks believed fire came from the gods. Other peoples have similar myths. Maybe there's a pattern here? Once we had technology advanced enough to pick up a signal from **beneath** the Moho—once we could actually dig down to the beacon—we would be considered ready for the next leap forward."

"And so this buried object you're digging toward contains useful technology of some kind? Benevolent technology we can discover once we're ready to make use of it?"

"Exactly. Such as the technology that created the device I just showed you. Something that would help humanity to develop further, make that next leap."

There was a silence as Crane digested this.

"So what's the problem?" he asked at last.

"At first, I was as certain of all this as the rest. But lately I'm not so sure. See, everybody **wants** to believe there's something wonderful down there. My scientists are starry-eyed, dreaming of entire new frontiers of knowledge. The Navy spooks are drooling over the possibility of new technology that might be weaponized. But how can we be **sure** what's there? These markers we've found are like a trail of bread crumbs, promising tastier things. But until their signals are translated, we can't know what's really buried below them."

Asher wiped his brow again. "Then something happened. We'd always assumed, Peter, that the artifact was buried millions of years ago. But a couple of days back we discovered the burial was relatively recent—around A.D. 1400. That's when I realized that sightings, actual **sightings,** of the burial event might be part of the written record. So I sent a researcher around the region, visiting libraries, abbeys, universities—any place that might have eyewitness accounts. And at Grimwold Castle, an old monastery off the coast of Scotland, we found one." A dark look crossed his face. "It made for disturbing, frightening reading."

"And you're positive? That this account you found describes the actual burial, I mean."

"There's no way to be sure."

"Can I read it?"

"I'll get a copy to you. But the point is this: assuming it **does** describe the burial event, this eyewitness account is about as clear a go slow message as I can imagine."

Crane shrugged. "Makes sense. Especially since you haven't yet deciphered the digital signal."

"Except the Navy keeps moving ahead with greater and greater speed. Admiral Spartan and I don't see eye to eye on the matter. His worst fear is that other nations will learn of the discovery. He wants the object exposed and penetrated with all possible speed, and samples of whatever's inside retrieved for study."

"Does anybody else outside the classified sector know of this?"

"A few. Rumors circulate. Most suspect it's more than Atlantis." Abruptly, Asher rose and began pacing. "Anyway, there's another reason for caution. We know that the crust is composed of three layers—the sediment layer, the basement layer, and the oceanic layer. We've dug through the first two and are almost into the third and deepest layer. Below that is the Moho. The thing is, nobody really knows for certain **what** the Moho is, or what will happen when we hit it. We need to proceed with caution. But the more I've protested, the more I and the NOS have been marginalized. More military are arriving now, and they're no longer regular Navy. They're 'black ops'—and very scary."

"People like Korolis," Crane said.

At the name, a look of anger passed briefly over Asher's face. "Korolis requested them, and they're reporting directly to him. In any case, my fear is that Spartan may soon take full command of the operation, with Korolis as his enforcer. If I object too loudly, I might be relieved of my position, expelled from the station." Asher stopped pacing and stared at Crane. "And that's where you come in."

Crane stared back in surprise. "Me?"

"I'm very sorry, Peter. I never wanted to burden you with this knowledge—or this responsibility. I'd hoped the medical problem would be solved quickly and you could return to the surface, still believing we'd found Atlantis. But with the discovery of this eyewitness account, and given Spartan's increasingly aggressive behavior . . . well, you're the only option I have left."

"But why me? You're taking a huge risk just by telling me all this."

Asher smiled wearily. "I did my homework, remember? My people are scientists. They're too intimidated by men like Korolis to ever help me. But you: you're not only qualified to treat undersea ailments, you also served on an intelligence-gathering submarine. And I'm afraid that's just what this might soon become: an intelligence mission. And maybe more."

"What do you mean?"

"I mean that every day, they're getting closer to the Moho. I can't wait any longer. One way or another, we **have** to know what's down there—before Spartan's digging machines get to it."

"What makes you sure I'll fall in on your side?

I'm ex-military, as you point out. I might agree with Admiral Spartan."

Asher shook his head. "Not you. Now, listen—don't repeat a word of this to anybody." He hesitated. "Maybe none of this will be necessary. Maybe our analysts will finish decrypting those markers tomorrow, or the next day, and all I've said will become moot." He nodded at the man standing beside the evidence locker, who throughout the conversation hadn't said a single word. "This is John Marris. He's my own cryptanalyst, and he's working night and day on the problem. Now, what I want you to do—"

At that moment, a sharp rap sounded on the door. It was repeated again, and then again.

Crane looked at Asher. The chief scientist had frozen in place beside the chair, his lined face suddenly pale. He gave his head a violent shake.

Another rap, louder, more insistent. "Dr. Crane!" boomed a gravelly voice from the corridor.

Crane turned toward the door.

"Wait!" Asher said in a low, urgent voice.

But at that moment the door opened. And Admiral Spartan stood silhouetted in the light of the corridor, a red all-access passcard in his hand, flanked by marines with M1 carbines in their hands.

21

Spartan looked from Crane to Asher and back again, his expression unreadable. Then he took a step into the room.

"Am I interrupting something?" he asked.

The room fell uncomfortably silent. Crane glanced at Asher, who had the stunned look of a deer caught in a pair of headlights.

When there was no answer, Admiral Spartan turned to the marines. "Take him outside," he said, pointing at Crane.

One of the marines beckoned Crane forward

with his rifle barrel. Crane swallowed painfully. The wonder of the last several minutes had evaporated, replaced by a painful sense of vulnerability.

He stepped into the hall with a sinking feeling. Spartan closed and locked the door behind him.

Crane waited in the narrow passageway, the marines standing silently on either side. His mouth was dry, and his heart raced uncomfortably in his chest. Sounds of raised voices began to filter through the door; he listened intently but could not make out the words. **What is happening?** He wasn't sure who to feel more worried about: himself or the old man in his room.

Five dreadful minutes passed. Then the door opened and Spartan emerged. He glared at Crane. "Come with me, Doctor," he said.

"Where are we going?"

"You will find it easier to just follow orders" was the clipped response.

Crane's eyes strayed back to the rifles in the hands of the marines. Clearly, he had no recourse but to obey. He marched down the corridor behind Spartan, the marines swinging into place behind him. A few passing technicians stopped to stare at their little parade. "Where—?" Crane began again, then stopped himself. Anything he said now would just dig the hole even deeper. Far better to say nothing, nothing at all . . . until he had to.

But the silent questions remained. **How much does Spartan know? What did Asher tell him?** They'd no doubt looked guilty as hell: three conspirators, meeting in secret . . .

This was, at heart, a military operation. He'd signed an awful lot of agreements up on the oil platform: God only knew what kind of personal rights he'd waived. It occured to him, with an unpleasant chill, that even if Spartan didn't know everything he no doubt had the means, the techniques—and, most likely, the right—to find out whatever he wanted.

They stopped before an elevator. The guards took up positions on either side while Spartan pressed the down button. Within moments the doors whisked open; Spartan stepped in, waited for the guards to usher Crane inside, then pressed the button for deck 7—the lowest non-classified level on the Facility.

What was it Asher had just told him? **Spartan may soon take full command of the operation, with Korolis as his enforcer.** Crane struggled to regulate his breathing, appear calm.

The elevator drifted to a stop and the doors rolled back onto deck 7. Spartan stepped out and led the way to an unlabeled door. He opened it with his red passcard while the marines once again took up positions on either side.

The room beyond was small and bare, the only furniture a long table with two chairs set along the near side. Behind the chairs were two huge, free-standing lights, their bulbs backed by metal reflectors. They were both aimed at a spot on the far wall—a spot that was approximately head level. Seeing these lights, Crane felt his heart begin to race even faster. His worst fears were confirmed.

"Walk over to the far wall, Dr. Crane," Spartan said in an expressionless voice.

Crane walked slowly to the wall.

"Turn around, please."

Crane did as ordered.

There was a sudden, metallic snap as both lights burst into brilliance, almost physically pinning him against the wall with their candlepower. He squinted and instinctively raised his hand to his eyes.

"Stand still, Dr. Crane," came the voice of Spartan, invisible behind the wall of white light.

Crane's mind began to work frantically. **Stay calm,** he told himself. **Stay calm.** What did he have to worry about? He was a member of the medical staff. He was supposed to be here. It wasn't like he was a spy or anything . . .

But then he remembered the deadly serious security at the Barrier, the fear he'd just seen on Asher's face.

From behind the wall of light came a single click. There was a moment of stasis. And then, one after the other, the spotlights went out.

"Have a seat, Doctor," said Spartan. He was seated at the table now, and a folder Crane had not noticed before was open in front of him.

Warily, heart still hammering, Crane took the empty seat. Spartan put his hand on the folder and pushed it toward him. It contained a single sheet of paper with about four paragraphs of text beneath a Department of Defense letterhead.

"Sign at the bottom, please," Spartan said. And he placed a gold pen carefully on the table.

"I already signed everything when I was topside," Crane said.

Spartan shook his head. "You didn't sign this."

"May I read it first?"

"I wouldn't suggest it. You'll just frighten yourself needlessly."

Crane picked up the pen, reached for the paper, hesitated. A little distantly, he wondered if he was signing an admission of guilt **pro res** before he'd even confessed to harboring secret knowledge. He realized it made little difference. Taking a deep breath, he signed the sheet and pushed it back to Spartan.

The admiral closed the folder and squared it sharply on the table. Just at that moment, a knock sounded on the door.

"Come in," Spartan said.

The door opened and a naval officer stepped inside. He saluted Spartan, handed him a white envelope, saluted a second time, then turned and left the room.

Spartan held up the envelope, letting it dangle from his thumb and index finger. Then—almost teasingly—he extended his arm toward Crane.

Crane took the envelope gingerly.

"Open it," Spartan said.

After a moment's hesitation, Crane tore away one edge of the envelope and upended it into his hand. A plastic wafer—like a credit card, only thicker—fell out. One side was clear, and he could see a forest of microchips embedded within. He turned it over to find his own face staring up—as he had looked minutes before, blinded by the lights. There was a bar code beneath this photograph and the words RESTRICTED ACCESS printed in red beside them. A brass clip was fastened to one end.

"That, along with retinal and finger-matrix scans, will allow you past the Barrier," Spartan said. "Keep it safe, Doctor, and on your person at all times. There are very severe penalties for losing such a card or letting it fall into the wrong hands."

"I'm not sure I understand," Crane said.

"I'm authorizing you access to the classified section of the Facility. Over the advice of Commander Korolis, I might add."

Crane stared at the ID card as relief flooded over him. **Oh, God,** he thought. **Oh, my God. This place is making me paranoid.**

"I see," he said, still a little stupid from surprise. Then: "Thank you."

"Why?" Spartan asked. "What did you think was happening?"

And Crane could have sworn that—just for an instant—a bemused smile flitted across the admiral's features before they dissolved once again into impassivity.

22

Forty miles off the coast of Greenland, the Storm King oil platform hovered stoically between squall-dark skies and the angry sea. A passing vessel—or, more likely, a reconnaissance satellite, its orbit re-tasked by a curious foreign government—would notice nothing unusual. A few riggers moved slowly around the platform's superstructure, appearing to work the derricks or inspect equipment. But by and large, Storm King seemed as quiet as the surrounding sea was restless. It looked as if the giant platform was asleep.

But within its steel skin, Storm King was a hive of activity. The LF2-M Deeply Submersible Resupply Unit—the Tub—had just returned from its daily journey to the Facility, two miles below. And now almost three dozen people were in the Recovery Chamber, waiting, as a giant winch hoisted the unmanned supply module up through an oversized hatch in the lowest level of the oil platform. Gingerly, the ungainly vessel was plucked from the ocean, then swiveled away from the hatch and lowered into a receiving bay. Under the watchful eye of a marine, two supply officers unsealed the hatch in the Tub's nose, revealing an access bulkhead. Opening this in turn, the officers began unloading the Tub, removing everything that had been stowed inside at the Facility. A remarkable diversity of objects emerged: large black waste containers, bound for the incinerator; carefully sealed confidential packets; medical samples in biohazard boxes, heading for testing too exotic to be performed in the Facility itself. One by one, the items were passed out to the waiting crew, who in turn began to disperse throughout the oil platform. Within fifteen minutes, the Recovery Chamber was empty except for the marine, the winch operator, and the two supply officers, who closed the access bulkhead and sealed the Tub's forward hatch, readying it for the next day's journey.

One of the waiting crew, a Science Services courier, had come away from the Recovery Chamber with a half dozen sealed envelopes under his arm. The courier was a relatively recent arrival on the platform. He wore tortoiseshell glasses and limped slightly as he walked, almost as if one leg was a little shorter than the other. He gave his name as Wallace.

Returning to the science facilities set up on the rig's Production Level, Wallace moved briskly from lab to lab despite his limp, delivering the first five envelopes to their intended recipients. But he did not immediately deliver the last. Instead, he retreated to his tiny office, which was tucked away in a far corner.

Wallace carefully closed and locked the door behind him. Then he opened the envelope and let the contents—a single CD—drop into his lap. Turning to his computer, he eased the disc into the drive. A quick examination of the contents revealed a single file, labeled "108952.jpg"—an image, probably a photograph. He clicked on the file icon and the computer obediently displayed it on the screen: sure enough, a ghostly black-and-white image that was clearly an X-ray.

But Wallace was not interested in the image—only in something it contained.

Although his credentials had been excellent and the checks on his background impeccable, Wallace was nevertheless a new arrival on the Deep Storm project, and thus held a low security rating. This meant, among other things, that his computer was only a dumb terminal, slaved to the rig's mainframe, without a hard disk of its own and crippled from running executable CD files. As a result it could run only approved software; no rogue programs could be installed on the machine.

At least, that was the theory.

Wallace pulled the keyboard to him, opened the primitive text editor that came pre-installed with the operating system, and typed in a short program:

```
void main (void)
    {
    char keyfile = fopen ('108952.jpg');
    char extract;
    while (infile)
            {
            extract = (asc ( (least_sig_bit
            (keyfile) )/2)^6);
            stdoutput (extract);
            }
    }
void least_sig_bit (int sent_bit)
    {
    int bit_zero;
```

```
bit_zero = << (sent_bit, 6);
return (bit_zero);
bit_zero = >> (sent_bit, 6);
}
```

Wallace examined the program, running through its steps in his head and making sure the logic was sound. He gave a grunt of satisfaction, then glanced once again at the X-ray image.

Each screen pixel of the image occupied a single byte in the jpeg file on the disc. His short but powerful program would strip out the two least significant bits from each byte, convert them from numbers to their ASCII equivalent, then display the resulting letters on the screen.

Quickly, he compiled and ran the program. A new window opened on his monitor, but it did not contain the X-ray image this time. Instead, a text message appeared.

REQUEST DELAY ON MAKING 2ND BREACH
ATTEMPT PENDING NEW DEVELOPMENTS
IN CLASSIFIED SECTION

He read, then reread the message, lips pursed.

With computers, it was possible to hide secret messages almost anywhere: in the background hiss of recorded music or the grainy texture of a digital photograph. Wallace was using the ancient spy technique of steganography—**hiding** secret information where it wouldn't be noticed instead of **encrypting** it—and bringing it into the digital age.

He cleared the screen, erased the program, and placed the disc back in the envelope. The entire process had taken less than five minutes.

Back in the science labs sixty seconds later, a radiologist looked up as an envelope was quietly slipped onto his desk.

"Oh, yes, I've been waiting for this X-ray," the radiologist said. "Thank you, Wallace."

Wallace simply smiled in reply.

23

Passing through the Barrier into the restricted section of the Facility was much less traumatic the second time: with the newly minted ID card clipped to his breast pocket and a near-silent Admiral Spartan at his side, the process took just a few minutes. The MPs guarding the airlock stepped back smartly; the two made the brief descent to deck 6; the hatch sprang open onto a narrow corridor. Spartan stepped out and Crane followed.

The last time he had been down here, he'd

been running to a floridly psychotic Randall Waite, and he'd had little time to notice anything. This time, Crane looked curiously around. Yet as they passed through the corridors the only outward indication they were inside the classified area was the abundance of warning signs on the pearlescent walls, the marines that seemed to be posted everywhere—and the heavy rubber seals around all the door frames.

Spartan led the way to a waiting elevator, ushered Crane inside. Unlike the elevators in the upper floors, the control panel here had buttons for only decks 1 through 6. Spartan pressed the button labeled **2** and they began to descend.

"You still haven't told me," Crane said, breaking the silence.

"There are a lot of things I haven't told you," Spartan said without looking at him. "Which one are you referring to, exactly?"

"Why you changed your mind."

Spartan considered this. Then he turned and gazed impassively at Crane. "You know I've read your dossier, right?"

"Asher said as much."

"The captain of the USS **Spectre** was most impressed with your conduct. He said you single-handedly saved the sub."

"Captain Naseby likes to exaggerate."

"I have to say, Dr. Crane, I'm a little unclear on what you did."

"The mission was classified. I can't speak about it, sir."

Spartan gave a mirthless chuckle. "I know all about the mission. It was to provide firsthand intel on the construction of a uranium enrichment plant on the shores of the Yellow Sea. And, if necessary, destroy it with a dirty torpedo in such a way as to make it look like an accidental explosion."

Crane looked at Spartan in surprise. Then he realized the government probably had very few secrets from the military leader of something as classified as the Facility.

"I didn't mean the mission," Spartan continued. "I meant, I'm unclear as to your role in saving the vessel."

Crane was silent a moment, remembering. "Crewmen began to die," he began, "in a particularly horrible way. Their sinuses were eaten away, and their brains turned to a kind of furry jelly. It happened in a matter of hours. Two dozen died on the first day alone. We were operating under a communications blackout, couldn't leave our patrol. There was panic on board, talk of sabotage, of poison gas. When a dozen more died overnight, chaos resulted. There was a breakdown in the chain of command, incipient mutiny. Lynch mobs began roaming the sub, looking for the traitor."

"And your role?"

"I realized that what everyone assumed to be the effect of some kind of poisonous gas might instead be mucormycosis."

"I'm sorry?"

"A rare but deadly fungal disease. I was able to cobble together the necessary materials to test tissue from the dead crew members, and I found their bodies were riddled with **Rhizopus oryzae,** the fungus responsible."

"And that's what was killing the crew of the **Spectre**."

"Yes. A particularly noxious variant of the fungus had incubated in the bilges of the sub."

"How did you stop its spread?"

"I medicated the rest of the crew. Brought them into a state of controlled alkalosis that the spores could not tolerate."

"And saved the ship."

Crane smiled. "Like I said, Admiral. Captain Naseby likes to exaggerate."

"It doesn't appear to be exaggeration. You kept your head, found the cause, then worked with the materials at hand to effect a solution."

The elevator doors whispered open and they

stepped out. "What does that have to do with our current problem?" Crane asked.

"Let's not be disingenuous, Dr. Crane. The parallels are numerous, and you can see them as well as I." Spartan walked briskly to an intersection, turned down another corridor. "I've been monitoring your progress, Doctor. And I've decided it would be prudent to afford you another level of trust."

"That's the reason you've given me classified access," Crane said. "It'll help me crack this more quickly."

"The **reason,** as you say, lies beyond that door." And Spartan pointed to a hatchway at the end of the corridor, flanked by the omnipresent marines.

At a gesture from the admiral, one of the marines cranked open the hatchway and pulled it wide. Crane began to move forward, then stopped again. Beyond the hatch lay a well of blackness.

Spartan stepped through the hatch, then glanced back. "Coming?"

Crane ducked through the dark hatchway. He looked around in astonishment.

They were in a long, narrow observation chamber, overlooking a vast equipment hangar that stretched beneath them. Technicians sat in two long lines on either side of Crane, monitoring banks of terminals. There was a beeping of electronics, the clatter of keys, the murmur of hushed voices. Beyond the glass wall of the observation chamber, down on the hangar deck, other technicians in white coats scurried around, pushing equipment or making notations on palmtop computers. But Crane ignored all this. His eyes were focused on the thing suspended by incredibly heavy cable, just over the floor of the hangar.

It was a sphere of metal—titanium, perhaps, or something even more precious—roughly ten feet in diameter. It was polished to a mirror finish, so bright it shone like a second sun within the confines of the bay, and Crane could only look at it through squinted eyes. It appeared to be absolutely round. The only blemish on its surface was a tiny forest of sensors, lights, and robotic equipment that hung from its underside like moss on a ship's hull. Two other identical metal spheres sat in cushioned and reinforced berths against a far wall.

"What is that?" he asked in a whisper.

"That, Dr. Crane, is the Marble. It's what everything else here—**everything** else—works in support of."

"Is that what is doing the digging?"

"No. A double-shielded tunnel-boring machine, depth modified, does that. The Marble's current job is to follow the boring machine, shoring up the fresh sections of shaft with steel bands. Later—when the shaft is complete—the Marble's job will shift to exploration and, ah, recovery."

"Is it autonomous?"

"No. There is no way all its functions can be automated. It has revolving crews of three."

"Crews? I don't see any hatch."

Admiral Spartan gave a dry bark that might have been a laugh. "At the depths we are working, Doctor, there can be no 'hatch.' Because of the pressure, the Marble must be perfectly round—it can't depart from the spherical in any way."

"So how do you get the crew in and out?"

"Once the crew is inside, the skin of the Marble is welded shut, then the weld is polished to a mirror finish."

Crane whistled.

"Yes. That's why each shift is twenty-four hours: entry and exit is so time-consuming. Luckily, as you can see, we have two backups, so while one is at work another can be prepped and resupplied. That way, work can continue around the clock."

They lapsed into silence. Crane found himself unable to take his eyes from the brilliantly shining sphere. It was one of the most beautiful things he had ever seen. Even so, it was hard to imagine three people crammed into such a tight space. He noticed a nearby viewscreen, showing a grainy image of the technicians hovering around the Marble: apparently, it was a video feed from inside the Marble itself.

"I gather you're not convinced it's Atlantis we're after," Spartan said drily. "But what we're after is not your concern. The medical situation, on the other hand, is very much your concern. You're not just answering to Asher anymore—you're answering to me. It goes without saying that you are to discuss none of what you see here with anyone in the unclassified section. Your movements here will be monitored and you will need escorts to the more sensitive locations—at least at first. We'll of course provide the tools or instruments you require. You've done classified work before, so you know the privilege—and responsibility—it entails. Abuse that privilege, and the next set of lights you're hauled before won't be for taking your photograph."

At this, Crane at last pulled his eyes from the Marble and glanced at Spartan. The admiral wasn't smiling.

"What has happened, exactly?" Crane asked.

Spartan swept his hand across the wall of glass, down toward the hanger deck below. "Until now, the Drilling Complex has been unaffected by whatever is making our people sick. But over the last twelve hours, three people in the complex have fallen ill."

"What are the symptoms?"

"You can ask them yourself. There's an emergency medical station on deck four. We've activated it, and you can use that as a temporary infirmary. I'll have the workers report to you there."

"Why wasn't I told about these new cases?" Crane asked.

"You **are** being told about them. The workers are high security and, as such, aren't permitted access to the unclassified levels."

"I could use Dr. Bishop's help."

"She has limited access beyond the portal, on an emergency-only basis and accompanied by marines. We'll deal with that situation if and when it becomes of critical importance. Now, if I may continue. In addition to the cases I mentioned, I have noticed others in the Complex who are becoming . . . psychologically affected."

"Does Corbett know?"

"No, and he's not going to. Corbett is, shall we say, porous. Any expertise he can offer should be filtered through you." Spartan glanced at his watch. "I'll have a detail take you back to your quarters. Get some sleep. I want you back at nine hundred hours tomorrow, and I want you fresh."

Crane nodded slowly. "So that's it. You've given me access because the rot's setting in here, too."

Spartan's eyes narrowed. "You have a new job

now, Doctor. It's not enough just to learn what's making people sick. You have to **keep them** healthy." And he gestured again toward the Marble and the technicians that surrounded it. "Because everything, and everyone, in this Facility is dispensable—**except** the drilling. That must continue at all costs. This work is of vital importance, and I will not allow anything or anyone to slow us down. I'll drive the Marble myself if I have to. Do I make myself clear?"

For a moment, the two men stared at each other. Then Crane gave a small nod.

"Crystal clear, sir," he said.

24

Crane lay back wearily in his bed. It was almost three in the morning, and the Facility was quiet. He could just make out the slippery, seductive sounds of a jazz clarinet filtering through the shared bathroom: Roger Corbett was a fan of Benny Goodman and Artie Shaw.

The day had been filled with more surprise and wonder than any other he could remember. And yet he was so weary that the moment he closed his eyes he felt sleep steal toward him. But he could not sleep, not quite yet. There was one thing he had to do first.

He reached toward the desk and retrieved a manila folder. Opening it, he pulled out a short document: the eyewitness account Asher had mentioned of the actual sea-burial event. Rubbing his eyes blearily, he glanced at the top page. It was a large photograph of a sheet of illuminated manuscript: tiny blackletter script offset by colorful—if disquieting—border illustrations and a lavish initial capital. The vellum was badly worn along two horizontal lines where the sheet had apparently been folded, and its edges were darkened with handling and long years. The text was in Latin, but thankfully Asher's researcher had supplied an English translation, which was appended to the photograph. Crane turned to the translation and began to read.

It was in the year of our lord 1397 that I, Jón Albarn, fisherman of Staafhörn, was made witness.

I had broken my arm most grievously at that time and was unable to sail my boat or ply my nets. Being on a day gone out to walk the cliffs, I at once noticed the heavens grow full bright, albeit the sky was cloud obscured. There came to my ears the sound of strange singing, as if of a multitude of voices, which made the very empyrean tremble.

I tarried not, but ran back forthwith to acquaint all the people of this revelation. But many folk of the village had heard with their own ears and seen with their own eyes and were making their way to the shingle beach. It being a Sunday, all the men of the village were at home with their families. And it was in but short order that the village was empty and all had gathered by the waters.

The heavens grew yet brighter still. There was a heaviness in the air that was passing strange, and many amongst us remarked at how the hair on our flesh grew light and stood on end.

All at once there came many bolts of lightning and thunderclaps. Then the clouds over the ocean came asunder, casting off rainbows and boiling mists as they did fall back. A hole appeared in the heavens. And through that hole shewed a giant Eye, wreathed in white flame. Pillars of light shone down from it, straight as any column, and the seas upon which the holy light fell grew most strangely calm.

All the people of the village were passing glad, for the Eye was of a great and wondrous beauty, bright beyond measure and girdled with dancing rainbows. And they all did talk of how the Almighty God had come to Staafhörn to favor us with His grace and benediction.

The menfolk of the town began to speak amongst themselves of how we should sail out to the wondrous light, to praise the Lord and receive His blessing. One or two amongst us said, nay, the distance is too great across the sea. But the Eye was of such surpassing beauty, and the encircling fire of such purity and whiteness, that soon all had taken to the boats, eager to touch the divine light with their own hands and contrive that it should fall upon them. Only I was left behind: the boats were filled with all the town, men, women, and children, and with my arm sadly broken I could not sail myself. And so I made my way up to the cliffs in order to better behold this miracle.

In minutes the boats were laid out across the sea, three dozen or more, and all within singing hymns of praise and thanksgiving. And all the time from the cliff head I too gave thanks, that of all the towns in the Kingdom of Denmark the Lord had graced Staafhörn with His favor. It seemed as if the line of sailboats was being carried forthwith across the water at marvellous speed, despite a sore lack of wind, and whereas I prayed I also felt a melancholy in my heart, at being the only soul left behind.

Some short time passed, and the boats were less than a league away from land, when the great Eye began to slowly descend from the heavens. The clouds that wreathed it were still all a-boil, and great curtains of mist hung around it, shot through with countless rainbows. But now the column of white light that fell from the Eye to the surface of the sea was wont to change. I beheld that it began to twist, and bend, as if a living thing. And the face of the sea upon which it fell began to change also. Calm no longer, it started to boil, as if consumed by a great furnace. The sounds of ethereal singing grew louder, and yet the sounds no longer bespoke of heavenly voices. They rose higher and higher until they became like unto the shriek of a hare in a trap, so overmastering I fell to my knees and stopped my ears.

From the head of the cliff I could see the boats hesitate in their forward course. One or two stopped, while others tried to turn back. But it was as if the sea now lay in a great anger. Waterspouts began to appear around the column of light, rippling out with unseemly haste, like unto when a boulder is dropped into a small pond. And as the vast Eye descended, the column of light beneath turned into a pillar of white fire, all consuming and terrible to behold.

Now the boats were in full retreat. But then came a great earthquake, and the clouds parted with a monstrous roar, and it seemed that in an instant all the stars of heaven fell into the sea. Fantastical flames rose up where each fell, and there came a great multitude of steam, billowing outward from the center and obscuring all the boats from view.

I had fallen prostrate on the ground with the violence of the earthquake, but though I was sore afraid I could not take my eyes from the scene. The devouring mist was spreading even toward the shore, and through it I could see gouts of red and purple fire, shooting into the air like unto heaven, then falling back into the sea with a thousand tongues of flame. And through it all the great Eye descended, surrounded by flames so white and bright they pierced all, even the great mist. It seemed to me it dropped with a great deliberation. And when it did hit the surface of the sea, the firmament was riven by a shudder of such force and magnitude that it far surpassed any power of description. And these roars and quakes did continue for nigh unto an hour, shaking the earth with such violence I was certain the fabric of the land would tear itself apart. Only with the long passing of time did the groaning slowly pass away and the mists begin to clear.

O strange and terrible! It seemed the devil had falsely deceived the people of Staafhörn, luring them to a most lamentable end under angelic guise. Because when at last the mists did clear, the sea had turned a deep red and was covered as far as the eye could see with dead fish and other denizens of the deep—but of the fishing boats, or my fellow villagers, there was not the slightest sign. Yet in my lamentation and grief I was also sore perplexed, for would not Lucifer have stayed to gloat over his victory? But of the great Eye of white fire there was no sign. It was as if the awful fate of those in the three dozen boats was but a matter of indifference to the foul fiend.

For many days thereafter I wandered Denmark, telling my story to all that would listen and heed my warning. But forthwith, I was branded a heretic and quit the kingdom in fear of my life. I stop here at Grimwold Castle only briefly, for succor and sustenance; where I go from here I know not, but go I must.

Jón Albarn

Committed to paper by Martin of Brescia, who hereby gives solemn oath that this account

has been faithfully recorded. Candlemas, anno
Domini 1398.

When Crane at last put the pages aside, lay
back, and turned off the light, the great weariness
he felt had not abated. And yet he lay in bed,
awake, his head filled with a single image: a vast
eye, unblinking and wreathed in a pure white
flame.

25

The door to John Marris's lab was open, but Asher knocked anyway.

"Come in," the cryptologist said.

Marris had the neatest lab in the Facility. Not a speck of dust was visible. Other than a half dozen manuals stacked carefully in one corner, his desk was empty except for keyboard and flat-screen terminal. There were no photographs, posters, or personal mementos of any kind. But, Asher reflected, that was typical of Marris: shy, withdrawn, almost secretive about his personal life and opinions alike. Wholly devoted to his work. Perfect qualities for a cryptologist.

What a shame, then, that his current project—such a short and apparently simple code—was proving so elusive.

Asher closed the door behind him, sat down in the sole visitor's chair. "I got your message," he said. "Any luck on the brute-force attacks?"

Marris shook his head.

"The random-byte filters?"

"Nothing intelligible."

"I see." Asher slumped in the chair. When he'd gotten the e-mail from Marris asking him to stop by at his earliest convenience, he'd felt a surge of hope that the man had deciphered the code. Coming from the phlegmatic Marris, "earliest convenience" was practically a shouted plea for immediate consultation. "What is it, then?"

Marris glanced at him, then looked away again. "I was wondering if, perhaps, we were approaching this decryption from the wrong angle."

Asher frowned. "Explain."

"Very well. Last night I was reading a book on the life of Alan Turing."

This was no surprise to Asher. A consummate academic, Marris was working toward a second doctorate, this time in the history of computing—and Alan Turing was a seminal figure in early computer theory. "Go on."

"Well . . . do you know what a Turing machine is?"

"You'd better refresh my memory."

"In the 1930s, Alan Turing posited a theoretical computer known as a Turing machine. It was composed of a 'tape,' a paper ribbon of arbitrarily extendable length. This tape was covered with symbols from some finite alphabet. A 'head' would run over the tape, reading the symbols and interpreting them, based on a lookup table. The state of the head would change, depending on the symbols it read. The tape itself could store either data or 'transitions,' by which he meant small programs. In today's computers, the tape would be the memory and the head the microprocessor. Turing declared this theoretical computer could solve any calculation."

"Go on," Asher said.

"I started thinking about this code we're trying to decrypt." And Marris waved his hand at the computer screen, where the signal emitted by the sentinel's pulses of light sat, almost taunting in its brevity and opacity:

```
00000111110010101101010110011101110001010110001100010100011010011000010000000000
```

"I wondered: what if this was a Turing tape?" Marris continued. "What would these zeros and ones do if we ran them through a Turing machine?"

Slowly, Asher sat forward. "You're suggesting those eighty bits . . . are a **computer program?**"

"I know it sounds crazy, sir—"

No crazier than the very fact of our being down here, Asher thought. "Please continue."

"Very well. First, I had to break the string of zeros and ones down into individual commands. I made the assumption that the initial values, five zeros and five ones, were placeholders to signify the length of each instruction—each digital 'word' thus being five bits in length. That left me with fourteen five-bit instructions." Marris tapped a key, and the long string of numbers vanished, to be replaced by a series of ordered rows:

00101
01101
01011
00111
01110
00101
01100
01100
01010
00110
10011
00001

00000

00000

Asher stared at the screen. "Awfully short for a computer program."

"Yes. Clearly, it would have to be a very simple computer program. And in machine language—the most basic, and universal, of digital languages."

Asher nodded. "And then?"

"When I got to my office this morning, I wrote a short routine that would compare these values against a master list of standard machine-language instructions. The routine assigned all possible instructions to the values, one after another, and then checked to see if any workable computer program emerged."

"What makes you think these—whoever is sending us the message uses the same kind of machine language instructions that we do?"

"At a binary level, sir, there are certain irreducible digital instructions that would be common to any conceivable computing device: increment, decrement, jump, skip if zero, Boolean logic. So I let the routine run and went on with my other work."

Asher nodded.

"About twenty minutes ago, the routine completed its run."

"Did those fourteen lines of binary translate to any viable computer programs?"

"Yes. One."

Asher felt his interest suddenly spike. "Really?"

"A program for a simple mathematical expression. Here it is." Marris punched another key, and a series of instructions appeared on his monitor.

Asher bent eagerly toward it.

INST.	MNEMONIC	COMMENTS
00101	ADD	/ Set up a tally in the accumulator
01101	01101	/ from the number in position 13 (decimal).
01011	CNM	/ Reverse the number sign of the tally.
00111	PLC	/ Place the resulting number
01110	01110	/ in position 14.
00101	ADD	/ Subtract from
01100	01100	/ the number in position 12.
01100	ISZ	/ Increment tally and skip if zero.
01010	JMP	/ Return program control to
00110	00110	/ step 6.
10011	END	/ End program.
00001		/ Position 12
00000		/ Position 13
00000		/ Position 14

"What does the program do?" Asher asked.

"You'll notice that it's written as a series of repeated subtractions, coded in a loop. That's the way you do division in machine language: by repeated subtraction. Well, it's one way—you could also do an arithmetic shift right—but that would require a more specialized computing system."

"So it's a **division** statement?"

Marris nodded.

Asher felt surprise and mystification mingle with the sudden, intense excitement. "Don't hesitate, man. What's the number they're dividing?"

"One."

"One. And it's being divided by what?"

Marris licked his lips. "Well, you see, that's the problem, sir . . ."

26

The door was one of a half dozen along the corridor in the northeast quadrant of deck 3. It bore the simple legend RADIOLOGY—PING.

Commander Korolis nodded for one of the accompanying marines to open the door, then stepped inside. Glancing over the commander's shoulder, Crane made out a small but well-equipped lab. If anything, it was too well equipped: most of the available space was crammed with bulky instrumentation. Just inside the door, an Asian woman in a white coat was sitting before a computer, typing rapidly. She looked up at Korolis's entrance, then stood, smiled, and bowed.

Korolis did not respond to her. Instead, he swiveled around, one eye staring disapprovingly at Crane, the other looking at some point over his left shoulder.

"This should serve your purposes," he said. He glanced around the lab once more—as if mentally checking off items Crane might steal—then stepped back into the hallway. "Post guard outside," he said to the two marines, then turned his back and walked away.

Crane watched the commander's retreating form for a moment. Then he nodded to the marines and entered the lab, shutting the door behind him. There was a low squeal of rubber as the grommeted seal around the door snugged tightly into place. He then approached the female scientist, who was still standing at her lab table, smiling.

"Peter Crane," he said, shaking hands. "Sorry to barge in like this, but I don't have a work space down here and they said this lab had a light table."

"Hui Ping," the woman replied, her smile displaying brilliant white teeth. "I've heard of you, Dr. Crane. You are looking into all the sickness, right?"

"Right. I just need to examine a few X-rays."

"It's no problem; feel free to use anything." Hui was small and thin, with sparkling black eyes. She spoke flawless English with a strong Chinese accent. Crane guessed she was about thirty years old. "Light table's over there."

Crane glanced in the indicated direction. "Thanks."

"Let me know if you need anything."

Crane walked over to the light table, snapped it on, and then drew out the X-rays he'd just ordered on several of the workers in the Drilling Complex. It was as he suspected: no problems. The radiographs were depressingly unremarkable. Everything looked clear.

Over the last twenty-four hours, he had performed informal examinations on several people from the Drilling Complex. And he'd found their complaints were like those in the non-classified section of the Facility: amorphous and maddeningly diverse. One complained of severe nausea. Another, blurred sight and visual field defects. Some complaints appeared psychological—ataxia, memory lapses. None of the cases seemed in any way severe, and—as usual—there was no interrelation. Only one was genuinely interesting: a female worker who had exhibited remarkable disinhibition of character. Normally a timid, quiet teetotaler, she had over the last few days become profane, aggressive, and sexually promiscuous. The day before, she'd been confined to quarters after being found drunk while on shift. Crane had interviewed the woman and spoken to her coworkers, and would send a comprehensive report to Roger Corbett for evaluation—suitably filtered, of course.

Crane pulled the radiographs from the light table with a sigh. He had ordered MRIs and taken blood, and he would send them to the lab for analysis. But he feared the results would be the same as before: inconclusive. A part of him had hoped for a breakthrough here. Although the last thing he wanted to see was more illness, if there had been a disease cluster in the Drilling Complex—where the real work was being done—that would have provided a clue. But they seemed no worse off than their fellows upstairs.

No: it was clear to him that Spartan's sudden concern was not due to severity but selection. Before, only non-essential people had been affected, and the admiral had shown little interest. But now that people directly responsible for the digging were falling ill, Spartan was sitting up and taking notice.

He snapped off the light table. Even if these new complaints proved inconclusive, they had given him a major break: he now had access to the classified levels of the Facility. This effectively doubled the number of people he could monitor, not to mention more opportunities for seeking out possible environmental factors.

Hui Ping looked over. She was a study in black and white: black hair, eyes, and glasses; white lab coat and pale, almost translucent skin. "You don't look happy," she said.

Crane shrugged. "Things aren't fitting into place as quickly as I'd hoped."

Ping nodded as she pulled on a pair of latex gloves. "That goes for me, too." Her glossy hair, cut short, shook as she moved her head.

"What are you working on?"

"That." And Ping pointed toward the far side of a hulking piece of equipment.

Crane walked over, peered around its edge. To his surprise he saw another of the thin sentinels—twin to the one Asher had shown him—hovering in midair, shimmering with myriad shifting colors. The same whisper-thin beam of pure white light led from the object's upper edge up to the ceiling of the room.

"Jesus," Crane said, awed. "You've got one."

Ping laughed lightly. "They're not exactly rare. More than twenty have been retrieved so far."

Crane looked at her in surprise. "Twenty?"

"Yes, and the deeper we go, the more we find."

"If you've found so many just in the path of the

drill shaft, the crust around here must be saturated with them."

"Oh, they're not in the path of the drill shaft."

Crane frowned. "What do you mean?"

"Well, the first one was. But since then, the rest have come to meet us."

"**Meet** you?"

Ping laughed again. "I don't know how else to put it. They come to the Marble. Almost as if they're drawn to it."

"You mean these things drill through solid rock?"

Ping shrugged. "We don't know how they come, exactly. But they do."

Crane looked at the object more closely. It looked impossibly strange, floating there in the middle of the lab, coruscating with a deep inner glow: a glimmering rainbow of infinite hues. Staring at it, Crane felt a sudden, deep conviction that Asher's fears were unfounded. Perhaps the unsettling eyewitness report he'd read the night before was false or referred to something else entirely. Surely, whatever was making people sick here had its roots elsewhere. This object **had** to be benevolent. Only a morally advanced culture, beyond war or aggression or evil, could have fashioned something of such ineffable beauty.

"What are you studying?" he murmured.

"That tiny beam of light it emits. I've been running it through refractometers, spectral radiometers. Analyzing its components. But it's difficult."

"You mean, because you have to move your equipment around to suit it—not the other way around?"

Ping laughed again. "That, too. But no, I mean what's happening to you is happening to me as well. The pieces just aren't fitting together."

Crane folded one arm over the other and leaned against the bulky equipment. "Tell me about it," he said.

"I'd be happy to. Only the scientists are taking much interest in these sentinels. The rest are just eager to get to the mother lode. Sometimes I think I've been given this non-essential assignment just because Korolis wants me out of the way. I was brought down here to program the scientific computers, not run them."

For a moment, she was unable to hide the bitterness in her voice. **So Korolis has taken her off the important work and stuck her in this backwater of a lab,** Crane thought. **Wasting her talent on theories and secondary measurements.** "Why would he do that?" he asked. "Doesn't he trust you?"

"Korolis doesn't trust anybody, especially someone with a degree from the Beijing University of Technology." She stood up, came over, and pointed at the hovering object. "Anyway. That beam of light it's emitting? It appears to be steady, right? But when you process it, you can see it's actually pulsing on and off, incredibly quickly: over a million times a second."

"Yes. Asher mentioned that to me."

"That's not all. It looks like ordinary light, right?"

"Except for how white it is, yes."

"But it's far from ordinary. In fact, it's paradoxical. Just about every test I've run has come back with anomalous results."

"What? Light's just light, isn't it?"

"That's what I used to think. But my tests are proving otherwise. Here, I'll give you an example. That piece of equipment you're leaning against? It's a spectrograph."

"I've never seen one so big."

Ping smiled again. "Okay, it's a very special photoelectric spectrograph. But it does what all its brethren do, just a lot faster and with greater detail. You know how spectrographs work?"

"They break light up into its component wavelengths."

"Right. When matter is ionized—by heat, say— it throws off light. Different kinds of matter throw off different kinds of light. They're called 'line emissions,' and the spectrograph can pick them out and sort them. They're very important to astronomers. By studying the line emissions of a star, they can determine what that star is made of."

"Go on."

"So I used this spectrograph to analyze the beam of light that thing's throwing out. And **this** is the result." Ping reached around for a sheet of paper and handed it to Crane.

Crane scanned the readout. He didn't see anything particularly unusual. It showed an erratic line, full of peaks and valleys, wriggling from left to right across the page—not all that different, he thought, from an EKG.

"I don't know much about photoelectric spectroscopy," he said, "but I don't see anything strange about this."

"Not strange for a distant star, maybe. But for this little object? Impossibly strange. These"—she pointed at several sharp spikes on the graph—"are absorption lines."

"So?"

"You only get absorption spectrums when there is something **in front of** the star you're looking at. Like a cloud of gas, or something, that blocks some of the light, absorbs specific wavelengths. You would **never** see such results from a beam of light in the same room with you."

Crane looked at the plot spectrum again, frowning. "So you're saying the kind of light this thing is emitting could only be seen from a far-away star."

"That's right. The spectrum of light this sentinel is giving off is, fundamentally, **impossible**."

Crane fell silent. He handed the readout back to Ping.

"And that's just one of a dozen paradoxes I've discovered about this little fellow. Every test I try yields incomprehensible results. It's fascinating—but frustrating, too. That's why I bothered using a spectrograph in the first place—I figured something normally used by astronomers would be safe, at least." She shook her head. "And then, there are its physical components. Why is it emitting a beam of light in the first place? And did you notice how the beam always shines in the same direction—up—whatever way the object is rotated?"

"No, I didn't." Crane reached for the floating object and, half distractedly, turned it over with his fingers. Although it swiveled obligingly under the gentle pressure, the beam of light it emitted stayed in place, rock-solid, pointed constantly at the ceiling, its point of origin moving smoothly over its surface as it rotated. The object felt cold to his touch and strangely slippery.

"Curious," he said. "The light shines from the same relative position no matter how it's oriented in space. As if the entire surface is capable of illumination." He pulled the marker closer. No doubt it was his imagination, but it seemed to be growing a little warmer in his hand. He glanced over at Hui Ping. "I wonder if—"

Then he fell silent abruptly. She had stepped back from him, and a look of shock and dread had suddenly come over her face.

"What is it?" Crane asked.

Dr. Ping took another step back, moving behind a large piece of equipment. **"Gloves . . ."** she said in a strangled voice.

Suddenly, Crane became aware of an almost painful heat in his fingertips. He quickly jerked his hand away. Released, the sentinel glided smoothly back to its former position in the precise center of the room.

He stared at it, rooted in place by sudden fear. Ping had spoken only one word, but her meaning seared its way through Crane's consciousness: **Nobody has ever handled it without gloves . . .**

As the burning sensation in his fingers sharply increased, he felt his heart accelerate and his mouth go dry. He had just committed a cardinal sin, made the most glaring error any rookie researcher could. And now . . .

But further thought was cut short by the sudden call of a loud Klaxon. Metal screeched against metal: all around the lab, air vents slammed closed. The overhead illumination snapped off, replaced by red security lighting.

Ping had pushed an Emergency Alert button on the wall and sealed them both inside.

27

Crane stood, frozen. The sound of the Klaxon seemed to make the walls tremble, and the emergency lights daubed the lab the color of blood.

What had happened? He'd touched the alien device—and his touch had triggered some kind of reaction. **Oh, God,** he thought, fear spiking wildly. **Have I been irradiated? Some kind of alpha radiation, maybe, or low neutron radiation? How big a dose? And how will I even . . .**

He shook this speculation away, trying to fight

back the fear, trying to think logically. **What's the treatment for partial-body exposure?**

He backed away from the hovering object. "Bath!" he shouted. "I need a saline bath, **quick**!"

Glancing over at Hui, he noticed she was leaning over the equipment and speaking to him—yet he could hear nothing over the shriek of the Klaxon.

"What?" he said.

More shouting, gesticulating.

"What?" he called again.

Hui turned, pressed a button on the wall. Abruptly, the Klaxon fell silent. A moment later, normal light was restored.

"I said, it's okay!" she cried. "It's only infrared!"

Crane stared at her. "Infrared?"

"Yes. I've just now gotten the readings on this console. When you touched it, the marker began emitting infrared light." Ping watched her instrumentation a moment longer. Then she stepped around the equipment and, holding up a portable Geiger counter, ran it up and down Crane's front, letting it come to rest on his fingers. "Just trace background readings—the kind you'd find throughout the Facility."

At that moment, Crane became aware of loud voices and pounding on the door. Hui turned, trotted quickly over to a communications console, grabbed a handset. "Dr. Ping here," she spoke into it. "Erroneous alert. I repeat, alert sounded in error."

An incorporeal voice responded, toneless and mechanical. "Enter validation code."

Hui turned to a keypad, punched in a series of numbers.

"Validation code verified," the voice said. "Standing down."

With another clanging of metal, the coverings drew back from the ventilation ducts and fresh air drifted into the lab once more. Hui unlocked the door and opened it; the two marines, who had been hammering on it, almost tumbled inside.

"False alarm," Hui said, smiling deferentially and nodding. "I'm very sorry for the inconvenience."

The marines looked around suspiciously for a moment, rifles at the ready. Hui continued to smile and nod, and after a moment—with a last look at Crane—the two ducked back outside and resumed their positions flanking the entrance. Hui closed the door once again, then turned toward Crane. Her smile immediately turned sheepish.

"Sorry," she said.

"**You're** sorry? I just made a mistake that would put a schoolboy to shame."

"No. I thought you knew the guidelines. I overreacted, I . . . Well, I guess we're all a little tense down here. Every test we've done shows these things to be inert, benign. Still . . ."

Her voice trailed off and they stood a moment in silence. Crane exhaled slowly, feeling his heart decelerate. His fingertips still tingled.

Hui seemed to be pondering something. "Actually," she said slowly, "I think you might have just done me a favor, Dr. Crane."

"How's that?" Crane asked, absently rubbing his fingertips.

"You've given me something else to analyze. Because now, the marker is emitting two kinds of electromagnetic radiation."

Crane looked at her. "You mean—"

"Yes." Hui pointed at her instrumentation. "It's **still** generating infrared as well as visible light."

Once again, Crane approached the object, a little warily this time. It floated there before him, shimmering, its edges wavering ever so slightly, like the delicate, inconstant lines of a mirage. "Why would it be doing that?" he murmured.

"That's the question, isn't it, Dr. Crane?"

Crane peered at it. "It couldn't have anything to do with its method of propulsion—could it?"

"That seems highly unlikely."

"Self-defense mechanism?"

"You mean, to make you let go of it? Equally unlikely. Something as sophisticated as this would have more effective ways to protect itself. Besides, we **tried** to damage one—they're impervious to everything we've thrown at them. Your fingers couldn't be much of a threat."

Crane circled the marker, frowning. He still felt a little shaky from the adrenaline rush of fright. Picking up a plastic test tube, he very carefully maneuvered it up and around the floating sentinel, caught it, then sealed the tube with a red rubber stopper and paused to examine it. The tiny entity hovered at the precise center of the test tube, supremely oblivious.

"Asher thinks it's a message of some sort," he said. "The on-off pulses of light are a digital code."

Hui nodded. "A logical conclusion."

"I wonder how he's doing," Crane said, more to himself than her. He felt guilty for not connecting with the chief scientist. The last time he'd spoken to Asher had been in his stateroom, when Spartan and his marines had burst in. He'd been so busy since then that he'd simply had no time to contact the man or seek him out.

"I'll send him an e-mail," Ping said. She sat at her desk and began to type. She paused, frowned, then typed again. "That's funny," she said.

"What is?" Crane said, stepping toward her.

"I'm getting network errors." She pointed at the

screen. "Look. Maximum allowable dropped packets exceeded."

"What kind of network are you running?"

"Standard 802.11g wireless, the same kind the entire Facility uses." Hui typed some more commands. "There—same thing again."

"I've never had any problems with the network in the Medical Suite."

"First time it's ever happened to me. Always been rock solid before." Hui retyped the commands. "Okay. Got the e-mail through on the third try."

But Crane was still thinking. "What's the frequency band of an 802.11g wireless network?" he asked.

"Five point one gigahertz. Why?" Hui turned from the computer screen to face him. "You don't suppose—"

"That something's interfering with it? Good question. You have any other five point one gigahertz devices in this lab?"

"Nope. Only the wireless network is transmitting on that frequency . . ."

Hui's voice faltered. For a moment, scientist and doctor looked at each other. Then—as if with a single thought—they both turned toward the little marker hovering serenely in the test tube Crane was holding.

Hui rose from her chair, walked to a nearby lab table, and fished through an assortment of meters and handheld devices until she located an analyzer. She stepped up to the floating object, held the analyzer before it, peered at its tiny screen.

"My God," she said. "It's transmitting on five point one gigahertz, as well."

"It's communicating on **three** frequencies," Crane said.

"Three that we know of. But all of a sudden I'm willing to bet there are more. Maybe lots more."

"And you're sure this is a new phenomenon?"

"Positive. There was only the single visible band of light—nothing else."

Crane stared at the tiny hovering thing. "What do you think happened?" he murmured.

Ping gave him a curious smile. "It seems you woke it up, Dr. Crane."

Then she stepped back to her desk, sat down, and began to type feverishly.

28

"CO$_2$ scrubbers?"

"Check."

"Servo and gimbal control?"

"Check."

"Baffle integrity?"

"One hundred percent."

"Inertial guidance indicators?"

"Green."

"EM lock?"

"Maximum."

"Temperature sensor?"

"Check."

Thomas Adkinson swiveled toward his instrument panel, tuning out the inquisitional turn and counter-turn between the pilot and the engineer. His own board was green, the robot arms fixed to the underside of the Marble prepped and ready to go.

The series of echoing booms from outside the hull had ceased, replaced by a faint swishing noise: the entry plate had been welded back into place, and all traces of the weld were now being polished away. A newcomer to the Drilling Complex, walking around the outside of the Marble, would see only a perfectly smooth sphere with no indication that three men were inside.

Three extremely cramped and uncomfortable men.

Adkinson shifted on his tiny metal chair, trying to find a position in which he could be comfortable for the next twenty-four hours. Because getting into and out of the Marble was so time-consuming—ninety minutes prepping for descent, thirty minutes for extraction afterward—the crews had to take what were essentially triple shifts for maximal efficiency.

Maximal efficiency, my ass. Christ, there had to be an easier way to earn a living.

The comm-link chirped. "Marble One, this is

Dive Control," came the disembodied voice over the speaker. "Status?"

Grove, the pilot, took the mike. "This is Marble One. All systems nominal."

"Roger."

Adkinson snuck a look at Grove. As pilot, he was technically in charge of the dive, which was a joke because the guy had little to do other than watch a few gauges and make sure there were no screw-ups. The real work was done by himself and Horst, the engineer. Even so, Grove was the kind of guy who was always aware of the audio-video feed that was being transmitted not only back to the Drilling Complex, but to a secure base outside of Washington, as well. He had to act commanding for the camera . . .

The comm-link chirped again. "Marble One, water lock is open. You are cleared for descent."

"Roger that," said Grove.

For a moment, all was still. Then there was a sudden jerk as the Marble was swung away from its berth toward the water lock. This was followed by a gradual settling sensation, and then a sudden, short plummet as the clamps were released and the Marble dropped into the lock. There was a booming sound overhead as the pressure doors were sealed. Like all other sounds from the outside, it was strangely attenuated, echoing and reechoing faintly in a hundred crazy ways.

That was due to the unusual—bizarre, actually—construction of the Marble. It had a super-laminated outer hull of titanium-ceramic-epoxy carbide and an inner hull of reinforced steel. But double hulls were commonplace for submersible vessels. What made the Marble unique was the stuff **between** the two hulls. Adkinson had seen diagrams and photographs. There were struts in there: hundreds of struts, thousands of struts. Struts from one hull to the other, and struts in between the struts.

The designers of the Marble had taken their cue from nature. And this was what Adkinson found strangest of all. He'd thought they were kidding when they'd explained it. The incredibly complex bracing was modeled after a . . . **woodpecker**. Seems any normal bird, hammering away at a tree day in and day out, would have its brain turned to jelly in record time by the impacts. But the skull of a woodpecker was double layered, with—guess what?—lots of tiny struts in between.

Adkinson shook his head. A woodpecker. Jesus. Still, just like having to be completely sealed up inside this shiny metal ball, it was all because of the pressure . . .

The pressure. Adkinson always tried hard not to think about that.

"Marble One," the comm-link squawked, "this is Dive Control. You have cleared the water lock. Pressure seal activated."

"Roger that," said Grove. He replaced the radio and turned to Horst. "What's the status on the Doodlebug?"

Horst was bent over his console, which consisted of three screens, a keyboard, and two tiny rubber joysticks. "Acquiring now."

Adkinson watched idly as the engineer worked. Horst's eyes were on the screens. There were three objects visible on them, green-tinted sonar images, one for each screen: their own Marble on the first; the tunnel-boring machine on the third; and, on the middle screen, the oceangoing robot known as the Doodlebug. There was only one "real" external camera on board, a tiny wireless job with a view port barely bigger than a periscope's, and it was reserved for the pilot.

"Got a lock," Horst said.

"Roger." Grove flicked a few switches on his command console, then turned a large rotary pot ninety degrees clockwise. "Boosting gain to seventy-five percent."

There was a chirp from Grove's console, followed by a low humming that seemed to come from everywhere and nowhere. And then, a strange sensation in the pit of his stomach as the Marble bobbed sharply downward for a moment, like a balloon being given a sudden tug.

"Full acquisition," said Horst.

Grove plucked the radio from its mount. "Dive Control, this is Marble One. We have a lock on the Doodlebug. Descending now."

Horst went back to his joysticks. There was another, gentler downward tug, and then the Marble began its smooth descent down the excavated shaft to the dig face.

Adkinson shook his head again. As strange as the composition of the Marble was, its method of diving was stranger still. He was used to submarines, with their ballast tanks and trim controls. But there could be no ballast tanks on the Marble—holes in its outer skin, or even the smallest porthole, were out of the question. Instead, they had the Doodlebug, a robotic submersible that sat in the shaft beneath them and descended to the digging interface at the beginning of the shift. It was coupled to the Marble by a strong electromagnetic field: when the Doodlebug went down, it pulled the Marble down after it.

Before the dive, the barometric equilibrium of the Marble was set to that of the Facility. Then it descended to the bottom of the shaft, the magnetic link with the Doodlebug doing all the work. And then, at the end of the shift, Horst—whose job it was to control the Doodlebug—simply broke the magnetic link. The Marble rose back up again, seeking barometric equilibrium with the water around it, until it reached the safety of the Facility, where equilibrium was attained and it came to rest.

It seemed bizarre. Yet it had worked like a charm through progressively deeper dives. It even had a fail-safe mechanism: if the Doodlebug ever had a mechanical failure or malfunction, all the engineer had to do was break the electromagnetic link prematurely and the Marble would automatically rise. Adkinson hated to admit it, but the whole arrangement was pretty ingenious. And when you got right down to it, the pressure had allowed for no other solution . . .

There it was again—the pressure.

"Zero minus one thousand relative feet," Grove announced.

"EM link five by five," said Horst. "Steady rate of descent."

Adkinson licked his lips. The pressure not only forced them to come up with extravagant solutions for working at these depths, but also made the work itself slow and painful. First, the rugged, autonomous, virtually indestructible tunnel-boring machine extended the shaft downward by another dozen feet or so, allowing seawater to fill the deepening hole. Then they stabilized this freshly dug section with reinforcing steel bands, using the incredibly complex and finicky robotic arms attached to the Marble's underside. That was his job, along with sucking the excavated silt up the shaft with a vacuum tube device and out through a wide conduit to a vent in the ocean floor some hundred yards from the Facility. It all had to be done quickly and precisely, or rock and sediment would cave in and—God forbid—bury the boring machine.

"Zero minus two thousand relative," Grove intoned.

Of course, they were too well trained—and the process too carefully controlled—for that to happen. **His** training—thanks to a certain eccentric old fart—had been particularly onerous, unpleasant, and exacting.

By the end of their shift, the central shaft would have been extended an additional three hundred or more feet straight down beneath the Facility, nicely lined with reinforcing steel—and since the shaft was filled with ocean water, the steel bands themselves were not under any pressure.

"Our rate of descent has dropped," said Grove.

Horst peered at his screens. "The Doodlebug has slowed."

Grove frowned. "It's not like last time, is it?"

"Last time" referred to the prior day's mission, on which the Doodlebug had inexplicably ceased responding to commands for sixty seconds near the lowest point of the shaft. A little idly, Adkinson wondered what idiot gave the thing its nickname. "Doodlebug" sounded small and cute. But the real thing didn't look like a bug at all, and it certainly wasn't cute: it was a hulking, beastly-looking robot, when you got right down to it.

"Nope, not like last time," the engineer was saying. "It's just a temperature gradient. We'll be through it in a moment or two."

Adkinson delicately readjusted himself on the small seat. He recalled that today was a red-letter day of sorts. The night before, the tunnel-boring machine had punched through the bottom of the basement layer—the second stratum of the earth's crust. They would be the first crew to penetrate the oceanic layer—the third, and deepest, section of the crust. Beyond that lay the Moho . . . and whatever it was that awaited them.

Adkinson was curious about what they'd find in the oceanic layer. All he knew for sure was that it was by far the thinnest of the three layers and the least known. After all, even the Ocean Drilling Project had never dug this deep. They were going where no human had ever been—he needed to remember that.

He sighed, idly fingering the complex trigger

mechanism for the robot arm—controlled wire-lessly, of course, since no hydraulics or wiring could penetrate the skin of the Marble. The trip down would go a whole lot faster, he reflected, if the company was more interesting. But talking to Horst and Grove was the social equivalent of watching paint dry.

"Zero minus five thousand," Grove said.

Your sister, Adkinson thought grumpily.

Ten minutes passed in which the only breaks in the silence came from occasional radio squawks from the surface and Grove's relentless play-by-play. As they at last approached the base of the shaft, Adkinson perked up. Once he could begin his exacting work—receiving the semicircular steel bands lowered by cable from the Facility, slotting them into place with the countless tiny levers controlling the robot arm, sealing them—time would pass quickly.

"Initiate deceleration," Grove said.

Horst tapped on the little keyboard fixed between his joysticks. "Commencing glide down."

Grove grabbed for the radio. "Dive Control, this is Marble One. Approaching the dig interface now. Commence payload deployment."

"Marble One, roger," came the squawk from the speaker. "Initial load on its way in five."

Grove glanced at Adkinson. That was the signal to get his butt in gear. He nodded back, then began prepping his station. He switched his sonar into active mode, preparing to monitor the lowering of the steel bands. He carefully took hold of the trigger mechanism for the robotic arm, flexed it, checked the half dozen tiny joysticks, then began running the test suites, first for the gross motor, then the fine motor controls.

Strange. The arm seemed sluggish, almost lazy, in response to his movements of the trigger . . .

Grove's voice abruptly intruded on his thoughts.

"We've stopped," the pilot said. He turned to Horst. "What's up?"

"I'm not sure." The engineer tapped at his keyboard, peered at one of the screens.

"Is there a proximity warning with the tunnel-boring machine?"

"No," Horst replied. "It began work on schedule. It's dug four feet of fresh shaft already."

"Then why has the Doodlebug stopped?"

"Unknown." Horst's fingers flew over the keyboard. "It's only responding intermittently to commands."

"Christ. This is all we need." Grove slammed his hand against a bulkhead.

The pilot was bearable when things went well, but hit a snag and he became a prize asshole. Adkinson fervently hoped this shift wouldn't turn out to be one for the record books.

"Can you up the gain?" Grove asked.

"It's already at maximum."

"Well, damn it, you'd better—"

"There," Horst said. "It's moving again."

"That's more like it," Grove replied, tone settling back to normal. "Okay, Adkinson, prepare to—"

"Oh, **shit**!" Horst said. And the sudden urgency in the engineer's voice sent a stab of fear through Adkinson. "It's **rising**!"

"What is?" Grove asked.

"The Doodlebug. It's not descending. It's coming **toward** us!"

Adkinson swung to face the engineer's center screen. Sure enough: through the greenish wash of sonar, he could see the robotic creature moving upward. Even as he stared, it seemed to increase in speed.

"Well, stop it!" Grove cried. "Shut it down!"

Horst typed desperately. "I can't. It's not responding on any of the channels."

There was a sudden, shrill alarm. "Collision warning," said a disembodied female voice. "Collision warning . . ."

"It's no good!" Horst called out. "Fifty feet and closing."

Adkinson felt another, stronger stab of fear in his vitals. If the Doodlebug rammed them—if it damaged the exterior of the Marble—it could damage the complex webwork of struts that maintained their structural integrity . . .

In sudden panic he wheeled around, hands clenching and unclenching, looking illogically for an exit.

"I'm scrubbing the mission!" Grove shouted over the bleat of the alarm. "Horst, decouple the EM link. We're heading for the surface."

"It's **been** decoupled. The Doodlebug's still coming. Thirty feet away now and closing fast!"

"Shit." Grove grabbed for the radio. "Dive Control, this is Marble One. We're terminating the mission and returning."

"Marble One, say again?" the radio crackled.

"The Doodlebug's malfunctioning—we're making an emergency ascent."

Adkinson gripped his seat, desperately trying to keep himself under control. He could sense them ascending now with painful slowness. His eyes were riveted to Horst's screens. **Hurry up, goddamn it, hurry up . . .**

"Collision imminent," said the silky female voice. "Collision imminent."

"Ten!" Horst almost screamed. **"Oh, Christ!"**

"Brace for impact!" yelled Grove.

Adkinson hurled himself over his console, grasping the reinforcing bulkhead as tightly as he could. He clenched his jaw. For a strange moment, it seemed that all the furious noise within the Marble—the wail of the proximity warning, Grove's shouts—were muted in a suspended agony of waiting. Then from below came a wrenching impact; the Marble bucked, yawed sideways, metal squealing and shearing; a sudden, furious, uncontrolled ascent; Adkinson's skull banged violently against the floor . . . and then darkness closed in over all.

29

Crane trotted along the labyrinthine corridors of deck 3, accompanied by a young marine with close-cropped blond hair.

"What is it?" Crane asked. "What's happened?"

"I don't know, sir," the marine said. "My orders were to escort you to the Drilling Complex. On the double."

The marine stopped to open an unmarked door, which gave onto a narrow service stairwell. They took the metal steps downward, two at a time, until they reached deck 1. The marine threw open another door, and they ran through another warren of passageways. As he ran, Crane noticed that the walls of this—the lowest level of the Facility—were painted a dull red.

Ahead now lay a large set of double doors. As Crane approached, the marines stationed outside pulled the doors open for him. Beyond lay the Drilling Complex, the large equipment hanger he had seen from above the day before. Equipment bulkheads and racks of instrumentation lined three of the walls. Numerous open hatchways led to labs, equipment bays, monitoring stations, and breakout rooms. The ceiling—two levels high in this space—was festooned with cranes, gantries, heavy chains, and hydraulic equipment. Technicians hurried here and there, speaking in low tones, their faces drawn and worried. Somewhere in the distance, an alarm was sounding.

In the center of the hanger, people stood clustered around what was clearly the upper seal of a water lock. Among them was Admiral Spartan. Crane walked quickly over to them.

"What's going on?" he asked Spartan.

The admiral glanced at him for a moment before returning his gaze to the water lock. "There's been some kind of accident with Marble One."

"What kind of accident?"

"We've lost communication with the crew inside, there's no way to know for sure. Apparently, the robotic mechanism that pulls the Marble down the dig shaft malfunctioned. Rammed the Marble. And now, Marble One is rising out of control."

"Oh, Jesus. Did they lose pressure?"

"Exceedingly unlikely. Any injuries are more likely to result from . . . impact."

"Blunt trauma," Crane muttered. He glanced around, thinking quickly. "You said the Marble has a crew complement of three?"

"Correct."

"I don't have any medical equipment on hand."

"Emergency field kits are being brought as we speak."

A loudspeaker rasped, "Estimated time until impact, two minutes."

"A field kit's not enough, Admiral," Crane said. "I'm going to need to prep the site for emergency treatment. And I'll need Dr. Bishop to assist. Especially if there's triage to be done."

Spartan turned to look at him again. "Not in the Drilling Complex."

"But—" Crane began.

"You can use the temporary infirmary on deck four. I'll have Dr. Bishop brought there." Spartan beckoned to one of the numerous marines stationed nearby. "Locate Dr. Bishop and escort her to deck four," he ordered.

The marine saluted, then moved briskly away.

"What if there are neck injuries?" Crane demanded. "We can't just move those crewmen . . ." He fell silent when he saw the expression on the admiral's face.

A lab technician looked up from the nearby control console. "Admiral," he said. "Marble One's rate of ascent is slowing slightly."

"What's the current rate?"

"Thirty-four feet per second, sir."

"Equilibrium's off," said Spartan. "That's still too damn fast."

Crane waited, going over the stabilization procedures he'd need to follow once the Marble was secured. For all his specialized training, it would come down to the same procedure any trauma paramedic would follow. ABC: airway, breathing, circulation. If the collision with the robotic digger had been violent enough, there might be lacerations, contusions, possible concussions. Since he had to move the crew to deck 4, he'd need to get cervical collars fixed, place the men on short boards as a precaution against—

"Estimated time until impact, sixty seconds," came the disembodied voice from the loudspeaker.

"Isn't there any way to slow it?" Crane asked.

"Just before it impacts the water lock, we're going to discharge a cushion of CO_2" Spartan said.

"Theoretically, that will reduce the impact. But the timing has to be exact."

He walked over to the lab technician. "Release the gas at minus five seconds."

"Very good, sir." The tech looked pale.

Crane glanced around the large hangar. The frantic activity had ceased, and a hush had descended. Everybody was standing still—waiting.

"Thirty seconds," came the voice from the loudspeaker. "Pressure seal deactivated."

Spartan plucked a radio from the console. "All hands, brace for impact!"

Crane stepped over to a nearby bulkhead, took hold with both hands.

"Rate of ascent?" Spartan asked the tech.

"Steady at thirty-two feet per second, sir."

The loudspeaker crackled. "Fifteen seconds."

Spartan looked quickly around the Drilling Complex, pinning everyone in turn with a brief gaze, as if assuring himself all the necessary players were in place. Then he turned back to the tech. "Release the CO_2."

The tech snapped a series of buttons. "Released, sir—"

At that moment, Crane felt a sharp thump beneath his feet. The Facility shuddered slightly.

It was as if an electrical circuit had abruptly been completed. Instantly, the Complex leapt back into activity. Orders were shouted; technicians in white lab coats and marines in fatigues ran to their stations. The metal floor rang with the sound of heavy footsteps.

"Water lock integrity?" Spartan asked the tech.

"One hundred percent, sir."

Spartan picked up the radio, punched in a frequency. "Open the hatch," he snapped. "Get my men up here."

"Outer water lock doors opening now," said the tech at the control console.

Crane saw three workers wheeling a bizarre-looking contraption into place beside the water lock: a steel scaffold about seven feet tall, onto which was set a large metal ring with a toothed circumference. What looked like a pair of industrial-strength lasers had been fastened onto the ring, in 180-degree opposition to each other. Clearly, this was the device that would cut a circular hole into the side of the Marble, creating an exit hatch and releasing the crew inside.

"Marble One's in the lock now," the tech said. "Closing outer doors."

"How long will it take the laser to cut an exit hatch?" Crane asked.

"Eight minutes," Spartan said. "That's at two hundred percent normal operating speed."

Crane's attention was distracted from the laser gantry by a commotion at the main entrance.

Three marines entered, pushing makeshift gurneys ahead of them; another followed in their wake, medical field kits slung over his shoulder. Spartan looked over at Crane, made the slightest nod of his head in the direction of the Marble. **You're on,** the nod told him.

Crane walked over to the laser gantry, gesturing for the marines to wheel the gurneys and trauma equipment up behind him. He busied himself prepping the gurneys, opening the kits, and laying out instruments, readying the C collars and short boards for the upcoming extraction, running down mental checklists, preparing for the injuries that likely awaited.

"Lock sealed," said the tech. "Equalizing pressure."

"Bring the retractor into place," Spartan ordered.

There was a whirring noise, and Crane looked up to see a large robotic clamp being dollied into position over the water lock.

"Pressure equalized," said the tech.

"Open the lock," said Spartan.

For a moment, all fell silent again. Then Crane felt a rumbling beneath his feet. The two panels of the water lock drew back from the floor, revealing a surface of dark water. The clamp slowly descended with a mechanical whir, swaying back and forth beneath the heavy cable, jaws yawning wide. It reached the water and kept descending until fully submerged. The whirring noise ceased. Crane heard a muffled clunk. The cable began to rise again, more slowly this time. He saw the top of the clamp break the water's surface. Inch by inch it rose, revealing its webbing of hydraulics, its heavy jaws . . . and at last, very slowly, Marble One itself came into view, suspended between them.

There was a collective gasp from the assembled group; groans; a suppressed cry. Someone behind Crane started to weep.

He barely heard.

What lay between the jaws of the robotic clamp was not a shiny, gleaming sphere of transcendent beauty. It was a shrunken tangle of metal, horribly imploded, transformed by the appalling pressure into an unrecognizable grayish wad barely a third its former size. One section of the hull had been split apart explosively and petaled back against itself, exposing countless spike-like struts resembling the quills of a porcupine. Other sections had been compressed so violently they seemed almost to have melted. Not one of the torn and twisted lines was distinguishable as the Marble he'd seen before.

An awful pall of silence settled over the hanger, broken only by weeping. For a long moment, the clamp hung there, suspended over the water lock, the operator too shocked to act.

"Cut it down," Spartan ordered in a savage voice. Crane glanced over at him, but the expression on the admiral's face was too terrible to contemplate, and he returned his eyes to the Marble.

With a shriek of protesting metal and a clank of chains, the remains of Marble One were steered to one side of the water lock, where it sat suspended a foot over the floor of the Drilling Complex, seawater running from it in heavy streams. **And not only seawater,** Crane noticed with a visceral twinge of dismay: some of the streams that poured from the tangled ruin were thick and red.

It was obvious—all too obvious—that there would be no need for the cervical collars, the short boards . . . or anything else. Crane turned toward the marines, ready to tell them to secure the medical equipment.

But even as he did so, he saw a familiar face among the horror-struck crowd that watched from the perimeter of the Drilling Complex. A short man in faded bib overalls, with piercing blue eyes and an unruly cloud of silvery hair. It was Flyte, the strange old man who had approached him in his cabin. He was barely visible behind two technicians, staring at the scene with an expression of pity and almost childlike sorrow.

Then he turned toward Crane, catching him with his intense gaze. Slowly, deliberately, he mouthed silently the same words he had uttered before, standing uninvited in Crane's stateroom:

Everything is broken.

30

Howard Asher had two laboratories on the Deep Storm Facility: a cramped cubbyhole on deck 8 and a somewhat larger space on deck 4. They were very different. While the deck 8 lab had a lived-in, eclectic, inviting feel, the lab in the classified section was spare, businesslike, and clinical. He was in this lab—head in his hands, pondering a complex series of charts and equations that lay before him—when the door opened and Admiral Spartan stepped in.

For a moment, the two men stared at each other

like sparring partners. Then Asher's tense, drawn face relaxed a little.

"Seat?" he said in a sad, quiet voice.

Spartan shook his head. "The Magnetic Descent Unit—the Doodlebug—is in poor shape. We plan to use the spare while Fabrication does an overhaul."

"So you plan to continue the dives?"

"Of course. Why wouldn't we?"

Asher looked at him in disbelief. "Admiral, three men just **died**."

"I'm aware of that. Have your engineers come to any conclusions?"

"About what caused the Doodlebug to malfunction? Nothing definite."

"What about ensuring it doesn't recur?"

For a moment, Asher stared appraisingly at the admiral. Then he sighed. "Doubling—or, better still, tripling—the strength of the electromagnetic field should guarantee the link remains stable on future dives."

Spartan nodded. "Anything else?"

"Yes. Shut down all robotic or automatic processes that aren't absolutely necessary to the construction of the shaft. That goes for the remaining two Marbles as well as the Doodlebug: operate with a bare minimum of instrumentation. And critical instrumentation should use redundant packets, with checksums for validity."

"That's your recommendation?"

Asher frowned. "My **recommendation** is that we cease all operations until we have a thorough understanding of what caused this disaster and why."

"That's not an option, Dr. Asher. There's no telling how long it would take to arrive at such an understanding."

"But the deaths—"

"A tragic mishap. Grove, Adkinson, Horst—they knew the inherent danger of the work when they signed up. So did you, for that matter."

Asher tried again. "Admiral, listen—"

"No, Dr. Asher. You listen for a minute. Haven't people always been willing to die in the name of discovery and knowledge? Isn't that why we're all here? Look at Robert Falcon Scott, Amelia Earhart, the crew of the **Challenger**. We're all putting our lives on the line here to push the envelope, to better mankind."

Asher sighed, rubbed at his eyes with a weary hand. "There's the empirical evidence to consider."

"What evidence might that be?"

"Marble One just penetrated into the third, the lowest, level of the crust—the oceanic layer. Is it coincidence that this aberrant behavior occurred at the deepest depth we've achieved?"

"Pressure would not cause a malfunction like that."

"I'm not talking about pressure. I'm talking about getting closer to whatever's down there. The oceanic layer is the thinnest of all. Even if we put these deaths aside for a moment, don't all these strange sicknesses trouble you? Doesn't it bother you that people are beginning to whisper, that there are serious morale issues?"

When Spartan did not reply, Asher rose and began to pace the room restlessly. "Thanks to Dr. Crane, we've made a huge leap forward."

"Dr. Crane should stick to his assignment," Spartan said.

"He's provided us with the biggest break yet. Admiral, those sentinels aren't transmitting a signal on one wavelength anymore. They're transmitting **different** signals now, on **thousands** of wavelengths. Probably millions. In fact, it seems they're transmitting on every single band in the electromagnetic spectrum. Radio waves, microwaves, infrared, ultraviolet—you name it."

"And in so doing, they are disrupting our instruments and wireless networks," Spartan said. "If it's anything, it's probably a welcome of some sort."

"That's possible. But it could be something else."

"Such as?"

"I don't know. But what they have to say is so important they're exhausting all available bandwidths to broadcast it." Asher hesitated. "It's my strong opinion we should stop digging until we've translated the message. You've got more than your share of Naval Intelligence spooks aboard. If I could tap them, pool our efforts, we could decrypt this message faster."

"They have other tasks at present. And besides, you don't have proof there **are** any messages."

Asher threw up his hands in exasperation. "What do you think, then? They're broadcasting the top forty hits of Alpha Centauri?" And he began pacing again.

Spartan watched him for a moment. "Very well, Dr. Asher. Let's assume there are messages. As I said, chances are they're welcoming us. Or perhaps they are transmitting user manuals for whatever we're digging toward. Am I curious about that? Very. But am I going to drop everything, stop work, until you discover what they're trying to say? No. For one thing, you can't give me an estimate for cracking the code. Can you?"

"I . . ." Asher stopped, gave his head an angry shake.

"And for another, it **doesn't matter** what the message is. As you pointed out, we're into the oceanic layer now. We're only a week away from reaching the Moho, maybe less. Whatever is down there, we're going to extract its contents and study them—before anybody else can."

Asher opened his mouth to respond. But before he could speak, the floor trembled: first gently, then violently. Manuals and binders fell from the shelves, and there was a crash of breaking glass as a tray of lab equipment slid off the nearby work-table. Confused voices sounded from the hall, and an alarm sounded in the distance. Spartan leapt to his feet, running to Asher's phone and dialing as another shudder shook the Facility.

"This is Admiral Spartan," he said into the mouthpiece. "Determine the source of that. If there's any damage, I want instant reports."

He turned to look at Asher. The chief scientist had grasped the edge of the worktable for support. Now he stood quite still, head cocked as if listening. "Just aftershocks now," he murmured.

"What the hell was that, Dr. Asher?"

"The price we pay for working in an oceanic ridge. The upside is, the crust of the earth is shallow here—the Moho is less than five miles deep. The downside is, ocean ridges are prone to earthquakes."

"Earthquakes," Spartan repeated.

"Yes. Small in magnitude, generally—this is a divergent boundary, after all." He looked over his glasses at Spartan, half sadly, half quizzically. "You never read the white paper I sent you on plate tectonics and oceanography?"

But the admiral didn't answer. His gaze was focused at some indistinct spot beyond Asher's right shoulder. At last, he shook his head. "Perfect," he said. "Just perfect."

31

The temporary infirmary on deck 4 was as small as the Medical Suite upstairs was expansive. It reminded Crane of the diminutive sick bay on the USS **Spectre,** in which he'd toiled for the better part of a year: all bulkhead and conduit. And yet for all its tininess, at the moment it seemed depressingly empty. Crane had expected to fill it with the three men from Marble One. Instead, there had not been enough left of the crew even for red-bag waste: Marble One had been sealed in heavy plastic sheeting and placed in a low-temperature locker for later analysis.

He sighed, turned toward Bishop. "Thanks for coming down. I'm sorry I wasted your time."

"Don't be silly."

"Did you know any of the three?"

"I knew Horst. Had some trouble with sleep apnea, dropped by for a couple of consultations."

"I never got the chance to meet any of them." Crane shook his head.

"Don't beat yourself up about this, Peter. It's not your fault."

"I know. It just seems like such a tragic waste."

And it wasn't only the death of the three crew members that weighed on him. There was also the fact that he was making precious little progress. They'd run just about every test in the book—CT scans, MRIs, EKGs, CBCs. Nothing. Every fresh theory, every promising new avenue of research, had ultimately led to a dead end. It made no sense: he'd been following all the rules of diagnosis, yet the solution remained stubbornly out of reach. It was as if whatever was wrong down here was somehow playing out beyond the laws of medical science.

He shifted, made a concerted effort to change the subject. "How are things upstairs? It's been so busy down here I haven't even checked your current patient status."

"Two new cases in the last twenty-four hours: one complaining of severe nausea, another presenting with arrythmia."

"You put a Holter monitor on him?"

"Yes, twenty-four-hour cycle. Then, the cook, Loiseau, had another seizure—worse this time."

"You've admitted him?"

Bishop nodded. "That's about it. Actually, it's Roger who's been getting more of the action."

"How's that?"

"Seven—maybe eight—people have come to see him, complaining of general psychiatric disorders."

"Such as?"

"The usual. Problems with concentration and focus, lapses in memory, disinhibition of character. Roger thinks it's localized eruptions of accumulated stress."

"I see." Crane was hesitant to disagree without further examination. But his own experience on stealth submarines, working with men and women under constant pressure, didn't bear out such a conclusion. Besides, any questionable personality types would have been weeded out during the Facility's vetting process. "Tell me more about the disinhibition case."

"One of the librarians in the multimedia nexus.

Retiring fellow. Shy. Picked two fights in Times Square last night. When security arrived he was drunk and disorderly, screaming obscenities."

"That's very interesting."

"Why?"

"Because one of the patients down here in the classified sector recently displayed very similar changes in personality." He paused, thinking. "It seems that the number of psychological cases are beginning to outweigh the physiological cases."

"So?" Bishop sounded unconvinced. "We're all going crazy by degrees?"

"No. But maybe—just maybe—it's the common thread we're looking for." He hesitated. "Have you heard the story of Phineas Gage?"

"Sounds like a Hawthorne tale."

"Actually, it's a true story. In 1848, Phineas P. Gage was the foreman of a railroad gang, laying track bed for a railway company in Vermont. Seems there was an accidental explosion. The blast drove his tamping iron—a four-foot, thirteen-pound metal spike more than an inch in diameter—right through his head."

Bishop grimaced. "What an awful way to go."

"That's just it—he didn't die. He may not have even been rendered unconscious, despite the fact that the iron spike destroyed most of the bilateral frontal lobe of his brain. Within a few months he was able to resume work. But here's the thing: **he was not the same man.** Before the accident, Gage had been efficient, pleasant natured, polite, thrifty, savvy about business matters. Now he was profane, flighty, impatient, reportedly lewd, unable to keep any position of responsibility."

"Like some of the early radical resection patients."

"Exactly. Gage was the first patient to provide a link between the brain's frontal lobe and human personality."

Bishop nodded thoughtfully. "And where are you going with all this?"

"I'm not exactly sure. But I'm starting to wonder if maybe our problem here isn't neurological. Did that electroencephalograph unit ever come in?"

"Yes, just this morning. They raised holy hell about it, too: took up half the Tub on the trip down."

"Well, let's put it to use. I'd like to get EEGs done on the half dozen most serious cases. Symptomology doesn't matter—in fact, mix up the psychological with the physiological." He stretched, massaged his lower back. "I could use some coffee. You?"

"Sure. If you don't mind playing delivery boy." And she frowned, jerking her thumb in the direction of the door.

"Oh, yes. Of course." Crane had momentarily

forgotten the marine stationed outside the temporary infirmary; the man had escorted Bishop down from the unclassified section on Spartan's orders and would be escorting her up again when she left the room. Clearly, she wasn't happy about having a babysitter. "I'll be right back."

He exited the infirmary, nodded to the marine, and made his way down the hall. His own surveillance had been eased and it felt a little strange, having relatively unrestricted access to the entire Facility. Although there were still plenty of areas to which his mediocre security rating did not permit access, during the medical interviews of the last two days he had seen enough labs, equipment bays, offices, quarters, and machine shops to last a lifetime.

The same held true for the leisure spaces. The cafeteria on deck 4 was spartan in its decor, and had tables and chairs sufficient for perhaps only a dozen people. Yet Crane had found that its French roast was every bit as good as that served in the Times Square café.

He entered, walked over to the service counter, and placed his order. Thanking the woman behind the counter, he put a little milk in his cup— Bishop liked hers black—and turned to head back for the infirmary. But the sound of raised voices stopped him.

A group of men sat around a table in the far corner. They were a motley bunch: two wore the obligatory white lab coats of Facility technicians, while another wore a machnist's jumpsuit and the last, a petty officer's uniform. They'd been huddled together in subdued conversation when Crane entered, and he'd barely taken note of them, assuming they were discussing the tragedy of Marble One. But in the short span of time it had taken him to order the coffees, the conversation had apparently veered into argument.

"And just how would you know?" One of the scientists was saying. "It's an extraordinary opportunity for mankind, the most important discovery ever. It's proof—**final** proof—we're not alone in the universe. You can't just ignore it, bury your head in the sand."

"I know what I've seen," the machinist shot back. "And what I've heard. People are saying we weren't meant to find it."

The scientist scoffed. "Weren't **meant** to find it?"

"Yeah. It was an accident. Like, it's too early."

"If we didn't find it, somebody else would have," the petty officer snapped. "I suppose you'd rather the Chinese got their hands on that technology first?"

"What damn technology?" the machinist said, raising his voice again. "Nobody has a fucking clue what's **down** there!"

"Christ, Chucky, lower your voice," said the second scientist, moodily stirring his cup.

"I've worked with the sentinels," the first scientist said. "I know what they're capable of. This might be our only chance to—"

"And **I** just finished wrapping up what's left of Marble One," the man named Chucky shot back. "Trashed beyond recognition. Three of my friends, dead. I tell you, we're not ready for this. We're overextended down here."

"What happened to Marble One is a terrible thing," said the first scientist. "And it's okay to grieve. But don't let grief blind you to the larger issue: **why** we're down here. No advance was ever made without risk. These visitors clearly want to help us. They have so much to teach—"

"How the hell do you know they want to teach us anything?" Chucky demanded.

"If you'd seen how beautiful the markers are, how utterly—"

"So what? A black panther's beautiful, too . . . right up to the minute it rips your guts out."

The scientist sniffed. "That's an inappropriate comparison."

"The hell it is. You assume they're friendly. You think you know everything. Let me tell you something: nature is **never** friendly. Our own planet is full of life-forms, all busy trying to kill each other!" The machinist's voice was beginning to rise again.

"Don't blame others for the failings of our planet," said the first scientist.

"Maybe they seeded planets all over the universe with these things." Chucky's face was pale, and his hands shook slightly. "We uncover 'em, they beam a signal back to their masters—who then come and destroy us. Very efficient system for wiping out potential competition."

The second scientist shook his head. "That's a little paranoid, don't you think?"

"Paranoid? Then you explain what's happening here. All the accidents, the problems **nobody wants to talk about!**"

"Cool it," the petty officer growled.

Chucky stood up, knocking his chair over. "Then why are people dying? Why are people getting sick? Why am **I** getting sick? Because there's something wrong, something wrong with my **head . . .**"

Crane was about to step forward and intervene when, suddenly, the machinist fell silent. He righted his chair and sat down, the petty officer's restraining hand on his shoulder.

Commander Korolis had just entered the cafeteria, accompanied by two officers in black fatigues and combat boots.

For a moment, all was still. The only noise was the machinist's labored breathing.

The commander turned his pale, out-of-synch eyes toward Crane, and his expression hardened into disapproval. Then he turned his gaze to the group at the table, moving slowly from one person to the next, as if committing each face to memory. And then—very slowly and deliberately—he turned and walked out again without saying a word.

32

Three hours later, the summons from Asher came. Michele Bishop had left the deck 4 infirmary to oversee the electroencephalograms Crane requested, and he'd just finished logging the morning's events and was preparing to track down "Chucky," the machinist, for a mandatory physical and psychological evaluation when the telephone rang.

He walked across the small room, plucked the phone from its cradle. "Dr. Crane speaking."

"Peter? This is Howard Asher. I need your assistance, please."

"Of course. Are you in your office? I'll be right there—"

"No. I'm in Hyperbaric Therapy. Deck seven. You know the location?"

"Certainly. But—"

"Please come at once." The phone went dead.

Crane stared at the receiver in mystification. Why Asher would be there, of all spots, made no sense.

It was the work of ten minutes to pass through the Barrier and ascend to deck 7. The scientific level was full of activity, as usual, but the small suite of rooms on the dead-end corridor composing Hyperbaric Therapy was empty, almost ghostly. This, too, was expected: since the atmosphere on the Facility was not, in fact, pressurized in any way, there were no pressure-related ailments to be treated. Crane had found this out the hard way, with his original theory of caisson disease.

The therapy suite consisted of a tiny control room; a waiting area outside the hyperbaric chamber; and the chamber itself, a metal cylinder about six feet in diameter and ten feet long, with an observation porthole in the entrance hatch and another on one side. Within, two cushioned benches ran along each of the walls, set across from each other. Along the ceiling ran two identical control strips, housing the lighting as well as the emergency water deluge system.

Asher was standing in the waiting area, along with John Marris, the NOD cryptanlyst. Marris had a large satchel slung over one shoulder. Asher looked tired, almost haggard, and his left hand—which he held protectively against his side—was bandaged with gauze. He nodded distractedly at Crane as he entered.

"You're not looking especially good," Crane said. "Getting enough sleep?"

Asher's response was a wintry smile.

Crane nodded at the bandaged hand. "What happened?"

"Look for yourself. Gently, please." Asher turned to Marris. "We'll run those common-language routines once again, doubling the ply depth. Perhaps we'll get a different result."

Carefully, Crane unhooked the metal butterfly clip and unwrapped the bandage. Beneath the gauze, an evil-looking ulceration had formed on the back of Asher's hand.

Crane examined it closely. The surrounding skin was pale, almost alabaster. Yet—alarmingly—Asher's fingertips were bluish black around the nails.

"When did you notice this?" he asked, looking up sharply at the chief scientist.

"Last night."

"Well, it's no joke." Crane carefully rewrapped the bandage. "It's a result of the vascular insufficiency you're suffering from. Not only is the hand ulcerated now, but there are signs of incipient necrosis as well. You have to report to the Medical Suite. We need to run Doppler imaging on that hand, do a bypass procedure on the blockage—"

"**No!**" Asher said fiercely. He took a deep breath, got himself under control. "No. There's no time for surgery."

Crane looked at him appraisingly. "Why is that?"

"We need to decipher that code. Three men just died; it's **vital** we understand what the message is. Do you hear, Peter? Until we've done that, I can't afford the downtime."

Crane frowned. "But your hand—"

"I'm still taking Coumadin. When I got my hand bandaged in Medical this morning, the on-duty intern gave me a course of antibiotic therapy. And there's **this**." Asher waved in the direction of the Chamber.

Crane had wondered if this might be what Asher had in mind. Hyperbaric therapy was, in fact, often used as an adjunctive treatment for clinical conditions like arterial insufficiency or for necrotizing soft tissue infections. Pure oxygen, under pressure, penetrated tissue more effectively, rallied white blood cells to the body's defense. Yet it was no substitute for more aggressive, and more direct, treatment.

"Listen, Peter," Asher said, his voice growing low and persuasive. "We're close. It's thanks to you the sentinels are now transmitting on countless frequencies. That was a huge leap for us. And with different messages on each of the frequencies, we have that many more samples to work with. See, the trouble was we've been barking up the wrong tree for the last couple of days."

"How so?"

"We thought we'd cracked it. We thought the sentinels had been transmitting . . . well, a mathematical expression."

"A mathematical expression?" Crane repeated. He found it hard to keep the disbelief out of his voice.

For a moment, Asher's look became almost sheepish. "A very simple mathematical expression."

"What was it?"

When Asher did not answer, Marris reached into his pocket and handed Crane a printout.

Pass 1 of 1
Mode: reductive

$$x = 1 / 0$$

Pass complete
Integrity verified
Machine cycles: 236340

Crane handed the sheet back. "One divided by zero? The first thing I learned in math was that you can't divide by zero."

Asher began pacing restlessly. "Obviously you can't. Division by zero is forbidden by all the laws of the universe. But the hell of it is, the decoding went so smoothly, it all fit together so well . . . we thought we'd just made some minor miscalculation in our translation. That's why I didn't tell you earlier, that's why we've wasted all this time running computer simulations and cryptographic attacks trying to spot our error. But now I see that was the wrong direction **entirely**." Here he stopped and wheeled back toward Crane, his eyes on fire. "We're going to run the signals through a series of common-language analyzers. We'd have done it sooner if we hadn't been so hung up on that wild-goose chase." He waved at the paper in Crane's hand. "We've wasted time—time we don't have. That's why we can't stop now. That's why

I'm ordering you—no, I'm **asking** you—to prep the chamber for oxygen therapy."

Crane didn't move. "It's not a cure. It's only delaying the inevitable."

Asher made a visible effort to remain calm. "I know that. I just need time—maybe a few hours, maybe a day—to run the signals through the language analyzers. Then I'll go straight to Medical, submit to any treatment or procedure you want. Marris can take care of the other issue by himself, at least for the present."

"Other issue?" Crane asked.

"Marris thinks he's figured out the method of transmission the saboteur is using to get information on and off the Facility."

"Really? What is it?"

"No time to explain now. But once I'm out of the chamber he's going to test his theory, try to trace the transmissions to their source. Meanwhile, I've e-mailed all the department heads—Ferguson, Conover, Bishop, the rest—to be on the lookout for anything suspicious." He paused. "But that's for later. Right now, our top priority is to decipher these signals."

Crane sighed. "Very well. But the moment you emerge from the chamber, I expect you in Medical."

At this, Asher gave a fleeting smile—the old

smile Crane remembered from his first days aboard Deep Storm. "Thank you, Peter." He turned to Marris. "Got everything?"

Marris hefted the laptop, nodded.

"We'll be able to access the WAN wirelessly on the inside," Asher said. "The sentinels are all several decks below us; there won't be any interference here."

"I'll get the chamber prepped," Crane said, turning away. Then he stopped. "Wait a minute. What's this 'we'?"

"I'm going inside with Dr. Asher," Marris said.

Crane frowned. "That's highly unusual. You're not the one requiring therapy."

"It's the only way to continue our work without interruption," Marris said.

Crane hesitated a moment longer. Then he shrugged. **It's only oxygen, after all.** "Very well. Go ahead then, step into the chamber, please. I'll walk you through the setup procedures via the onboard microphone."

He stepped into the control room only to find that Asher had followed him. The chief scientist laid his right hand on Crane's arm. "Peter," he said, lowering his voice. "Don't tell Spartan."

"Don't tell him what?"

"About the wrong turn we took. Or about how close we are now."

This caught Crane by surprise. "I thought the whole point of this exercise was to tell Spartan what you find."

Asher shook his head vigorously. "No, not right away. I don't trust Spartan." His voice fell even further. "And I trust Korolis even less." His grip tightened on Crane's arm. "Promise me, Peter?"

Crane hesitated. Hearing this—seeing the strange light in Asher's eyes, the sheen of sweat on his brow—a new thought suddenly occurred to him. Vascular insufficiency might not be the only thing afflicting Asher. Perhaps what was striking the rest of the personnel was affecting him now, as well.

It was a profoundly depressing and disturbing thought.

Gently, he freed his arm from Asher's grasp. "Very well."

Asher nodded, smiled again. Then he turned away and walked toward the hyperbaric chamber. And as Crane ran through the control room setup—bringing the compressors online, ensuring the ASME storage tanks were topped up, checking the relief valves and pressure gauges—the haunted, hunted look in Asher's eyes remained always before him.

33

Charles Vasselhoff shuffled slowly and uncertainly toward Bottom, the mess hall located on deck 3. It wasn't so much that he was hungry—his mouth felt dry, as if moths had nested in it, and there was an unpleasant feeling in the pit of his stomach—it was simply that he had no place else to go. His large frame shook with chills, yet he felt so hot he'd had to unzip the top half of his orange jumpsuit. But what bothered him most was his head. The pain had begun like a normal headache, and he'd assumed it was just stress or maybe overwork. But then it had grown worse: a strange, irritating feeling of **fullness,** as if his brain had grown too big for his skull. His vision blurred, and his fingers grew tingly and numb at the tips. So he'd stopped work in the Electro-mechanical Machine Shop, where he'd been re-pairing impact damage to the alpha Doodlebug, and went to his quarters.

But that had been no better. He'd tossed and thrashed, soaking the pillow with a cold sweat and entangling his limbs in the sheets. Patroni, one of his bunkmates, had been there, big smelly feet up on the communal table, watching a cook-ing show on the Facility's internal cable network. The incessant drone of the cooking pro became more and more annoying. The strange sensation in his head increased, causing his ears to ring. And then there was the way Patroni looked at him—sidelong, sneaky glances, the way you'd look at somebody who was talking to himself just a little too loudly. Vasselhoff had been aware of people staring at him for the last couple of days—it started, he thought, around the same time the headaches began—but never his own bunkmates. And so with a whispered curse, he swung his legs out of the bunk, pushed himself to his feet, and stepped out into the hallway, shutting the door behind him without a word.

And now he found his feet taking him in the direction of Bottom. At least, he thought it was the direction of Bottom, but somehow he found himself in front of a Radiography Lab instead. He blinked, swayed slightly on his feet, turned around. Somewhere he'd taken a false step: he'd try again. Putting one foot deliberately in front of the other, he started back down the narrow corridor.

A man in a white lat coat passed by, digital clipboard in hand. "Yo, Chucky," he said without stopping.

Chucky took another two steps, then halted. Slowly, even stiffly, he turned in the direction of the technician, who was already halfway down the hall. The words had taken a second to register: the strange, crowded feeling in his head was causing his eyes to water slightly and the ringing in his ears to increase, and he was withdrawing into himself, preoccupied with the pain in his head and the chills that racked his body.

"Hey," he said tentatively, his voice sounding thick and strange. He licked his lips again but was unable to bring any moisture to them. Turning back, he made his slow, plodding way to the cafeteria, stopping at each intersection and blinking at the direction signs, forcing himself through the fog of confusion to make the necessary turns.

Bottom was crowded before the impending shift change. Some people were clustered before an easel sporting the evening's menu choices.

Others had formed a line for the serving stations. Chucky joined this line, wondering—remotely— why his legs felt so wooden and heavy. The buzz of conversation in the small cafeteria seemed to make the ringing in his ears worse. It was so loud, so distinct, he was certain the others must hear it, too. Yet nobody seemed to find anything strange or out of place. It was as if invisible beams of noise were being directed into his head alone.

Where was it coming from? Who was doing this?

He took a tray from the stack, shuffled ahead, bumped into the person ahead of him, mumbled an apology, lurched backward.

It took all the concentration he could muster to move forward with the line. He reached for a can of soda, then another and another, thinking they might wash the dryness from his mouth. He took a plate of watercress salad, looked at it uncertainly, put it back. He stopped at the carving station, where a chef wielding a heavy steel knife cut a thick slab of prime rib for him, forking it onto a plate and drizzling a brownish line of gravy over it.

Holding his tray with both hands, he made for the nearest empty seat and sat down heavily, the soda cans rattling against each other. He had forgotten to pick up a knife and fork, but it really didn't matter: the painful oppression in his head was spreading, causing his jaws to ache and his neck to feel stiff, and any trace of hunger he might have felt was now completely gone. Two women were sitting at the table, talking animatedly. They paused to glance at him. He remembered they were programmers in the research department but could not recall their names.

"Hello, Chucky," one of them said.

"Tuesday," Chucky replied. He tugged at one of the cans of soda, tugged again, and it opened, spraying a small jet of brown liquid over his hands. He raised it to his lips and took a long, greedy sip. It hurt just to fit his mouth to the can opening, and he did it imperfectly; soda dribbled down his chin as he swallowed. Even the swallowing hurt.

Damn it.

He put down the can, blinking, and listened to the ringing in his head. He'd been wrong, it was not a ringing: it was a voice. No, **several** voices, whispering to him.

Suddenly, he felt afraid: afraid of the numbness in his fingers; afraid of the chills that racked his body; and, most of all, afraid of the whispering inside his head. His mouth went dry again and he took another sip, heart pounding. He could feel the warm liquid going down, but it had no taste.

The voices grew louder. And as they did, Chucky's fear went away, replaced by a rising anger. It wasn't fair. Why were they doing this to him? **He** hadn't done anything. Beam signals into somebody else's head; there were plenty of assholes on the Facility ripe for it.

The women at the table were looking at him, frowning with concern. "Are you okay, Chucky?" the other programmer asked.

"Fuck you," Chucky said. They didn't give a shit about him. They just sat there staring, letting the signals fill his head with voices, fill his head until it exploded . . .

He rose abruptly, knocking over his tray and spilling soda and meat juices over the table. He swayed dangerously, righted himself. The cafeteria was spinning and the voices in his head were louder still. But that was suddenly all right: he knew now where the beams were coming from. They were radioactive, they had to be; he'd been a fool not to have realized it before. He lurched toward the carving station, grabbed one of the heavy knives lying there, still speckled with bits of meat and shiny gobbets of fat. The chef said something and reached forward, but Chucky slashed with the knife and the man shrank back. There was a scattering of screams, but they were barely audible beneath the voices in his head and Chucky paid no attention. He staggered out of the cafeteria and into the hallway, brandishing the knife. It was the radiation, he knew that now: getting into his head, making him strange, making him **sick**.

He would put a stop to that.

He lurched as quickly as he could down the hall. There would be no wrong turns this time: he knew exactly where he needed to go, and it wasn't far away. People he passed pressed themselves against the walls to avoid him, but they were now little more than fuzzy, monochromatic shapes and he paid them no heed.

As he half shuffled, half staggered down the corridor, the chills grew worse and the voices grew louder. He wouldn't listen; no, he would not do the terrible things they urged on him. He would stop them; he knew just what to do.

There it was, just ahead now: a large, shielded hatchway, with a burgundy-and-yellow radiation sign above it and two marines standing guard. Catching sight of him, they both started yelling, but Chucky could hear nothing over the chorus of voices. One of the marines dropped to his knees, still mouthing frantically, pointing something at him.

Chucky took another step forward. Then there was a brilliant flash of light and a roar so loud it overwhelmed even the babel of voices; pain blossomed in Chucky's chest; he felt himself driven backward with incredible violence; and then, slowly, the pain and the voices ebbed away into endless blackness and—at long last—he found peace.

34

The larger of the two operating bays in the Medical Suite had all the equipment and instrumentation necessary for major surgical procedures, from standard appendectomies to complex laparoscopic work. This evening, however, it had been appropriated for an entirely different function: that of temporary morgue.

The corpse of Charles Vasselhoff lay on the operating table, faintly bluish under the bright lights. The skullcap had been removed; the brain weighed, then returned. Now the metal walls of the bay rang with the sound of a Stryker saw as Crane attacked the breastbone, making the Y incision down the chest and across the abdomen. A female intern stood at his elbow, beside the tray of autopsy instruments. Just beyond was Michele Bishop. Her face was covered by a medical mask, but her brow was furrowed.

Near the door, and well back from the body, stood Commander Korolis. "When will the final report be ready, Dr. Crane?" he asked.

Crane ignored him. He turned off the vibrating saw, handed it to the waiting intern, then turned toward the microphone of a digital tape recorder and resumed dictation. "Penetrating gunshot wound to the right side of the chest. Injury to the skin and soft tissue. No perforation. There is no indication of close-range firing, such as powder residue or charring of the wound." He glanced at Bishop, who wordlessly handed him a pair of rib cutters. He snipped the remaining ribs, then carefully lifted off the chest plate.

Using forceps, he studied the devastation revealed by the overhead light. "Wound path is front to back, slightly downward. The wound itself consists of a ten-sixteenth-inch circular hole, with circumferential abrasion and a slight marginal radial laceration. There are injuries to the anterior right second rib, lower lobe of right lung, right subclavian vein, and lower gastrointestinal tract." He picked up an enterotome, inserted its bulb-shaped blade into the lumen, and gave it a gentle downward tug, pushing the viscera to one side. "Deformed large-caliber bullet embedded in tissue to the right side of the T2 vertebral body." Gingerly, he fished out the bullet with the forceps, then turned back to the recorder.

"Pathological diagnosis," he continued. "The entrance gunshot wound to the upper chest entered the right pleural cavity and lacerated the right subclavian vein. Cause of death: trauma and extensive bleeding into the right pleural space. Manner: homicide. Toxicology report to follow."

Korolis raised his eyebrows. "Homicide, Dr. Crane?"

"What would you call it?" Crane snapped. "Self-defense?" He dropped the bullet into a metal basin, where it clattered back and forth.

"The man was brandishing a deadly weapon in an aggressive and threatening manner."

Crane laughed bitterly. "I see. Those armed soldiers were in jeopardy."

"Vasselhoff was intent on trespassing into a highly restricted and sensitive area."

Crane handed the forceps to the intern. "What, he was going to carve up your precious reactor with a kitchen knife?"

Korolis's eyes darted quickly to the intern and

Dr. Bishop before returning to Crane. "It is made quite clear to everyone on sign-up: the strategic assets on this Facility will be protected at all costs. And you should be more careful what you say, Doctor. The consequences for breaching the agreements you signed are most severe."

"So sue me."

Korolis paused a moment, as if considering this. When he spoke again, his voice was softer, almost silky. "When can I expect that report?"

"When I finish it. Now why don't you get out and let us get on with our work?"

Korolis paused again. Then a small smile—little more than a baring of teeth—formed on his lips. He glanced down at the corpse. And then, with a barely perceptible nod to Bishop, he turned and silently left the operating bay.

For a moment, the three stood motionless, listening to the departing footsteps. Then Bishop sighed. "I think you just made an enemy."

"I don't care," Crane replied. And in fact he did not care. He felt almost physically sick with frustration—frustration over the climate of secrecy and military intolerance that hung over the entire Deep Storm project; frustration over his own inability to put an end to the affliction that had just, indirectly, caused the death of Vasselhoff. He pulled off his gloves, tossed them into the metal basin, and snapped off the recorder. Then he turned to the intern. "Would you mind closing up, please?"

The intern nodded. "Very well, Dr. Crane. Hagedorn needle?"

"That will be sufficient, yes."

He stepped out of the operating bay and into the central corridor of the medical suite, where he slumped wearily against the wall. Bishop came up beside him.

"Are you going to finish the report?" she asked.

Crane shook his head. "No. If I think about it any more right now, I'll just get too angry."

"Maybe you should get some sleep."

Crane gave a mirthless laugh. "Wouldn't happen. Not after a day like today. Besides, I've got Asher to deal with. He'll be coming out in about three hours."

Bishop looked at him. "Out of what?"

"You didn't know? He's in the hyperbaric chamber."

Bishop's look turned to one of puzzlement. "Asher? Why?"

"His vascular insufficiency condition. It seems to have gotten worse over the last couple of days. He's now presenting with ulcerations at the extremities."

"Is there a blockage? He shouldn't be in the

chamber—he should be here, undergoing a by-pass procedure."

"I know. I told him that. But he was insistent. He's . . ." Here Crane paused, remembering the code of silence to which he was bound. "He's apparently very close to a breakthrough, point-blank refused to stop working. Even took Marris into the chamber to continue the work."

Bishop didn't respond. She looked away, gazing thoughtfully down the corridor.

Crane yawned. "Anyway, I couldn't sleep if I tried. I'll catch up on some paperwork." He paused a moment. "Oh, yes—any of those EEGs come through yet?"

"One so far. Mary Philips, the woman who complained of numbness in the hands and face. I left it in your office. I'll go check the status of the others—I had the technician put a schedule together, and at least half a dozen should be done by now. I'll have her bring the printouts to you."

"Thanks." Crane watched her move briskly down the corridor. That was one blessing, at least: their relations had improved significantly.

He turned and walked slowly back to his cramped office. As promised, Bishop had left an EEG readout on his desk: a bulky packet of perhaps two dozen sheets of brain wave data, with a report clipped to the top sheet. He hated reading

EEGs: the art of detecting electrical abnormalities in someone's brain from the endless squiggly lines was a maddening one. Still, he'd been the one to request the tests; he couldn't afford to leave any avenue unexplored. And if there was anything to his premise that the problems at Deep Storm were neurological, the EEGs could confirm or deny it.

Crane took a seat, passed a weary hand over his eyes, then spread the readout across his desk. A welter of horizontal lines greeted him: the inner landscape of Mary Philips's brain, lines rising and falling with changes in amplitude and frequency. At first glance, all the lines seemed unremarkable, but Crane reminded himself it was always that way with electroencephalograms. They weren't like EKGs, where anomalies jumped out at you. It was more a question of relative values over time.

He turned his attention to the alpha rhythm. It displayed maximum amplitude in the posterior quadrants; this was normal for waking adults. He ran his eye along it for several sheets without seeing any abnormality beyond the kind of transients consistent with anxiety, perhaps hyperventilation. In fact, the woman's alpha PDR was quite well organized: very rhythmic, with no sign of admixed slower frequencies.

Next, he turned to the beta activity. It was present frontocentrally, in perhaps greater amounts than usual, but still within normal range. Neither set of waves displayed any particular amount of asymmetry or irregularity.

As he ran his eye across the sheets, following the thin black lines as they rose, then fell, a depressingly familiar sensation gathered within him: disappointment. This was proving, yet again, to be a dead end.

There was a knock on the door, and a lab technician appeared. She had a large stack of papers in her hand. "Dr. Crane?"

"Yes?"

"Here are the rest of the EEGs you requested." She stepped forward and put them on his desk.

Crane eyed the foot-high pile of printouts. "How many are there?"

"Fourteen." She smiled, nodded, and quickly left the office.

Fourteen. Great. Wearily, he turned back to Mary Philips's brain scan.

He moved down to the theta and delta waves, scanning from left to right, careful to interpret each ten-second digital epoch separately. The background activity seemed a little asymmetric, but that was more or less standard for the beginning of the test: the patient would no doubt settle down as the procedure continued . . .

Then he noticed it: a series of prefrontal spikes, small but definitely noticeable, among the theta waveforms.

He frowned. Theta activity, beyond a few random low-voltage waves, was extremely rare in adults.

He glanced through the rest of the readout. The spikes in the theta line did not go away: if anything, they increased. At first glance they were reminiscent of encephalopathy or perhaps Pick's disease, a form of cerebral atrophy that ultimately led to "flat affect" and dementia. The type of weakness Mary Philips had complained about was, in fact, an early symptom.

But Crane wasn't convinced. There was something about these spikes that troubled him.

Flipping back to the beginning of the printout, he turned the graph paper on its side. "Vertical reading"—examining the EEG from top to bottom rather than left to right—would allow him to concentrate on a particular brain wave and its distribution, rather than viewing the overall left-brain, right-brain picture. He turned the pages slowly, running his eye down the theta waveform.

Suddenly, he froze in place. "What the **hell**?" he said.

He dropped the printout on his desk and opened a nearby drawer, fishing for a ruler. Locating one, he quickly placed it against the paper, peering closely. As he did so, he felt a strange tingle start at the base of his neck and work its way down his spine.

Slowly, he sat back in his chair. "That's it," he murmured.

It seemed impossible—but the evidence lay right in front of him. The spikes in Mary Philips's theta waves were not the intermittent rise and fall of normal brain activity. They were not even random discharges of some physical pathology. The spikes were **regular**—precisely, inexplicably regular . . .

He pushed the Philips EEG aside and reached for the top readout from the stack the technician had brought him. It belonged to the man who had suffered the TIA, the ministroke. A quick examination confirmed it: the same theta spikes were present in his brain, as well.

It was the work of fifteen minutes to go through the rest of the EEGs. The patients had suffered from an incredible variety of symptoms: everything from sleeplessness to arrythmia to nausea to outright mania. And yet every one showed the same thing: spikes in their theta waveforms of a regularity and precision simply not found in nature.

He pushed the stack of printouts aside with a sense of unreality. At last he'd done it: he'd found the commonality. It **was** neurological. The theta waveforms of normal adults were supposed to be flatline. And even when they did spike, they were **never** supposed to fire in a precise, quantifiable rhythm. This was something utterly unknown to medical science.

He stood up and walked toward the internal phone, his thoughts piling up fast. He needed to consult with Bishop about this, and right away. With the autonomous nervous system affected, all these seemingly disparate symptoms suddenly snapped into place. He was a fool not to have seen it before. But how was it propagated? Neurological deficits on such a broad spectrum were absolutely unheard of . . .

Unless . . .

"Oh, Jesus," he breathed.

Quickly, almost frantically, he reached for a calculator. His gaze flew from the EEGs to the calculator as he furiously punched in numbers. Then he stopped abruptly, staring at the readout in disbelief.

"It couldn't be," he whispered.

The phone rang, shockingly loud in the quiet office. He jerked upright in his chair, then reached for it, heart racing. "Crane."

"Peter?" It was Asher's voice, sounding reedy and artificial in the oxygenated atmosphere of the hyperbaric chamber.

"Dr. Asher!" Crane said. "I've found the common vector! And, my God, it's something so—"

"Peter," Asher interrupted. "I need you to come

here right now. Just drop everything and get down here."

"But—"

"We've done it."

Crane paused, mentally struggling with this abrupt shift. "Deciphered the message?"

"Not message. Messages. It's all on the laptop." Asher's voice not only sounded thin—it had an air of desperation to it as well. "I need you here, Peter. Immediately. Because it's imperative, absolutely **imperative,** that we don't—"

There was a crackle, and then the phone abruptly went dead.

"Hello?" Crane frowned at the phone. "Dr. Asher? Hello?"

Silence.

Still frowning, Crane hung up the phone. He glanced at the pile of reports on his desk. Then he turned and quickly exited the office.

35

The last time Crane had been on deck 7—less than five hours before—the scientific level had been in its usual state of orderly bustle. But now when he stepped out of the elevator, he found himself in the midst of sudden chaos. Alarms were blaring; shouts mingled with cries; marines, technicians, and scientists ran past him. There was a feeling in the air very much like panic.

Crane stopped a maintenance worker. "What's going on?" he asked.

"Fire," the man said breathlessly.

Sudden fear lanced through Crane. As a sub-mariner, he had learned to dread fire underwater. "Where?"

"Hyperbaric chamber." And the man freed himself from Crane's grasp and ran off.

Crane's fear redoubled. **Asher . . .**

Without another thought, he tore down the hallway.

The hyperbaric suite was full of emergency response crews and rescue workers. As he pushed his way through the crowd, Crane caught the acrid scent of smoke.

"Doctor coming through!" he shouted, forcing himself into the control room. The tiny area was jammed with security personnel. Hopkins, one of the young medical technicians, was at the controls. Commander Korolis stood behind him. As Crane approached, Korolis glanced at him briefly, then returned his gaze to Hopkins without a word.

"What happened?" Crane asked Hopkins.

"Don't know." Sweat poured from Hopkins's forehead as his hands flew over the instrumentation. "I was down the hall in Pathology when the alarm sounded."

"When was that?"

"Two minutes ago, maybe three."

Crane glanced at his watch. It has been less than five minutes since Asher had telephoned him. "You've called in a paramedic team?"

"Yes, sir."

Crane looked through the glass partition toward the hyperbaric chamber itself. As he did so, he saw a gout of flame leap up the chamber porthole.

Jesus! It's still on fire!

"Why hasn't the water deluge system engaged?" he shouted at Hopkins.

"Don't know," the medic repeated, still feverishly working the controls. "Both the primary and backup extinguisher systems have been overridden somehow. They're not responding. I'm doing a crash depressurization now."

"You can't do that!" Crane said. "The chamber would have been at peak pressure!"

It was Korolis who answered. "With the sprinklers out, it's the only way to get the hatch open and extinguishers at the fire."

"The pressure in the chamber was set at two hundred kilopascals. I did it myself. You dump it suddenly, you'll kill Asher."

Korolis raised his eyes once again. "He's dead already."

Crane opened his mouth to speak, then stopped. Whether or not Korolis was right, they could not let the fire continue to burn: if it reached the oxygen tanks, the entire level might be threatened. There was no choice. Crane slammed his fist against the bulkhead in rage and frustration, then forced his way out into the waiting area.

Rescue teams were clustered around the entrance to the chamber, readying extinguishers and snugging oxygen masks over their mouths and noses. A small speaker above the glass partition to the control room squawked into life. "Full decompression in fifteen seconds," came the electrified voice of Hopkins.

The rescue crews checked their equipment, donned their masks.

"Decompression complete," said Hopkins. "Locks disengaging."

With a snap of electronic bolts, the entrance to the chamber sprang open. Immediately, heat and black smoke flooded into the waiting area. The stench of acrid smoke and burnt flesh suddenly became overpowering. Crane turned away involuntarily, eyes welling over with sudden tears. From behind came the sound of running feet, shouted orders, the sharp nasal gush of fire extinguishers.

He turned back. The extinguishers were still going. The crews were inside the cylinder itself now, and the dark plumes of smoke had been replaced by a thick fog of flame retardant. Stepping forward, he clambered into the chamber and forced his way past the rescue workers. Then he stopped abruptly.

Asher was lying on the floor, curled up around his laptop. Marris was lying nearby. They had crouched on the floor in an attempt to avoid the flames and smoke. A futile attempt: Asher's clothes hung in charred flakes from his limbs, and his skin was horribly blackened. His mane of gray hair had been burned away, and the bushy eyebrows singed to tiny curls.

Crane knelt quickly for a gross examination. Then he reconsidered. It seemed inconceivable Asher could have survived. Blood was flowing freely from his ears, but that was the only sign of movement. Barotrauma—the sudden loss of pressure—had ruptured his middle ear. And that would have been the least of the effects: the emergency depressurization would have caused massive gas embolisms, basically carbonating his blood. And the smoke inhalation, the massive third-degree burns . . .

The suddenness of this tragedy, the loss of a friend, the sheer waste of it all, staggered Crane; and yet part of him almost felt glad Asher was dead. The burns and the embolisms would have left him in unimaginable pain . . .

The emergency crews were receding now, the

palls of fog rolling away. Fire suppressant dripped from every surface. Outside the chamber, Crane heard a scattering of voices as the paramedic team arrived. Gently, he laid a hand on Asher's shoulder. "Good-bye, Howard," he said.

Asher's eyes flew open.

For a moment, Crane thought it was muscle contraction, the nucleotide ATP running down after death. But then the eye fixed itself on him.

"Fluids!" Crane called immediately to the paramedic team. "I need massive saline, **now**! Ice compresses!"

Slowly—agonizingly—Asher raised a claw that was little more than singed meat on bone. It gripped Crane's shirt collar, pulled him close. The chief scientist struggled to move blackened lips; they cracked with the effort, weeping clear fluid.

"Don't try to talk," Crane said in a low, soothing voice. "Lie still. We'll get you to Medical, get you comfortable."

But Asher would not lie still. His hand tightened around Crane's shirt. "Whip," he said in a desiccated whisper.

An EMT came up behind Crane and, with gloved fingers, began pulling back Asher's charred clothing and prepping an IV. Another one bent over the still form of Marris.

"Relax," Crane told Asher. "You'll be out of here in a moment."

Asher's grip grew tighter still, even as his limbs began to convulse. **"Whip . . ."**

He let out a high-pitched gasp and shuddered. His eyes flew up in his skull; there was a gargling in his ruined throat. Then his grip relaxed, his arm slid to the floor, and he spoke no more.

36

Crane sat at the desk in his quarters, staring at the computer monitor but seeing nothing. Several hours had passed since the accident but he was still numb. He'd taken a long shower, and he'd delivered his clothes to the laundry, yet his room still stank of charred hair and skin.

He felt a sense of disbelief that was almost paralysis. Was it really only eight hours since he'd performed the autopsy on Charles Vasselhoff? At the time, they'd had one postmortem report to write.

Now they had three.

In his mind, he kept seeing Howard Asher as he'd first appeared: an image on a screen in the Storm King library, tanned and smiling. **What we have here, Peter, is the scientific and historical discovery of all time.** Asher had never smiled again as much as he had on that first day. In retrospect, Crane wondered how much of it had been a show put on to make him feel welcome, feel comfortable.

There was a soft rap on the door, then it pushed open to reveal Michele Bishop. Her dark blond hair was pulled back severely, exaggerating her high cheekbones. Her eyes looked reddened and sad.

"Peter," she said, her voice low.

Crane wheeled his chair around. "Hi."

She stood in the doorway, uncharacteristically hesitant. "I just wanted to make sure you were okay."

"I've been better."

"It's just that you never said a single word. Not when we moved Asher's body to the Medical Suite. Not when we performed the final examinations. I guess I'm a little concerned."

"I can't understand what went wrong in the hyperbaric chamber. What caused the fire? Why was the sprinkler system off-line?"

"Spartan's ordered an investigation. He'll find out what went wrong."

"I should have done more. Checked the chamber myself. Tested the water deluge system."

Bishop took a step forward. "That's exactly what you **shouldn't** be thinking. You did everything you had to. It was an accident, that's all. A terrible accident."

There was a brief silence before Bishop spoke again. "I guess I'll head back to the Medical Suite. Can I bring you back something from the pharmaceutical locker? Xanax, Valium, anything?"

Crane shook his head. "I'll be fine."

"I'll look in on you later, then." And Bishop turned away.

"Michele?"

She looked back.

"Thanks."

She nodded, then left the stateroom.

Crane turned slowly back toward the terminal. He stared at it, without moving, for several minutes. Then he pushed himself roughly away from the desk and began pacing. That didn't help, either: he recalled how Asher had paced in much the same way on the day he'd revealed what Deep Storm was really about.

That had been just four days ago.

It was all so horribly ironic. Here, at last, he'd made the breakthrough—only for Asher to die before he could hear about it. Asher, who had brought him down to solve the medical mystery in the first place.

Of course he wasn't the only one who'd made a breakthrough. Asher had as well. But now he was dead: spontaneous pneumothorax, gas emboli, and third-degree burns over 80 percent of his body.

Bishop was right: he **had** been unnaturally silent in the aftermath of Asher's death. It wasn't only the shock, though that was part of it. It was also because of what he couldn't say. He'd wanted so badly to tell her what he'd discovered, to share it with someone. But she didn't have the necessary clearance. Unable to speak of it, he'd found himself saying nothing.

He couldn't put off the PM reports any longer.

He sat back down at his terminal, brought up his desktop. A blinking icon told him he had incoming mail.

With a sigh, he booted up his mail client, moused his way to the in-box. There was one new piece of electronic mail; curiously, no sender was listed.

"There is a time for many words, and there is also a time for sleep."
Homer, **Odyssey**, Book XI

Dr. Asher was a man of many words. Important words. Now, he can only sleep.

It is a tragedy indeed.

Too much death—and we have not even reached it yet. I fear the worst.

The burden is all on you now, my dear doctor. I'm forced to stay here; you are not. Find the answer, then leave, quick as you can.

If one must labor in darkness, one should not labor alone. Find a friend.

I'm afraid our irrational numbers here on the Facility have grown since we spoke in your cabin. But perhaps there's a silver lining, because, after all, the answer to your puzzle lies with them.

I bid thee good morrow.

F.

Crane frowned at the computer screen, unsure what to make of this cryptic message. **Find a friend . . .**

There was another knock on his door: Bishop, no doubt, returning with the meds he'd said he didn't need. "Come in, Michele," he said, closing the note.

The door opened. Hui Ping stood in the entrance.

Crane looked at her in surprise.

"I'm sorry," she said. "I hope I'm not disturbing you."

"Not at all," Crane said, recovering. "Come in."

Ping stepped in, took the seat Crane offered. "I just learned of Dr. Asher's death. I would have found out earlier, but I'd stumbled across something strange in the lab. Anyway, as soon as I heard . . . well, funny, but you were the only person that came to mind to talk to."

Crane inclined his head.

Abruptly, Ping rose. "It's selfish of me. After all, you were there. You must be feeling—"

"No, it's all right," Crane said. "I think I need to talk, too."

"About Dr. Asher?"

"No." **That's still too raw,** he thought. "About something I discovered."

Ping sat down again.

"You know how I've been running every test I could think of, following up leads, looking for the cause of what's making people ill."

Ping nodded.

"I was getting nowhere until something occurred to me: people were complaining about two completely different **kinds** of symptoms. Some were physiological: nausea, muscle tics, a horde of others. Others were psychological: sleeplessness, confusion, even mania. I'd always believed there had to be a common factor involved. But what kind of factor could cause both? That's when I got the idea the underlying cause had to be neurological."

"Why?"

"Because the brain controls both the mind and the body. So I ordered EEG tests. And just today I got back the first set of tests. Every patient had spikes in the theta waves of their brains—waves that are supposed to be quiet in adults. Even stranger, the pattern of spikes was exactly the same **for every patient**. That's when I got a crazy idea. I plotted the pattern of spikes. And you know what I discovered?"

"I can't imagine."

Crane opened the drawer of his desk, pulled out a manila envelope, and handed it to Ping. She opened it and pulled out a computer printout.

"This is Asher's digital code," she said. "The one the sentinels are transmitting."

"Exactly."

She frowned in incomprehension. Then, suddenly, her eyes widened. "Oh, no. You don't mean . . ."

"I do. The spikes in the theta waves **match** the pulses of light. **It's the same message as the one the sentinels were first transmitting.**"

"But how is that possible? Why didn't we detect anything?"

"I'm not sure. But I have a theory. We already

know those sentinels are broadcasting their message on every conceivable wavelength of electromagnetic radiation—radio waves, microwaves, ultraviolet, infrared. We also know whatever created those sentinels has technology far beyond our own. So who's to say they're not also broadcasting their messages on other channels, other types of radiation **we don't even know how to detect yet**?"

"Such as?"

"Quark radiation, maybe. Or a new type of particle that can pass through matter, like Higgs bosons. The point is it's some unknown form of radiation, undetectable by our instruments, that interferes with the electrical impulses in our brains."

"Why doesn't it affect everybody?"

"Because biological systems aren't equal. Just as some people have heavier bones, some people have more resistant nervous systems. Or perhaps there are structures in the Facility that inadvertently act as Faraday cages."

"As **what**?"

"Faraday cages—enclosures built to isolate things from electromagnetic fields. But I think everybody here **is** affected—just in different degrees. I haven't exactly felt like myself recently . . . have you?"

Hui thought a moment. "No. No, I haven't."

There was a brief silence.

"So are you going to take this to Admiral Spartan?" Hui asked.

"Not yet."

"Why not? Sounds to me like your work is done."

"Spartan hasn't been very sympathetic to any viewpoint other than his own. I don't want to tell him prematurely, give him an excuse to dismiss it. The more evidence I have, the better. And that means finding the other piece."

"What other piece is that?"

"Before he died, Asher discovered something. There, in the hyperbaric chamber. I know, because he told me so, over the phone. It's all on the laptop, he said. I need to get that laptop, find out what he discovered. Because he was desperate to tell me something, there at the end. He kept repeating one word: **whip.**"

Hui frowned again. "Whip?"

"Yes."

"Whip who? Or what? And why?"

"The secret to that's on his computer—if the hard drive is salvageable."

Another thoughtful silence fell over the stateroom. At last, Crane roused himself and turned toward Hui Ping. "Want to head down to Times Square, get an espresso?"

Hui brightened. "Sure."

They stepped out into the hall. "Perhaps I can help you," she said.

"How?"

"As part of my computer science degree, I spent a summer interning at a data recovery facility."

Crane turned to her. "You mean, you can retrieve data off ruined hard drives?"

"I didn't actually do the recovery myself—I was just an intern, after all. But I watched the process plenty of times, assisted in several."

They stopped at the elevator. "Earlier, you said you'd stumbled over something strange in the lab," Crane said. "What was it?"

"Sorry? Oh, yes. Remember those absorption lines I showed you? The ones the sentinal in my lab was emitting?"

"The ones you said could only come from a distant star?"

"Right."

The elevator doors whispered open, they stepped in, and Crane pressed the button for deck 9. "Well," Hui continued, "just for kicks, I ran that set of absorption lines against a database of known stars. You see, every star has a unique absorption signature. And guess what? I found an exact match."

"Between your little sentinel and a faraway star?"

Hui nodded. "One hundred and forty light-years away, to be exact. Cygnus Major, otherwise known as M81."

"You think that's where the marker came from?"

"Well, that's just it. That star, Cygnus Major, has only one planet. A gas giant, with oceans of sulfuric acid and a methane atmosphere."

Crane felt puzzled. "No mistake?"

Hui shook her head. "Absorption line signatures are as unique as fingerprints. No mistake."

"You think that—on top of everything else—they're trying to tell us where they come from?"

"Looks that way to me."

"Well, that's strange. Because what could a planet of methane and acid possibly see in the oxygen and water of Earth?"

"Exactly." And as the elevator doors opened onto Crew Support, she turned and gave him a speculative look.

37

The floor of the hyperbaric therapy suite was thick with debris: empty extinguisher casings, bandage wrappers, disposable gloves. Commander Terrence W. Korolis stepped around it all with the finicky precision of a cat.

Two commandos in black ops fatigues stood outside the doorway, barring entry to what was being treated as an active crime scene. Another stood guard by the control room. Korolis found their chief, Woburn, in the waiting area next to the hyperbaric chamber itself, speaking to a technician. The entrance hatch to the chamber was open; heavy scorch marks ran along its upper edge and across the nearby ceiling, which was caked with soot.

When Woburn caught sight of Korolis he nodded to the technician and stepped away, following Korolis into the control room. The commander waited until Woburn had shut the door behind them.

"Update, please, Chief," Korolis said.

"Sir." Woburn carried his well-muscled body with stiff precision. "The safety circuits were deliberately bypassed."

"And the internal sprinklers?"

"Deactivated."

"What about the fire? Any theories how it started?"

Woburn jerked a thumb in the direction of the observation window. "The compressor, sir. The technician believes it was tampered with."

"How?"

"It seems the step-down transformer was disengaged while the compressor was running at maximum."

Korolis nodded slowly. "Forcing the RPMs to spike."

"And the compressor to overheat, first, then basically explode into flame. Yes, sir."

"Where could this have been performed?"

"There's a support closet beyond the hyperbaric suite, tucked between two of the science labs. All the work could have been done from there."

"Would it have taken long?"

"The technician said if the person knew what he was doing, it might have taken two, maybe three minutes, tops."

Korolis nodded. The person knew what he was doing, all right. Just as he'd known how to score the inside of the dome with a laser cutter. A good saboteur was trained in how to wreck or blow up almost anything.

Korolis knew all about that kind of training.

He turned back to Woburn. "Any cameras tasked on that support closet?"

"Negative, sir."

"Very well."

Korolis paused to glance out the observation window. The technician had ducked inside the hyperbaric chamber and was now out of visual contact. Aside from the operatives in dark fatigues, there were no witnesses.

He turned to Woburn again. "You have it here?" Although the door was closed, he spoke in a tone even softer than before.

Woburn gave a slight nod.

"Nobody saw you take it?"

"Only our own men, sir."

"Excellent."

Woburn knelt beside the control console, reached underneath it, and extracted a slim case of black ballistic nylon. He handed it to Korolis, along with a key.

"Do you want us to conduct a further investigation, sir?" Woburn asked. "Inquire whether any of the scientists saw anything, or anyone, unusual?"

"There's no need for that, Chief. I'll take over from here and relay my findings to the admiral."

"Very good, sir." And Woburn executed a superbly crisp salute.

Korolis regarded him a moment. Then he returned the salute and left the hyperbaric suite.

Korolis's private quarters were in a special section of deck 11 reserved for military officers. He stepped inside, then closed and carefully locked the door before moving toward his desk. The stateroom was dimly lit. Where others might have set framed pictures or light reading, Korolis had security monitors and classified manuals.

He placed the nylon case Woburn had given him on the desk, then unlocked it with the key. Unzipping the case, he reached inside and pulled out a laptop computer, badly scorched along one side.

The stateroom filled with the acrid stench of burnt plastic and electronics.

Korolis turned to his environmental control panel, put its air-scrubbing filter on full. Then he took a seat and pulled the terminal keyboard toward him. He entered the password for his private computer, then entered a second, much longer passphrase to enter a secure area of the Facility's military network, accessible only by him. Next, he loaded a forensic audio program of the type used by audio restoration engineers and wiretappers. Then, bringing up a list of files, he paged through the entries until he found the one he wanted. Loading this into the forensic program brought up a complex screen dominated by an audio waveform: a mono sound file captured by a tiny microphone.

Korolis plugged a pair of headphones into the computer. Then he adjusted the program's spectral filter to remove extraneous noise, boosted the gain, and clicked the playback button.

Over the headphones came Crane's voice, remarkably clear given the low fidelity of the surveillance microphone.

"Before he died, Asher discovered something . . . I know, because he told me so, over the phone. It's all on the laptop, he said. I need to get that laptop, find out what he discovered. Because he was desperate to tell me something, there at the end . . ."

Then came another voice: a voice the program's soundprint analyzer had identified as Hui Ping's. Korolis's face darkened as he listened.

"The secret to that's on his computer," Crane went on.

With a click of his mouse, Korolis stopped the playback. Another click closed the file and exited the program.

Korolis stood, carrying Asher's damaged laptop over to a far corner of the room, where a gray locker sat on the floor. Kneeling, he unsnapped its clasps, opened it, and pulled out a bulky object: a degaussing magnet.

Once again, he made sure the door to his stateroom was locked. Then—slowly and deliberately, and careful to stay well away from his own computer—he held the magnet close to the laptop, passing it over the hard disk. Even if it had survived the fire, this would certainly scramble its data beyond all recognition.

Crane and Hui Ping were serious security risks—and one couldn't be too sure. This step was a start. And Korolis knew exactly what to do next.

38

Cold Storage Locker 1-C, on the lowest level of the Facility, was a grim place. The temperature was regulated to a precise 38.5 degrees Fahrenheit. The flooring consisted of wooden pallets, placed over a bilgelike inch of cold, dirty water. The lighting was faint, throwing the claustrophobic space into heavy gloom. The air smelled of mold and butchered meat. The only sound was the faint dripping of water.

Admiral Spartan stood in the center of the locker, staring at the horribly mangled remains of

Marble One. It hovered before him like a crum-
pled foil ball, lashed around by heavy chain and
suspended from the ceiling by a large, cruel-
looking hook. To one side lay the heavy blue tarp
he'd just pulled away.

What flaw caused this disaster? As a military officer, he'd made it his life's work to achieve victory
by anticipating failure—his own or an enemy's—
and either forestalling or exploiting it. But how
could you anticipate failure when you were working with a rule set that was utterly, incomprehen-
sibly foreign?

It was true that, since Marble One had been
destroyed, Marble Two and Marble Three had
continued operations without delay. They had
implemented the changes recommended by Asher
and his scientific team, and there had been no further problems. If anything, the work was going
even more swiftly than anticipated: the third,
lowest layer of the crust had proven to be of a
softer, almost siltlike material that could be excavated very quickly, and they were on track to
reach the Mohorovicic discontinuity in days now.

Asher. The chief scientist's warning, in the wake
of Marble One's destruction and the deaths of its
crew, sounded again in the admiral's head: **My
recommendation is that we cease all operations
until we have a thorough understanding of
what caused this disaster.**

And now Asher, too, was dead.

There was a screech of metal behind him, and the door to the locker opened, throwing a stripe of yellow light across the dark interior. Commander Korolis—who had a feline distaste for being either cold or wet—wedged the door open and stepped inside.

Spartan glanced at him. "Your report, Commander?"

Korolis approached. "The sprinkler system in the hyperbaric chamber was compromised. And the compressor was overloaded, causing an explosion and fire inside the chamber itself. No question about it: this was an act of sabotage."

"An act of murder," Spartan said.

"As you say, sir."

Spartan turned back toward the ruined Marble. "This time, it seems a particular person was targeted rather than the entire Facility. Why?"

"I don't have an answer to that yet, sir. Perhaps we simply caught a break."

Once again, Spartan glanced over at Korolis. "Caught a break, Commander?"

"In terms of the target. We were lucky the saboteur didn't go after a more strategic asset."

"I see. And just how much more strategic an asset could we have than Dr. Asher?"

"Asher's usefulness to the project was growing questionable. He'd become a Cassandra, sir—his talk of gloom and doom, his eagerness to derail the excavation schedule, wasn't good for morale."

"Indeed." Spartan reflected that if Korolis had any personal failings, frankness was not one of them.

"That's my opinion anyway, sir. To be honest, I'm surprised it's not yours as well."

Spartan ignored the innuendo, instead waving a hand at the remains of Marble One. "And what of **this**?"

"Tapes of the transmissions have been carefully analyzed, along with the black box from the Doodlebug. Unlike the hyperbaric chamber, there's absolutely no sign of tampering or foul play. Equipment malfunction, plain and simple."

Spartan fell silent for a moment, contemplating the obscene tangle of metal. Then he roused himself. "Any progress on identifying the responsible individual?"

"Yes. We've isolated one individual who was in both locations—Outer Hull Receiving and the hyperbaric oxygen suite—directly before the sabotage incidents took place."

"And who would that be?"

Wordlessly, Korolis drew an envelope out of his breast pocket and handed it to Spartan. The admiral opened it, gazed at the contents for a moment, then handed it back.

"Dr. Ping?" he said.

Korolis nodded. "Her Chinese background always struck me as a little suspicious. And wasn't it your opinion, sir, that the saboteur must be in the employ of a foreign government?"

"She was thoroughly vetted, just like everybody else."

"Things can slip through the cracks sometimes. Especially if somebody wants them to slip through badly enough. You know that as well as I do, sir."

"Your recommendation?"

"That she be detained in the security brig until a thorough interrogation can be undertaken."

At this, Spartan turned toward Korolis, eyebrows rising. "Isn't that rather precipitous?"

"The safety of the entire Facility hangs in the balance."

Spartan's lips twitched in a small and bitter smile. "What about her right to habeas corpus?"

Korolis stared back in surprise. "Under the circumstances, sir, that's not a consideration."

When Spartan didn't answer, Korolis spoke again. "There's something else. Remember Asher's last word, the one he repeated to Crane?"

Spartan nodded. " 'Whip.' "

"What if he wasn't saying 'whip' at all? What if he was **trying** to say Hui Ping?"

Looking at Korolis, Spartan's eyes narrowed.

"That's right, sir. 'Hui P . . . Hui P . . .' It sounds exactly the same—**'wee P.'**"

At last, Spartan roused himself. "Very well. But there's no need for the brig. Just have her confined to quarters until the matter can be resolved."

"Sir, with all due respect, I think the brig would be—"

"Just follow orders, Commander."

There was a flicker of movement over Korolis's shoulder. Spartan glanced up to see Peter Crane standing in the open doorway.

"Dr. Crane," he said, raising his voice a trifle. "Don't stand on ceremony. Come join us."

Korolis turned quickly, sucking in his breath with a hiss of surprise.

Crane came forward, his short dark hair and dark eyes in sharp contrast to the white of his medical coat. Spartan wondered how long he'd been standing there, and how much he had heard.

"What can we do for you, Doctor?" he asked.

Crane's gray eyes moved from Spartan, to Korolis, to what was left of the Marble, before returning to the admiral. "I was looking for Commander Korolis, actually."

"You seem to have found him."

Crane turned to Korolis. "Those characters you have guarding the hyperbaric therapy suite told me to speak with you. I want Asher's laptop."

Korolis frowned. "Why?"

"I think he discovered something just before the accident happened. Perhaps the meaning of the signals the sentinels are transmitting."

"The laptop was severely damaged in the fire," Korolis said.

"It's worth a shot," Crane replied quickly. "Wouldn't you agree?"

Spartan watched the exchange with curiosity. Clearly, these were two men who had very little use for each other.

Now Korolis lifted his gaze to Spartan, who nodded almost imperceptibly.

"Very well," the commander said. "Come with me. It's being held in an evidence locker."

"Thanks." Crane glanced at Spartan, nodded, then turned to follow Korolis out of the locker.

"Dr. Crane?" Spartan said.

Crane glanced back.

"If you find anything, report it to me immediately, please."

"Very well."

Korolis saluted and the two men stepped out of the locker. But Spartan stood there in the chill air, looking thoughtfully after them, for a long time.

39

Crane found Hui Ping in her lab, scrutinizing an absorption line printout and making notations on the pale green datasheet with a felt marker. She looked up as he entered, smiled.

"Oh, good," she said. "You got the laptop."

The smile faltered as she caught the expression on his face. "Peter. Something wrong?"

Crane stepped forward. He glanced up at the security camera mounted in the ceiling, stayed carefully out of its field of view. "I have to ask you something. Have you ever been to Outer Hull Receiving?"

"You mean, the place where the Tub docks with fresh supplies?" She shook her head. "Never."

"Where were you around the time Asher died?"

"Here, in my lab. I was studying these absorption lines, remember? I told you that."

"So you were nowhere near the hyperbaric chamber."

"No." Ping frowned. "Why? What are you getting at?"

Crane hesitated. He was about to take a calculated risk—and, very probably, break every rule in the lengthy agreements he'd signed when he came here. It was true he could think of no reason why Korolis would lie about Ping's involvement. And aiding a suspected saboteur was a treasonable offense. But his gut told him she was trustworthy.

Besides, she was the only person who could help him learn what Asher had discovered.

He licked his lips. "Listen carefully. Korolis claims you're the saboteur."

Ping's eyes widened. "Me? But—"

"Just listen. He's convinced Spartan to put you under house arrest. A detail will be down here to escort you to your quarters at any moment."

"That can't be." Her breathing grew fast and shallow. "That's not right."

He gestured her toward him, out of camera range. "Calm down, it's okay. I'm getting you out of here."

"But **where**?"

"Just relax. I need you to think. Is there a lab or some other place where you can work on the laptop? Somewhere isolated, out of the way, without security cameras?"

Hui didn't answer.

"Look, I'm not going to let them take you. But we have to get out of here. Now do you know of a place like that?"

She nodded, making an effort to calm herself. "On deck six. The Maritime Applied Physics Lab."

"Okay. But there's something I need to do first. Step over here, out of the camera's view." And—reaching into the pocket of his lab coat—he pulled out a sterile wrapper. As Hui drew close, he tore away the wrapper, exposing a number 12 scalpel that gleamed in the artificial light.

When she saw the scalpel, Hui stopped. "What's that for?"

"I need to remove the RFID tags they inserted in us," Crane said, pulling out additional medical equipment and laying it on the table. "Otherwise, they'll find us anywhere."

He pulled up the sleeve of his lab coat, swabbed the dimpled area on his forearm with disinfectant.

He let the scalpel hover over his skin a moment as he held his breath.

The first incision sliced through the epidermis. The second penetrated the dermis and exposed the RFID tag, embedded amid yellow subcutaneous fat. Hui looked away as he plucked out the radio tag with tissue forceps, then let it drop to the floor of the lab and crushed it underfoot.

"There," he said. "Now I can't be tracked like some migrating fowl."

He dressed and sterilized the wound, applied a butterfly closure, and tossed the scalpel in the wastebasket. Then—pulling another sterile scalpel from his pocket—he turned toward her.

She took an involuntary step backward.

"Don't worry," he said. "I've got an anesthetic pad to numb your skin. The only reason I didn't use one on myself was because I accidentally grabbed just one from the dispensary in the temporary infirmary."

Still, she hesitated.

"Hui," he said. "You've **got** to trust me."

She sighed, nodded. Then she stepped forward again, pushing up her own sleeve as she did so.

40

"Ready?" Crane said, disposing of the medical instruments. "Then take what you need and let's go."

Hui hesitated a moment. Then she walked to her desk, pulled open a drawer, and removed a bulky tool kit. Next, she disconnected her laptop from the network, unplugged it, and tucked it beneath her arm.

"What's that for?" Crane asked, nodding at her laptop.

"Spare parts." She straightened. "Ready."

"Lead the way, then. Avoid marines and security cameras."

They left the radiology lab and made their way down the narrow corridors of deck 3. At the first intersection, Hui stopped, then chose the right-hand path to avoid a security camera. They followed the corridor to the end, where it dog-legged left.

Crane turned the corner, then stopped. Ahead of them, to one side of the hallway, two marines stood on guard outside a closed, red-painted door.

He thought quickly. The marines had radios clipped to their belts. But chances were very good there hadn't been any general announcement made about a search for Hui. If they were to back up it would look far more suspicious.

He reached for Hui's hand, gave it a brief, in-conspicuous tug. Then he started forward, swing-ing Asher's laptop case with what he hoped was the right degree of indifference. After a moment, he saw—from the corner of his eye—Hui begin to follow him.

Crane passed the marines, who eyed him but said nothing.

They passed a half dozen closed doors, then arrived at another intersection. To the left, more marines were stationed.

"I can't do this," Hui whispered to Crane.

"You've **got** to."

She paused for a moment, clearly trying to think. "There's a maintenance stairway behind Bottom we can take to deck six. This way." She turned and started down the right-hand corridor.

The cafeteria was relatively quiet, a dozen people sitting in small clusters at the white-topped tables. Hui led the way along one wall to the swinging doors that opened onto the cramped kitchen. It was as crowded as the cafeteria was empty. In one corner, Crane saw Renault, the executive chef, but the man was busily plating a meal and did not look up.

Hui walked across the tiny kitchen, past the cold storage unit, and pulled open a metal hatch in the rear wall. A narrow metal stairway lay beyond. Ducking through and closing the hatch behind them, they made their way quickly up three flights of stairs to deck 6. The stairway ended here—no doubt, Crane realized, because directly above lay the Barrier, the no-man's-land between the classified and non-classified areas.

On the landing, Hui paused to collect herself. She reached for the handle, took a deep breath. Then she opened the hatch.

An empty corridor lay beyond.

She gave a sigh of relief. "The lab's just down this hallway."

She led Crane past a maintenance room and an unoccupied office, then stopped outside a door labeled MARITIME APPLIED PHYSICS and opened it briskly. Crane made a final scan of the hall, making doubly sure there were no witnesses or security cameras. Then he followed her into the darkened lab, closing the door quietly behind him.

Hui snapped on the lights, revealing a large, well-appointed space. There was a central table on which sat a stereozoom microscope and an autoclave. A couple of lab stools were snugged up to one side. An open door in the rear wall led to an equipment locker; to either side stood racks of oscilloscopes, galvanometers, and other gear Crane couldn't identify. A large drop cloth of some unusual material hung from a hook beside one of the equipment racks. It gave off a silvery sheen under the fluorescent light.

Crane walked over to the drop cloth, rubbed it between his fingers. "What's this?" he asked.

"Fire suppressant cloth. Just in case an experiment goes awry."

He nodded. "And why isn't this lab being used?"

"Dr. Asher had planned to take this opportunity—being on the Facility, I mean—to run some deep-water tests. Capillary-gravity wave analysis, current sedimentology, that sort of thing. After all, having a resource like this is the chance of a lifetime."

"What happened?"

"He was overruled by Spartan. Needed extra

manpower for the excavation, it seemed. Lost bunk space for half a dozen of the scientists he'd been counting on." She walked over to the lab table, placed her laptop and tool kit on it. "You can set Asher's laptop here," she said. "As gently as possible, please. This kind of work should really be done in a class one hundred clean room: if we raise any dust, or if dirt gets on the exposed media, our chances of retrieving any data will become that much slimmer."

Crane set the laptop case carefully on the table. Hui rubbed her hands together for a moment, orienting herself. Then she began rummaging through various drawers, assembling a small arsenal of equipment: latex gloves, surgical masks, scalpels; a high-intensity work lamp; a magnifying lens in a tabletop stand; cans of compressed air. She opened her tool kit and spread the contents out on the table. Then she slipped a grounding strap over her wrist and glanced at him.

"What are we looking for, exactly?" she asked.

"I don't know for sure. Somehow, we have to reconstruct Asher's final journey of discovery."

Hui nodded. As Crane watched, she slowly unzipped the case and pulled out the damaged laptop. One end was badly burned, the plastic housing partially melted. Scorch marks and smoke covered its surface. Crane's heart sank.

Hui pulled on the pair of gloves, fixed the surgical mask over her face. She handed another mask to Crane, gesturing for him to follow suit. Using the can of compressed air, she gave the already-spotless table a cleansing blast. Then she used a screwdriver from her tool kit to remove the laptop's back plate. This was followed by the motherboard and the power supply. Now the hard drive itself was exposed.

"We might be lucky," she said. "The hard drive was away from the worst of the damage."

Moving to her own laptop, she disassembled it in turn. The work, the challenge, seemed to calm her. Watching, Crane was impressed by how quickly and skillfully she was able to break the computer down into its component parts.

Now, taking Asher's hard drive carefully in hand, she carried it over to her own laptop and substituted it for her drive. She quickly reassembled her laptop, plugged it in, turned it on. There was a loud clicking sound, followed by several beeps. An error message appeared on the screen and the computer refused to boot.

"What's that noise?" Crane asked.

"At the data recovery facility I interned at, they called that the Click of Death. It usually means a servo failure or something similar."

"That's bad, right?"

"I don't know yet. We've got to open up the drive."

She powered down her laptop, disassembled it again, and removed Asher's hard drive. Setting it carefully on the table, she motioned Crane to step back. Using a series of tiny screwdrivers, scalpels, and some tools that to Crane looked more suitable for a dentist's office, she coaxed off the top half of the housing. Bringing the work lamp close, she aimed it at the hard drive. The inner workings stood revealed in the glare: a series of thin, gold cylinders stacked one atop another, each sporting a tiny read/write arm, the whole surrounded by a tiny green forest of integrated circuits.

Hui leaned in with the magnifying lens, giving the drive a close inspection. "There doesn't appear to have been a head crash," she said. "The platters look like they're in good condition." A pause. "I think I see the problem. There are burned chips on the PCB."

"PCB?"

"Primary controller board."

"Can you repair it?"

"Probably. I'll swap out the board with the one from my laptop."

Crane frowned. "You can do that?"

"Every laptop on the Facility is precisely the same model. You know the government—always buy in bulk."

Working through the magnifying lens, Hui used jeweler's tools to remove a tiny portion of the drive mechanism. "It's really fused," she said, holding it up to the magnifying lens and turning it this way and that with a pair of tweezers. "We're lucky the platters themselves weren't melted."

She put it aside. Opening the hard drive from her own laptop, she carefully removed the same piece, attached it to Asher's drive, and replaced the top of the housing.

"Moment of truth," she said, returning the damaged drive to her laptop. She quickly re-assembled the computer, plugged it in, gave the interior a gentle blast of canned air, and switched it on again.

Crane drew close, staring eagerly at the screen. The same error message reappeared.

"Damn," he said.

"But the Click of Death is gone," Hui replied. "And did you notice there were no warning beeps during the POST?"

"What's that mean?"

"The laptop sees the hard drive now, no prob-lem. It just can't find any data."

Crane swore under his breath.

"We're not done yet." She slipped a jewel case from her tool kit, opened it, and took out a CD. "This is a bootable disc with an assortment of di-agnostic tools. Let's take a closer look at Asher's hard drive."

She slipped the disc into the laptop and re-started it. This time the screen came to life. The disc drive trundled for a moment, then several windows opened. Hui took a seat at the lab table and began typing. Crane peered over her shoulder.

For several minutes, Hui moused her way through a variety of windows. Long series of bi-nary and hexadecimal numbers appeared, scrolled up the screen, then disappeared again. At last, she sat back.

"The hard drive is operable," she said. "I can't detect any further physical damage."

"Then why can't we read it?" Crane asked.

Hui looked at him. "Because it appears some-body has erased all the data on it."

"Erased?"

She removed her face mask, shook out her hair, and nodded. "Based on the electromagnetic pat-tern, it seems somebody used a degausser on it."

"And this was done **after** the fire?"

"Must have been. Asher wouldn't have done it himself."

"But why?" Crane felt stunned. "That makes no sense. For all anybody knew, the laptop was ru-ined."

"I guess somebody wanted to make sure of that."

Slowly, Crane pulled out the other lab stool and sat down. He took off his own mask and dropped it on the table. All of a sudden, he felt very old.

"That's it, then," he said. "Now we'll never know what Asher found."

He sighed. Then he glanced at Hui. What he saw surprised him. She was looking back, a small smile on her face that—at any other time—he might have termed mischievous.

"What is it?" he asked.

"I still have one or two tricks up my sleeve."

"What are you talking about? The hard drive's been erased."

"Yes. But that doesn't mean the data's gone."

He shook his head. "I don't understand."

"It's like this. When you erase data on a hard drive, you're really just overwriting that data with random zeros and ones. But you see, when the read/write head writes that new data, it uses **only enough signal** necessary to set the bit. That's the way hard drives work: just enough signal, and no more."

"Why is that?"

"To make sure that adjoining bits aren't affected. Anyway, because the signal isn't powerful enough to fully saturate the platter, whatever data was previously there is—like a ghost—going to affect the **overall** strength of the signal in that location."

Crane looked at her, uncomprehending.

"Let's say you have two positions on a hard drive, side by side. The first contains a zero, the second contains a one. Then somebody comes along and overwrites those two positions with two ones. So now we have a one in **both** positions. But guess what? Because the read/write head uses the **bare minimum of signal** to write those ones, the position that had a **zero** in it before has a weaker signal strength than the position that had a **one** in it."

"So the data that was there before affects the new data that overwrites it," Crane said.

"Exactly."

"And you've got a tool that can resurrect that old, overwritten data?"

Hui nodded. "It takes an absolute value of the signal and subtracts it from what's actually on the hard disk. That leaves us with a shadow image of what had been there before."

"I had no idea that was possible." Crane paused. "But wait a minute. The data wasn't overwritten. You said it was degaussed. Demagnetized. How can you restore that?"

"Whatever kind of degausser was used, it doesn't seem to have been very powerful: probably a hand-held model. Or maybe the person who did this didn't take into account that the platters of the hard disk have a small amount of shielding.

Anyway, a light degaussing is the equivalent of overwriting the hard disk two, maybe three times. And my equipment has the capability of restoring data that's been overwritten **twice** as many times as that."

Crane could only shake his head.

"But the process is destructive. We'll only have one pass at it—and that means we'll need another hard drive to dump the reconstructed data onto. I trashed mine when I removed the PCB." She glanced at him. "Can I borrow yours?"

Crane smiled. "Seems we're going through laptops pretty fast. Sure, I'll get it now."

"I'll get the data recovery started." Hui pushed the magnifying glass aside and reached for her tool kit.

"You be safe." And Crane turned and quietly left the lab.

41

The man calling himself Wallace limped quietly through the maze of passages making up the science facilities of the refitted Storm King oil platform. He moved more quickly than usual: he had only now received a message in his quarters—a coded signal, transmitted via low-frequency radio—and he had to pass it on to the operative on Deep Storm immediately.

The Tub left in twenty minutes, bound for the ocean floor. If he hurried, he might just make it.

Reaching his office, he turned on the light, then

shut and locked the door. The courier bag sat on his desk, ready to be delivered to the Recovery Chamber on the lowest level of the platform. He opened it, rummaged through its contents, then pulled out a CD hand-labeled RADIOGRAPHS 001136–001152.

Image files—precisely what he needed.

He inserted the CD into his computer, loaded one of the images at random into memory. He removed the CD, placed it back in its jewel case, and returned it to the courier bag. Next, he wrote a short routine that would embed a message into the least significant bits of the pixels of the radiograph image. It was the work of five minutes to type in the computer program and double-check it for bugs.

The man pressed a function key, causing the short routine to execute. A question mark appeared on screen: the routine was requesting input. He carefully typed in the message he'd been ordered to relay. Then he paused, finger hovering over the enter key, while he examined the message for accuracy:

IF WORK IS NOT STOPPED
DESTROY FACILITY WITHIN 24 HOURS

Satisfied, he pressed the key. The message disappeared from the screen; there was a brief pause as the program converted the message into its binary equivalent, then hid it within the digital code of the radiograph. A short chirp indicated that the process had been completed successfully.

Wallace smiled.

Opening a drawer, he pulled out a writable CD, slid it into the drive, and instructed the computer to burn a copy of the doctored radiograph. While the machine worked, he sat back in his chair, cleaning his glasses with his shirttail. The image was not large, and within a few minutes the new disk had been burned. He ejected it and quickly powered down the computer, instantly destroying all traces of his work. Pulling a fresh jewel case from the open drawer, he inserted the CD, wrote the recipient's name on it with a black marker, then slipped it into the courier bag.

He stood up, slung the bag over his shoulder, glanced at his watch.

Twelve minutes to spare. Excellent.

Unlocking his door, he stepped out, whistling to himself as he made his way to the Recovery Chamber and the waiting Tub.

42

Hui Ping sat bolt upright on the lab stool, dropping a screwdriver on the table with a clatter, as Crane crept into the lab.

"God!" she said. "You practically scared me to death."

"Sorry."

"You took so long. What happened?"

"I just had to return a few messages, back in my stateroom." Crane didn't bother to mention the ten-minute questioning he'd just endured on his way back through the Barrier: two marines who were very eager to discover the location of Dr. Ping. There was no point making her more nervous than she already was.

"How are you coming?" he asked, stepping forward and placing his laptop on the table.

Hui was laboring over a complex contraption that, to Crane's untrained eye, appeared to be several lab instruments joined by a forest of ribbon cables. In response to his question, she pushed herself away from the table.

"Just finished the last test."

"Looks like rocket science to me."

"It **is** rocket science. Almost. A magnetometer, chained to an A/D converter, and both in turn slaved to a timecode striper. The whole thing's capable of making a bit-by-bit copy of Dr. Asher's erased hard drive."

Crane whistled. "Trust Asher to fit his labs up properly. What if you didn't have all these cool toys?"

"The magnetometer is vital. I could do without the rest, but it would take a lot longer." She reached for his laptop, then paused. "I'm going to have to wipe your hard drive. Sure you don't mind?"

Crane shrugged. "Go ahead. All my files are on the network, anyway."

Hui booted up his laptop and typed in a series of commands. "This may take a few minutes."

A silence settled over the lab while the hard drive trundled.

"While retrieving my laptop, I did some thinking," Crane said at last. "Whoever degaussed Asher's computer wanted to make ultra sure what Asher discovered remained a secret."

"I was thinking the same thing. But that person also didn't want anybody to **know** he was trashing it."

"Precisely my point. Otherwise they could have simply taken a sledgehammer to the laptop."

"But who? And why?"

"The saboteur?" Crane said.

"Seems unlikely, doesn't it? I don't know his motives, but if I was the saboteur, I'd want that data for **myself**." Hui stood up.

"My money's on Korolis," Crane said.

"Why's that?"

"As far as I can tell, he lied about your presence at Outer Hull Receiving and in the hyperbaric suite." He hesitated. "Does your resumé mention that internship at the data recovery facility?"

Hui nodded.

"So he knows about that, too. I don't think he wants anybody learning what's on this laptop."

"I hope you're wrong. He'd make a very dangerous enemy." Hui stood up. "We're set."

Removing the case from his laptop, she attached the end of a ribbon cable to the hard drive, leaving the power cables connected. Then she powered up the chain of devices, made a few adjustments, and simultaneously engaged switches on the magnetometer and the digital timecode device. A low whirring filled the lab.

"How long will this take?" Crane asked.

"Not long. Apparently, Dr. Asher was like you—he did most of his work via dumb terminal on the Facility's mainframe. I doubt the laptop holds more than his personal e-mail, Internet files, and the work on the codes."

Ten minutes went by in which little was said. Hui monitored the extraction process while Crane puttered around the lab, picking up instruments and replacing them, trying not to grow impatient. At last the whirring noise stopped.

"That's it." Hui turned off the devices, removed the ribbon cable, placed the case back on Crane's laptop. She turned toward him. "Your hard drive should now be a replica of Asher's. Ready?"

"Fire it up."

She pressed the power button and they both crowded around, watching the screen. For a moment, it remained black. Then there was a brief chirp and the OS splash screen appeared.

"Bingo," Hui said softly.

Crane waited as she loaded a file management

utility from one of her CDs and began exploring Asher's documents.

"Everything appears to be intact," she said. "No data dropouts."

"What's there?"

"It's as I suspected. E-mail, a few scientific articles in progress. And then a large folder titled 'decrypt.'"

"Take a look at that."

Hui typed a series of commands. "It contains several utilities I'm not familiar with—probably language translators or decryption routines. There are three subdirectories, as well. One called 'initial,' another called 'source,' and a third called 'target.'"

"Let's see what's in 'initial.'"

Hui moved her mouse over the icon. "It contains just one file, 'initial.txt.' Let me bring it up." She clicked the mouse and text window opened.

```
10000001110000000000000000000011000000010
00000000000000000001100000000000000000000
00000000011000000000000000000000011000001
10000000000000000000000000000011000000000
00000000000000000001100000000000000100000
00000000011000000000000011100000000000001
10000000000000100000000000000011000000000
00000000000000000001100000000000000000001
```

00000000011000000000000000000000000000001
10000011000000000000000000000011000000000
00000000000000110001100000000000000000000
00000000010000100100000000000001110001
00100000000000000001000000000000000000000
01001000010000000000001010000000000000000
00010001000000000000000000000000000000000
10000000010000000000001000000001000000000
00010000100010000001000010000000000000100
00000010001000000010000000000000000000100
00000000000000000100000000000100001000000
00000010000100000000010000000010000100000
00000000000000010000000000001000010000000
00000010000000000000000000000000000001010
00000000010000010

"Judging by the length," she said, "I'll bet it's the very first signal the platform workers discovered, the high-frequency seismic ping. The one that led us here in the first place."

"You mean, the one transmitted from **beneath** the Moho."

"That's right. Dr. Asher doesn't seem to have made an attempt to decipher it."

"He was concentrating on the signals the sentinels were transmitting. They were shorter, easier to work with. And my guess is they're located in the 'source' subfolder."

"Let's check." A brief pause. "Looks like you're right. There are about forty files here, much shorter."

"So Asher and Marris only parsed forty of the signals for decryption. What do you want to bet the other subfolder holds the translations?" Crane felt his excitement grow.

"I wouldn't take that bet. Let's check the contents." Hui moused over the screen. A new folder opened, containing a list of the contents of "target":

1_trans.txt

2_trans.txt

3_trans.txt

4_trans.txt

5_trans.txt

6_trans.txt

7_trans.txt

8_trans.txt

"There they are," Hui said, her voice almost a whisper.

"So Asher and Marris had translated eight of the forty messages when they called me. Hurry, open the first one."

Hui moused over the icon, clicked. A new text window opened, containing a single line:

$$x = 1/0$$

"Wait a minute," Crane said. "There's something wrong here. That's Asher's old, original translation. The one he got wrong."

"I'll say he got it wrong. Anybody who could build something as complex as those sentinels must know you can't divide by zero."

"He told me the decryption had gone so smoothly at first they figured they'd made some tiny mistake. So they wasted days trying to figure what they did wrong. When they went into the hyperbaric chamber, they'd given up on that and were taking a new direction entirely." Crane frowned at the screen. "This is old news. There must be another folder somewhere."

There was a pause while Hui consulted her file utility. "Nope. This is the only viable folder."

"Take a look at the second file, then. Maybe he just didn't bother to erase his wrong guess."

Hui opened "2_trans.txt":

$$x = 0^0$$

"Zero to the power of zero?" Crane said. "That's just as undefined as division by zero."

Another thought struck him. "Can you check the time and date stamp on those files?"

A few clicks of the mouse. "Yesterday after-noon."

"All of them?"

"Yes."

"That was when he was inside the chamber, all right. So they **are** new, after all."

Crane lapsed into silence while Hui opened the six other files. Again and again, they were simple mathematical expressions; again and again, they were illogical, impossible.

$$a^3 + b^3 = c^3$$

$$\pi = a/b$$

$$x = \ln(0)$$

"**A** cubed, plus **b** cubed, equals **c** cubed?" Hui shook her head. "There are no three numbers that will satisfy that expression."

"Or how about the natural logarithm of zero? Impossible. And pi is a transcendental number. You can't define it by dividing one number into another."

"And yet it seems Dr. Asher was right the first time. About the translations, I mean."

"He clearly **thought** he was. But it makes no sense. Why would those sentinels be broadcast-ing a series of impossible mathematical expres-sions? And why would they consider them so important they'd be transmitting on every known frequency . . . and then some? I think that—"

Crane abruptly fell silent. From outside in the corridor he could hear muffled conversation, the sound of tramping feet.

He turned toward Hui. She looked back, eyes wide.

He pointed toward the back of the room. "Into that closet. Quickly."

She ran to the equipment closet and slipped inside. Crane turned off the lights with a quick slap of his palm, then followed as quickly and silently as he could. At the last minute he stopped, stepped back out of the closet and into the room, and plucked the fire-suppressant drop cloth from its hook.

The footsteps came closer.

Crane spread the drop cloth as evenly as he could over the laptops and equipment on the table. Then he raced to the closet and shut them both in. A moment later, he heard the lab door open.

He peered out of the grille in the closet door. Two marines stood in the entrance of the lab, silhouetted by the glow of the corridor.

One of them snapped on the lights. Crane leaned back into the darkness. He could feel Hui's warm, rapid breath on his neck.

Footsteps again as the marines stepped into the room. Then silence.

Slowly—very slowly—Crane leaned forward again, until he could just peer through the grille. He saw the marines standing by the lab table, doing a slow recon of the room.

"There's nobody here," one said. "Let's try the next lab."

"In a minute," the other replied. "I want to check something out first." And—with cautious deliberation—the man stepped toward the closet.

43

Crane shrank back into the darkness. Behind him, Hui caught her breath. He reached down, took her hand, squeezed it tightly.

The thin rays of light filtering through the grille were now obscured by the approaching figure. Crane heard the footsteps stop just outside the door.

Suddenly, a radio squawked. There was a brief fumbling, the snap of a button. "Barbosa," came a voice, so close it seemed almost to come from inside the closet. Another brief squawk. Then: "Aye, aye, sir."

"Let's go," Barbosa said.

"What is it?" asked the other marine.

"Korolis. There's been a sighting."

"Where?"

"Waste Reclamation. Come on, let's move out." There was the sound of retreating footsteps, the closing of a door—then silence once again.

Crane realized he was holding his breath. He let it out in a long, shuddering gasp. Then he released Hui's hand and turned to face her.

Hui looked back, her eyes luminous in the dim light.

Five minutes passed without another word. Slowly, Crane felt his heartbeat return to its normal speed. At last, he put his hand on the closet door and pushed it quietly open. Legs still feeling like jelly, he emerged and switched the lights back on.

Hui pulled the drop cloth off the instruments and computers, her movements slow and mechanical. "What now?" she asked.

Crane tried to force his brain back on track. "We keep going."

"But where? We've gone over all the decryptions. They're just a lot of impossible math expressions."

"What about that other file, 'initial.txt'? The

longer one that's being transmitted from beneath the Moho. You're sure there's no translation on the laptop?"

Hui shook her head. "Positive. Like you said, Dr. Asher must have concentrated on the shorter ones the sentinels were emitting."

Crane paused. Then he turned toward the laptop. "What could he have discovered?" he said, almost to himself. "He was beside himself with excitement when he called me from the oxygen chamber. There must be **something**."

He turned back to Hui. "Can you retrace his final steps?"

She frowned. "How?"

"Check the time and date stamps of the computer files. Figure out what he was doing in the minutes before he called me."

"Sure. Let me get a listing of all the files, sorted by date and time." Hui turned to the computer, opened a search window, and—moving a little more quickly now—typed in a command.

"Most of the files he was working on were in the 'decrypt' folder." She pointed at the screen. "But for the last fifteen minutes the laptop was operational, it appears Dr. Asher was surfing the Web."

"He was?"

Hui nodded. "I'll open the browser, bring up the history." A brief clatter of keystrokes. Crane rubbed his chin, puzzled. **We'll be able to access**

the WAN wirelessly, Asher had told Marris, just before they entered the hyperbaric chamber. It was certainly possible they had accessed the Internet . . . but why?

"Here's a list of sites they visited," Hui said. She stepped back to give Crane room.

He leaned in toward the screen. The list contained a dozen Web sites, most with dry governmental names. "A few sites at the Environmental Protection Agency," he murmured. "The Nuclear Regulatory Commission. The Ocotillo Mountain Project."

"The list is chronological," Hui said. "The last sites he visited are at the bottom."

Crane scanned the remainder of the list. "Department of Energy. The Waste Isolation Pilot Plant. That's it."

He stared at the screen. Then, all of a sudden, he understood.

"My God," he breathed. Comprehension burned its way through him.

"What?" Hui asked.

He wheeled toward her. "Where is the network port in this lab? I need access to the Internet."

Wordlessly, she took a category-5 cable from her tool kit and connected the laptop to the Facility's WAN. Crane moused to the last entry in the history display, clicked on it. A new browser window opened, displaying a text-heavy official site, topped by a Department of Energy seal and a title in large letters:

WIPP—Waste Isolation Pilot Plant
Carlsbad, New Mexico

"Wipp," Hui said in a very quiet voice. "**That's** what Asher meant. Not 'whip.' "

"But what is it?"

"A series of huge caverns, dug within a massive salt formation deep beneath the Chihuahuan Desert in New Mexico. Six million feet of underground storage space. Very remote. It's going to be the nation's first disposal facility for transuranic waste."

"Transuranic waste?"

"Nuclear garbage. Radioactive by-products of the cold war and the nuclear arms race. Everything from tools and protective suits to old spacecraft batteries. Right now, the stuff is stored all over the place. But the new plan is to store it all in one central location: far beneath the desert." He glanced at her. "And Ocotillo Mountain: that's a heavily guarded site in southeastern California, a geologic depository for spent nuclear fuel and decommissioned weapons of mass destruction."

He turned back to the screen. "I attended a medical conference on the dangers of nuclear garbage and deactivated weaponry. Where to dump something so lethal is a huge problem. Hence, repositories like Ocotillo Mountain. But what's the connection to the Deep Storm project? What was Asher driving at?"

There was a brief silence.

"Did he say anything else?" Hui asked. "When he called you, I mean."

Crane thought back for a second. "He said it was imperative, absolutely imperative, that we didn't . . . and then he stopped."

"That we didn't **what**? Continue the dig?"

"I'm not sure. I never stopped to consider."

And then—suddenly—Crane understood. And as he did, he felt an almost physically overwhelming mix of triumph and fear.

"Oh, **no,**" he breathed.

"What is it?"

"The Waste Isolation Pilot Plant? Ocotillo Mountain? **That's** what we're sitting on top of."

Hui turned pale. "You don't mean—"

"That's **exactly** what I mean. All this time, we've been positing some benevolent, paternal race that's planted some wondrous technology deep in the earth for mankind to discover when we've become sufficiently advanced to appreciate it. But that's not it at all. The truth is the Earth has been used **as a dumping ground for**

weapons or toxic waste—unimaginably dangerous toxic waste, too, given how advanced your
friends from Cygnus Major are."

"That's what Asher was trying to tell you?"

"It's got to be—there's no other answer. That
thing encased below the Moho, the thing Spartan
is digging toward right now? It's a time bomb."

He paused a moment, thinking fast now. "That
medical conference I mentioned? Finding a place
to dump nuclear garbage is only part of the problem. The real problem is that the stuff is going to
stay radioactive **for longer than recorded history.** How are we going to warn somebody, ten
thousand years in the future, that they'd better
stay away from Carlsbad or Ocotillo Mountain?
Civilization as we know it will have been transformed utterly. So the Department of Energy is
seeding the sites with what they're calling 'passive
institutional controls.'"

"Warning markers."

"Exactly. Not just one kind, either, but a wide
variety—pictures, symbols, text. To tell our de-
scendants the site has been isolated and sealed off
for good reason. There were rumors of active controls, as well."

"But how can you be sure what's below **us** is
dangerous?"

"Don't you see? Those sentinels we uncovered as

we've dug—they're 'institutional controls,' too, in their own way. And those signals they're sending out are warnings."

"They're just mathematical expressions."

"But think what kind of expressions they are. They're **impossible**. When Asher first decrypted the message and thought he'd gotten it wrong, you know what he said? 'Division by zero is forbidden by all the laws of the universe.' And that's the key word: **forbidden.** Every single expression those sentinals are transmitting—zero to the power of zero, the others—they're **all** forbidden."

"Because whoever did this couldn't use a warning that was language based."

"Precisely. Only mathematical formulas are universal." He shook his head. "And to think of Flyte, and his talk of irrational numbers. He was more right than he knew. I think."

"Who?"

He gave a soft laugh. "Never mind."

Hui thought for a moment. "Why did they start with just one expression—and then begin broadcasting thousands?"

Crane shrugged. "Maybe they thought that division by zero was the simplest, most basic—that's why it was so pervasive. Maybe my touch triggered new behavior in the sentinel. Or maybe the fact that we hadn't stopped digging convinced the devices that we hadn't taken the hint—that we needed supplements."

He turned abruptly, took a step toward the door. All of a sudden, a sense of terrible urgency filled him: with every new minute, the digging brought them closer to an unthinkable oblivion.

"Where are you going?" Hui asked.

"You're looking at one guy who finally **has** taken the hint."

"What about me? Where should I go?"

"Stay here. It's as safe as anywhere—probably safer, because it's already been searched." He took her hand again, gave it a reassuring squeeze. "I'll be back for you—soon."

She took a deep breath. "Okay. Maybe I'll take another look at that initial transmission. The one Dr. Asher didn't translate."

"Excellent idea," Crane smiled. Then he stepped up to the lab door, paused to listen, and quickly slipped out into the corridor.

44

Admiral Spartan stood silently, looking at Crane. They were standing in a quiet corner of the observation chamber, and the only light came from the long window overlooking the Drilling Complex. The light was not sufficient to betray the expression on the admiral's face.

Crane glanced at the technicians and engineers, sitting at their monitoring stations. Then he looked down into the hangar. A crew of workers was prepping one of the remaining two Marbles for its descent. Even from this vantage point, there seemed to be a palpable excitement in the air: it seemed they were now just days, perhaps hours, from reaching the Moho, and any of the next few trips could be the breakthrough dive.

He returned his gaze to Spartan.

The admiral seemed to rouse himself from deep contemplation. He clasped his hands behind his back. "Let me get this straight. All the mysterious illnesses, the psychological problems, are the result of a signal?"

"It's the same digital signal the sentinels first transmitted via light waves. Except this other signal is transmitted in some way our technology can't pick up. And it triggers a highly abnormal spiking of theta waves in the brain. See, the brain works on electricity," Crane explained. "When that electricity misfires, it affects the autonomous nervous system. That in turn can cause nausea, visual field defects, arrhythmia—all the neurological deficits we've been seeing. It can also affect the frontal lobe of the brain. And that in turn accounts for the problems with memory and concentration, changes in character, even psychotic episodes."

"How can we counteract it? Negate its effects?"

"The signal? We can't even track it. The only solution is to avoid it. Stop the dig, get people to the surface, away from the source."

Spartan gave a dismissive shake of his head.

"And this signal is transmitting a mathematical expression."

"Asher decoded several signals. All mathematical expressions, all impossible."

"You're saying they're a warning of some kind."

"The expressions are all forbidden by universal law. What better way to signal danger, when language isn't an option?"

"What better way, Doctor? Something more articulate. More direct."

Crane thought he heard skepticism in Spartan's tone. "Whoever planted these objects beneath the Moho—whoever created the sentinels—is clearly far, **far** more advanced than we are. Who's to say they aren't transmitting signals that are, as you say, more articulate—but we just aren't smart enough yet to intercept them?"

Spartan pursed his lips. "And we're the proud owners of an interstellar toxic dump. Or, perhaps, a cache of doomsday weapons from some distant arms race."

Crane didn't answer. The silence lengthened. Over his shoulder, he could hear the distant murmur of conversation, the clicking of keyboards.

At last, Spartan exhaled slowly. "I'm sorry, Doctor, but it all sounds very circumstantial to me. In fact, I have to wonder whether your own theta waves aren't beginning to spike. An alien civilization uses Earth as a waste repository, then sends out signals to warn us."

"No, not us. They couldn't care less about us— the violence of the original burial event proves that. We're insects to them. The civilization that did this probably comes from an environment of methane and sulfuric acid. Oxygen and nitrogen may even be toxic to them. They're not concerned about us; to them the Earth is a useless planet, and we're too primitive to deserve consideration. It's only a freakish chance we discovered their message in the first place. They're concerned about civilizations **far more advanced.** They're warning **them** to stay away from Earth."

Spartan did not reply.

After a moment, Crane sighed. "You're right. It is circumstantial. There's no way to conclusively prove what's down there without penetrating the Moho. But that's like saying a grenade is circumstantial until you pull the pin."

Still, Spartan did not respond.

"Look," Crane went on, hearing the urgency in his own voice. "I don't know what's down there exactly—I only know that it's unimaginably dangerous. Is it worth jeopardizing the Earth to find out what's down there? Because the stakes might be **at least** that high."

At last, Spartan roused himself. "And you're convinced of that?"

"I'd bet my life on it."

"And this deliberate erasing of Asher's hard drive—are you sure of that, as well?"

Crane nodded.

"Your talents seem to extend beyond the medical profession. Did you resurrect the data yourself?"

Crane hesitated. "I had assistance."

"I see." Admiral Spartan looked back at him, expression still unreadable. "Would you know where Hui Ping is?"

Crane kept his tone neutral. "No idea."

"Very well. Thank you, Doctor."

Crane blinked. "Excuse me?"

"You may go. I'm rather busy at the moment."

"But everything I've said—"

"I'll consider it."

Crane looked at Spartan in disbelief. "You'll **consider** it? Another dive, maybe two, and it'll be too late to **consider** anything." He paused. "Admiral, there's more at stake here than your mission, than what's down at the bottom of that shaft. There's also the lives of everyone on board this Facility. You have a duty, a **responsibility,** to them as well. Even if there's only a remote chance that I'm right, you owe it to them to examine my findings, the report I'm preparing. Because the risk is simply too great to do otherwise."

"You're dismissed, Dr. Crane."

"I've done my job—I've solved the mystery. Now you do yours! Stop this fool's task, save this Facility, or I'll—"

Dimly, Crane became aware that he was raising his voice, and heads were turning. He abruptly fell silent.

"Or you'll what?" Spartan asked.

Crane did not reply.

"I'm glad to hear you've done your job. Now I suggest you leave the Drilling Complex on your own accord, Doctor. Before I have an armed detail escort you out."

For a moment, Crane stood where he was, rooted in place by anger and disbelief. Then, without another word, he spun on his heel and exited the observation chamber.

45

Michele Bishop sat at the desk in her tidy office. She was intently scrutinizing an X-ray on her monitor, her dark blond hair falling over her eyes, chin perched lightly on carefully varnished fingernails. Outside, the Medical Suite was draped in a profound stillness.

Inches from her elbow, the phone rang, shattering the silence. Bishop jumped in her seat. Then she reached for the phone. "Medical, Bishop."

"Michele? It's Peter."

"Dr. Crane?" She frowned. It sounded like him, all right; but his normally phlegmatic, almost lazy voice was rushed and breathless. She pressed the power button on the edge of her monitor, then sat back in her seat as the screen went black.

"I'm in the temporary infirmary on deck four. I need your help, badly."

"Very well."

A pause. "Are you okay? You sound . . . preoccupied."

"I'm fine," Bishop said.

"We've got a crisis on our hands." Another pause, longer this time. "Look. I can't tell you everything yet. But what's down below us—it isn't Atlantis."

"I guessed that much."

"I've discovered what we're digging toward is something incredibly dangerous."

"What is it?"

"I can't tell you that. Not yet, anyway. There's no time to waste. One way or another, we have to make Spartan stop. Look, here's what I need you to do. Round up the scientists and technicians—the ones you know best. Rational, nonmilitary. Reasonable people you can trust. People who are well connected. Any names come to mind?"

She hesitated a moment. "Yes. Gene Vanderbilt, head of Oceanographic Research. And there's—"

"That's fine. Call me back on my mobile when they're assembled. I'll come up and explain everything then."

"What's going on, Peter?" she asked.

"I've figured it out. What's making people sick. I've told Spartan, but he won't listen. If we can't convince Spartan, we'll have to get a message to the surface, tell them what's happening down here, get them to exercise higher authority. Can you do this?"

She did not reply.

"Michele, look. I know we haven't always seen eye to eye. But it's the safety of the entire Facility we're talking about here—and maybe a lot more than that. With Asher gone, I need help from his staff—those that believed in him and what he stood for. Spartan's men are only days, hours, away from their goal. We're doctors, we took an oath. We **have** to keep the men and women in our care out of harm's way—or at least try our best. Will you help me?"

"Yes," she murmured.

"How long will it take?"

She paused, eyes darting around the room. "Not long. Fifteen minutes, maybe half an hour."

"I knew you'd come through."

She bit her lip gently. "So Spartan's not going to stop the dig?"

"You know Spartan. I gave it my best shot."

"If he won't stop of his own accord, nobody else is going to be able to convince him."

"We have to try. Look, call me back, all right?"

"I will."

"Thanks, Michele." And the phone abruptly went dead.

Silence returned to the office. Bishop sat in her chair, motionless, looking at the phone for perhaps sixty seconds. Then, slowly, she returned it to the cradle, a thoughtful—almost resigned— expression on her face.

46

By Facility standards, Admiral Spartan's quarters on deck 11 were relatively commodious. The fact they were so sparsely furnished made them appear even larger. The suite of rooms—office, bedroom, conference area—were dressed in a rigidly militaristic style. Instead of paintings, the walls were decorated with commendations. An American flag hung limply beside the brilliantly polished desk. The single bookshelf behind it held numerous Navy manuals and treatises on strategy and tactics. In addition—the only evident window into Spartan's private soul—it also held half a dozen translations of ancient texts: the **Annals** and **Histories** of Tacitus, the **Strategikon** of Emperor Maurice, Thucydides' account of the Peloponnesian war.

Korolis had seen it all before. His good eye took everything in, while the other drifted away in a myopic haze. He closed the door quietly behind him and stepped forward.

The admiral was standing in the middle of the office, his back to Korolis. At the sound, he turned. And now Korolis stopped in surprise. Because he now saw, over Spartan's shoulder, one of the sentinels their excavation had uncovered. It hovered placidly in the center of the room, white light pointing toward the ductwork on the metal ceiling. The admiral had apparently been studying it.

Korolis reflected that perhaps he should not be surprised, after all. The admiral had been behaving a little out of character the last day or two. Normally, Spartan took his recommendations almost automatically, without question. But recently the admiral had been overriding his suggestions, almost taking him to task on certain issues. Like that business about putting Ping in the brig, for example. His change in behavior seemed to date from the time of that business with Marble One. Or perhaps the admiral, too, was being affected by . . .

But Korolis decided not to follow that thought to its logical conclusion.

Spartan nodded at Korolis. "Have a seat."

Korolis walked past the sentinel without giving it another look and seated himself at one of two chairs before the admiral's large desk. Spartan walked around the far side of the desk and settled himself slowly into his leather armchair.

"Everything is proceeding according to schedule," Korolis said. "In fact, far ahead of schedule. With the retasked procedures in place, there have been no further, ah, glitches. It's true that operating in manual mode, with checksums on vital processes, has slowed the digging somewhat, but this has been more than offset by the lack of xenoliths in the sediment, and—"

Spartan raised a hand, stopping Korolis in midsentence. "That will do, Commander."

Korolis felt another faint stirring of surprise. He had assumed the admiral had summoned him, as usual, for a progress report. To hide his discomfiture he picked a paperweight from the desk—a large metal cleat, a relic from the Revolutionary War frigate **Vigilant**—and turned it over in his hands.

There was a brief silence in which Spartan brushed back his gunmetal-gray hair with a heavy hand. "When is Marble Two due back from the digging interface?"

"ETA is ten hundred hours." Korolis replaced the cleat, checked his watch. "Fifty minutes from now."

"Have the recovery unit do the normal post-op. Then have Marble Two secured. And tell the Marble Three team to stand down until further orders."

Korolis frowned. "I'm not sure I heard you correctly, sir. Have Marble Three stand down?"

"That is correct."

"Stand down for how long?"

"I can't answer that yet."

"What's happened? Have you received some word from the Pentagon?"

"No."

Korolis licked his lips. "Begging your pardon, sir, but if I'm to have the men call off the dig, I'd appreciate an explanation."

Spartan seemed to consider this request. "Dr. Crane has been to see me."

"Crane, sir?"

"He believes he's found the cause of the medical problems."

"And?"

"It has to do with the emission signals from the anomaly. He's preparing a report; we'll get the details then."

Korolis paused. "I'm afraid I don't follow. Even if Crane's right, what does the source of the illnesses have to do with the dig?"

"In the course of his research, he's made another discovery. A translation of the alien signals."

"A translation," Korolis repeated.

"He believes them to be a warning."

"Asher believed the same thing. Crane always was his errand boy. They never had any proof."

Spartan looked at Korolis appraisingly for a moment. "They may have some now. And it's funny you should mention Asher. As it turns out, it was the data on his laptop that fueled Crane's discovery."

"That's impossible!" The words were out before Korolis could stop himself.

"Indeed?" Spartan's tone grew milder, almost gentle. "And why is that?"

"Because . . . because of the fire damage it sustained. The computer couldn't possibly function."

"It turns out it wasn't just the fire. According to Crane, somebody demagnetized the hard drive, as well." The appraising look remained on the admiral's face. "You wouldn't know anything about that, would you?"

"Of course not. Anyway, it doesn't seem possible Crane could have pulled any data from that hard disk. The laptop was burnt, destroyed."

"Crane had help."

"From who?"

"He wouldn't say."

"It sounds like a lot of crap to me. How do you know he isn't just making it all up?"

"If that was his intention, he wouldn't have waited this long to tell me. Besides, I'm not sure why he'd do that. And in any case his findings appear to have a troubling degree of consistency."

Korolis realized he was breathing quickly. He felt an unpleasant chill shudder through him; a moment later, it was followed by a sensation of intense warmth. Sweat popped out on his forehead.

He sat forward in his chair. "Sir," he said. "I must ask you to rethink this decision. We're only one or two dive sessions away from the Moho."

"All the more reason to be cautious, Commander."

"Sir, we're so close. We **can't** stop."

"You saw what happened to Marble One. It's taken us eighteen months to get where we are; I don't want to put all that progress in jeopardy. Another day or two will make little difference."

"Every **hour** makes a difference. Who knows what foreign governments might be plotting against us? We have to get down there, harvest what we can, as **quickly** as we can. Before that saboteur tries again."

"I will not have this entire project imperiled by rash or impetuous actions."

"Sir!" Korolis shouted.

"Commander!" Spartan raised his voice only slightly, but the effect was startling. Korolis forced himself into silence, his breath still faster now, and shallow.

Spartan was staring at him again.

"You don't look very well," the admiral said evenly. "I'm forced to wonder if perhaps the illness that's spread throughout the Facility isn't affecting you as well."

At this speculation—so ironically close to his own, earlier diagnosis of Spartan—Korolis felt a surge of real anger. He hadn't mentioned the recent and worsening headaches to anyone; they were just due to tension, he was sure of that. He gripped the arms of his chair with something close to ferocity.

"Believe me, I'm as eager to reach the anomaly as you are," Spartan continued. "But we brought Dr. Crane down here for a reason. **I** helped pick him. And now I have no choice but to pay attention to his findings. I'm going to assemble a team of our top military scientists to review his conclusions. We can proceed from there. Meanwhile, I want you to report to Dr. Bishop for a full—"

With a sudden move that was half instinct, half unconscious, Korolis leapt out of his chair, scooped the heavy cleat from the desk, and dashed it against Spartan's temple. The admiral went gray; his eyes rolled back to unbroken white; and he slumped out of his chair, falling heavily to the floor.

Korolis stood over him, breathing hard, for close to a minute. Then, his calm returning, he placed the cleat back on the desk, smoothed down his shirt front. He glanced at the phone, paused briefly to collect his thoughts, then picked up the receiver and punched in a number.

It was answered on the second ring. "Woburn."

"Chief."

"Sir!" Korolis could almost hear the black ops leader snapping to attention.

"Admiral Spartan has become mentally incompetent. He is no longer himself. I am therefore assuming command. Please have a watch set outside his quarters."

"Very good, sir."

"And meet me in the Drilling Complex, on the double."

47

Roger Corbett was in his office, making notes on the patient who had just come in complaining of panic attacks and agoraphobia, when the phone rang. He put his digital notepad and stylus aside and picked up the handset.

"Dr. Corbett," he said.

"Roger? It's Peter Crane."

"Hi, Peter. Let me guess—my snores have been filtering through our shared bathroom, right?"

It had been meant as a bit of levity, but somehow Crane didn't sound interested in small talk.

"I've been waiting to hear from Michele. Any idea where she is?"

"No. I haven't seen her for some time."

"She was supposed to get back to me forty-five minutes ago. I've tried her mobile, but she isn't picking up. I'm a little concerned."

"I'll see if I can't track her down. Anything I can help with?"

There was a pause. "No thanks, Roger. Just see if you can locate Michele, please."

"Will do." Corbett replaced the phone, then stood up, stepped out of his office, and walked down the hall.

In the reception area, four people were waiting. This in itself was very unusual—Bishop ran a tight, efficient ship, and normally there was never more than one patient waiting to be seen. Corbett stepped into the nurse's station. His psychiatric intern—a gravely serious young man named Bryce—was seated beside the receiving nurse, filling out a supplies request form.

"Any idea where Dr. Bishop is?" Corbett asked.

Bryce shook his head. "Sorry."

"She stepped out over an hour ago," the nurse offered.

Corbett turned to her. "Did she say where she was going?"

"No, Doctor."

Corbett stared out at the reception area. Then he

retreated back down the hall to his office. He brought up the internal directory on his digital notepad, looked up an extension, picked up the phone, and dialed.

"Monitoring Services, Wolverton," came a gruff voice.

"This is Dr. Corbett in the Medical Suite. I need you to run a trace on Michele Bishop."

"Can I have your passphrase, Doctor?"

Corbett gave it. The faint sound of keystrokes filtered over the phone. Then Wolverton spoke again. "She's currently in the Environmental Control spaces, deck eight."

"Environmental Control?" Corbett wondered aloud.

"Is there anything else, Doctor?"

"That will be all, thanks." Slowly, thoughtfully, Corbett hung up the phone. Then he picked up his mobile and—stopping just long enough in reception to tell Bryce he was temporarily in charge—left the Medical Suite.

Environmental Control was a large, essentially unmanned warren of dimly lit compartments in a far corner of deck 8. It was filled with furnaces, compressors, humidification systems, electrostatic precipitators, and other devices designed to make the air on board the Facility as comfortable and germ free as possible. Although the floors and walls hummed with the spinning of a dozen turbines, there was remarkably little noise. The watchful, listening silence felt oppressive to Corbett. He opened his mouth to call Bishop's name, but something about that silence made him reconsider. He moved quietly through the first compartment, into a second, and then into a third.

This last space was full of massive air ducts and steel-encased "filter farms" that rose from floor to ceiling. It was even darker than the previous two compartments, and Corbett threaded his way slowly between the ducts, looking from one side to the other. Had Bishop already left? Perhaps the tech in Monitoring had been mistaken and she'd never been here. It seemed a highly unlikely spot, and . . .

Suddenly, Corbett caught sight of her. She was kneeling before a bulkhead at the far end of the room, back to him, utterly absorbed in something. For a brief moment he thought she must be administering CPR; but then, squinting through the dim light, he realized what he'd thought was a body was actually an oversized black duffel bag. He took a step closer. Strange: her elbows were rocking back and forth as if she were, in fact, performing cardiac massage. Corbett frowned, perplexed. Judging by the faint grunts of effort, whatever she was up to took some doing.

Corbett took another step forward. Now he could see over her shoulder. She was kneading a long, claylike brick, stretching it out into a thick, off-white rope about two feet long.

Two other such ropes had already been pressed against the steel bulkhead in front of her.

Before he could stop himself, Corbett drew in a sharp breath. Instantly, Bishop dropped the puttylike brick and jumped to her feet, whirling to face him.

"You're the saboteur," Corbett said, obviously. "The one who tried to rupture the dome."

Her nostrils flared, but she said nothing.

Corbett knew he should do something—run, call for help—but he felt dazed, even paralyzed, by shock. "What is that?" he asked. "Semtex?"

Still Bishop said nothing.

Corbett's mind reeled. It's true that, despite working with her for months, he really knew very little about Michele Bishop. Even so, it seemed impossible. **It can't be, it can't be. Maybe there's some mistake.**

"What are you doing?" he asked.

At this, she finally spoke. "I should think that would be obvious. The southern pressure spoke is just on the other side of this bulkhead."

Somehow, hearing her speak—hearing this affirmation of treachery from her own lips—broke Corbett's mental logjam. "The pressure spokes are full of seawater," he said. "You're going to rupture the hull. Flood the Facility."

He took a step backward.

"Stay where you are." Something in her voice made Corbett freeze.

"Why are you doing this?" As he spoke, he put his hands behind his back as casually as possible.

Bishop didn't reply. She seemed to be debating her next move.

Slowly, stealthily, Corbett slipped his cell phone out of his back pocket. He opened it as quietly as possible, then dialed 1231 with the edge of his thumb. It was the extension of his intern, Bryce: a number that could be entered quickly and easily, without looking. He fumbled for the mute switch; not finding it, he moved his thumb over the cell phone's speaker, muffling it.

"We don't have any Composition-4 on this side of the Barrier," he said. "How'd you get it?"

Any indecisiveness had now left Bishop's face. She laughed mirthlessly at the question. "A lot of medical by-products get transported back and forth in the Tub. You know that. The guards aren't too eager to paw through a lot of red-bag waste. It's possible to get all sorts of things through that way. Such as this." And she dipped her hand into a pocket of the lab coat and pulled out a gun.

Corbett, still numb with surprise, looked at the gun with something like detachment. It was an ugly little weapon with an unusual glossy texture and a silencer snugged onto the barrel. He was about to ask how she'd gotten it through the metal detectors, but the glossy look provided an answer: it was a ceramic-polymer composite, expensive and illegal.

"If you flood the Facility, you'll die too," he said.

"I'm setting the detonators for ten minutes. By that time I'll be on deck twelve, headed for the escape pod."

He shook his head. "Michele, don't. Don't betray your country like this. I don't know what country you're working for, but it isn't worth it. This isn't the way."

Bishop's face abruptly darkened. "What makes you think I'm working for a foreign government?" she asked fiercely. "What makes you think I'm working for a **government** at all?"

"I—" Corbett began, then stopped, taken aback by this sudden outburst.

"The United States can't be allowed to get its hands on what's down there. America has already shown, time and time again, how it abuses the power it's given. We got the atomic bomb, and what did we do? Within six months we'd nuked two cities."

"You can't compare that to—"

"What do you think America will do with the technology that's down there? America can't be trusted with that kind of power."

"Technology?" Corbett asked, genuinely confused. "What technology are we talking about?"

As quickly as the outburst began, it ended. Bishop didn't answer, simply shaking her head angrily.

Into the silence came the squawk of a male voice.

Now for the first time Corbett felt real fear grip his vitals. In the heated exchange he'd forgotten to keep his thumb pressed over the cell phone's speaker.

Bishop's expression hardened further. "Let me see your hands."

Slowly, Corbett raised his hands. The cell phone was in his right.

"You . . . !" With a sudden movement, fast as a striking snake, Bishop pointed the gun at him and pulled the trigger.

There was a puff of smoke; a sound remarkably like a sneeze; and then a terrible burning sensation exploded in Corbett's chest. A massive force threw him backward against a ventilator housing. He sank to the floor, wheezing and gargling. Just before an irresistible blackness enveloped him, he saw—dimly—Bishop stomp brutally on the cell phone, then kneel again and continue molding the brick of plastique against the outer bulkhead as rapidly as possible.

48

Crane stepped into the elevator, pressed the button labeled 1. Even before the doors had slid shut he was pacing restlessly.

What was taking Michele Bishop so long?

He'd spoken with her more than ninety minutes before. She'd said it would take no longer than half an hour to assemble the scientists.

Had something gone wrong?

At last he'd grown tired of cooling his heels in the temporary infirmary and decided to take one more crack at convincing Admiral Spartan. He

had to try; the stakes were too high for him not to try. And anything—even an argument—beat sitting around.

As the elevator doors opened again, something occurred to him. He stepped out, plucked his cell phone from his pocket, dialed Central Services.

"May I help you?" a neutral female voice asked.

"Yes, I need to speak with somebody named Vanderbilt. Gene Vanderbilt, in Oceanographic Research. I don't have access to a directory."

"One moment, I'll connect you."

As Crane walked briskly down the pale red corridor, his phone clicked audibly a few times. Then a man's voice sounded: "Oceanography, this is Vanderbilt."

"Dr. Vanderbilt? Peter Crane here."

There was a brief pause. "You're Dr. Crane, right? Asher's man."

"That's correct."

"He's greatly missed."

"Has Michele Bishop contacted you?"

"Dr. Bishop? No, not recently."

Crane stopped dead. "She **hasn't**? And you've been in your lab?"

"Yes. For the past several hours."

Crane began to walk again, more slowly this time. "Listen, Dr. Vanderbilt. Something's happening, but I can't talk about it over the phone.

I'm going to need your help, and the help of the other top scientists."

"What is it? Is there a medical emergency?"

"You could say that. I'll tell you the details in person. For now, all I can say is that it concerns the safety of the entire Facility and maybe a lot more besides."

Another pause. "Very well. What is it you want me to do?"

"Gather your senior colleagues together as quickly and quietly as possible. When you've done that, ring me back."

"It may take a few minutes. Some of them are in the classified section."

"Then get to them as quickly as possible. Tell them not to say anything to anybody. Believe me, it's **vitally** important, Dr. Vanderbilt—I'll explain when I see you."

"All right, Doctor." Vanderbilt's voice had become slow, thoughtful. "I'll see if I can't assemble a group in the deck twelve Conference Center."

"Call my cell, it's in the directory. I'll come up." He hung up, then clipped the phone to the pocket of his lab coat. **If Spartan comes through, I'll just tell Vanderbilt everything's been resolved,** he thought.

Ahead lay the double doors of the Drilling Complex. To his surprise, Crane noticed the doors were no longer guarded by marines but rather by two black ops agents armed with M16s. As he approached, one of them raised a hand for him to stop. The agent gave Crane's ID badge a careful scrutiny, then at last stepped back, pulling one of the doors open as he did so.

The complex was bustling. Crane paused just inside the entrance, looking around. Marines and black ops agents were stationed in strategic locations. Technicians and maintenance crews moved briskly about the crowded hangar. The greatest concentration of activity was at the center, where one of the two remaining Marbles hung from its robotic clamp. The laser scaffold stood nearby.

Loudspeakers in the corners of the ceiling coughed static. **"Attention,"** came a clipped voice. **"Marble Three descent initiating in ten minutes. Dive control officers, report to your stations."**

Crane took a deep breath. Then he began walking toward the Marble, where the three-person crew—wearing distinctive white jumpsuits—were surrounded by technicians. If Spartan wasn't nearby, he knew, at least somebody could point him in the right direction. . . .

As he approached, one of the crew members turned to look at him. Crane stopped in surprise. Above the white jumpsuit, he recognized the lined face and unruly white hair of Dr. Flyte.

Seeing him, Flyte's eyes widened. He separated himself from the group and walked over to Crane.

"Dr. Flyte," Crane said. "Why are you wearing a uniform?"

Flyte looked back at him. His delicate, birdlike features seemed drawn and nervous. "I do not wish to wear it—oh, **no**! My job is to repair the arm, improve the arm, teach others of its mysteries—not to wield it myself. But **he** would insist. 'The Olympian is a difficult foe to oppose.'" He glanced over his shoulder furtively, lowered his voice. "I have to be here, but **you** don't. You must leave. It's as I told you: **everything** is broken."

"I need to find—" Crane began. Then he fell silent abruptly. Because somebody else was approaching: Commander Korolis. With fresh surprise, Crane saw he, too, was wearing the white jumpsuit of the Marble crew.

"Get back to the Marble," Korolis told the old man. Then he turned his pale, exotrophic eyes to Crane. "What are you doing here?" he said.

"I'm looking for Admiral Spartan."

"He's unavailable." Korolis had dispensed with his earlier, hypocritical veneer of civility. Now his tone, his expression, his very manner, exuded hostility and suspicion.

"I need to speak with him."

"Impossible," Korolis snapped.

"Why is that, Commander?"

"He's had a breakdown. I've assumed command."

"A breakdown?" **Could this be what was keeping Bishop?** But as soon as the thought occurred to him, he rejected it. If the head of the Facility had suffered some kind of seizure or collapse, Corbett, or one of the medical interns, or Bishop herself would have told him.

And that meant only one thing: none of the medical staff had been notified.

Alarm bells went off in Crane's head. Suddenly he realized just how precarious his present position had become.

"Attention," came the voice from the loudspeaker. **"Crew insertion now commencing. Sealant team, prepare to restore and verify hull integrity."**

"Don't do it," Crane heard himself say.

Korolis frowned. "Don't do what?" His eyes were red rimmed, and his voice, normally soft, was loud and breathless.

"Don't make the dive."

"Sir!" a worker from a monitoring station called out to Korolis.

The commander turned toward him. "What is it?"

"There's someone who needs to speak with you. Bryce, an intern in the Medical Suite."

"Tell him I'm busy."

"Sir, he says it's of the utmost importance—"

"That"—and here Korolis shot out an arm, pointing it daggerlike at Marble Three—"is the **only** important thing at the moment."

"Very good, sir." The man hung up the phone, returned to his instruments.

Korolis turned back to Crane. "And why shouldn't I make the dive?"

"It's too dangerous. It's a fool's errand."

Korolis took a step closer. Beads of sweat were visible on his forehead and temples. "I heard about your little theory. You know what **I** think, Doctor? I think **you're** the one that's dangerous. A danger to morale. A danger to this very mission."

He stared at Crane a moment longer. Then, abruptly, he wheeled toward a brace of marines. "Hoskins! Menendez!"

They shot to attention. "Sir!"

Korolis jerked a thumb at Crane. "This man is under military arrest. Once the Marble is safely launched and the all clear is sounded, take him to the brig and post an armed guard outside his cell."

And before Crane could protest, the commander walked back to Marble Three, where an unhappy-looking Dr. Flyte and his fellow crew member were already slipping into its silvery maw.

49

Roger Corbett lay in a spreading pool of his own warm blood, wrapped in a fog of pain. At times it seemed he was dreaming; at others, as if he were already dead, floating in some limitless dark oblivion. Thoughts, feelings, associations drifted in and out, seemingly without his ability to control them. A minute might have passed, or ten; he didn't know. There was only one thing he was certain of: he could not let the crouching figure with the gun realize he was still alive.

The pain was intense now, but pain was good:

it helped him fight against the terrible lassitude that kept trying to drag him down forever.

As he lay there, he felt a pang of regret. His three o'clock appointment would be waiting for him. She was probably there now, tapping her foot and glancing at her watch. She'd been making such progress in anger management it seemed a pity that . . .

Then the faintness returned, washing over him, and he surrendered to dark dreams. In them, he was a diver who had swum too deep. And now the surface was a mere smudge of faint light far, far above, and his lungs were already bursting as he kicked his way upward, swimming as fast as he could, yet with so very much farther to go . . .

He forced himself back to consciousness. The figure in the corner was done.

She rose in the darkness and turned toward him, her eyes shining faintly with the light from the adjoining chamber. Corbett held his breath and lay motionless, his own eyes mere slits. Leaving the duffel where it lay, she took a step toward him, then another. Then she stopped once again. There was a dull gleam as the barrel of her gun rose toward him.

Suddenly she turned sharply. A moment later, Corbett heard it, too: voices, sounding faintly over the whine of compressors.

Others—two at least, maybe more—must have

entered the first compartment of Environmental Control. Sudden hope brought a measure of clarity back to him, helped steady his flagging senses. His gambit had worked. Bryce was sending help.

The voices came closer.

She stepped over him, gun at the ready, and slid up to the hatch leading to the second chamber. Opening his eyes a little wider, Corbett watched her peer carefully around the corner. The curved line of her hair, the barrel of the gun, were silhouetted by the yellow halo of light. Then she slipped through the hatch into the second chamber, ducked behind a turbine, and was lost from his view.

The voices continued. They no longer seemed to be getting any closer. He guessed they were still in the first compartment, somewhere between Bishop and the main exit from Environmental Control. From the few words he could make out, they sounded like maintenance workers, checking one of the innumerable pieces of equipment.

That meant the cavalry hadn't arrived—at least, not yet. Maybe it wasn't going to.

Corbett put out a hand, tried to raise himself to a sitting position, but his hand slipped and skidded on the bloody floor. A spear of pain lanced through his chest, and he bit his upper lip savagely to keep from crying out.

He lay there, breathing shallowly, letting the

pain ease somewhat. Then, planting his feet on the metal floor, he pushed himself forward, slowly, toward the far bulkhead.

It was agonizingly slow. One foot, two feet, a yard. Bloody bubbles frothed in the back of his throat. His shirt and coat were sodden with blood and acted like a dragline, slowing him still further. Halfway to the far wall he stopped briefly when faintness threatened to engulf him again. But he could not stop for long; if he did, he knew he would never start again. Once more, he planted his feet, forced himself a few inches at a time across the floor.

Now at last his head bumped against the far wall. With a sob of pain, he forced his gaze upward. Just above were the fat ropes of Semtex, four in all, pressed against the metal bulkhead in parallel lines. Into each had been set a detonator.

Focusing his strength, Corbett lifted an arm, fumbled for the nearest detonator, and plucked it from the shaped charge. Searing pain filled his chest again and he fell back, gasping. He could hear blood dripping from his elbow and wrist onto the bare floor.

From his supine position he examined the detonator. He could dimly make out a battery, a manual timer, two thin plates of metal separated by foil, a coil of optical fiber. Everything was miniaturized. He knew only a little about explosive ordnance but it looked like a long-period-delay "slapper." When the timer went off, the foil would be exploded electrically, and the plates would deliver the initial shock to the charge.

He placed the detonator as gently as possible on the floor. Ten minutes, she'd said; he figured he had maybe four or five left.

Three detonators to go.

Marshaling his strength, he lifted his arm again, strained for the next detonator, plucked it free— careful not to accidentally readjust its timer—and fell heavily back again.

This time the pain was much worse and he almost slipped into unconsciousness. The blood boiled in his throat and he choked and coughed. A minute passed while he recovered enough strength to continue.

The third shaped charge was out of reach. Digging in his heels once again, he pushed himself along the floor until he was near. Then he looped his hand upward a third time, pulled the detonator free, swung it back to the floor.

The pain was now so intense he did not think he could move to the fourth. He lay in the darkness, struggling to remain conscious, listening to the low murmur of voices. They seemed to be involved in an endless argument over some bit of engineering trivia.

How much time did he have left? A minute? Two?

He wondered where, exactly, Bishop was. No doubt she was crouched behind some piece of machinery, listening impatiently to the chitchat, waiting for the workers to move on so she could safely escape.

Why hadn't she just shot them? The gun was silenced. There could be only one reason: the hybrid weapon had a small magazine, maybe just two rounds. And she couldn't run past them; that would give the game away. She still had a chance to escape. But not if two more people took up the hue and cry . . .

No. She wouldn't run past them. She'd retreat to the Semtex and readjust the timers on the detonators, buy herself some more time.

He realized he'd been too preoccupied with his task, too overwhelmed by pain, to grasp this before. She'd be back—and at any moment.

Desperation gave Corbett renewed conviction. With his last reserves of energy he swung his arm up one more time, his hand closing over the fourth and last detonator.

Just as he did so, a shape appeared in the hatchway to the second compartment, silhouetted in deep black relief. Catching sight of him, she gave a muttered curse and leapt inward.

Corbett jerked in surprise and dismay. As he did so, his fingers pinched together involuntarily; there was a crackling sound and a tiny puff of smoke from the detonator—a terrible suspension of time that lasted a millisecond, yet that to Corbett seemed to go on and on and on—and then, with an unimaginably violent scream, the universe came apart in an apocalypse of fire and steel. And water.

50

"Outer doors closed," a voice droned over the speaker system. "Pressure seal activated. Marble Three in the pipeline. Estimated time to dig interface: nineteen minutes, thirty seconds."

From a far corner, Peter Crane watched in frustrated rage as the huge robotic clamp—now empty of its burden—swung away from the water lock and back to its resting position. While the Marble was being painstakingly sealed, then lowered through the lock, he'd looked around at the Drilling Complex staff, hunting for a sympathetic glance, a furtive nod, anything that might signal a potential accomplice. But there had been none: the engineers, technicians, and support staff were already resuming their normal duties, busying themselves with the familiar motions of a dig session in progress. Nobody seemed to notice he was there.

Except for the brace of marines who stood at his shoulders. The all clear sounded, and one of them nudged him. "All right, Doctor. Let's move out."

As they walked toward the doors that led into the corridors of deck 1, a sense of unreality settled over Crane. Surely this was all a dream. It certainly had all the skewed, misshapen logic of a dream. Was he really being marched to the brig by two armed marines? Were they really still digging toward some terrible retribution? Had Korolis really taken over military command of the Facility?

Korolis . . .

"You don't want to do this," he said in a low voice to the marines. Their response was to pull open the double doors, escort him through.

"It's not the admiral who's unfit for command," he went on as they marched down the corridor. "It's Commander Korolis."

No answer.

"You see the pallor of his skin? The hyperhidrosis—excessive sweating? He's got the sickness that's going around. I'm a doctor; I'm trained to notice these things."

Ahead, the corridor forked. One of the marines nudged Crane's shoulder with his rifle butt. "Turn right."

"Since I've arrived at the Facility, I've seen many cases. Korolis is a classic presentation."

"You'll be better off if you button your lip," the marine said.

Crane glanced at the pale red walls, the closed laboratory doors. His thoughts returned to the other forced march he'd made: the one with Spartan, when he'd been processed and cleared for the classified sector. At the time, he hadn't known where he was being taken. This time it was different. The sense of unreality grew stronger.

"I was in the military, too," he said. "You're soldiers, you've taken an oath to serve your country. Korolis is a dangerous and unstable man. By taking orders from him, what you're doing is no better than—"

The rifle butt slammed into his shoulder, much more violently this time. Crane sprawled onto his knees, neck snapping forward painfully.

"Take it easy, Hoskins," the second marine said gruffly.

"I'm tired of his mouth," Hoskins said.

Crane picked himself up and wiped his hands, staring at Hoskins through narrowed eyes. His shoulder blade throbbed from the impact.

Hoskins nodded with the barrel of his gun. "Get moving."

They continued down the corridor, made a left. Ahead lay the elevator. They approached it and Hoskins pressed the **up** button. Crane opened his mouth to reason with them again, thought better of it. Maybe the brig guards would listen to reason . . .

With a low chime, the elevator door slid open.

At the same moment, a tremendous boom came from somewhere far overhead. The entire Facility seemed to briefly rise off its footings. The lights dimmed, brightened, dimmed again. There was a secondary explosion that shook the installation as violently as a dog might shake a rat. With an ear-splitting shriek, a piece of gray metal ducting fell from the ceiling, pinning Hoskins to the floor.

Crane acted without conscious thought. He gave the second marine a quick, disabling downward kick to the knee, then dove headlong into the elevator, pressing the floor buttons indiscriminately. His lab coat tore against the metal grille and his cell phone was knocked from its clip, skittering away across the floor.

The emergency lighting came on, and in its orange glow he could see Hoskins struggling to sit up. Blood from a scalp wound flowed over the marine's nose and mouth but he was standing now, a grim expression on his face. As warning sirens began to sound in the distance he leveled his rifle, took aim. Crane ducked back behind the closing elevator door as a bullet whined past . . . and then the doors shut and he felt himself ascend.

51

Gordon Stamper, machinist first class, ran down the steps from deck 9 two at a time. The yellow turnout gear clung heavily to his back and shoulders; the hooks, portable radio, and other equipment clipped to his nylon gut belt rattled with every footfall. The rest of the rescue team followed, carrying oxygen supplies, tubular webbing, pick-head axes, and supplemental gear.

The call that had gone out over the emergency channel said this wasn't a drill. And yet Stamper wasn't so sure. Oh, it was clear **something** had happened: there'd been that godawful explosion, the brief loss of power. But the lights had come back and the Facility didn't seem any the worse for wear. He sure as hell didn't put it past the powers that be to stage something like this just to see if Rescue Operations was on its toes. The brass was always looking for ways to bust the balls of the enlisted men.

He threw open the door to deck 8. An empty corridor greeted him, doors on both sides of the hall all shut. This wasn't surprising: the end of the shift was approaching, and most administrators and researchers working on this floor would be elsewhere, grabbing a meal inside Central or, more likely, conducting wrap-up meetings in the conference rooms on deck 7.

The microphone for his portable radio was clipped to a shoulder epaulet. He clicked it on with a press of his thumb. "Stamper to Rescue One."

The radio crackled. "Rescue One, roger."

"We're on deck eight."

"Roger that."

Stamper clicked the radio off with a certain grim satisfaction. They sure as hell couldn't complain about the response this time: the call had come through only four minutes before and they were already on the scene.

Their objective was Environmental Control,

which was at the other end of the level. Stamper glanced around at his team, made sure they were assembled and ready, then gave the signal to move out.

The more he thought about it, the more he was sure this was bogus, a drill. The call—as he understood it, there had only been one, frantic and half incoherent, and it had been terminated prematurely—had said something about a breach; about **water**. And that was bullshit, plain and simple. Everybody knew there was a protective dome between the Facility and the North Atlantic and the space between was pressurized and dry. And if it wasn't a drill, it was probably just a broken water pipe; this floor was manned by pencil-necked scientists and paper pushers, apt to faint or cry wolf at the first bead of moisture.

They moved down the corridor, gear clanking, and paused when they reached a T-shaped intersection. The left passage led to the administrative sector, a complicated warren of offices and narrow passageways. By turning right and heading through the research labs, they could reach Environmental Control faster, and—

There was a clang of metal from the direction of the labs, followed by a frantic babel of voices. He paused, listening. The voices were low, but they seemed to be coming nearer.

He cupped a hand to the side of his mouth. "Yo!"

The voices stopped.

"This is Rescue Operations!"

The excited, nervous chatter resumed, and now Stamper heard the sound of running feet. He turned back toward his team, jerking his hand in the direction of the voices.

As he rounded the corner into the research sector, Stamper caught sight of them: maybe five or six scientists, running toward him. They were wild-eyed, clothes and lab coats in disarray. One of them, a middle-aged woman, was crying softly. Their leader—a tall, thin man with curly blond hair—was half drenched in water.

About fifty feet down the corridor beyond them, the watertight hatch had been sealed.

Stamper stepped forward as the group came running up. "Gordon Stamper, team leader," he said in his most authoritative voice. "What's the problem?"

"We've got to get out of here—**all** of us!" the tall man said breathlessly. The woman's cries increased in volume.

"Just what, exactly, has—"

"There's no time to **explain**!" the man interrupted. His voice was high and uneven, perched on the edge of hysteria. "We've dogged all the hatches we could, but the pressure's just too great. They won't hold, they'll go any second—"

"Just a minute," Stamper said. "Get a grip on yourself, settle down, and tell us what's happened."

The man turned to the rest of the scientists. "You get up to deck nine, quick as you can."

The panicked group needed no further encouragement. Without another word they ran past the rescue party and disappeared down the hall, heading for the stairwell.

Stamper watched them flee, an impassive expression on his face. Then he turned back to the blond man. "Let's hear it."

The man swallowed, made a visible effort to master himself. "I was in the corridor outside the Seismo-Acoustic Sonar Lab. I had an end-of-shift meeting, and I was just verifying which conference room before heading down to deck seven. There was this . . ." His voice faltered, and he wiped his mouth with the back of his sleeve. "This huge explosion. It knocked me to the ground. When I got up, I saw . . . a wall of water, flooding the Environmental Control spaces at the end of the corridor. There was blood in the water, body parts. **Lots** of body parts."

He swallowed again. "A colleague and I ran to the outer Environmental Control hatch, dogged it shut. Then we retreated down the hall, checking the labs and gathering anyone we could find. Just as we were leaving, the hatch we'd shut blew open, water started pouring in, and the research labs started to flood. We dogged the inner hatches of the research sector as we fell back. But the pressure's just too great, they're going to go any moment, and—"

Suddenly, his voice was drowned out by a terrific boom from the spaces up ahead.

The scientist started, gave a small cry of terror. "You see! There goes the hatch! We have to get out, get out **now!**" And he turned and fled in the direction of the rear stairwell.

Stamper watched his retreat. Then, very deliberately, he clicked his microphone into life once again. "Stamper to Rescue One."

"Rescue One, your signal is five by five."

"Be advised we have intercepted personnel retreating from the Research sector. They have retreated up stairwell bravo two. Intel obtained from deck eight indicates a large-scale breach in the vicinity of Environmental Control."

There was a pause. "Will you repeat that last, please? Over."

"A **large-scale** breach. Recommend you seal off this entire grid section and send down containment crews to repair the breach and secure the deck."

Another pause. "Have you verified this your-self?"

"No."

"Please perform a visual and give us a sit rep. Over."

"Roger and out." **Shit.**

Stamper stared down the corridor, in the direction of the dogged hatch. He wasn't nervous, not exactly; he'd performed this drill so many times it was hard for it to seem anything but routine, even now. Yet there was something about the terror that had radiated from the group of scientists, something about the naked fear in the blond man's eyes . . .

He turned to his team. "Let's go."

But even as his words died away, he became aware of another sound, coming from the research spaces ahead: a low groaning, gurgling, **rushing** unlike anything he'd ever heard before. It spiked in volume abruptly and the hairs on the nape of his neck stood on end.

Almost without realizing it, he took an involuntary step backward.

"Stamper?" one of the rescue crew said behind them.

And then, with an almost animal squeal, the dogs securing the hatch ahead of them flew out of their housings, one after the other, with reports like pistol shots. The hatch popped from its housing like a champagne cork. And a living mass of water boiled toward them.

For an instant, Stamper just stared, frozen with shock and horror.

It was terrifying, the way it came at them with single-minded, predatory hunger. It ate up everything in its path with a rushing, hissing, sucking noise. Stamper had no idea water could make that kind of a sound. And it was a horrible color, a slippery reddish black, with spumes of blood-colored froth throwing off a misty spindrift. Its violence was appalling. **Things** bobbed in the water, chairs and lab tables and instruments and computers and other matter he did not care to look at. The smell filled his nostrils: a chill, salty, coppery odor that—with its promise of great inky depths—was somehow even more frightening than sight alone . . .

. . . And then the spell was broken and he was scrambling backward, falling over himself and the rest of the team, slipping and cursing and staggering in a mad rush to gain the stairwell and escape the horror rushing up behind them.

His radio was squawking but he paid no attention. There was a sharp clang directly behind as one of the rescue crew slammed and dogged the hatch leading to the rear hallway. Stamper didn't even bother to look around. They could shut half a dozen hatches if they wanted to; in the end it would make no difference. Because now it was all too clear to him there was no way in hell that the breach was going to be sealed—or that deck 8 was ever going to be secured.

52

Crane ran down the corridors of deck 6 as quickly as he dared. At each intersection, he slowed; once past it, he broke into a jog again. The halls were quiet: he encountered a maintenance worker trundling a cart, two scientists murmuring to each other in low tones. Whatever loud noise had shaken the Facility so severely just minutes before seemed to be causing little alarm. The warning sirens had been silenced, and there was no anxiety in the faces he passed.

Ahead lay the cul-de-sac that housed the Maritime Applied Physics lab. He paused outside the door, glanced back down the corridor: still deserted. The lab itself seemed silent. He opened the door and quickly slid inside.

Hui Ping was standing beside the lab table. "Where have you been?" she asked. "I was sure something happened to you. And then that explosion just now . . ."

"I'm sorry, Hui, I was held up. How's it been here?"

"Quiet. Until a minute ago." She gave him a mirthless smile. "Actually, the time wasn't really wasted. While waiting, I think I deciphered that first signal, the one coming from beneath the Moho. And when you see—"

"There's no time for that. We've got to get out of here, and fast. The security cameras will have picked me up by now."

"Security cameras? What's happened?"

"Korolis has happened. He's taken command of the Facility."

"What about Spartan?"

"God only knows what's happened to him. It gets worse: Korolis is insisting the digging proceed on schedule. He seems obsessed with it, even manned Marble Three himself. I think the illness is beginning to affect him, too. When I tried to stop him, he had me arrested."

"What?"

"I managed to get away before I was thrown in the brig. But we have to get to deck twelve. I've mobilized some of the top scientists—they're gathering in the conference center there. I intend to explain everything to them: the dig, Asher's discoveries, Korolis—everything. We have to get word up to the surface, get the attention of people who can put a stop to all this madness—"

Suddenly, he stopped. "Oh, **shit**." His shoulders slumped.

She looked at him in mute inquiry.

"The Barrier," he explained.

In his haste, he'd forgotten about the checkpoint between the secure and nonsecure zones. The guards were probably still on the lookout for Ping—and they'd sure as hell be looking for him.

"**Damn** it!" He turned, slamming a fist against the lab table in frustration. "We'll never get past the Barrier."

He turned back to look at Ping. What he saw startled him. The computer scientist had gone a little pale. Surely, she hadn't forgotten about the Barrier as well . . . had she?

"What is it?" he asked.

When she replied it was in a very small voice. "There's another way. One possible way. An emergency exit hatch on deck two."

"Emergency exit? From the Facility?" Suddenly, Crane remembered the rungs he'd seen, bolted to the outer hull of the Facility, as he'd climbed the catwalk on his way to meet the Tub.

"Is it guarded?" he asked.

"I don't think so. It's a one-way hatch—you can't get back in, so there's no security issues with avoiding the Barrier. Not that many people know about it. The only reason that I do is because it's located in the maintenance spaces just below my lab."

He paused only another second. "Let's go."

Crane followed Ping as she began retracing the route they'd taken from her lab earlier in the day. **Was it really only seven hours before?** he reflected bitterly. In terms of everything they'd discovered since—and what had gone down within the Facility—it seemed ages.

Gaining the stairwell, they descended quietly and cautiously, pausing before each landing to make sure they remained alone and unobserved. They passed deck 3, the clang of pans from the Bottom kitchen clearly audible, and descended one more level. Hui put her hand on the exit bar, took a deep breath, then pushed it open.

Crane peered out. Ahead lay a short corridor that ended in a T. Between them and the junction was a group of men in lab coats, standing in the doorway of an office labeled SEDIMENTATION AND STRATIGRAPHY. At the sound of the stairwell door opening, they glanced over, expressions curious.

Crane sensed Ping hesitating. "Go on," he said in a low voice. "Just walk past them."

Ping stepped into the corridor. Crane followed as casually as he could, nodding to the group as he passed by. The faces weren't familiar, and he hoped none of them had been in the Drilling Complex when he'd been put under arrest. He had to force himself not to look back over his shoulder. But there was no clatter of feet, no shouted demands for them to stop.

At the intersection, Ping turned left, passing a series of small labs and offices. Then she stopped abruptly.

"What is it?" Crane asked.

Wordlessly, she pointed. About ten yards ahead, a security camera was fastened to the ceiling.

"Is there another way around?" he asked.

"Very circuitous. And we'd probably pass other cameras, anyway."

He thought for a moment. "Is it far?"

"Just around the next corner."

"Okay, then. Quick as you can."

They trotted ahead, keeping their heads down as they passed the camera. Ping turned another corner, stopped outside a gray door. She pulled it open and they ducked inside.

Crane found himself in an equipment store-
room; tools and light machinery sat on deep
metal shelves that rose from floor to ceiling. Ping
led the way to the rear, where there was a heavy
unmarked hatchway.

"Help me undog this," she said.

With effort, they pushed the four heavy drop
bolts out of the way, then opened the hatch. Beyond was a small, dim space, lit only by a caged
red bulb. There was another hatch here: round,
much smaller and heavier, with a servo-controlled
opening mechanism. WARNING, read a sign above
it. EMERGENCY EXIT ONLY. NO REENTRY AT THIS
LEVEL.

Crane put his hand against the hatch. It felt
cold and damp. From beyond it came a faint roaring sound he couldn't quite identify.

Behind him, Ping was breathing rapidly. He
turned toward her. "Are you ready?"

She shook her head. "I'm not sure I can do
this."

"You **have** to. This is the only chance we have
of getting past the Barrier. You've got a better
chance on deck twelve, among scientists, far from
the classified sector. Stay down here, and it's only
a matter of time until Korolis's goons find you
and lock you up."

She steadied herself. "Okay. Let's go."

Once she pulled the hatch closed behind them,

Crane undogged the exit portal, and then—putting his hands on a spoked wheel at its center—turned it counterclockwise. One revolution; two; then, with a chuff of air, it sprang free in his hands.

There was a small control box beside the hatch, housing a single red button marked ENGAGE. Crane glanced at Ping, who nodded. He pressed the button and the servos stirred to life, pulling the hatch inward toward them.

The roaring sound suddenly increased an order of magnitude. A sharp smell of brine and bilge wafted in on a chill breeze.

Beyond—in the strange twilight of the interior of the dome—lay a narrow platform, no more than four feet square. Quickly, Crane backed himself onto it, helping Ping out after him. Satisfied she was safely on the platform, he turned around.

And froze in shock and disbelief.

53

"We're six minutes out from the interface, sir."

"Thank you, Dr. Rafferty." Commander Korolis shifted on the small pilot's seat, nodding his satisfaction. He glanced approvingly at the dive engineer. The man was not only extremely loyal to him but also was one of the top military scientists on the Facility, a physicist by training. Handpicked by him and 100 percent dependable. Only the best talent was good enough for this particular dive.

Descent number 241 was well under way, and there would be no screw-ups this time.

Korolis glanced over the controls once again. He'd run them in the simulator a dozen times, and in any case they weren't all that different from those of a submarine. There would be no surprises.

As he looked at the gauges he felt a spike of pain at his temples. He winced: had he thought of it, he'd have taken a handful of Tylenol before boarding. He straightened, forcing the pain away: no headache was going to detract from this moment.

He turned back to Rafferty. "Doodlebug status?"

"Green across the board, sir."

"Excellent."

The descent was going like clockwork. In just a few minutes, they would arrive at the dig interface. And then, with any luck, soon . . . **soon** . . .

He spoke to Rafferty again. "Has that reading been confirmed?"

"Yes, sir. Sensor reports from Marble Two's last dive indicate the oceanic layer is at maximal penetration."

Maximal penetration. They had done it. They had bored through the third—and deepest—layer of the earth's crust.

No, there would be no surprises. Except for the

most important one: the riches that lay in store directly below, at the Mohorovicic discontinuity.

Whoever said the price of freedom was eternal vigilance was right—as far as that went. But Korolis knew there was more to it than that, much more. It was not enough to be watchful—one had to **act,** to seize the nettle. If the opportunity presented itself, it had to be taken, no matter what the difficulty. America stood alone, the only remaining superpower; the rest of the world, out of either jealousy or hatred, was arrayed against her, hoping for her to fall. Hostile governments were bleeding her dry through trade imbalances while at the same time increasing their armies and refining their own weapons of mass destruction. In such a desperate climate it was his duty—it was **all** their duties—to do **whatever** was necessary to ensure America stayed strong.

The nuclear fraternity was large, and getting larger. Nukes were no longer enough to intimidate or impress or keep at bay. What was needed was something new—something whose power was so awesome it would guarantee America's position for the indefinite future.

And that meant appropriating—by any and all means necessary—technology to keep her ahead of the herd. And that technology lay directly beneath them. Technology that could transmit messages from beneath the earth's crust. Technology that could store almost infinite reservoirs of energy in a tiny, iridescent chip.

The thought of passing up such technology was inconceivable. The thought of **someone else** claiming it was unacceptable.

"Four minutes out," said Rafferty.

"Very well." Korolis glanced from the engineer to the third occupant of Marble Three: the wiry old man with the blizzard of unruly white hair. Dr. Flyte, for once saying next to nothing. Korolis frowned. The man's presence on the Facility had been an unfortunate necessity: as the foremost authority on cybernetics and miniaturization, he'd been the only person capable of devising the complex robotic arm the Marble employed. The man might have been a genius, but he was notoriously eccentric, and—in the opinion of Korolis—a security liability. As a result, he had been kept secretly aboard the Facility, more or less against his will. It seemed the best solution: not only had it kept the all-too-talkative old fellow from speaking to the wrong people, but also Flyte's presence on the Facility meant he could maintain the robotic arms and train others in their complexity.

Korolis shifted in his seat. He'd chosen Flyte for this dive because—as with Rafferty—he'd wanted the very best. And who better to man the controls of the robotic arm than its inventor?

Another throb of pain seared his temples, but Korolis willed himself to ignore it. Nothing was going to get in the way of completing this dive; he would not allow his work to be impeded by human frailty. Something momentous was about to happen.

And it was entirely fitting that **he** be here in person, to make the discovery himself. After all, nobody else could be trusted. Admiral Spartan had proven himself weak—dangerously weak. This was not a time for going soft or for second-guessing. Spartan had been doing too much of both, lately, to retain the helm of an operation as critical as this one.

In recent days, it had grown clear to Korolis that the admiral was becoming unfit for command. The surprise, even dismay, he'd shown at Asher's death—the single greatest impediment to their progress—had been only the first sign. And his unmanly grief over what happened to Marble One, in truth just a casualty of war. But the admiral's willingness to listen to the poisonous, traitorous words of Peter Crane—that could not be borne.

At the thought of Crane, Korolis's expression darkened. He'd known Crane would be a troublemaker from the first time he'd met him in the Medical Suite. Monitoring the doctor's quarters, overhearing the long conversation with Asher, had merely cemented his conviction. All that cowardly talk about danger, about scrubbing the mission . . . Erasing Asher's hard disk, as he himself had done—and isolating the equally suspicious Hui Ping so she could not assist with any data retrieval—should have been enough to keep the old crackpot's crazy ideas, his alarmist pet theories, from infecting others. How was he to know that bastard Crane would be able to retrieve the data? If in fact he had, if it wasn't all a lie; no doubt the man was capable of anything . . .

He calmed himself with the thought that the man was in the brig by now. There would be plenty of time to deal with him later.

The radio crackled. "Dive Control to Marble Three."

Korolis took the mike. "Dive Control, go ahead."

"Sir, there's a situation we need to brief you on."

"Proceed."

"A few moments ago, the Facility was hit by what appears to have been an explosion."

"An **explosion**?"

"Yes, sir."

"What kind of explosion? Machinery failure? Detonation?"

"Unknown at the present time, sir."

"What was the location?"

"Deck eight, sir."

"What's the present status?"

"No damage reports have come back yet, sir—automatic detectors are off-line and the situation's still a little fluid. Power has been fully restored. There seems to be some issues with the environmental controls. Damage control and rescue teams have been dispatched; we're waiting for a sit rep."

"Well, pass it on when you get it. Meanwhile, have Chief Woburn take a squad up to do his own recon."

"Very good, sir."

"**'Hades is relentless and unyielding,'**" Dr. Flyte said, more to himself than anyone else. Then he lapsed into a quiet, singsong recitation in what Korolis assumed to be ancient Greek.

"Over and out." Korolis replaced the mike. Woburn could be relied on to deal effectively with the situation—he and his agents had been carefully selected for their reliability and their devotion to him, forged over countless clandestine missions in past years.

He now realized that, in the back of his mind, he'd always known this would happen: that he would need the loyalty and support of the black ops team; that at the ultimate moment he would be here, inside the Marble, to claim the prize.

Rafferty looked over from his perch. "Two minutes to interface."

"Spin up the tunnel-boring machine." Korolis turned to the old man. "Dr. Flyte?"

The cybernetics engineer fell silent, glancing back with his bright blue eyes.

"Commence final diagnostics on the robotic array, if you please."

The response was another quotation. **"'Son of Atreus, what manner of speech has escaped the barrier of your teeth?'"** But—a little grudgingly—Flyte busied himself at his station.

As Korolis turned back to his own control panel, he allowed himself a grim little smile. Let Chief Woburn clean up the mess overhead. His own destiny lay **below**—three hundred meters beneath their feet.

54

Crane took an involuntary step backward, bumping his shoulders hard against the metal flank of the Facility. He stared in disbelief.

The platform they stood on jutted out roughly thirty feet over the sea floor, into which the base of the Facility had been embedded. Below, a bizarre, almost lunar landscape spread out toward the dome: the exposed sea bed. It rose and fell crazily, in small, alien hills and valleys and ripples, partly submerged. It was a dark-chocolate color, and in the half-light of the dome it shone with an eerie luminescence. It appeared to be made up of a fine, muddy, foul-smelling silt.

But this was not what arrested his horrified gaze. It was the view **above**.

The dome that surrounded and protected the Facility rose in a gentle curve until it was almost lost from sight, far above. To one side of their little platform, a vertical line of heavy rungs had been bolted onto the Facility's outer skin. These rose, in a straight and unbroken line, up the sheer metal face. Near the top of the Facility, Crane could barely make out the narrow catwalk that led out to the receiving platform for the Tub—the catwalk he himself had crossed the week before. Between this catwalk and their own small ledge, Crane could see one of the massive, tube-shaped pressure spokes that ran like a hollow skewer between the dome and the Facility. This, too, he had seen before.

Except now it looked very different. At the spot where the spoke met the wall of the Facility, torrents of water were spitting and boiling outward and downward in huge, angry spumes. **This** was the source of the awful roar: a violent cataract of water, jetting from a rent in the pressure spoke with the murderous intensity of a machine gun. Even as he stared, the tear seemed to widen and the gush of seawater increase.

Although half dazed by the awful sight, Crane

was immediately aware of several things. Whether structural failure or sabotage, this was the explosion he'd heard. And despite the business-as-usual atmosphere inside the Facility, things were far from all right; if damage control hadn't realized that by now, they would at any second.

With this single glimpse, all Crane's fears, hopes, and goals reversed themselves in an instant.

For a moment he turned instinctively toward the hatch, as if to duck back inside and warn the workers in the Drilling Complex of their peril. Then he remembered that the escape hatch was one-way: reentry at this level was impossible. Besides, the sea floor beneath them was now almost entirely covered in black water, and more was raining down all around them from the widening breach above; within minutes, their tiny platform and the exit hatch would surely be underwater . . .

He suddenly became aware of a sharp pain in his hand. He looked over to see that Hui Ping was squeezing it as she stared upward at the whirling kaleidoscope of water, her face and hair damp from spray.

He gently freed his hand. "Come on," he said. "We can't stay here."

"I can't do this," she murmured.

She had said much the same thing within the airlock. "We have no choice," Crane replied.

Her eyes moved to his for a moment. Then she lowered them. "I'm afraid of heights," she said.

Crane stared at her. **Shit. Oh, shit.**

He took a deep breath. Then—trying to ignore the furious storm of water overhead and the icy rain that fell around them—he put a hand on her shoulders and stared kindly into her eyes. "There's no choice now, Hui. You've **got** to."

"But—"

"It's the only way. I'll be right behind you. I promise."

She looked at him a moment longer, water streaming down her cheeks. Then she swallowed, gave a faint nod.

He turned her toward the gray metal wall of the Facility, placed her right hand on the lowest rung. "Just take it one step at a time."

For a moment she remained motionless, and Crane wondered if her fear had immobilized her. Then—slowly, tentatively—she placed her left hand on the next rung; tested her grip; pulled herself up, fitting her left foot onto the lowest rung.

"That's it," he said encouragingly over the roar of water. "That's it."

She pulled herself up another few rungs and he

began climbing as well, staying as close to her as possible. The rungs were cold and treacherously slippery. The smell of salt water was thick in his nostrils.

They climbed very slowly, their silence broken only by Hui's faint gasps of effort. The roar grew louder, and Crane ventured another glance upward. Vast sheets of water were coruscating out from the breach now, curling and twisting away in downward spirals. A faint mist, born of the violently atomized water, was rising everywhere in ragged sheets; illuminated by the weak sodium lights, it looked ethereal and strange, treacherously beautiful.

Hui's foot slipped, her shoe skidding dangerously close to Crane's face. She let out a cry and pressed herself tightly against the rungs.

"I can't," she said. "I can't."

"Just take it easy," Crane said soothingly. "Nice and slow. Don't look down."

Hui nodded without turning her head. Taking a fresh grip on the rungs, she began climbing again, breathing hard.

They continued upward at the same, plodding pace. Crane estimated they'd climbed about forty feet so far. The torrents of water were growing stronger, spattering hard against his hands and face. The closer they got to the actual breach, he knew, the more violent it would get.

Another minute or two of climbing, then Hui stopped, gasping. "Need to rest."

"No problem. Make sure you've got a secure grip, then lean in against the rungs. You're doing great." Secretly, Crane was glad for a break, as well: his chest was heaving, and his fingers ached from gripping the cold metal rungs.

He guessed they were now probably just outside the Barrier. The skin of the Facility stretched out from them in all directions, a vast, gray monolithic cliff face of metal. Crane looked down, between his feet. The rungs they had already climbed fell away, a straight line leading into the spray and mist below. He could just make out the small platform they had first emerged onto, barely more than a speck far beneath him. Still farther down, at the extreme limits of visibility, the sea floor was now entirely covered by restless, roiling ocean.

"There's something I haven't asked," he shouted over the roar of the water.

Hui kept her gaze on the metal rungs. "What?"

"Where do we reenter the Facility?"

"I'm not sure."

This stopped him. "Excuse me?"

"I know there's one, maybe two access hatches on the upper floors. But I don't know what decks they're on."

"Fair enough." Crane wiped his dripping eyes, shook the water from his hair.

They had, he estimated, perhaps as many as a hundred more feet left to climb. From his precarious vantage point, he glanced uneasily up at the damaged pressure spoke. It was just two floors or so above them now, a massive, horizontal spar half obscured by the cascades that jetted from the rupture in its skin. The blizzard of water was so intense Crane was unable to tell if the Facility had been punctured, as well. He let his eye travel farther up the line of rungs. Luckily, they were bolted at some distance from the spoke. Even so, the rungs directly overhead were being lashed and buffeted by wave after wave of black seawater.

It would be a bitch to climb through that.

He felt his heart accelerating, and the muscles of his legs begin to spasm. He glanced away. The sight was paralyzing; if he didn't start moving again right away, he never would.

"Let's get going," he called out over the cataract.

They resumed their slow climb. With each new rung they ascended, the force of water against them grew stronger. Where before it had felt like a drenching downpour, now—as they began to draw level with the breach—the water was coming at them more and more horizontally.

Crane could barely see Hui's legs amid the water. "Careful!" he shouted. "Be sure you're secure before taking a new step!" He opened his mouth again to say more, but salt water abruptly filled it and he turned away, coughing and choking.

Pull up . . . anchor feet . . . reach for a rung . . . pull up again. Crane tried to think of nothing but climbing, to lose himself in the rhythm. The water was driving straight at him, filling his eyes and ears, tugging at his fingers, trying to pluck him bodily from the face of the Facility. He had lost track of how far they'd ascended now; and with water all around him— flooding over his limbs, blinding him, chilling him to the bone—it was impossible to determine by sight. It seemed his whole world was water. The very breaths he gulped were more water than air. He began to feel light-headed, disoriented.

He stopped, shook his head to clear it. Then he reached up, grabbed another rung; his hand began to slip and he grasped the rung tighter, steadying himself. Turning his face away from the water, he took a deep breath, then pulled himself up. **We must be opposite the spoke by now,** he thought. **This can't go on much longer. It can't.**

Suddenly, he heard a shriek directly above him, the sound all but lost in the thunder of the water. A moment later something struck him violently in the head and shoulders, and he almost let go of the rungs. A weight now hung around his neck, jerking and thrashing. He stood in the blinding, choking whirlwind of water, fighting to keep his hold.

Then there was another cry, almost in his ear, and he abruptly understood. Hui had slipped and fallen. In a desperate attempt at self-preservation, she'd managed to grab him.

"Hui!" he yelled.

55

"**Hui!**" he shouted again.

She moaned, her cheek cold and wet against his.

"**Hold on!** Tight as you can! I'll try to climb out of this!"

He steadied himself on the rungs, the muscles of his calves and arms screaming under the extra weight. Summoning all his energy, he freed one hand and reached up, feeling for the next rung. With her arms around his neck, it was torture; his fingertips touched the rung, then slipped away. With a grunt of effort he tried again, grabbing it this time. He half pushed, half jerked himself upward with his legs, grabbed another rung. He felt her knees press hard against his hips, her ankles lock around one of his knees.

Another grab for the next rung, another heroic thrust upward. And suddenly he realized that the awful torrent of water was ebbing slightly. This brought renewed hope, and he pulled upward again. Now his head and shoulders were above the jets of water. He paused to rest—chest heaving, every muscle dancing and jerking—then he pulled the two of them up another couple of rungs.

Now they were above the water, which ran like a surging river a few inches beneath their feet. Anchoring himself as best he could, Crane took Hui's hand in one of his and guided it to the nearest rung. Slowly, gently, he helped her gain her own footing.

And then they stood there—gasping, sobbing—as the cataract screamed directly beneath them.

It seemed that hours passed while they clung to the side of the Facility, motionless, without speaking. Yet Crane knew it could not have been more than five minutes. At last, he forced himself to stir.

"Come on," he shouted. "We're almost there, we must be."

Hui did not look at him. Her clothes and white lab coat were plastered to her narrow frame, and she was shivering violently.

He wondered if she had even heard him. "Hui! We have to keep going!"

She blinked, then nodded absently. The fear in her eyes was gone; shock, and exhaustion, had driven it away.

Slowly they continued to climb. Crane felt almost stupefied with cold and weariness. Once— only once—he looked down again. The rungs led into a perfect chaos of water. Nothing else could be seen. It seemed impossible they had managed to climb through that hell.

Above him, Hui was saying something, but he couldn't make it out. Languidly, as if in a dream, he looked up. She was pointing to a spot ten feet above her, where another small platform had been set into the wall of the Facility.

With the last of their strength they pulled themselves onto it. There was another hatch here, unmarked. Crane raised his hands to open it, then stopped. What if it was sealed? If they could not get back inside, they were dead. If the rising water didn't drown them, they would die of cold.

He took a deep breath, grabbed the bolts, and bore down hard on them. They turned smoothly. He spun the access wheel, then threw his weight against the hatch. With a squeaking of rubber, the seal parted and the door opened inward. Crane helped Hui step into the small airlock beyond, then he followed her, sealing the hatch securely behind them.

They were back inside.

56

They stepped out of the airlock into a narrow, dark chamber. Crane paused a minute to catch his breath. From beyond came the **whoop, whoop** of an alarm.

Crane opened the door and they emerged into an empty hallway. Here, the cry of the alarm was much louder.

"Deck eleven," Hui said, taking a quick glance around. "Staff quarters."

"We need to get to the conference center on

twelve," Crane said. "Dr. Vanderbilt's waiting for me there."

At random, Crane ducked into a stateroom, plucked a towel from the bath, and wrapped it around Hui's shoulders. Then they ran for the nearest stairwell. The floor seemed deserted, and only once did they pass someone: a man in a maintenance jumpsuit who stopped to stare, openmouthed, as they went past, drenched and dripping.

Reaching the stairwell, they dashed up a flight to the top level of the Facility. Unlike 11, deck 12 was crowded: people stood in the corridors and in open doorways, faces tense and drawn.

The conference center consisted of a central space that resembled a lecture hall, surrounded by a few small breakout rooms. Half a dozen people stood huddled together in the central hall, talking quietly. When Crane entered, they fell silent. One man detached himself from the crowd. He was tall and thin, with red hair and a closely cropped beard. A pair of black glasses poked out from the pocket of his lab coat.

He stepped toward them. "Dr. Crane?" he said.

Crane nodded.

"I'm Gene Vanderbilt." The oceanographer gave them a quick once-over. His eyes widened a little at their appearance, but he made no comment. "Come on—I'll introduce you to the others."

They walked over to the group. Crane waited impatiently through the introductions, then quickly shook hands.

"Frankly, I'm surprised to see you at all," Vanderbilt told him. "I didn't expect you to make it."

"Why is that?" Crane asked. He wondered if Vanderbilt already knew he was a wanted man, that he'd never make it past the Barrier.

"Because deck eight is completely flooded. The watertight doors are all sealed, the elevator shafts closed down."

"Completely flooded?" Crane felt shocked. **So the Facility was breached, after all,** he thought. Now there was no way for anybody on the classified floors to reach the upper levels.

"Some compartments of deck seven, as well. Isn't that right?" And Vanderbilt turned to a short, swarthy machinist who'd been introduced as Gordon Stamper.

Stamper nodded vigorously. "About sixty percent of deck seven is underwater at present. Compartments seven-twelve through seven-fourteen flooded in the last five minutes."

"Seems you found a different route," Vanderbilt said to Crane, with another appraising glance.

"And that's inaccessible now, too," Crane

replied. "One of the pressure spokes has ruptured, and water's flooding in between the Facility and the dome. The emergency exit on deck two is already underwater."

"Yes, we know about the spoke," Vanderbilt said. "Containment crews are on their way."

"It's a pretty serious breach," Crane said dubiously.

"Tell me about it," Stamper replied. "If you all will excuse me, I need to rejoin my team."

"Get back to me in fifteen with another report," said Vanderbilt.

"He's reporting to you?" Crane asked.

Vanderbilt nodded. "I'm the ranking science officer on the decks above eight."

"What about the military?"

"Fragmented. At work trying to contain the breach and ensure hull integrity."

Crane glanced back at Stamper's retreating form. "You said you know all about the breach. Any idea what caused it?"

"Sabotage," Vanderbilt said.

Crane looked back at him. "You're sure?"

"It seems Roger Corbett stumbled upon the saboteur as she was placing the explosive."

"**She?** You mean the saboteur was a woman?"

"Michele Bishop."

Hui Ping gasped.

"No," said Crane. "It's not possible."

"Corbett managed to dial his cell phone while he was confronting Bishop. Called his own intern, Bryce. He heard it from her own lips."

Too much had happened, too quickly, for Crane to even begin absorbing such a terrible shock. He felt a deep chill that had nothing to do with his sodden clothes. **Michele? No, it simply can't be.**

"Where are they now?" he asked mechanically.

"Neither one escaped deck eight. We think they were both killed in the explosion."

As if from a great distance, Crane realized he could not think about this. Not right now. With a tremendous effort, he pushed it aside, then took a deep breath. "The breach isn't our only problem," he said. "In fact, it may not even be the biggest."

"I gather that's what you're here to tell us about."

Crane glanced around at the assembled scientists. "How many of you here have classified clearance?"

Two—Vanderbilt included—raised their hands.

Through his shock and weariness, Crane realized he was about to break all the security protocols he had signed. He also realized that he did not care in the slightest.

Quickly, he sketched out their current situation: the true nature of the dig; Asher's suspicions; the medical problem and its solution; the decrypted messages. Hui interjected here and there, clarifying a point or adding an observation of her own. As he spoke, Crane watched the faces of the scientists. A few—including those who had classified access—nodded now and then, as if some of their private suspicions were being confirmed. Others looked astonished, even incredulous, and—in one or two instances—a little skeptical.

"Korolis has taken military command of the Facility," he concluded. "I don't know what he's done with Admiral Spartan. But Korolis is in Marble Three now, hell-bent on penetrating the Moho. From what I understand, it could happen during the current dive—at any moment, in fact."

"So what do you suggest we do?" Vanderbilt asked.

"We need to contact the surface. AmShale, or even better, the Pentagon. Get in touch with the people in charge, the ones that can put a stop to this madness."

"That's going to be difficult."

Crane glanced at the oceanographer. "Why?"

"We can't contact the surface. Not at present. I've already tried."

"What's wrong?"

"The Facility-to-surface communications gear is on deck seven. It's underwater."

"Damn," Crane muttered.

For a moment, nobody spoke.

"The escape pod," Ping said.

Everyone looked in her direction.

"What about it?" one of the scientists asked.

"If we can't contact the surface, then we'll just have to deliver the message in person."

"She's right," another scientist said. "We can't stay here. Not if what Dr. Crane says is true."

"And there's something else," Hui added. "If they're unable to repair the breach, the water level will keep rising outside."

"The Facility wasn't built to withstand the pressure at this depth," someone added. "It'll implode."

"The pod will hold a hundred people, give or take," said Vanderbilt. "That should easily accommodate everybody on the upper decks."

"What about the people in the classified areas?" Crane asked.

"Another reason for us to get to the surface as quickly as possible," Vanderbilt replied. "Communications are down. The faster we get topside, the faster they can get back here to effect rescue and repair."

Crane glanced around the group. People were nodding.

"It's settled, then," said Vanderbilt. "Let's start transferring personnel to the escape pod. I'll need some volunteers to make sweeps of decks nine through eleven, send any stragglers here."

"I'll take deck nine," Crane said. "I know it better than I know the others."

Vanderbilt nodded. "Meet us back here as quickly as you can."

Crane turned to Ping. "You'll help with the boarding?"

She nodded.

"I'll be right back." He gave her hand a brief, reassuring squeeze. Then he turned, jogged quickly out of the hall, and vanished from sight.

57

In the cramped, sweat-heavy confines of Marble Three, Rafferty swiveled his shaggy head to one side. "Sir."

Korolis glanced at the engineer.

"Sensors are registering an anomaly in the sedimentary matrix."

"Where?"

"Less than two meters below the present dig interface."

"How's the tunnel-boring machine behaving?"

"A little ornery, sir. We're dropping the check-sum on every other data packet now."

"Ease it back to half speed. We don't want any foul-ups."

"Half speed, aye."

"Any specifics on the anomalous readings?"

"Nothing yet, sir. The water's too sedimented; we need to get closer."

"What about the ultrasound?"

"Unknown interference from below, sir."

Korolis massaged his temples, cursing the limitations of the equipment. The closer they got to the anomaly, the less reliable their instruments became.

It was hot inside the Marble, and he wiped the sweat from his forehead before fitting his eyes to the rubber housing of the external viewscreen. He activated the spotlight beneath the Marble. Instantly, the tiny screen displayed a perfect hurricane of silt and rock: with the boring machine digging away the sediment beneath them and the vacuum tube unit sucking it up for distribution across the seabed, the water surrounding them was completely opaque. **Too sedimented, hell.** He snapped off the spotlight and pulled back, fingertips tapping impatiently on the viewscreen handles.

From outside there came a muffled boom, as if

from a great distance away. Dr. Flyte had fitted another reinforcing band into place.

The radio squawked. "Marble Three, this is Dive Control."

Korolis plucked the radio from its cradle. "Go ahead, Dive Control."

"Status report on the explosion, sir."

"Let's have it."

"Apparently, there was a breach in the south pressure spoke."

"And the Facility?"

"Deck eight is flooded and almost fifty percent of deck seven is underwater."

"Deck seven? That's not possible—each floor is designed to be absolutely watertight."

"Yes, sir, but because of the location of the breach, water's been coming down through the ventilation shafts. There's a report the explosion was caused by—"

"What about the repair parties? Is it under control?"

"The watertight hatches on the decks immediately above and below the breach have all been sealed. The inflow of water has been stopped."

"Good work."

"But water is rising within the dome cavity, sir. And if any more of deck seven becomes flooded, the Barrier will potentially come under stress."

Korolis felt pain throb across his scalp. "Then the breach in the pressure spoke must be repaired, and fast."

"Sir—"

"I don't want to hear any excuses. Take as many repair crews as you need. Get it done."

"Commander," Rafferty murmured in his ear.

"Stand by," Korolis snapped into the radio. "Yes, Dr. Rafferty?"

"I read incoming movement."

"From where?"

"I'm not sure, sir. A minute ago, nothing. They just appeared."

Korolis blinked. "Sentinels?"

"Unknown. If they are, they're much larger than the others, sir. And moving fast."

Korolis snugged his face against the eyepiece once again, snapped on the exterior light. "Secure the boring machine. I can't see a damn thing in all this murk."

"Aye, aye. Securing tunnel-boring machine."

Korolis peered into the viewscreen. Slowly, the storm of sand and sediment subsided. And then **they** appeared, like apparitions emerging from a fog.

There were two of them. They had the same ineffable exteriors as their smaller brethren in the Facility: a dazzling, unearthly kaleidoscope of shifting colors, amber and scarlet and hyacinth and a thousand others, so bright in the black depths they threatened to overload the camera's CCD sensors. But these were much larger—three feet long, perhaps four, with glittering crystalline tails that whipped and twitched behind them and dozens of tendrils floating out on all sides. They drifted to a stop just below and to each side of the Marble. As Korolis stared, they floated languorously, as if waiting.

He had never seen anything so beautiful. Korolis felt his headache, the unpleasant prickly warmth that enveloped him, every physical irritant, begin to fall away under their spell.

"They've come to greet us," he whispered.

His radio squawked again. "Sir?"

Korolis forced himself away from the viewscreen. As he did so, the headache returned, full force, so strong that he felt a spasm of nausea. He picked up the radio with a stab of anger.

"What is it?" he barked.

"Sir, we've received a report from the upper decks. It appears some of the scientists are mobilizing."

"Mobilizing?"

"Yes, sir. They are rounding up staff and crew and directing them to the staging area outside the escape pod. They appear to be planning a mass evacuation."

At this, Flyte gave a delighted cackle. "'Gray-eyed Athena, send them a favorable breeze,'" he intoned quietly.

Korolis held the mike close to his lips, spoke in a controlled voice. "Nobody is abandoning this Facility on my watch. Doesn't Chief Woburn have personnel on the upper decks?"

"Yes, sir. They're in the stairwells to deck eight, assisting in the damage control efforts."

"Well, deal with the situation. Korolis out."

"Very good, sir." The radio gave a chirrup, then lapsed into silence.

Korolis turned back to Rafferty. "Distance to the anomaly?"

"One meter directly beneath the dig interface."

"Can you get a read on it?"

"Checking." The engineer bent over his instrumentation. "It appears to be composed of some super-dense material."

"Size?"

"Unknown. It extends in all directions."

"A new layer of strata?"

"Highly unlikely, sir. The surface appears to be perfectly regular."

Perfectly regular. One meter directly beneath. The words set Korolis's heart racing.

He absently wiped his forehead again, licked his lips. "What's the status of the air-jetting system?"

"One hundred percent operational."

"Very well. Have the tunnel-boring machine

dig the lateral retaining tunnel. Then maneuver it and the Doodlebug into the tunnel and deploy the stabilizer arm."

"Aye, sir."

Korolis looked from the engineer to Dr. Flyte and back again. Then, without another word, he swiveled back to the eyepiece.

58

It took Crane twenty minutes to complete his sweep of deck 9. Normally bustling at all hours of the day and night, it now looked like a ghost town. The theater was a graveyard of empty seats; the library, utterly deserted. The PX was closed, its windows dark; the tables of the sidewalk café unused and lonely. Crane found a worker sleeping in a carrel in the multimedia nexus, and a lone technician in the Medical Suite, where he stopped to retrieve a portable medical kit. He sent both on ahead to deck 12.

He ducked into the laundry—empty—and grabbed another towel. Then he returned to Times Square, giving the shopfronts one last appraising glance. The stillness was eerie. The smell of roasting coffee hung in the air, and music filtered out from the café. And there was another sound, as well: a faint groaning from deck 8, directly beneath. It reminded him irresistibly of his submarine duty, and the strange—almost sinister—creaking of the ballast tanks as they filled with seawater.

As he climbed the stairwell, his thoughts returned to Michele Bishop. He did not want to believe it. And yet a part of him realized it was, perhaps, the only explanation for why she hadn't organized the scientists herself; why she had not called him back as promised. Someday, he would try to figure out her motivation. Right now, he could not even begin to.

He thought back to their final, brief phone conversation. **So Spartan's not going to stop the dig?** she had asked. One thing, at least, was painfully clear: it was not idle curiosity that had prompted this question.

Reaching deck 12, he made his way quickly through the now-hushed corridors. The staging area for the escape pod was a large chamber adjoining the Compression Complex. As he entered, he found two dozen people lined up before a metal ladder bolted to the wall. It disappeared up through a hatchway in the ceiling. A faint bluish light filtered down, throwing the ladder into spectral relief.

Vanderbilt was supervising the boarding, Hui Ping at his side. When they saw Crane enter, they came over.

"Anyone?" Vanderbilt asked.

"Only two."

The oceanographer nodded. "That's everyone, then. The sweeps of the other three decks are complete."

"What's the head count?" Crane asked.

"A hundred and twelve." Vanderbilt nodded toward the line that snaked its way toward the ladder. "Once these last are aboard, we'll initiate the launch sequence."

"Where's Stamper?"

"He and the rest of his crew are already in the pod. There's nothing more they can do from this side of the breach."

Vanderbilt headed back to the ladder, and Crane turned to Hui Ping. "Why aren't you aboard?" he asked, removing the damp towel from around her shoulders and replacing it with the dry one.

"I was waiting for you."

Silently, they joined the end of the line. As they waited, Crane found thoughts of Michele Bishop creeping back into his head. To distract himself, he turned back to Hui.

"What was that you were going to tell me?" he asked.

Hui was absently clutching the towel, her gaze far away. "I'm sorry?"

"Earlier, you said you'd deciphered that transmission. The longer one, the one they first received from beneath the Moho."

She nodded. "Yes. Well, it's a theory, anyway. I can't prove it, but it seems to fit."

She dug into the pocket of her lab coat, pulled out a dripping palmtop computer. "This thing is drenched. I'm not even sure it will work." But when she snapped the power button, the display flickered to life. Taking the stylus, she opened a window of binary numbers:

```
10000001110000000000000000011000000
01000000000000000000011000000000000
00000000000000011000000000000000000
01100000110000000000000000000000000
01100000000000000000000000000110000
00000000010000000000000110000000000
01110000000000001100000000000010000
00000000001100000000000000000000000
00011000000000000000001000000001100
00000000000000000000000011000001100
00000000000000000011000000000000000
```

```
00000001100011000000000000000000000000
00000100000100100000000000000011100010
01000000000000000001000000000000000000
00010010001000000000001010000000000
00000001001000000000000000000000000
00000001000000001000000000010000000
01000000000001000100010000001000010
00000000001000000010001000000010000
00000000000001000000000000000000100
00000001000010000000000010000100000
00001000000010000100000000000000000
01000000000001000010000000000100000
00000000000000000000000000000101
10000000000010000010
```

"Here it is," she said. "The digital stream Dr. Asher saved as 'initial.txt,' the one he never tried to decrypt. While I was waiting for you I tried a variety of cryptographic attacks on it. Nothing worked. It seemed to have nothing in common with all the mathematical expressions he deciphered."

The line for the ladder was slowly growing shorter; there were perhaps ten people ahead of them now. "Go on," Crane said.

"I was about to give up. Then I thought of what you'd said about WIPP, and how they were employing not one but several types of warnings. 'Pictures, symbols, text,' you said. And I got to thinking. Whoever planted this stuff beneath the Moho, maybe **they** used several types of warnings, too. Maybe they weren't all just forbidden mathematical expressions. So I started experimenting. First I attempted to play the message back as an audio file. That didn't work. Then I wondered if it might be a graphic image, or images. I broke it up in various ways. Those repeated pairings of ones in the first half of the sequence intrigued me. So I divided it into two equal parts. You'll note that the first image is delimited by ones. And there is precisely the same ratio of ones to zeros between the two images. It seemed it was **meant** to be divided in half."

She tapped the stylus on the screen. The binary sequence reappeared, this time broken in two:

```
100000011100000000000000000001
100000001000000000000000000001
100000000000000000000000000001
100000000000000000000011000001
100000000000000000000000000001
100000000000000000000000000001
100000000000010000000000000001
100000000000011100000000000001
100000000000010000000000000001
100000000000000000000000000001
100000000000000000010000000001
100000000000000000000000000001
```

```
10000011000000000000000000000001
10000000000000000000000110001
100000000000000000000000000001

00000100100000000000000001110001
00100000000000000000001000000000
00000000000100100001000000000000
00101000000000000000000001000100
00000000000000000000000000000000
10000000010000000000100000000
10000000000001000100010000001
00001000000000001000000001000
10000000100000000000000000100
0000000000000000100000000010
00010000000000001000100000000
0100000001000100000000000000
00000100000000001000010000000
0000010000000000000000000000
00000001011000000000010000010
```

She glanced at Crane. "See anything different about the top image?"

Crane peered at the screen. "The ones are clustered together."

"Exactly." With her stylus, Hui circled the groupings.

```
10000001110000000000000000000001
10000000100000000000000000000001
10000000000000000000000000000001
10000000000000000000011000000 1
10000000000000000000000000000001
10000000000000000000000000000001
10000000000000010000000000000001
10000000000000111000000000000001
10000000000000010000000000000001
10000000000000000000000000000001
10000000000000000000010000000001
10000000000000000000000000000001
10000011000000000000000000000001
1000000000000000000000000110001
100000000000000000000000000001
```

"Now, does that suggest anything to you?" she asked.

He shook his head. "No. Not really."

"Well, it does to me. I think it's an image of the inner solar system." She tapped the large cluster. "There, dead center, is the sun. And circling it are the inner five planets. And I'll bet that if you checked the star charts, you'd find they had been spun back to their positions of six hundred years ago."

"The time of the burial event."

"Precisely."

"What's the second image, then?" Crane asked. "It looks random. Like noise."

"That's it exactly. It **is** random—and in fact, it's perfectly random. I checked."

Crane frowned at the storm of ones and zeros. Then a sudden, chilling thought struck him. "Do you think it means . . . Armageddon?"

She nodded. "I think it's another kind of warning. If we disturb what's down there . . ." Her voice trailed off.

He looked up from the screen and stared at her. "The solar system will be blown to bits."

"Literally and figuratively."

Now Vanderbilt was helping a female scientist directly ahead of them ascend the ladder into the escape pod. As Hui stepped forward and grasped the ladder, Crane stopped her. "That was impressive, you know."

She turned to him. "I'm sorry?"

"You, hiding in that lab, having the presence of mind not only to work on this problem, but to figure it out . . ."

At that moment, the door to the staging area flew open. A marine in black fatigues stepped in, M-16 assault rifle in his hands. His gaze went from Crane, to Hui, to Vanderbilt, to the scientist halfway through the hatch.

"Step away from the ladder," he barked.

Crane turned to him. "We're evacuating this station, going for help."

"There will be no evacuation. Everyone is to disembark and return to their stations, and the escape pod is to be secured."

"On whose orders?" Vanderbilt said.

"Commander Korolis's."

"Korolis is unwell," Crane said.

"I'm the senior scientist here," Vanderbilt said. "With the lower decks inaccessible, I'm in charge. The evacuation will proceed."

The marine unshipped his weapon and aimed it at them. "I have my orders," he said, his voice perfectly flat and even. "Everyone **will** leave the escape pod. One way or the other."

Crane's looked from the barrel of the rifle to the soldier's flinty, impassive eyes. There was no doubt in his mind—none at all—that this was not an idle threat.

The woman on the ladder had frozen in place. Now, slowly, sobbing quietly, she began to descend once again.

59

Crane stared at the marine. The man was standing inside the doorway, perhaps fifteen feet away.

He felt his hands ball into fists. Unconsciously, a plan had formed in his mind. He glanced at Vanderbilt. The oceanographer looked back and a silent understanding passed between them. Almost imperceptibly, Vanderbilt nodded.

Crane's eyes returned to the automatic rifle. There was no way he could reach it, he knew, without being gunned down. But if he could keep the marine busy, at least it would give Vanderbilt a chance to move in.

He took a step forward.

The black ops agent turned toward him. The man's eyes widened slightly, as if sensing the agent's design. Quickly, the weapon swung up to Crane's chest.

At that moment a shape came into view in the corridor beyond the staging area. "Secure that weapon," a familiar voice boomed.

The agent turned. Admiral Spartan stood in the doorway, a large gash across his forehead. The upper portion of his uniform was stiff with dried blood. A heavy sidearm lay in his right hand. He looked pale but determined.

"I said secure that weapon, soldier," he said quietly.

For a moment, nobody moved. Then the black ops agent abruptly swung the M-16 in Spartan's direction. In a fluid motion, the admiral raised his pistol and fired. In the enclosed space, the explosion was deafening. The marine flew backward under the impact, his weapon clattering across the floor. The woman on the ladder screamed.

Spartan remained where he was a moment, his gun trained at the motionless form. Then he stepped forward, picked up the automatic rifle, and turned to Crane. Silently, Vanderbilt helped the woman back up the ladder, then motioned for Hui Ping to follow.

Crane opened his medical bag for a dressing kit, but Spartan waved it away. "Where have you been?" Crane asked.

"Locked in my cabin."

"How'd you get out?"

The admiral brandished the handgun with a mirthless smile.

"You know what's happened?"

"I know enough. Is everybody aboard the escape pod?"

"Everybody from decks nine through twelve. A hundred and twelve in all. Deck eight is completely flooded. Nobody below there can get past."

A look of pain crossed Spartan's face. "It's vital you get these people away from here as quickly as possible."

"No argument here. Let's get aboard."

The admiral shook his head. "I'm staying here."

"You can't. There's no guarantee rescue will arrive in time. Besides, Korolis is down in Marble Three right now. He could reach the Moho at any moment. God only knows what will happen then."

Spartan pointed his handgun at the marine. "More like him are on their way. They'll stop the pod's disengage sequence, prevent you from leaving. I won't allow that."

Crane frowned. "But—"

"That's an order, Dr. Crane. You're to save as many as you can. Now get aboard, please."

Crane hesitated a moment longer. Then he snapped to attention, gave the admiral a salute. Spartan returned it, a wintry smile gathering on his face. Crane turned to follow Vanderbilt up the ladder.

"Doctor?" Spartan called.

Crane glanced back.

Spartan pulled a card from his pocket, held it out. "When you reach Storm King, call this man. Tell him everything."

Crane glanced at the card. It was embossed with a Department of Defense seal and it read only MCPHERSON, (203) 111–1011.

"Aye, sir," he said.

"Good luck."

Crane gave the admiral a final nod. Then, quickly, he climbed the ladder and pulled himself through the hatchway.

He was in a small, vertical tube, illuminated by recessed blue LEDs. The ladder continued upward, flanked on both sides by heavy ductwork. There was a hollow clang from below as Spartan closed the outer hatch.

Climbing another two dozen steps, Crane passed through an immensely thick, collarlike portal and emerged into a low, teardrop-shaped enclosure. It was dimly illuminated in the same faint blue wash as the access tube. As he stood at the top of the ladder, letting his eyes adjust, he saw he was surrounded by two tiers of circular benches, one behind and above the other, that ran completely around the pod. A safety railing was positioned before each. Both tiers were crowded with people, some holding hands. The atmosphere was strangely hushed; hardly anyone spoke, and those who did conversed in whispers. Crane's eyes moved from face to familiar face. Bryce, the psychiatric intern. Gordon Stamper, machinist. Lab techs, pizza flippers, mechanics, librarians, PX cashiers, food service staff: a cross section of Facility workers he'd treated, worked with, or brushed elbows with over the past ten days.

Two people were conspicuously absent: Roger Corbett and Michele Bishop.

To his right was a small control panel, manned by Vanderbilt and a technician Crane didn't recognize. Vanderbilt rose and came forward.

"Admiral Spartan?" he asked.

"He's staying behind," Crane replied.

Vanderbilt nodded. Kneeling, he closed and carefully sealed the hatch. Then he turned and nodded at the tech, who worked the panel controls briefly.

A low tone sounded overhead. "Disengage now under way," the tech said.

Vanderbilt rose, wiped his hands on his lab coat. "There's a five-minute countdown while the compression sequence is completed," he said.

"Time to the surface?"

"Once we disengage from the dome, just over eight minutes. On paper, anyway."

Slinging his medical kit over his shoulder, Crane scanned the seated people on the two tiers of benches, checking for injuries. Then he returned to the control panel. Directly behind Vanderbilt sat Hui Ping. She smiled faintly as Crane took a seat beside her.

"Ready?" he asked.

"No."

A small circular porthole had been set into the portal hatch. It looked exactly like the one Crane had sat next to during his initial descent in the bathyscaphe. Now he leaned forward, looked down through it. He could see the ladder descending toward the sealed outer hatch, outlined in the pale blue light.

"Two minutes," the technician at the control panel said. "We've got good pressure."

Beside him, Hui stirred. "I've been wondering about something," she said.

"Shoot."

"Remember when you explained about Ocotillo Mountain? You said that there were two kinds of countermeasures to prevent anyone, intentionally or unintentionally, from intruding into the vaults full of old nuclear weapons—passive security measures and active ones."

"That's right."

"I can understand what the passive measures would be—warning signs, images etched on metal, things of that sort. But what would the **active** countermeasures be?"

"I don't know. There was little talk about them at the conference, other than to note their existence. I gathered that information about them was classified." He turned toward her. "Why do you ask?"

"Those sentinels we found—those are passive measures in their own way, like you said. They simply beam out warnings. I guess I was wondering if **they** have active countermeasures, as well."

"I don't know," Crane replied slowly. "That's a very good question."

"One minute," the tech murmured.

And in the silence that followed, Crane could now hear distinctly—filtering up from the hatchway beneath his feet—the sharp, steady cadence of automatic weapon fire.

60

The tunnel-boring machine and the Doodlebug had been secured in the lateral retaining tunnel. The stabilization arm had been deployed, locking Marble Three into position directly above the anomaly. These final steps had been simulated many times; the actual procedures had been executed flawlessly. From here on, they were proceeding like surgeons, using only compressed air and the robotic arms. It had gone deathly silent inside the Marble.

"Give it another shot," Korolis whispered. "Gently. Gently."

"Aye, sir," Rafferty whispered back.

The three men communicated by looks and brief murmurs. Even Dr. Flyte seemed caught up in the moment. Again Korolis wiped the sheen of sweat from his face, then pressed his eyes to the tiny view port. A kind of awed reverence hung in the air, as if they were archaeologists excavating some supremely holy tomb. His pounding headache and the strange, metallic film that coated his tongue had vanished completely.

As he watched, Rafferty sent another puff of compressed air over the bottom of the hole. A small storm of sediment and loose gabbro erupted into the yellow glow of the Marble's exterior light, to be quickly sucked away by the vacuum unit.

"Careful," Korolis murmured. "What's the distance?"

"We're there, sir," Rafferty replied.

Korolis turned back to the viewscreen. "Another jet," he said.

"Another jet, aye."

He watched as another stream of compressed air shot over the bottom of the dig interface. He could see the two large sentinels floating on either side, glittering tails moving restlessly back and forth, tendrils drifting lazily. They were like spectators at a show. And why not? It was only right they should be here. They had come not only to witness his triumph, but also to guide him through the fabulous technological riches that awaited. It was not chance that brought him here on this most critical of dives: it was destiny.

"Again," he whispered.

Another jet of air; another gray storm of matter. The viewscreen quickly cleared as the vacuum unit sucked away the particulate. Korolis gripped the control handles even more tightly.

The radio on his control panel squawked into life. "Marble Three, this is Dive Control. Marble Three, this is Dive Control. Please acknowledge—"

Without taking his eyes from the viewscreen, Korolis reached down and snapped off the radio. He could see something now—a bright sheen, almost like the reflected gleam of metal.

"One more shot," he said. "Very carefully, Dr. Rafferty. Smooth as glass."

"Very good, sir."

A ripple of compressed air shot through the dark water beneath them; a fresh confusion of gray and brown particles. And then, as it cleared, Korolis gasped.

"My God," he breathed.

The air-jetting system had cleared the base of the shaft, revealing a smooth, glassy surface. To Korolis, pressed up against the eyepiece, it looked

almost like someone blowing dust from a tabletop. Beyond lay an illusion—at least, he thought
it was an illusion—of nearly infinite depth: a
black infinity extending below. His searchlight
was reflecting from the glassy surface, but he
thought he could make out another light source,
dim and strange, beyond and below the bright co-
rona.

On either side of the Marble, the large sentinels
had grown agitated. No longer content to simply
drift, they were moving back and forth across the
narrow diameter of the tunnel.

"Extinguish the light," Korolis said.

"Sir?" Rafferty said.

"Extinguish the light, please."

Now Korolis could see more clearly.

They were suspended above a massive cavity, of
which only the smallest speck had been exposed.
Whether the cavity was hollow—or whether the
glassy surface directly below them filled it, like
glue forced into a hole—he could not be sure.
The velvety blackness gave no distinct impression, save that of vast depth.

But no . . . a faint light appeared from far below. As he stared, barely able to breathe, it slowly
brightened.

It was coming closer.

"Sir!" said Rafferty, his normally reserved voice
tense.

Korolis glanced at him. "What is it?"

"They've stopped broadcasting their signals."

"You've regained full control?" Korolis asked.

"Yes, sir. Wireless and remote systems, as well. Sensors, too: ultrasound, radiation, magnetometer, everything."

Korolis turned back to the viewscreen. "They're showing themselves to us," he murmured.

The light was closer now. Korolis noticed that it was wavering slightly: not in the lazy, undulant way of the sentinels' silhouettes, but in a sharp, almost fierce pulsation. And it was a color he had never seen before: a kind of deep metallic sheen, like the glow of black light on a knife blade. It seemed he could taste it as much as see it. This was a strangely unsettling sensation. Something about it made the hairs on the nape of his neck stand up.

"Sir!" said Rafferty again. "I'm picking up radiation signatures from below."

"What kind of radiation, Dr. Rafferty?"

"Every kind, sir. Infrared, ultraviolet, gamma, radio. The sensors are going crazy. It's a spectrum I don't recognize."

"Analyze it, then."

"Very well, sir." The engineer turned to his station and began punching in data.

Korolis turned back to the viewscreen. The glowing object was still rising toward them out of the rich blackness. Its strange color deepened. It was shaped like a torus, its outline pulsating ever more brilliantly. As he stared, openmouthed, the lambent otherworldliness of it brought back a sudden memory of childhood, long forgotten. When he was eight, his parents had taken him to Italy, and they had attended a papal mass at St. Peter's basilica. When the pontiff had brought out the host and raised it toward the congregation, Korolis felt himself galvanized by something like an electric shock. Somehow, the richness of the baroque spectacle brought the true import of it home to his young consciousness for the first time. There, at the tabernacle, the pontiff was offering them the most wonderful gift in the universe: the sacred mystery of the consecrated host.

Of course, organized religion had long since lost its usefulness for Korolis. But, staring at the wondrous, shimmering thing, he felt the same blend of emotions. He was among the chosen. And here was the offering of a higher power, the most wondrous of gifts.

His mouth was dry, and the coppery taste had returned. "Either one of you want to take a look?" he asked huskily.

Rafferty was still hunched over his laptop. Dr. Flyte nodded, then slid his way across the cramped interior and took up a position at the view port. For a moment, the old man said nothn his jaw worked briefly. **" 'No light; but darkness visible,' "** he murmured.

ptly, Rafferty looked up from his laptop.

mander!" he barked. "You need to see this,

rolis bent over the screen, which showed two

ges, each one a blizzard of narrow vertical

s.

At first I couldn't identify the spectrum of elec-

magnetic radiation," Rafferty said. "It made no

nse; it seemed impossible."

"Why?" Korolis found his glance stealing back

oward the viewscreen.

"Because the spectra contained wavelengths of

both matter and antimatter."

"But that can't be. Matter and antimatter can't exist together."

"Exactly. But that object you see on the screen? Sensors said it was composed of both. Then I separated the matter signature from the antimatter signature. And I got this." Rafferty waved toward the computer screen.

"What is it?"

"Hawking radiation, sir."

At this, Dr. Flyte turned from the viewscreen in surprise.

"Hawking radiation?" Korolis repeated.

Rafferty nodded. Sweat had appeared on his forehead, and there was a strange brightness to his

eyes. "It's the thermal radiation that e
from the edges of a black hole."

"You're joking."

The engineer shook his head. "The spect
instantly recognizable to any astrophysicist.

Korolis felt his growing sense of euphoria t
to dissipate into disbelief. "You're saying that
ject we're looking at is a black hole? Compose
both matter **and** antimatter? That just isn't po
ble."

Flyte had returned his gaze to the viewscree
Now, he pushed himself back, blue eyes flashir
in his pale face. "**Ehui!** I think I understand."

"Then explain, please, Dr. Flyte."

"Gentlemen, gentlemen. That torus-shaped object down there isn't a single black hole. It's two."

"**Two?**" Korolis repeated, his incredulity deepening.

"Two, yes! Imagine two black holes—they'd
each be extremely small, perhaps the size of a marble—in very tight orbit around each other.
They're orbiting at a furious rate, a thousand a second or more."

"Orbiting how?" Korolis asked.

"Not even **I** have all the answers, Commander
Korolis. They must be held in that orbit by some
force, some technology, we don't understand. To
the naked eye, they appear to be a single body.

And to Rafferty's instruments, they appear to be emitting Hawking radiation of both matter and antimatter."

"But in reality they are two separate entities," Korolis said.

"Of **course,**" Rafferty breathed. "Just as the individual spectrum readings on my laptop indicate."

All of a sudden, Korolis understood. It wa unimaginably powerful, and yet so elegant in i simplicity. His euphoria returned. "Two bla holes," he said, more to himself than the othe "One matter, one antimatter. Locked toget but not touching. And if the force that held tl in orbit was removed . . . or, as it were, **off . . .**"

"The matter and antimatter would col' Rafferty said grimly. "Utter and complete co sion of matter into energy. It would release energy per unit mass than any other re n known to science."

"Let me see that." Korolis replaced Dr. F at the viewscreen. His heart was hammering his chest, and his hands were slick on the c trol handles. He stared at the glowing, pulsating ing below him with new reverence.

When this descent had started, he'd had pes of discovering some new and revelatory te nology; something so awesome and overwhelming it would guarantee America's supremacy. Now he had succeeded beyond his wildest dreams.

"A bomb," he whispered. "The greatest bomb in the universe. And it fits in a matchbox."

"A **bomb**?" said Rafferty. There was a note of concern, even fear, in his voice. "Sir, as a weapon, what we're looking at is of no practical use."

"Why is that?" Korolis said, not taking his eyes from the viewscreen.

"Because it could never be used. If those two black holes ever collided, the resulting explosion would be staggering. It would destroy the solar system."

But Korolis was no longer listening. Because the dark infinitude in his viewscreen was now subtly changing.

Where before there had been inky blackness— broken only by the shimmering light of the single artifact—now a faint, even blush of light was suffusing the spaces below. It was like the light of pre-dawn. And Korolis caught his breath at what it revealed. There was not one artifact, but hundreds—**thousands**—held in the clear matrix that spread out beneath him. The nearer ones glowed with their strange, alien light, while those farthest away were mere pinpricks, almost invisible to the eye. Between them all, sentinels prowled, tendrils rippling, ceaselessly vigilant.

It was a prize beyond all hope, beyond all imagining, beyond all measure.

Korolis leaned back, wiped the sweat from around his eyes with the back of a hand, leaned in again. "Return to your station," he told Flyte. "Ready the robot arm."

The cybernetics engineer blinked. "I beg your pardon?"

"Ready the robot arm. Extend it down one meter."

"But that would put it in contact with the surface of—"

"Exactly."

There was a pause. Then Rafferty spoke up. "Forgive my saying so, sir, but are you sure that's wise, given the apparent nature of—"

"I'm letting them know that we're accepting their gift."

Another pause. Then, murmuring something in Greek, Flyte turned to his station, grasped the arm's trigger mechanism.

On the screen, Korolis watched as the robotic arm came into view below the Marble. It moved forward hesitantly, a little jerkily, one steel finger extended. And once again his mind flashed back to his childhood trip to Rome. He remembered standing in the Sistine Chapel, staring upward, mouth agape, at Michelangelo's depiction of the Creation of Adam: the fingertips of God and man about to touch—the first moment of life—the start of a universe . . .

The arm came in contact with the glasslike surface. It dimpled inward, like transparent gelatin.

Korolis thought he heard a faint singing, a low susurrus of sound like a choir atop a distant mountain. **This is what it is like to touch eternity . . .**

Instantly, the two sentinels floating on either side winked out of sight. One moment they were there; the next they were gone, ghostly reflections now of mere memory. As he stared, a bright light bloomed deep within the cavity below them. It had the golden brilliance of a tiny sun. And its fierce light suddenly revealed all the secrets of that deep void. Korolis gasped, stunned, as its true enormity—and the staggering, **overwhelming** number of artifacts contained within it—was laid bare.

This was a cache of death that could threaten the entire cosmos.

"If just one could blow up a solar system, why do they need thousands?" he muttered.

In the sudden silence, Flyte asked a question. "Do you know why the Parthenon is such a ruin?"

This was so bizarre that Korolis turned toward the old man despite himself.

"The Turks," he went on, once again sounding

serious. "They used it as a munitions depot in the eighteenth century. A stray shell blew it up. This is the same thing, Commander. It's a weapons dump, the fruit of some intergalactic arms race. Something far beyond our technical comprehension."

"That's rubbish," Korolis said. "Has Dr. Crane been talking to you?"

"I'm afraid it's not rubbish. We were never meant to find this. These weapons were buried so they could never be found or used. Because they could absolutely destroy not only the world, but this **section of the universe**."

"Sir!" Rafferty said. "I'm getting some very strange readings."

"What kind of readings?"

"I've never seen anything like it. A completely alien energy signature. And it's moving toward us at a tremendous rate of speed."

"**'A generation of men is like a generation of leaves,'**" Flyte sang in a low, mournful, dirgelike voice. "**'And the season of spring comes on.'**"

As he turned back to the viewscreen, Korolis realized the sun that had blossomed into existence far below them was not so tiny, after all. The singing grew louder, became an unearthly shriek. A moment later, Korolis realized the sunlike object was **moving**—passing by the sentinels and the artifacts, **bomb** artifacts, so quickly now they were mere blurs of color. For a brief moment, something about its single-minded trajectory reminded him of an antiaircraft missile. And then, as it drew closer and became clearer, it no longer looked like anything he'd ever seen before; racing up through the void toward him, growing and still growing until its fiery light filled the entire viewscreen, flinging off tongues of flame in bright angry curls like molten shavings . . .

. . . And then—as it engulfed Marble Three and erupted up the tunnel, vaporizing Korolis's flesh and carbonizing his bones in less than a millisecond—there was no time to feel surprise, or fear, or even pain.

61

"Thirty seconds," the tech at the control panel said. "Maximum buoyancy achieved."

Vanderbilt looked up from the instrumentation. "Hang on, people. This is going to be a rough ride."

Below, the sounds of gunshots had ceased.

Crane looked around. The escape pod had gone utterly still now, and in the faint blue light the sea of faces looked drawn, tense, worried.

"Ten seconds," the tech said.

"Ejection sequence initiating," said Vanderbilt.

Now Crane could hear—echoing up through the entrance tube—the clang of some metallic object against the outer hatch. Over his shoulder, somebody began to pray loudly. Crane reached over and took Hui Ping's hands in his.

"Ejection under way," said the tech.

There was a sharp jolt, the grinding of metal on metal, and then the escape pod shot upward like a cork. Crane felt himself pressed into his seat as they rocketed toward the surface. He glanced down through the porthole but could see only a storm of bubbles, illummated by the pod's running lights.

At that moment, he heard a strange sound. It was low, almost at the threshold of audibility, and it seemed to come from far below. It sounded as if the earth itself was crying out in pain. The escape pod trembled in a way that had nothing to do with their rapid ascent.

There was a sudden confusion of shouts and groans. Beside him, Hui suddenly raised a hand to her face. "My ears," she said.

"Change in air pressure," Crane told her. "Try swallowing or yawning. Or the Valsalva maneuver."

"The what?"

"Pinch your nose and shut your mouth, then try forcing air through your nostrils. It helps equalize the pressure in your ears."

He glanced downward through the porthole again, searching for the source of the strange roar. The welter of bubbles had cleared and he could just make out the curve of the dome, already hundreds of feet below them now, its cluster of lights like the faintest of stars in a black sky. As he watched, they faded from view, and all was dark.

Then—just as he was about to look away—an explosion of light came from below.

It was almost as if the entire ocean had suddenly been illuminated. Crane had a brief vision of the sea floor—stretching away in all directions like a grayish lunar plain. Countless bizarre and alien-looking deepwater fish hung below him. Then the brightness became too intense and he had to turn away.

"What the **hell**?" he heard Vanderbilt say.

The porthole was like a lightbulb, bathing the inside of the escape pod in brilliant yellow. But even as he looked, Crane noticed that the light was beginning to fade. More sounds came from below now: sharp booms and rat-a-tats like a legion of enormous fireworks. He leaned forward again, squinting into the porthole. He caught his breath.

"Oh, my God," he breathed.

In the light reflecting upward from the ocean floor, he could just make out the dome. It had been abruptly blown open, peeled back like a banana. Inside it, he could see unearthly flashes of red and brown and yellow, a furious cascade of explosions as the Facility tore itself apart.

And there was something else: a massive shock wave—roiling and churning like a living thing—boiling upward toward them at a furious rate.

He sat up instantly, grabbing Hui Ping with one hand and the safety railing with the other. "Brace for impact!" he yelled.

A moment of terrible anticipation . . . and then the pod was abruptly thrown on its side, nearly upended by the force of the wave. There were cries, screams. The lights went out, and the only illumination was the dying yellow light from below. Crane clung grimly to Hui as they were shaken violently back and forth. Someone went tumbling across the cabin, colliding with a safety railing and sinking to the floor with a groan. More screams, shouts for help. There was a popping sound, then a hiss of water.

"Seal that breach!" Vanderbilt shouted to the tech above the tumult.

"What is it?" Hui asked, her face pressed against Crane's shoulder.

"I don't know. But those active controls you were asking about? I think Korolis might have just run into them."

"And—and the Facility?" she asked.

"Gone."

"Oh, no. No, **no**. All those people . . ." Softly, she began to weep.

Slowly, the buffeting abated. Crane glanced around the dim space. Many were sobbing or moaning; others, frightened and agitated, were being restrained and comforted by their neighbors. There seemed to be only one casualty: the man who had tumbled across the cabin. Gently, Crane freed himself from Hui and went to tend him.

"How much farther?" he called out to Vanderbilt.

The oceanographer had risen to help the tech deal with the breach. "Unknown," he called back. "Power's out; all systems have failed. We're rising on our own buoyancy now."

Crane knelt before the injured man. He was dazed but conscious, struggling to get up. Crane helped him to a sitting position, then dressed a nasty gash across his forehead, another on his right elbow. The light from below had faded completely now, and the escape pod was pitch black. Crane felt his way through ankle-deep water back to Hui.

As he took a seat, he felt someone else move past him in the dark. "We can't seal the breach," came Vanderbilt's voice. "We'd better hope we reach the surface soon."

"Eight minutes have passed already," the tech said. "They **must** have."

Even as he spoke, Crane noticed—or thought he noticed—the oppressive blackness of the cabin giving way to the faintest light. He felt Hui press his hand: she had noticed it, too. The headlong upward rush seemed to slow, then falter. A lambent light began to suffuse the cabin, flickering in patterns of green and deep blue.

And then came a sensation that was unmistakable. They were bobbing in a gently rolling swell.

A ragged cheer erupted across the escape pod. Hui was still weeping, but now, Crane realized, they were tears of joy.

Vanderbilt waded through the water to the escape hatch in the roof of the pod. But even as he did so there was a muffled shout from above. The clatter of footsteps sounded on the roof; the handle of the hatch turned; there was a metallic squeal as it was raised.

And then Crane saw—for the first time in almost two weeks—bright sunlight and a brilliant blue sky.

62

There was a confusion of rooms and cubicles, murmured questions. Someone shone a bright light into his left eye, then his right. A heavy terry cloth robe was draped over his shoulders. And then—full circle, as in a dream—Crane found himself back in the Storm King library, alone, facing the same computer monitor he had faced twelve days ago, the afternoon he first arrived.

He licked his lips. Perhaps it **was** a dream; perhaps none of this had happened. It had all been some fabulous mental confection that started out full of light and promise but slowly devolved into nightmare. And now consciousness would return; bits and fragments of the illusion would fall away like chunks of an old facade; reason would reassert itself; and the entire structure would be revealed for the preposterous dreamscape it really was.

Then the monitor winked into life, revealing a tired-looking man in a dark suit, wearing rimless glasses and sitting at a desk. And Crane knew that this, in fact, was no dream.

"Dr. Crane," the man said. "My name's McPherson. I understand Admiral Spartan gave you my card."

"Yes."

"And you're alone?"

"Yes."

"Why don't you begin at the beginning, then? Leave nothing out."

Slowly—methodically—Crane related the events of the last two weeks. For the most part, McPherson merely listened, motionless, but the occasional question he posed made it clear that much of what he was hearing was not entirely new to him. As Crane's recitation neared its end—the vindication of Asher's theory, the actions of Korolis, the final meeting with Spartan—McPherson's tired face grew even wearier. The bags beneath his eyes seemed to grow darker, and his shoulders sagged.

Crane stopped speaking, and for a time the room fell into a profound silence. At last, McPherson roused himself. "Thank you, Dr. Crane." He reached toward a control box that sat beside him, preparing to break the video connection.

"Just a minute," Crane said.

McPherson glanced back at him.

"Can't you tell me anything about the saboteurs? I mean, why would anybody do something like this?"

McPherson gave him a weary smile. "I'm afraid there are many reasons somebody would do such a thing, Dr. Crane. But to answer your question, yes, I can tell you a little. You see, we'd been tracing their lines of communication, just as Marris was planning to do. And just an hour ago, an arrest was made on Storm King."

"Here?" Crane said. "On the oil rig?"

"Dr. Bishop's contact. We don't know everything yet, but we know we're dealing with a cadre of ideologues, fiercely opposed to American interests and dedicated to neutralizing our ability to protect ourselves. Their members are mostly recruited out of colleges and universities, much as Kim Philby, Guy Burgess, and the other Cambridge spies were recruited—young people, impressionable and full of high ideals, who can easily be influenced and preyed upon. The group is very well financed, whether by a foreign government or private individuals we're not yet sure. But we'll find out soon enough. Either way, they were committed to preventing us from taking possession of whatever technology was buried down there."

There was a brief pause. "So what happens now?" Crane asked.

"You'll remain with us for a few days. You, Ms. Ping, some of the others. Once the processing and debriefing is complete, you'll be free to go."

"No. I mean, what will happen to the project? Deep Storm?"

"Dr. Crane, there **is** no more project. Deep Storm is gone." And with that, McPherson removed his glasses, rubbed his eyes, and terminated the feed.

Crane left the library and walked down the drab metal corridor beyond. He passed an office in which a small group of people sat together, speaking in low voices. In another office, a woman sat at a desk, her hands clasped together, head bowed in contemplation or prayer. Everybody seemed to be in shock. A technician walked by him, the man's gait slow, almost purposeless.

Reaching the end of the corridor, Crane pulled open the hatch. Outside, beyond the metal guardrail of the walkway, the blue-black sea ran away to infinity. He stepped out into the sea air and climbed several sets of steps to the top level of the superstructure. About a dozen of the Deep Storm survivors were clustered beside the helipad, waiting for the AmShale chopper to make its next trip back from Iceland. Standing apart from them, wearing handcuffs and leg irons and chained to a stanchion, stood a pale-skinned man with thick tortoiseshell glasses. He was flanked by two armed marines.

At the edge of the platform, away from the others, stood Hui Ping. She was staring out into the distance, watching the sun sink into the restless waves. Crane walked over to join her, and together they stood a moment in silence. Far below, in the slick of oil that lapped around the rig's support pillars, two Navy cutters prowled back and forth through a widening debris field, stopping now and then to retrieve an object.

"Done?" Hui said at last.

"For now."

"What's next?"

"We're guests of the government for a couple of days. Then I guess we go home. Try to get on with our lives."

Hui pushed a stray hair back behind her ear. "I've been trying to make sense of it all. I think I understand why Dr. Bishop killed Asher—when she heard he and Marris were tracing the saboteur's communications lines, she must have felt she had no choice. She couldn't allow herself to be stopped preemptively."

"That's how it seems to me. Asher told me he alerted all the department heads to be vigilant—including her. That was his own death warrant."

"But there's one thing I don't understand. Why we're all still here."

Crane turned toward her. "What do you mean?"

"The Facility was destroyed by a massive explosion. That means Korolis must have reached the anomaly. If we were right about what's down there, why do we still have an earth to stand on?" She pointed at the sky. "Why can I still see Venus on the horizon?"

"I've been thinking about the same thing. The only explanation I can come up with is that it has to do with the active security measures we talked about."

"So the explosion that destroyed the Facility was a protective mechanism of some kind."

Crane nodded. "Exactly. To keep that repository from being tampered with. A dreadful explosion, to be sure, but a pinprick in comparison to what would have happened otherwise."

They fell silent. Hui continued gazing out toward the horizon. "It's a beautiful sunset," she said at last. "You know, for a while there, I never thought I'd see another one. Even so . . ." She sighed, shook her head.

"What?"

"I can't help feeling just a little disappointed. That we'll never see that technology again, I mean. Even the little bit we came in contact with was—was wondrous. And now it's gone from us forever."

Crane did not answer immediately. He turned back toward the railing, slipped his hand into his pocket. "Oh, I wouldn't be too sure."

Now it was Hui's turn to glance at him. "Why not?"

Slowly, he withdrew his hand. In his palm, winking in the orange light of the sunset, lay a plastic test tube with a red rubber stopper. And the thing that floated lazily within it was aglow with strange and enchanted promise.

• EPILOGUE •

Crane rinsed his razor under a stream of hot water, gave his face a cursory examination in the bathroom mirror, then stowed his toiletries away and stepped back into the bedroom. He dressed quickly in white shirt, brown tie, and tan chinos: civilian attire, or as near as the Navy could come to it. Plucking the oversize ID badge from a nearby bureau, he clipped it to the pocket of his shirt. He gave the room a last once-over, then dropped his toilet kit into the suitcase and lifted it from the bed. Like everything else, it had been issued to him by a Navy quartermaster, and it weighed next to nothing in his hand. **Not surprising,** he thought, since it contained next to nothing: he'd taken nothing with him from Deep Storm except the sentinel, and even that he'd handed over—after a little soul-searching—to McPherson.

McPherson. The man had called just a few minutes earlier, asking Crane to stop by before heading to Administration.

Crane hesitated a moment longer. Then, taking a final look around, he exited the room, walked down the dormitory corridor, and stepped out into the July sunshine.

He'd been at the George Stafford Naval Base, twenty miles south of Washington, for just three days. Yet already he felt familiar with the layout of the small, highly secure facility. Squinting in the bright light, he walked past the motor pool and the machine shop to the gray, hangarlike structure known simply as Building 17. He showed his ID to the armed marine stationed outside, but this was a mere formality: Crane had come and gone so frequently in the last few days everyone knew him by sight.

Inside, Building 17 was brilliantly lit. There were no internal walls, and the cavernous space had the hollow echo of a basketball court. At the center, in a cordoned-off area guarded by more marines, lay a vast riot of mangled metal: the remains of Deep Storm, or at least those portions safe to retrieve—most remained on the sea floor, too radioactive to approach. It looked like some kind of giant's nightmare jigsaw.

At first—when it had been necessary for him to help with tagging and identification—he'd been overcome by a sense of horror. Now, the sight merely made him sad.

At the far end of Building 17, a series of cubicles had been assembled, tiny in the huge space. Crane walked across the concrete floor to the closest one, and—though it was doorless—rapped on its wall for formality's sake.

"Come," said a familiar voice. Crane stepped inside.

The cubicle's furniture consisted of a desk, a conference table, and several chairs. Crane saw that Hui Ping was already seated at the table. He smiled, and she smiled back: a little shyly, he thought. Immediately, he began to feel better.

Since their arrival at Stafford, the two had spent most of their waking hours together: answering endless questions, reconstructing events, explaining what had happened—and why—to a succession of government scientists, military brass, and several mysterious men in dark suits. This time

had only served to cement the bond that, in retrospect, had already begun to form on the Facility. While Crane didn't know exactly what the
future held for him—a research position, probably—he felt confident that Hui Ping would enter
into it in one way or another.

McPherson sat behind the desk, gazing at his
computer screen. One end of the desk was piled
with classified documentation, the other with
graphs and bulky printouts. In the center sat a
hollow cube of clear Plexiglas. Inside it, Crane's
sentinel hovered.

Crane supposed McPherson must have a first
name; that he must have a house in suburbia
somewhere, perhaps even a family. But if
McPherson did have a life beyond the naval base
it seemed to have been put on permanent hold.
Whenever Crane had been in Building 17,
McPherson had been there as well, attending
meetings, writing reports, or huddling in whispered consultation with naval scientists. As the
days had passed, the man—reserved and formal
to begin with—had grown more and more remote. Lately, he'd taken to watching the video
feed from the Marble's final descent again and
again, the way someone might worry at a sore
tooth. Crane noticed it playing on the monitor
even now. He wondered, in passing, if the Facility

had been McPherson's responsibility; if he might ultimately be held accountable in some way for the tragedy.

"Mind if I sit down?" he asked.

For a minute, McPherson remained glued to the grainy video feed. Then he pulled himself away. "Please." He paused, glancing from Crane to Ping and back again. "You're all packed?"

Hui nodded. "It didn't take long."

"You'll be processed at Administration. Once the exit interviews are completed, a car will take you to the airport." Then McPherson reached into his desk. Crane assumed that yet more forms requiring their signatures would be forthcoming. But instead the man drew out two small black leather cases and handed them formally across the desk. "There's just one more thing."

Crane watched as Hui opened hers. Her eyes went wide, and she caught her breath.

He turned to his own case. Inside was an official commendation, signed not only by half a dozen of the highest-ranking admirals in the Navy but also by the president himself.

"I'm not sure I understand," he said.

"What's there to understand, Dr. Crane? You and Dr. Ping determined the true nature of the anomaly. You kept your heads when others didn't. You helped save the lives of—at the very least—one hundred and twelve people. For that, this government will be eternally in your debt."

Crane closed the lid. "This is what you wanted to see us about?"

McPherson nodded. "Yes. And to say good-bye." He stood up, shook their hands in turn. "They're waiting for you in Administration." And he sat down, returning his gaze to the monitor.

Hui rose, headed for the cubicle exit. Then she turned to wait for Crane. He rose slowly, his gaze moving from McPherson to the monitor. He could just make out the image of Korolis, hunched over the Marble's viewscreen; Flyte working the robotic arm. McPherson had the volume low, but Crane could nevertheless make out the old man's birdlike voice: **"It's a weapons dump, the fruit of some intergalactic arms race . . ."**

"Let it go," Crane said quietly.

McPherson stirred, glanced over at him. "Sorry?"

"I said, let it go. It's over."

McPherson returned his gaze to the monitor. He did not reply.

"It's a tragedy, but it's over now. There's no need to worry about others accessing the site. No foreign government can approach the dig interface; it's too heavily irradiated."

Still McPherson did not reply. He seemed to be struggling with some inner conflict.

"I can guess what's eating at you," Crane said gently. "It's the thought of a weapons dump like that, something capable of such extreme destruction, buried within our own planet. It bothers me, too. But I remind myself that whoever entombed those devices also has the power to protect them—to make sure they are never tampered with. Korolis found that out the hard way: the video you're watching proves it."

McPherson stirred again, seemed to come to a private decision. He glanced over at Crane once more. "That's not what's bothering me."

"Then what is?"

McPherson gestured at the screen. "You heard Flyte. It's a weapons dump, he said. A burial spot, off-limits, never to be broached again."

"Yes."

McPherson reached for the keyboard, typed in a command. The video rewound, characters moving furiously backward across the screen. With another command, he restarted the playback. Crane listened to the taped conversation: **". . . two black holes in very tight orbit around each other . . . at a furious rate . . . one matter, one antimatter . . . if the force that held them in orbit was removed, the resulting explosion would destroy the solar system . . ."**

McPherson stopped the playback. He plucked a tissue from a box on his desk, wiped his eyes. "We have dumping grounds for our old nuclear weapons, too," he said in a low voice.

"Like Ocotillo Mountain. Asher was researching the site. That's how we—"

"But you see, Dr. Crane," McPherson interrupted, "here's what keeps me up at night. Before we dump our old weapons, **we disarm them.**"

Crane stared silently at McPherson for a moment, processing what he'd just said.

"You don't think—" Hui began. Then she fell silent.

"What's buried down there, beneath the Moho?" McPherson asked. "Oh, yes. Thousands of devices. **Active** devices. Unimaginable weapons, black holes locked together in rapid orbits. To de-arm the weapon, you'd simply decouple each pair so they could never touch. Right?" He leaned across his desk. "So if this is just a dumping ground, **why wasn't that done?**"

"Because—" Crane found that his mouth had suddenly gone dry. "Because they **haven't** been decommissioned."

McPherson nodded very slowly, "Maybe I'm wrong. But I don't think it's a dump."

"You think it's an active storage facility," Crane said slowly.

"Hidden away on a useless planet," McPherson replied. "Until . . ."

He didn't finish the sentence. He didn't need to.

Slowly, Crane and Ping walked through the echoing hangar. They passed the wreckage that had once been the Facility, heading for the security exit in the far wall. As they walked, Crane found his mind drawn irresistibly to the eyewitness account left behind six hundred years before by Jón Albarn, the Danish fisherman: **A hole appeared in the heavens. And through that hole shewed a giant Eye, wreathed in white flame . . .**

They navigated the security exit and stepped out onto the tarmac, into pitiless light. The sun was a ball of fire in a field of perfect cerulean. And as Crane glanced up toward the sky, he wondered if he would ever be able to look at it in quite the same way again.